Praise for the novels of
USA TODAY bestselling author Delores Fossen

"This is a feel good, heartwarming story of love, family and happy endings for all."
—*Harlequin Junkie* on *Christmas at Colts Creek*

"An entertaining and satisfying read…that I can highly recommend." —*Books & Spoons* on *Wild Nights in Texas*

"The plot delivers just the right amount of emotional punch and happily ever after."
—*Publishers Weekly* on *Lone Star Christmas*

"Delores Fossen takes you on a wild Texas ride with a hot cowboy." —*New York Times* bestselling author B.J. Daniels

"Clear off space on your keeper shelf, Fossen has arrived."
—*New York Times* bestselling author Lori Wilde

"This is classic Delores Fossen and a great read."
—*Harlequin Junkie* on *His Brand of Justice*

"This book is a great start to the series. Looks like there's plenty of good reading ahead."
—*Harlequin Junkie* on *Tangled Up in Texas*

"An amazing, breathtaking and vastly entertaining family saga, filled with twists and unexpected turns. Cowboy fiction at its best." —*Books & Spoons* on *The Last Rodeo*

D0189799

DELORES FOSSEN

MORNINGS AT RIVER'S END RANCH

HQN

ISBN-13: 978-1-335-62398-0

Recycling programs
for this product may
not exist in your area.

Mornings at River's End Ranch
Copyright © 2022 by Delores Fossen

Second Chance at Silver Springs
First published in 2022. This edition published in 2022.
Copyright © 2022 by Delores Fossen

For questions and comments about the quality of this book,
please contact us at CustomerService@Harlequin.com.

HQN
22 Adelaide St. West, 41st Floor
Toronto, Ontario M5H 4E3, Canada
www.Harlequin.com

Printed in Lithuania

MIX
Paper from
responsible sources
FSC® C021394

CONTENTS

MORNINGS AT RIVER'S END RANCH   7

SECOND CHANCE AT SILVER SPRINGS   319

MORNINGS AT RIVER'S END RANCH

CHAPTER ONE

"HEY, DO YOU believe in that whole kill-the-messenger thing?" Wyatt Buchanan heard the woman call out.

Wyatt looked up from the fence repairs he'd been checking and spotted the rider coming across the pasture toward him. Even though he already knew who his visitor was because he recognized the voice, he picked through the thick glare of the late-afternoon sun and saw her. Nola Parkman, a blast from his past, an often pain in his ass and, sadly, the love of his life.

Lost love, that was. And the "life" part was probably an exaggeration.

Probably.

But Nola was at least the love of part of his life, anyway.

Nola was astride Honey Bee, one of his prized palominos that she'd obviously borrowed from his stables and was in no sense of the word *gracefully* riding the normally graceful mare. In fact, Wyatt was surprised Nola hadn't pingponged right out of that saddle and busted her butt. Or lost that precarious grip on the wicker picnic basket she was balancing in her lap.

"Well?" Nola prompted. She reined in, sort of, fumbling and nearly dropping the basket before Wyatt took it. Nola's dismount wasn't pretty either, and it seemed to him that Honey Bee did the equine equivalent of an eye roll. "Are you in the mood for messenger murder, or will you grant me a pardon?" she asked.

"Depends on the message," he grumbled.

Because Honey Bee looked annoyed enough to give Nola a hard tail flick and maybe even a harder nip, Wyatt tucked the basket under his arm and took hold of Nola's elbow to move her away from the mare. Once he had her out of flicking and nipping range, he let go of her so he could push up the brim of his Stetson and give Nola the once-over. To see if he could figure out what this visit was really all about.

Her long blond hair was scooped in its usual disordered ponytail, with just as many strands falling out as there were gathered up. No makeup. That was usual, too. And judging from her stained jeans and old Roper boots with burnt specks, she'd been blowing her glass art in her workshop. Again, that was usual. But there was a wariness in her blue eyes.

Hell yeah. Something was wrong.

Of course, her impromptu visit alone had already told Wyatt that. The messenger question and that wariness were only like a PS at the bottom of an email with bad news. She was here to tell him something he didn't want to hear, and it was dire enough news that she'd brought along food. He was betting the contents of that basket included his favorite ham and Swiss on rye, no mayo, which she'd picked up from the TipTop Diner.

"Don't you have ranch hands to do this sort of thing since you're the owner of River's End?" she asked, tipping her head to the fence he'd been inspecting when she'd arrived. "There was a whole bunch of them by the barns and stables. One of them even saddled the horse for me."

Wyatt had known with complete certainty that she hadn't saddled Honey Bee herself because Nola didn't know squat about tack. If she'd done the saddling, she wouldn't have made it all the way to the pasture.

"I had a new crew doing fence repairs, and I wanted to check their work," he explained.

He'd chosen to spot-check this area because this particular pasture wasn't in use for the next three weeks, when some new horses would be moved here. If someone wanted to go the lazy route, then this would have been the place to do a half-assed job. Thankfully, the job had been full-assed, so he wouldn't have to chew anyone out. Or fire someone.

"Either you're two weeks early or this is about something else," Wyatt commented, still studying her, still waiting.

No need for him to clarify the two-weeks comment. They both knew, down to the hour, the anniversary that they anticelebrated each year. In thirteen days and nine hours, it would be the birthday of the child they'd made together. Their daughter, who'd been born nearly seventeen years ago, when Nola and he had been sixteen.

A daughter in *DNA only*.

That was something Wyatt had had to repeat to himself like a mantra over the years. It was the easiest way to put a pause on the whole eating-away-at-him deal. Yeah, they'd made the kid, and Nola had pushed all six pounds and eleven ounces of her out into the world after a long, grueling labor. But within minutes, they'd had to give her to someone who stood a hundred percent chance of doing a better job with her than they could have.

Which wasn't exactly a high standard.

They'd both been high school juniors back then, and he'd still been eight days away from his seventeenth birthday. Nola had been a month away from hers. And Wyatt had had less than five hundred dollars to his name. The only job he could have gotten was something at minimum wage. Despite her highborn Parkman surname, Nola had been in the same proverbial boat. So, they'd made the only choice they could and that was to give her up.

It was because of that hundred percent belief that someone else could do a better job than them that Nola and he had made a pact. They had agreed they would never look for the girl or her adoptive parents. No ancestry DNA tests to see if she popped up as a match. No peeks at adoption connection sites where there were posts of children looking for bio-parents and vice versa.

Added to that, the only time Nola and he had allowed themselves to talk about the DNA-only was on the birthday. One day a year of rubbing their noses in the penance that was silently simmering and jabbing there the other 364 days of the year.

Sometimes, they hadn't been able to do that penance face-to-face, like when Nola had been in Italy training to make her glass, but they'd still managed some long phone or email conversations. No matter the format, though, the mood had always been miserable.

"I'll be back in two weeks for that," Nola murmured, scooping up the basket and heading to the lone tree in this particular part of the pasture.

A sprawling oak he'd named Nine Months Later.

Because it'd likely been where he had gotten Nola pregnant all those years ago. Of course, it could have also happened at one of the other comfort-lacking places where they'd had a go at each other. Teen hormones were a greedy, insatiable son of a bitch. And sometimes a "gift" that just kept on giving. But Nola and he had paid a billion times over for their lack of self-control and a discount condom that obviously hadn't been worth squat.

Because of that, Wyatt had never had much faith in condoms, or any other form of birth control, for that matter. He'd also decided he had never wanted to risk getting another girl or woman pregnant. Never. So, he'd had a vasectomy when he'd turned twenty-one.

While Honey Bee cropped some grass and moseyed over to Moonlight, the gelding that Wyatt had ridden out to the pasture, Nola took a thin blanket from the basket, spread it out under the shade of the tree. A shade that still didn't block off much of the heat. It was August when the sweltering Texas heat could be a son of a bitch, too.

He'd been right about her choice of sandwiches, but she'd also brought along at least a half dozen little bags of her favorite cheddar-cheese-and-onion potato chips. And beer. A six-pack. Since Nola didn't drink beer, that meant she'd felt he might need to be on his way to getting drunk to deal with whatever news she'd come to deliver.

"Just tell me why you're here," he insisted, popping the top on one of the beers.

She didn't even hesitate. "Today is August first, the drawing of the Last Ride Society."

Of all the things he'd steeled himself up to hear her say, that wasn't anywhere on his steel-required radar.

The Last Ride Society had been formed decades ago by the town's founder, Hezzie Parkman. Hezzie apparently had a thing about her silver-spoon descendants preserving the area's history by having a quarterly drawing so that one lucky/unlucky Parkman would then in turn draw the name of a local tombstone to research. Research that required the drawer to dig into the person's history and write a report for all the town to read—

"Hell," Wyatt said when it hit him. "You drew my brother's name."

Nola nodded, sighed, ripped open a bag of chips and funneled some straight from the bag into her mouth. "It was Griff's name all right. I wasn't actually at the drawing, but my mom was, and she accepted the *honor* for me."

Yeah, her mom, Evangeline, would have done that all right. The civic-minded Evangeline, who counseled troubled teens, arranged food drives, donated most of her income to the needy and probably walked on water every now and then, wouldn't have considered that Nola might want to shirk duty and tradition. Even if that duty and tradition meant poking around in Griff's life.

And his death.

Even if it meant Wyatt would have to relive things he'd barely survived.

"Evangeline asked me to tell you if you needed someone to talk to about this, about Griff," she clarified, "that her door is always open."

Wyatt scowled. Not because it was lip service. It wasn't. Evangeline would go out of her way to help him deal with this, even though she had to secretly be holding a grudge against him.

Had to be.

After all, he'd knocked up her teenage daughter and had created the juiciest kind of gossip that still sparked every now and then even after seventeen years. Added to that, he wasn't to the manor born. In fact, in those days, Griff, their brothers, Jonas and Dax, and he had been the poor pitiful kids, orphaned after their parents had drowned on a fishing trip when their boat had capsized.

Long before the time Wyatt had done the knocking up, he and his siblings had been living on River's End Ranch, which was then run-down in every way possible, while being raised, in a very general sense of the word, by a mean-as-a-snake cousin. The cousin, Maude Muldoon, had taken them in only because of the monthly social security checks paid out since they were orphans. The state had allowed that because they'd apparently thought Maude having a uterus and some shared DNA were ample qualifications for raising four grieving boys.

Now Wyatt owned Maude's ranch, which he'd bought by paying off the back taxes after she'd died, and over the past decade, he'd built it into something that took him way, way out of the poor-pitiful-kid income bracket. He didn't have more money than God, but he likely had more funds than plenty of the Parkmans did.

And he had the ranch.

It was the lottery of pipe dreams for him because it was big, profitable and incredibly beautiful. There were lots of pretty ranches in and around Last Ride, but he'd always thought River's End had gotten the long end of the stick in that particular department. The narrow Rocky River with its clear blue water coiled and cut through the pastures like a Wish You Were Here picture on a postcard.

Well, he was here. And it was his. That was one wish he could tick off his bucket list.

"I just want to know your ground rules for the report I'll be writing about Griff," Nola went on, funneling in more chips and washing them down with an orange soda. She might be thirty-three now, but she had the taste buds of a twelve-year-old.

"Well, sure as heck don't mention that he made a habit of doing the nasty with your sister Lily," he said right off the top of his head. "Learning about that would give your grandparents a stroke." The couple was well into their late eighties and the very definition of old money, old school.

Nola made a sound of agreement. "Best to leave out Lily's and Griff's underage drinking, too. And that time Griff gave her so many hickeys that she went through a tube of concealer a day for an entire week just to cover them up."

True. There were just some things family members didn't need to know. In fact, he was betting that was something Evangeline and her snooty parents wouldn't want to have anywhere in their memory banks. Evangeline was already dealing with the fact that none of her daughters had chosen a life of service, what with Lily raising horses, Nola with her glass workshop and Lorelei owning and running the shop that sold Nola's glass creations. At least with Nola there was the artist factor, but with Lily's knack for breeding quarter horses, Wyatt considered her an artist as well.

"What are Lily's ground rules?" he asked.

Nola shook her head. "Haven't had a chance to ask her yet. She's tied up with some business stuff. But I'll check first chance." She paused and nudged him with her elbow in what he recognized as a gesture of comfort. Attempted comfort, anyway. "What about you? How much is it going to eat away at you to have the town talking about Griff again?"

The eating away would be huge, along with bringing back the mother lode of bad memories. But that wasn't what he told Nola. No need to make her feel worse about this than she already did. Added to that, the timing sucked with their annual pity party only two weeks away.

"You could maybe do the research fast," he suggested. "Just like ripping off a bandage. Then people can move on and talk about something else."

She made a sound of agreement. "News of this will stir up the Sherlock's Snoops," Nola pointed out.

It sure would, but then, it didn't take much to stir up that lot. They were basically a group of nosy people who had way too much time on their hands and fancied themselves to be Sherlock Holmes. And when Griff's life had ended one pretty spring evening when he'd been just nineteen, the Sherlock's Snoops had refused to accept that it was anything but foul play.

Wyatt didn't want to believe there'd been foul play or suicide, but each time he had to deal with memories of his brother, he slid into a dark hole. A hole that seemed to get darker and deeper each time he went there, so he'd pulled back and stopped taking their calls or reading their emails. He'd also tried, as much as possible, not to think about it.

"When I come back for our noncelebration in two weeks, I can let you know how the research on Griff is going," Nola continued, then paused. "If that's what you want."

That would make for one miserable visit since it'd be a double punch to the gut. *DNA-only*, Wyatt reminded himself. He didn't have a mantra that worked for Griff, though.

"I'll want to know," he assured her. He didn't. That was a big-assed lie, but it wasn't right to put all of this on her shoulders, especially since Nola didn't want this any more than he did.

"Monkey balls," Nola muttered. Her version of profanity, something she'd started shortly after Lily's daughter, Nola's niece, had started repeating everything she'd heard her beloved aunt say.

Nola went quiet, staring out at the pasture while she sipped more of her orange soda. Wyatt could hear the carbonated bubbles pinging against the inside of the metal can, could smell the fruity scent mix with the grass and sandwich he'd yet to eat. Picnic smells for a nonpicnic mood.

"Why couldn't I have been matched up with the tombstone of somebody with no connection to us?" Nola complained. "Or somebody fun like that woman who used to live behind the motorcycle repair shop?"

"The one who raised pygmy goats and dressed them up,"

he remarked. She'd gained some fame with her pygmy pair reenacting *Star Trek*'s Spock and Captain Kirk. A San Antonio newspaper had run a story on it.

"Exactly! Her or Ella Lou Devers, who claimed she'd had Al Capone's love child. I heard they found all kinds of interesting porn in her house after she passed."

Wyatt looked at her. "If you want to research porn, all you have to do is turn on your computer."

Nola shook her head. "Not the same. The cheap thrill comes from running across it unexpectedly when it's supposed to be secret. Speaking of the unexpected and secrets, look what I found the other day." She pulled out an envelope from her back pocket and handed it to him.

He opened it, looked in and had a *holy hell* moment when he spotted the pictures that'd been taken a lifetime ago with an instant camera. Specifically, nearly naked pictures of Nola and him.

"Why the heck would you keep these?" he snarled, but since he wasn't blind and was a guy, he knew why. Because this was about that cheap-thrill stuff she'd just mentioned. This was about seeing Nola pose for him while wearing only panties and a smile.

Since she would have been only sixteen at the time, it felt a little pervy to look at them, but then he flipped to one of his sixteen-year-old self. He'd been trying to show off muscles he hadn't had yet on that rangy body.

He continued to flip through and found one of them French-kissing while Nola was also trying to push the button on the camera. They were off-center and too close to the lens, but he didn't get a pervy feeling this time. It was a punch-to-the-gut reminder that he'd kissed her like that often. Had put his hands on every inch of her body.

But that had ended after she'd gotten pregnant.

And, sticking to the promise she'd made to her grandparents, Nola hadn't kissed or touched him since. At the time, it had seemed like the right decision. Still probably was. Being together like that would no doubt make them think of their hearts being ripped apart because of the *DNA-only* they'd had to give up.

"It was interesting to see us like that," Nola went on. "And I had to take a really long, cold shower after I looked at them awhile." She laughed. "After I kept thinking about them."

He'd be taking some cold showers, too. And would be thinking about them as well.

"I figure I shouldn't keep these," she went on, and he noted her breathing was a little heavier now. Or maybe that was his. "After all, someday someone might be researching me for the Last Ride Society, and I wouldn't want this included. Would you?"

It sounded like such an innocent, no-brainer question, but hell, here he was, looking at the nearly naked pictures now, knowing that he should stop so he wouldn't have the images of her small perfect breasts in his head.

Too late.

The images were there.

"Would you?" she repeated.

This time it sounded dirty, and when he looked at her, he spotted the tiny crumb of potato chip on her bottom lip. It was just perched there, practically begging Wyatt to remove it.

With his tongue.

In that instant, Wyatt knew he was going to make a mistake. One that he was one hundred percent sure he'd regret.

That didn't stop him.

CHAPTER TWO

NOLA MADE THE first blow into the carbon steel pipe that she'd named Harry Potter after her favorite wizard. She watched the magic happen when she pressed her thumb to the top of the pipe to trap her breath in the metal tube. The glass bubble came to life at the bottom, and she began to turn it to see what it would become.

She needed this. The escape. The flow inside her that warmed the places that needed warming. There was sure plenty of warming both inside and out while in a glass-blowing workshop.

This was her space, though it probably looked way too industrial for most, what with its exposed-beam ceiling, concrete floor and metal-studded walls. And the stuff, of course. Buckets of broken and crushed glass, pipes, scissors and other well-used tools she needed to shape, snip and stretch whatever she'd just blown.

Unlike some other artists in her profession, she wasn't a planner, didn't have grand visions of a piece that she then just set out to make. Instead, she let the glass and Harry Potter talk to her, let them and her breath give the glass some life before she moved the hot blob to the graphite marver table. There, she'd nudge the piece into the right dance that would create whatever this was supposed to be.

Apparently, this one would be a vase.

An opalescent one with a long neck and the color of ripe

peaches. It wouldn't be a masterpiece, but it would sell in her sister's shop, the Glass Hatter. Sooner or later, everything sold there, and the better pieces, those that had more than their fair share of the magic, would go to the Waterstone Gallery in nearby San Antonio, where there was a wait list of buyers for her work.

People often dubbed her with the charmed-life label because they considered her glass to be art that was worthy of an astonishingly high price tag. Nola just considered herself lucky. Most didn't get to earn an embarrassingly cushy living by doing something they loved. Then again, most hadn't gotten her training or opportunities either, and those opportunities had started with a summer glass program in Austin, where she'd apparently shown some promise.

After that, she'd spent two years at a prestigious glass school in Italy, where she'd gone only weeks after giving up Wyatt's and her baby. Evangeline had probably agreed to her going so far from home because she'd known how depressing it would be for Nola to stay in Last Ride.

And maybe because her mother realized Nola had some raw talent.

After all, not many sixteen-year-old kids got offered that kind of opportunity, on scholarship no less, and with the plan to continue her high school classes via email. No virtual classrooms in those days, but she'd managed to finish.

"Yoo-hoo?" she heard her twin sister, Lily, call out.

"Close the door," Nola automatically reminded her, and she counted off the handful of seconds before Lily also did something automatic and complained of the heat.

"Sheez Louise, it's hot in here," Lily grumbled.

Nola continued one more leg of their usual start to a conversation when Lily made a visit to the workshop. "It's hotter over here."

Two thousand degrees, to be exact. Well, that was the temp inside the glory hole that melted the glass. The breeze from the six huge industrial fans that Nola had set up prevented heatstroke, but anyone who entered would be sweating like a proverbial pig in just a couple of minutes.

Nola finished rolling and shaping the vase before she tapped it to detach it. A step she always equated to cutting a newborn's umbilical cord. Then she took it to the smaller of her two annealer ovens, where it would slowly cool for the next twenty-four hours. A slow cool was needed to keep it from shattering back into the tiny pieces it'd been when she first started it.

Soon after the vase had cooled, it would be put up for sale for whatever price tag her other sister, Lorelei, slapped on it. The shop was Lorelei's. Her *baby*, Nola decided, going with that whole birthing-and-infant theme that was on her mind.

The infant theme was no doubt the reason Lily had braved the heat and sweaty armpits to come here. Because Lily would have remembered that it was the dreaded birthday. Seventeen years, or it soon would be in two hours.

"I wanted to catch you before you showered and changed to go to Wyatt's," Lily commented. She pulled Nola into a hug. A really short one before Lily pulled back and waved her hand in front of her face. "You are going to shower and change before you see him, right?"

"Of course." Though there had been a time or two she'd forgotten. Not today, though. She'd need the cool stream of the shower to settle her before she carried this doom-and-gloom mood of hers over to Wyatt's.

Lily sighed when she glanced at the shelves of finished pieces. The rows of other vases, glasses, paperweights, critters and doodads that she'd blown and completed over the past two weeks. Throwing herself into her work. Or rather, *blowing* herself into it, anyway.

"I'm sorry," her sister murmured.

Obviously, Lily could count, and she knew this was far more than Nola's usual output. The two weeks before the birthday was always like that. A frantic hamster wheel race *running, running, running*—to try to keep her mind jammed with her fragile little creations.

And in this case, one big creation.

"How's the research coming on Griff?" Lily asked.

Now it was Nola's turn to do sisterly-sympathy duty. Not with a hug because, hey, sweaty armpits, but with what she hoped was a consoling look. Some people only loved once, and they loved hard. That'd been Griff and Lily. And when he'd died at nineteen, Lily's heart, life and future had been crushed.

On the surface, it didn't seem as if that crushing had lasted, because within two months, Lily had jumped into marrying a man after a whirlwind romance. But even at that tender age, Nola had known a rebound reaction when she'd seen it. Lily had been trying to add some balm onto the grief that was too hard for her to bear. The balm hadn't worked, though, and Lily had gotten a divorce less than a year later.

On the bright side, Lily had gotten something really great out of that brief marriage. A daughter, Hayden, who was now thirteen. So, all had turned out well enough. Ditto for their older sister, Lorelei, who was in the process of adopting an adorable little baby munchkin she'd fostered since birth. It had made Nola see that it was what she wanted.

Correction, it was what she'd *always* wanted.

And Nola had given up waiting for a suitable partner to come along and make a baby with her. Instead, she'd already gone through the steps to make an adoption happen.

If all went well, in another year or less she'd be the mother of a child she could actually keep.

"I haven't even started the Last Ride Society research yet," Nola confessed. "I figured I'd wait until after today."

Of course, then she'd have to mentally patch herself up. That'd take a week or so. And then she could start.

Lily made a sympathetic sound of agreement as she began sweeping her gaze around the rest of the workshop. "If there's anything I can do to help—" Her sister's eyes went saucer size when they landed on the piece by the side wall.

The *one big creation*.

At nearly four feet tall, it was too big to have tucked out of sight, and it stood out like a megawatt beacon in the jammed-to-the hilt workshop of already sparkling, beaconing glass. Nola had been stunned, awed even, when she'd blown those breaths and watched it form. The endorphins and years of blowing had allowed her arms to bear the weight when she'd gone back for gather after gather of more crushed glass and then turn after turn to keep up the magic.

In the end, it had become two thin, breathe-on-it-wrong-and-it'd-probably-shatter entwined columns of shimmering fire-red glass. Not tear or S shaped. More like two drops of rain that had slid together in a fluid, sinuous spiral on their way down. She'd captured that moment, that merging spiral right before it would have metaphorically splatted on the ground.

Nola knew without a doubt it was the best thing her breath had ever made. And that her chances of being struck by lightning were higher than her ever making anything this good again. That made her both happy and sad. Reaching pinnacles at thirty-three wasn't fun to crow about.

"You slept with Wyatt," Lily blurted out.

Nola whipped toward her and frowned. "How the heck did you get that from that?" She flung an accusing finger at the piece.

"Because that's sex and that's Wyatt." Lily flung her own accusing finger at the left, slightly large column. "And that's you." The accusation turned to the other column.

It was. Nola had seen it in between the blows, the sweat, the gathers and the turns. She had felt the slide of heat that it'd caused in her body when she'd watched the slow dance of the glass.

But she sure as heck hadn't counted on anyone else seeing or feeling it.

"You went over to tell Wyatt about drawing Griff's name, and you ended up sleeping with him," Lily went on, but she stopped with her uncanny—aka unwanted—summary of events and sighed. "Are you okay?"

"I'm okay-ish," Nola said. The *ish* made it less of a lie. Of course, Lily knew it for the whopper that it was, because she risked another hug.

"You slept with Wyatt," Lily repeated in a soothing, sympathetic tone.

"Well, actually, it was just sex under a tree in the pasture. I left shortly thereafter, so there was no sleeping."

Lily eased back to give her the flat-eyed, level look that only a sibling who was two minutes older and an elementary teacher could pull off. "You left because you thought you'd made a mistake, or because it was bad?"

Nail on the head with the first part. Massive miss with the last. It'd been earth-moving sex, but then, it was Wyatt, who was a master at moving earth for her and giving her incredible orgasms. He had plenty of experience in that arena since he'd given her the first such experience. And the second, third, etc.

"I honestly don't know why Wyatt and you didn't get together again after you came back from Italy when you were eighteen," Lily remarked.

"Well, for one thing, he wasn't here." Before Nola had returned, Wyatt had already left to go work at a big ranch over in Wrangler's Creek. "Then, after Maude died, and he came back to buy River's End, I was engaged."

There was no need for Nola to verbally go over the rest, but in the sanitized, *won't dwell on it now* summary, she'd ended her engagement after a year to Mistake Number One only to learn that Wyatt was getting married to a woman he'd met in Wrangler's Creek. That hadn't lasted for him either, but right about the time he was filing for a divorce, Nola had gotten engaged to Mistake Number Two.

By the time that second one had run its course and she'd disentangled herself from the stalker-hell, smothering relationship, she had pretty much sworn off men. That had coincided with Wyatt pretty much swearing off women.

"Well, there's no time like the present," Lily pointed out. "You could be ready for a do-over."

This was the easy part to argue. Well, not easy, but Wyatt had taken any future do-overs off the table by telling her about his vasectomy.

"Wyatt doesn't want kids," Nola spelled out. "I do. I can promise you he won't want to play daddy to the child I intend to adopt."

Before Lily could spout *Never say never* or some other such nonsense that people spouted, the door opened again, the light spearing through the workshop, and their big sis, Lorelei, came in.

"God, it's hot in here," Lorelei complained.

"It's hotter over there," Nola and Lily said in unison, both hiking their thumbs toward the furnace. "And there," Lily added, motioning toward the red sculpture.

"I came over to check on you before you went to Wyatt's," Lorelei said, looking at the time and turning toward the sculpture in the same motion. "I'm glad I caught you. Shouldn't you be leaving—"

Her oldest sister stopped, her mouth dropping comically open. "Oh, my God." Lorelei didn't take her eyes off it. "It's amazing. Incredible—you had sex with Wyatt."

Great. Two out of two had picked up on it. Of course, they were two of the four people who knew her best, and Nola made a mental note not to let her mother or Wyatt see it since they were the remaining two.

"Are you guys back together?" Lorelei asked, not in the eternally optimistic tone like Lily's. This tone fell more into the *Have you lost your mind?* zone.

"We're not back together," Nola assured her while she started shutting down for the night. "It was more of an impulsive thing. A one-off that we won't be repeating."

"It happened when she went over to tell Wyatt about drawing Griff's name," Lily supplied.

The dirty pictures she'd found had played into that, too, but there was no need for Nola to announce that.

Lorelei made a sound of relief. "Good. Because your name moved up on the adoption list, and it won't be long now before you get that baby."

Even though it was month-old news, that brought on a group hug, one that Lorelei ended just as fast as Lily had when she got a whiff of Nola's ripe BO.

"Soon, we'll all be mothers," Lorelei added, doing a little bobble to substitute for jumping up and down. "Just like we used to talk about when we were kids."

They had indeed had those conversations, complete with

names that they'd thankfully rethought. Lorelei had named her daughter Estella instead of her teenage top pick of Holiday for a girl, and Lily had gone with Hayden instead of Jagger as an homage to Mick Jagger. That was back when Lily went on a listening spree of the Rolling Stones.

Nola had worked hard to forget any name she'd come up with back then because those memories had gotten tied up with her pregnancy, but she was pretty sure there'd been a Wyette and a Wyatt Jr. It made her wonder what the adoptive parents had named the child they'd been given, but then, she'd wondered that a lot.

"Well, I won't keep you," Lorelei went on when Nola put away the last of her equipment. "You should be on your way to get that shower." But her gaze drifted back to the sculpture. "Hard to believe you can create something like that with sand, fire and breath. What are you going to call it?"

Nola's first thought, one that was worse than their teenage choices of baby names, was titling it *Wyatt's Junk*, because the more she looked at it, there was a phallic vibe to it.

"Call it *Love Rediscovered*," Lily suggested.

"Lustful Longings," Lorelei countered. "Or just *Longings*."

Nola preferred *Wyatt's Junk* to any of those. "I'll give it some thought and let you know," she settled for saying while she swiped some of the sweat off her face and grabbed her purse.

"You'll send it to the gallery in San Antonio, then?" Lorelei asked as the three of them headed to the door.

Nola didn't require any thought for this. "No."

It'd be akin to passing around those old pictures of Wyatt and her. It was best to find a place for this in her house. Maybe tucked away in her bedroom where no one would see it.

But she would see it.

And there'd be plenty of dirty thoughts about Wyatt followed by cold showers in her future.

She considered the dirty-thoughts angle after she said goodbye to her sisters, used the app on her phone to shut down the furnace, turn off the lights and fans and lock up. Then Nola hurried toward home.

It'd been two weeks since she'd seen Wyatt. Two weeks since they'd given in to those lustful longings, so it was going to be awkward between them later. No doubts about that. But there wouldn't be any repeats. She was sure of that because these noncelebrations were the very definition of gloom and doom.

Of course, she'd thought the same about her visit to tell him of the drawing, so she needed to stay on guard. With the adoption on the horizon, it wouldn't do for her to dive into the head-over-heels thing for Wyatt again. They weren't the kind of friends who could have benefits.

Well, except for that one time five years ago.

That had happened on one of the nonbirthday, noncelebration dates, too. Just a kiss, though. A tipsy, sloppy one. Well, tipsy on her part. Wyatt had been as sober as a judge, whatever that meant. He always was around her, and she suspected that was because he wanted to be in control when they were together. Unlike the times when they'd been teenagers and had gone at each other when the mood struck.

It had struck often.

Wyatt probably thought it was his lack of control that'd caused the pregnancy, but she was just as much to blame for that as he was.

Since her workshop was only three blocks from her house, she made her way there on foot, waving and nodding while moving quickly, to let those who greeted her see that she was in a hurry. She went even faster when she saw her distant cousin Derwin Parkman trying to flag her down from the other side of the street. Derwin was head of the Sherlock's Snoops and therefore would want to talk about Griff and the research.

"Sorry, I'm running late," she shouted to him and barreled up the steps to her home, a Victorian cottage surrounded by mansions.

This was Parkman Row, the glitziest street in town. But that wasn't why she lived here. In fact, that distinction had been a deterrent. She was here because it had once belonged to her father, and he'd lived in this house before marrying Evangeline. Since her father had died of Hodgkin's before Lily and she had even been born, Nola had wanted this small piece of him.

Well, more of a piece of him than the Parkman DNA she'd inherited, anyway.

Nola had his blond hair. His blue eyes. But she'd wanted to walk in his steps, brush against the same walls and breathe a trace of his scent that maybe, hopefully, still lingered after all these years. That was why she'd jumped to buy the cottage five years ago when it'd finally come up for sale, and she had used her father's old pictures of the place to make it resemble what it was when it had been his.

Of course, she was also walking in the steps and breathing scents left by the two owners who had lived there in between her father and her, but she liked to think she could filter out what was him and what was everything else.

The place was messy. Not that unusual when she was on a glassblowing binge, so she had to dodge clothes she hadn't put away and ignore the smell of the pizza she'd left on the coffee table. She stripped while she ran to the shower and made it fast, though she did take the time to wash her hair.

Her phone rang the second she got out of the shower, and she saw her mom's name pop on the screen. No way did she want to get into a conversation with her right now, so she waited until it went to voice mail, and while she dressed, she listened to the message.

"Bright Blessings, Nola. I know you can't do it tonight because you're heading to Wyatt's," her mother said, "but please make time for us to talk. It's important."

Crud. Had Lorelei blabbed about the sculpture already? If so, her sister would pay for that. So would Nola, since she'd be forced to listen to Therapist Mom. Of course, Evangeline was actually a therapist, and while she rarely shifted into that mode with her daughters, she would almost certainly make an exception if she knew about the Wyatt sex.

Repeating her "crud" and thinking up some punishment for Lorelei, Nola yanked open the drawer on the vanity to locate her hairbrush. And she froze. Just froze. Her vision pinpointing at what she saw there.

She shook her head, thinking, and her heart started to race. Seconds later, the panic set in.

Oh, mercy.

No.

CHAPTER THREE

NOLA WAS LATE.

Not time-to-worry late yet, only by five minutes, but each minute that passed gave Wyatt too much time to think.

He'd screwed up big-time by having sex with her, and it could give their friendship a mule kick in the gut. A friendship that meant a lot to him. It'd been hard-fought to find that balance between holding the leash on the old heat and being there for each other while not intruding, and he needed to get that balance back. With no more lapses.

Before two weeks ago, the lapse had been that kiss.

It'd been hot, greedy, ill-timed and something they'd vowed to wipe from their memories. He would have had an easier time forgetting he was a man. And as ill-timed and completely wrong as that unforgettable kiss was, it'd been a drop in the bucket compared to the sex they'd had two weeks ago. It was going to take a whole lot of groveling and maybe a sworn statement signed in blood that it'd never ever happen again.

Well, it would take all that and more if Nola didn't duck out and actually showed for this noncelebration. Even though it was important to both of them, necessary even, he would understand if she didn't want to see him.

Wyatt paced across his kitchen, looking out at the horses in the pasture and drinking the too-sugary orange soda he didn't even want. He wanted a beer or some tequila shots, but the last thing he needed was a cloudy mind when he started that groveling.

Normally, it soothed him being in his house, seeing his horses, looking out at his ranch. It anchored him. That wasn't by accident. He'd had the white stables and fences built because of their clean lines. Straight, simple and ordered. He'd done the same to the house. Not Maude's house. He'd had that one torn down, not even leaving the foundation because he hadn't wanted to have any trace of her in his space.

Yes, Maude had once owned the bit of land near the house, but she'd never worked it. Had maybe never stepped foot out on it since she'd always complained the only reason she was there was because her late husband had dragged her to it and had then died on her. As if that'd been the man's intentions all along.

The ranch, such as it was back then, hadn't even had a name. In Wyatt's mind, a ranch was like a ship. Names were needed for tradition, for luck, and so there'd be something to put on a sign in front of the property to let everybody know it wasn't just land.

His phone rang, the sound shooting through the quiet house, and he spilled some soda when he fumbled to get it out of his jeans pocket. He figured it was Nola calling to cancel, but nope.

It was Evangeline's name on the screen.

Since she was probably calling to tell him "Bright Blessings" or some such commiseration, he let it go to voice mail. He couldn't deal with Nola's mom tonight, even if he suspected that Evangeline could have used some commiserations as well. After all, she'd lost a granddaughter when Nola and he had given up the baby.

He saw the little bubble on his phone to indicate Evangeline had left a voice mail, so he played it in case Nola had asked her mom to call him with an excuse for her not coming. Not that Nola would have done that in a million years, but he listened to it anyway.

"Wyatt," Evangeline said in the message, "I suspect you're with Nola now and that's why you're not answering. Could you please call me when you get a chance? Oh, and Bright Blessings."

Hell, maybe Evangeline had heard about Nola and him having pasture sex. Not that she would have heard it from Nola. That was another not-in-a-million-years kind of deal. But it was possible, likely even, that Nola had told one of her sisters, who in turn had let it slip to Evangeline. If so, Wyatt suspected there'd be more Bright Blessings phone calls and chats in his future so that Evangeline could do her nonlecture lecturing about the dangers of opening up old wounds.

He deserved those lectures and a whole lot more. It wouldn't surprise him if the calm-as-a-lake, nonjudgmental Evangeline wanted to neuter him with rusty farm tools.

Wyatt felt the relief when he heard the car pull into his driveway. He didn't rush to the door but had to fight an impulse or two to do just that. Instead, he walked into the adjoining living room and waited for the knock. Just a knock before Nola would stick her head in and call out something like "Are you decent? If not, I'll avert my eyes until you've covered that superior hiney of yours."

Except she probably wouldn't do that this time.

Nope, because he'd gone and screwed up. It likely had put an end to the playful banter between them that was just as comforting and anchoring as his ranch.

The knock came. Wyatt's stomach tightened. The door opened. But it wasn't Nola.

His brothers, Jonas and Dax, came in.

"What the hell are you two doing here?" Wyatt snarled, but he already knew. They didn't show up at every non-celebration, but they did every now and then because they were both well aware that this was a day from hell for him.

Wyatt appreciated that. Mostly. But he didn't appreciate it now, not with the talk he needed to have with Nola. And speaking of Nola, where the heck was she?

"I came to give you relationship advice about women," Dax said in his usual cocky tone. "Oh, wait. You'd need a relationship and a woman first before you can get advice."

Dax laughed even though it was an old, lame joke, and they all knew it. A joke told so often that Jonas had quit rolling his eyes at their kid brother, who had earned oh so many eye rolls in his life.

"We won't stay." Jonas spoke up. "I wouldn't have even stopped if I'd seen Nola's car in the driveway."

He was the big brother, four years older than Wyatt and seven years older than Dax. Jonas was rock-solid and a whole bunch of other such clichés, and because he was a recent widower, he didn't have a current relationship or a woman, either. However, since he did have a stepson who'd just turned thirteen, that gave him a free pass from Dax's jokes about the lack of a sex life.

As the oldest, Jonas had been the one to take on the father role after their parents died. The father role and the buffer to protect them as best he could from Maude's vile moods. He'd done a decent enough job of it that when Wyatt saw Father's Day cards in the stores, he always thought of Jonas.

When he saw cards like Have a Great Day Celebrating the Result of Your Parents Having Hot, Dirty Sex, he thought of Dax.

Not that Dax talked about sex all the time, but his kid brother didn't seem to go a week without someone to warm his bed. That was probably because he was a rodeo champion with the rock-star looks to go along with it. He had his own buckle-bunny fan club.

"Didn't know you were in town," Wyatt commented to Dax.

Dax shrugged. "Bruised my tailbone when a bull named Ass Kicker truly did kick my ass, so I'm taking a few days off. Thought I'd swing back and see those in my gene pool." He gave Wyatt's arm a punch, which was the brotherly equivalent of a hug and shout that he was worried about him.

Yeah, even cocky kid brothers could care.

Jonas substituted the arm punch for a direct question. "You okay?" Jonas asked him, and he glanced at the can of orange soda Wyatt was holding. A red flag since Jonas knew he didn't drink such things.

"I'm fine," Wyatt lied, and he didn't dodge Jonas's gaze, which lingered on him. He was in the dad mode now, worried about one of his chicks. Since Jonas had enough of his own worries, aka the whole widower deal, Wyatt repeated the lie, hoping that the second time around it sounded more believable. "How about the two of you?"

"Okay," Jonas said, obviously going with a lie of his own, and he hitched his thumb to their brother. "Some teenage girls at the gas station asked Dax for his autograph."

Dax shrugged and slipped right back into his cocky grin. "What can I say? Women want me and men want to be me."

"I don't want to be you," Jonas and Wyatt said in unison. "And as for the women," Jonas went on, "these were girls who haven't fully developed the lobe in their brains to make rational decisions."

That didn't deter Dax one bit. He just kept on grinning while subtly glancing at Jonas and Wyatt. The grinning and glancing stopped, though, when they heard the sound of a car approaching the house.

"It's Nola," Wyatt told them when he glanced out the window.

"All right, let's get out of here," Jonas said, already heading for the door. Dax was right behind him. "Hang in there," Jonas added to Dax's parting shot of "Don't do anything that starts with a *c*."

Of course, Wyatt's mind immediately went to such words as *copulate* and *coitus* and others that he thankfully managed to push out of his head before they took hold there.

Wyatt watched Nola bolt from her car, the body language, gestures and flustered urgency of someone running late. That didn't stop her, though, from pausing to give his brothers a hug. Dax said something to her that Wyatt couldn't hear, something that made her laugh, but even from a distance, Wyatt was pretty sure her laughter was more than a bit hollow. Probably because she was about to face the man who'd lost his mind and had sex with her in the pasture.

Nola continued all those gestures and that speed as she moved away from his brothers and came toward the house. She practically ran those last steps, a surprise because Wyatt had expected some hesitancy.

She moved Wyatt away from the door so she could shut it, and then she leaned her back against it while she seemingly tried to recover her breath.

"I'm late," she said.

"Yeah, by nearly a half hour." He was about to launch into the groveling, but Nola started talking before he could say another word.

"No, I'm laaate." She stretched out that last word and then gestured to the front of her jeans.

Wyatt was sure he raised an eyebrow or two. And equally

sure everything inside him ground to a halt when that stretched-out word and her gesture sank in.

"Late," he managed to say, though he wasn't sure where he'd gotten the air to form human speech. His lungs had clamped into a vise, and all the oxygen in the house had vanished.

She dropped her purse and grabbed on to two handfuls of the front of his shirt. "Confession time. Did you really have a vasectomy, or was that malarkey so that women who wanted kids would leave you alone?"

Again, oxygen was an issue, and that accounted for why he had to croak out a response. "Not malarkey." And he was reasonably sure that was the first time he had ever used that particular word.

Reasonably sure, too, that he had to sit down, so that was what Wyatt did. He sank down onto the foyer floor and kept shaking his head until he came up with something that might unclench his lungs.

"Maybe you're just late," he threw out there, though he was way out of his depth here.

"I'm never late." And she certainly didn't sound out of her depth with that. Muttering her usual "Monkey balls" profanity, she kept her back against the door and slid down to the floor across from him. She pulled up her knees to her chest and groaned, a long stream of the sound that echoed through the house.

"Maybe just this one time you are." He hoped, and then he moved on to prayer. This was one hell of a déjà vu that Nola and he didn't need.

"My cycle is like clockwork, and I was so busy at the workshop that I didn't notice I should have started my period a week ago," she went on. "But trust me when I say I noticed it when I was getting dressed and saw the unopened box of tampons in my drawer. A box I'd just bought the day I came out here to tell you about drawing Griff's name."

Wyatt held back asking her if it was possible she had forgotten about it. That probably wasn't something a woman would forget. But he could give her a stat that suddenly seemed like a glimmering light at the end of a dark tunnel.

"A vasectomy is effective nearly 999 times out of a thousand," Wyatt threw out there.

"One in a thousand," she murmured like profanity. Nola groaned and banged the back of her head against the door. Hard. "This is like the condom fail all over again."

"No, it's not." Wyatt refused to believe that, and he started grasping at straws. "Maybe you're going through menopause."

Okay, maybe he should have left that straw ungrasped, so he tried again. "Perhaps the stress of the drawing, the non-celebration and us having sex created so much anxiety that it caused you to be late. That could happen, right?" he asked.

He watched her latch on to that glimmering thought he'd just tossed her. "I suppose. I have been stressed," she admitted.

Great! Really great. They had a theory now, and he could breathe again.

"I stopped at the pharmacy on the way here to buy one of those pregnancy tests," Nola went on, "but two women from the Sherlock's Snoops were in there, and they followed me around asking questions about the research. I couldn't shake them, so I couldn't get it. The pharmacy is still open. You could go and get one of the tests and bring it back here."

"Me?" And it shocked him that his voice hadn't actually cracked. "Why the hell me?"

"Because if someone sees me get it, everyone will start

gossiping." Her logic was a little shaky, but it came through as the voice of reason.

Bad reasoning as far as Wyatt was concerned. "And they won't gossip about me?" he argued.

"If anyone sees it, you could say you were picking it up as a favor to Dax. Everybody's always gossiping about his quick zipper."

That was true, and even though he'd never purchased such a test for his little brother, Wyatt had bought Dax plenty of condoms—not the discount kind—in that particular pharmacy. Still, he had to think of a reason why he couldn't do that.

The thinking stopped, though, when he looked at Nola's face.

Crap. She was blinking back tears and chewing on her bottom lip. And the reason she was doing that was all his fault. His and maybe the doctor who'd done his vasectomy. But Wyatt wasn't going with that one-in-a-thousand possibility right now. He would get that test, Nola would pee on the stick and it'd be negative. Then they could have a laugh of relief and get on with grieving the loss of the only child they'd made on another of those long-shot fails.

"Stay here," Wyatt told her. "If someone sees you waiting in my truck, they might put two and two together."

She didn't object to that, but when she moved to get away from the door, Nola caught on to his hand and gave it a gentle squeeze. "It'll be negative," she said. "It'll be because of stress."

Wyatt had heard enough wishful thinking to know when he heard it, but he gave Nola the best confirming nod he could manage and went out to his truck. He had a couple of ranch hands who lived in the bunkhouse behind the stables, but if they saw him, they'd maybe think he was headed into town to pick up beer or a pizza.

Forcing himself to remain calm, he made the short one-mile drive into town, and not for the first time in his life, he was glad Dobb's Pharmacy was on this end of Main Street. The other times he'd been in that "glad" mode were when he'd been on those condom-buying runs for Dax. For himself, too, when Nola and he had been teenagers. The location meant he stood the chance of fewer people spotting him.

Wyatt thanked a couple of lucky stars that there were no vehicles out in front of the pharmacy. There was only a beat-up truck in the back that he thought belonged to the night clerk, who was one of Asa Palmer's kids. There were at least a half dozen of them, and they all must have had bad eyesight, because they wore thick glasses. But Wyatt wasn't going to rely on poor vision to stop gossip tonight. He intended to use the self-checkout that the owner had had installed a year earlier.

Wyatt grabbed a shopping basket so he wouldn't have to walk around with the test in his hand, and he went on the hunt. He finally found an unmarked section for feminine hygiene products, various creams and period meds. He'd been worried that he would have to pick and choose which one, but there was only one brand called One-Step Pregnancy Test, which he thought was good marketing. Nobody would want to go through a whole bunch of steps to learn their fate.

He dropped the test kit into the basket, grabbed a large box of condoms to cover it, and he headed to the front.

"Wyatt," someone called out, causing him to drop the f-bomb. Because it was Nola's sister Lorelei.

He didn't have to look far to see Lorelei making her way toward him. She was a slightly older version of Nola, with the Parkman signature blond hair and blue eyes. But Nola had always been far prettier, softer and more casual around the edges. Lorelei always looked as if she was on the way to a business meeting.

Not tonight, though.

She was carrying a cute baby that Wyatt knew she was in the process of adopting, but beneath the front carrier thing that reminded him of a high-waisted kangaroo pouch, Lorelei was dressed to the nines, probably because she'd been at work in the retail shop where she sold Nola's completed glass pieces.

"I'm surprised to see you," Lorelei remarked. "I figured you'd be with Nola."

"I will be, but I forgot a few things," he said before he realized just what a stupid thing it was to blurt out.

That was because Lorelei's gaze drifted into his basket. He had a look, too, and was partly thankful the pregnancy test wasn't visible. So, instead of Lorelei considering why Wyatt would be buying a pee-stick test, she now believed Nola and he had a night of safe sex planned.

"These are for Dax," he said, hoping to recover himself. "He's in town."

The baby stuck out her tongue and blew a raspberry at him. It sounded like one of those buzzers on a quiz show when a contestant got a wrong answer.

"Yes, I saw him earlier at the gas station. Some girls were following him around," Lorelei added.

"I need to get a few things for Nola, too," Wyatt went on, and he walked a few steps away to grab several handfuls of the chips Nola liked. He already had a boatload of them, in anticipation of her needing some comfort food during the noncelebration, but the bags would ensure the pee stick was covered.

"She'll love those," Lorelei remarked, following him. "Oh, did Nola tell you?"

Wyatt felt his stomach slide to his kneecaps. "Tell me what?"

The baby blew another raspberry and farted.

Lorelei didn't seem to notice the fart or the fact that Wyatt had started to sweat both literally and figuratively. Her face brightened. "About the glass piece she made. It's amazing, Wyatt. The best I've ever seen. I know this is a tough night for Nola and you, but you should celebrate the piece. You should get a bottle of champagne," she added in a bubbly gush.

But she stopped bubbling and gushing, and she frowned when she glanced in the direction of the refrigerated area. To say there was a limited selection was a huge understatement.

"Or you could drop by my house and I'll give you a bottle," Lorelei amended. "I always keep a couple on hand."

"That's all right. Nola prefers the cheap stuff." And because Nola might indeed need some alcohol when the pee stick proved this lateness was truly nerves and to put some distance between Lorelei and him, Wyatt went to the refrigerated booze section and grabbed a bottle of sparkling strawberry wine.

"I'll be seeing you," he called out to Lorelei, hoping she didn't follow him to the front. Thankfully, she headed to the back, where there was ice cream and milk.

Since he wasn't sure how long it'd take Lorelei to gather what she wanted, Wyatt rushed to check out. And cursed when he had to scan all eight of the little bags of chips. Then he cursed when the damn machine wouldn't read the barcode on the condoms. The bored-looking Palmer kid looked over from his seat from behind the counter. A glance before he went back to reading a gaming magazine.

Wyatt set the condoms on the rack with the gum and candy bars, raked the pee-stick box over the scanner and nearly whooped when it rang right up. He didn't have as much luck with the wine, though, because the screen gave him a warning that his ID would need to be checked before he could purchase it. The warning must have also alerted the clerk, because he looked up again and pressed something on the register in front of him.

"You're good," the clerk said in the same tone as *You're old*.

Wyatt didn't care one bit about the insult. He swiped his credit card, signed the screen and got out of there fast.

Somehow, he managed not to wreck on the way home, but he accomplished that only by yelling and cursing at the top of his lungs. It not only made it impossible to think about anything else, but it also burned off some of the nerves. Like primal therapy. He hurried in the house and found Nola exactly where he'd left her. Sitting on the floor in the foyer.

Since everything in the bag was for her, he handed her the entire thing, and she looked through it as she got to her feet. She didn't question the extras. On a sigh, she opened one of the bags of chips while she read the instructions on the test box.

"Three minutes after I pee on it," she said, and carrying her stash, she went into the hall powder room.

He didn't hear the actual peeing part, but he did hear the toilet flush and Nola washing her hands. Then the wait started. He set the timer on his phone, even though Nola had likely already set hers. She wouldn't want to wait any extra time to get the verdict.

Stress. That was all. Stress, stress, stress, which, of course, was only creating more stress.

"I ran into Lorelei at the pharmacy," he said. Not exactly small talk. More like that earlier primal therapy, but at a much lower volume and without the curse words. "She doesn't know you're late."

"No, and you better not have told her," Nola said on a gasp.

"I didn't." Wyatt wasn't sure he could tell anyone because he wasn't able to say the words aloud. As far as he was concerned, there were no spoken words in the English language that started with *p*. "But she mentioned something about a glass piece you'd made."

"She didn't call it *Lustful Longings*, did she?"

"No." But that caught his interest and distracted him for a moment. It must be some piece of glass to earn a name like that. "What name did you give it?"

"*Wyatt's Junk*, but obviously I'll have to rethink that."

Now it really had his interest, but so did the timer. Two minutes left. "What about it makes you think of my junk?"

"It's phallic."

He waited for more, but apparently that was it. If he'd been Dax or in a better mood, he would have joked if she was going to call it after his man parts, then it'd better be big and impressive, but considering they were waiting on a pee-stick verdict, it would have been in poor taste.

"Lily wants to call it *Love Rediscovered*," Nola said. Then she paused a long time. "FYI, they figured out we'd had sex. Recent sex," she clarified.

"What?" he snapped. "How?"

"From the glass piece. Apparently, it reminded them of us."

Now he really had to see it, but before he could even try to form an image of it in his head, he heard the police siren, and it took him a moment to realize it wasn't an actual siren but Nola's choice of timer. His went off, too, and he heard her moving around in the bathroom. He didn't have to listen that hard to hear the other sounds Nola made.

Because the f-bomb she yelled could have been heard all the way to Kansas.

CHAPTER FOUR

NOLA WAS CERTAIN she was feeling a whole boatload of emotions, but it was hard to tell which particular one was leading the pack. There was a good argument for panic being the first-place winner here. But mind-numbing fear and complete shock weren't that far behind.

It was kind of comical in a noncomical kind of way that the little plus sign on the stick could cause such a tsunami of feelings. Of course, that plus sign wasn't just a little symbol. It was proof positive that there was a reason for her being late. And that reason was because she was pregnant.

Again.

"Oh, my God," she managed to say, and she just kept repeating it, well aware that she sounded as if she were losing it. There was probably a reason for that tone. Because she *was* losing it.

"Uh, are you okay?" Wyatt asked from the other side of the door.

"No," she answered.

Nola couldn't even lie about that or soft-pedal her response because she was nowhere close to being okay and might never be again. She was pregnant. With Wyatt's baby. Again.

Pregnant. Pregnant. Pregnant.

She was certain—well, hopeful, anyway—that she would eventually be able to get past the tsunami that had now merged with a tornado or two and sort out what she was feeling. But Nola didn't have a clue when that would happen. For now, she just continued to sit on the bathroom floor, hugging her knees to her chest while she rocked back and forth. She kept her gaze glued to the plus sign. Didn't have much of a choice about that. Her eyes wouldn't budge.

Wyatt cursed and announced, "I'm coming in," a split second before he did just that. He looked at her. Then swung his gaze to the thermometer-sized stick she had vised in her right hand.

He must have been able to see the little plus sign, too, because he went through the same panicking motions she had. Profanity, groans, legs giving way, which required him to sit on the floor. His butt landed next to hers.

Nola had no idea what to say. Or if she could speak. It really didn't seem necessary, but she was sure Wyatt was the only other person on earth who was feeling what she was feeling.

But she rethought that.

No, they weren't on the same emotional plane here. In fact, they weren't even at the same table. She wanted kids. Not like this, that was for sure, and sure as heck not with a man who didn't want them.

Actually, not with a man at all.

Nola realized she'd written that part out of the mental picture of her life. In that picture, she was raising her beautiful son and daughter as a single mom. And with occasional help from her family, of course. But since it was highly likely she'd never totally get over Wyatt, it seemed best to leave a husband/daddy out of the scenario. Any man she brought into her life would always pale in comparison to hot cowboy Wyatt, and that just wouldn't be fair.

The silence came, stayed. It hung in the air like wet cotton balls. And speaking of balls, she finally came up with something to say to him.

"You should get your money back from that doctor who did your vasectomy," Nola grumbled.

"I should kick his ass," Wyatt added to her grumble.

If she had been in his boots, she would feel the same way. After all, he'd endured what had likely been a painful procedure to ensure he didn't knock up anyone else, and here it had failed him with the very person he'd experienced a failure with before. But his comment told her something else.

Or rather, confirmed it.

He hadn't changed his mind about his no-kids rule, because he certainly wasn't doling out any *it'll be okay* or *we'll get through this* platitudes.

"How accurate are those tests?" he asked. "Because there's a big chance it could be wrong, right?"

She heard the desperation in his voice. Not a smidge of it either, but gallons and gallons of it. The reality of that plus sign was sinking in fast but not well.

Nola picked up the box, pulled out the instructions and read through them again. It took her a while to get through the tiny print, but her attention landed on something she knew was only going to add to Wyatt's desperation.

"It says it's ninety-nine percent accurate at the two-week point after conception," Nola relayed to him.

Two weeks. Not that many days, but it suddenly seemed a long time to walk around without knowing she was pregnant.

"I'll take another because sometimes there are false positives," she explained after going through more of the small print. She checked the time. "But it'll have to wait until tomorrow because the pharmacy just closed."

"Take three or four more," he insisted. "I'll pay for them."

That caused her to frown, and she wasn't sure why. But it seemed as if Wyatt wanted her to keep testing until he got a result he wanted. She wanted different results, too.

Didn't she?

Of course she did, and Nola went back to that *doing this by myself* plan. However, she knew in her gut, or maybe that was a different organ of her body, that this hadn't been a false reading, that she had indeed gotten pregnant under the very tree in the very pasture where she'd likely conceived their daughter.

Fate was probably laughing its butt off over that coincidence. But since she didn't want any of the folks in town to be doing a similar kind of laughing or gossiping, she would need to drive elsewhere to get the tests. That meant going into San Antonio, something she wasn't steady enough to do tonight, and she doubted Wyatt was, either. Still, she couldn't put it off. Nola definitely didn't want word of this getting back to anyone in her family before she'd gotten the chance to tell them first.

And oh what a joy that would be.

Her sisters would be sympathetic, of course, and Lily would dole out her usual *let's look on the bright side* stuff. Lorelei would be partly judgy because Wyatt was involved. But her mother… Oh, mercy. She was going to have to tell Evangeline once again that she had gotten pregnant.

Nola cut off the flashbacks of the last time that'd happened. She didn't need to see a repeat of the not-so-subtle disappointment in her mother's eyes. And besides, maybe her gut was wrong and this was a false positive. Maybe there was no baby to obsess over after all, so she shouldn't borrow trouble until she knew for certain that trouble was around to be in such a borrowing state.

Her phone rang, the sound shooting through the wet-cotton-ball silence. Since she was holding her cell in her left hand with a now-stopped timer on it, she saw the name flash on the screen.

Derwin Parkman. The current president of Sherlock's Snoops.

"You have his name in your contacts?" Wyatt muttered after he glanced at the screen and cursed.

"He was interested in commissioning me to do some art pieces for the new Last Ride Society library, so we exchanged contact info." But it wouldn't be glass he'd want to discuss tonight.

Nope. It'd be the research on Griff, something Nola was not in the mood to talk about, so she let the call go to voice mail. However, when the little red light indicated he'd left a voice mail, she played it, only so she could get her mind off that plus sign for just a couple of seconds.

"Nola," Derwin greeted, his voice already grating on her nerves with just that one word in his overly enthusiastic tone. "I wanted you to know we're starting a fundraiser to get the money to have Griff's old car hauled up from the bluff. I'd like to get together and talk about that. Call me."

She deleted the message and had no intention of returning his call to discuss that, especially since Derwin would make sure he tracked her down over the next few days. But Wyatt had obviously heard the message, and that was probably what got his attention off the plus sign long enough for him to give her a questioning look.

"No, I didn't ask him to do a fundraiser," she supplied before Wyatt could even ask.

Though this wasn't the first time the subject had come

up. In the fourteen years since Griff had died, there'd been talk on and off about the car. Nola had never actually seen it herself. She didn't like giving her nightmares any fodder, and that would be a certain way to do it.

But from what she'd been told, the old Ford Taurus was apparently wedged, front end down, sticking up between two massive boulders the size of elephants. Or mountains, depending on who was telling the story. No matter what the actual size, though, it was the spot where the car had lodged after Griff had driven into, or lost control and had bashed through, the double fence barriers set up on the dirt road. The road that led to the bluff that folks called Lover's Leap.

Yeah, not very original.

And to the best of her knowledge, no lover had actually ever leaped from there. Well, except for Griff, and at the time, she wasn't even sure he'd qualified for the lover status.

Anyway, the car was still there and had been for fourteen years. Once someone had spotted the car, it'd taken the better part of a day for rescuers to get down to the scene and retrieve Griff's body from the canyon below, but the county didn't have the special equipment it would take to haul out the vehicle. Hence, the fundraiser to pay for the equipment and the team to do the job. A fundraiser that almost certainly wouldn't have come to fruition if she hadn't drawn Griff's name for the Last Ride Society.

"Sorry," she told Wyatt. "You didn't need to hear that particular message, what with that going on." She tipped her head to the pee stick.

"No," he agreed, and that was all he said for a while. Enough of a while for the wet cotton balls to start accumulating again. "If you have any say in the matter, the car should stay put."

Nola didn't ask him his reasoning on that. Didn't need

to know. But she suspected it would stir up the mother lode of gossip, which in turn would stir up yet more grief for Wyatt. She had a twin sibling and couldn't imagine the pain she'd feel at losing her.

Especially the way Griff had died.

Maybe as long as the car was stuck between the two stone elephants, then Wyatt could let himself believe it was an accident. That Griff hadn't meant to end his life. But if the vehicle was raised and examined, then maybe someone could determine that Griff hadn't even hit the brakes and had in fact accelerated to his death. Or perhaps determine what the Sherlock's Snoops touted.

That someone might have tampered with the car.

Nola doubted it was in the cards to determine any of those possibilities. The brakes, the acceleration or the tampering. And that might be playing into the reason why Wyatt wanted to leave things as they were. Because all the testing and analysis would scrape away at him, leaving him raw but still with no definitive answers.

"I'm sure I'll run into Derwin soon," she remarked. "Sooner than I want," Nola amended. "I can tell him it's a no-go on the car."

Whether Derwin or the rest of the Snoops would listen to her or not was anyone's guess, but she'd have to try. At the moment, Wyatt had way too much to deal with to add that. Heck, so did she.

She was about to ask him if he could get her a stiff drink. Maybe a quadruple shot of anything from a liquor bottle, but the little plus sign seemed to flash with neon-quality lighting. A reminder that she couldn't booze out, but she was pretty sure large amounts of chips and orange soda could serve as a substitute by giving her a sugar high and a carb crash.

Somehow, she got to her feet, and put her phone in her pocket so she could extend her hand and help Wyatt up. It took him a couple of seconds, some more muttered profanity and a groan before he finally took hold and stood.

Nola tucked the test stick back into the box and tossed it in the small empty trash can, the thud of it echoing when it hit the metal. Since it would obviously be a while before there was enough trash to empty and because she didn't want Wyatt to have to look at it, she retrieved it, crammed it into the back pocket of her jeans and washed her hands.

She met Wyatt's gaze in the mirror.

It was an all-doom-and-gloom expression on his hot face. Oh, yeah. Even now she could see the hotness first and the gloom and doom second. Apparently, even in a time of crisis, Wyatt could still tick off all of her fantasy-guy boxes, what with that tousled black hair and dreamy green eyes.

It'd been those eyes she'd first noticed about him. That'd been when he'd moved to Last Ride as a kid after his parents had died. She hadn't known them since they weren't from Last Ride, but Nola did remember Maude, the woman who'd raised him.

Wyatt and his brothers looked nothing like the crotchety old woman. Maude had been squat, barely five feet tall and had had stringy graying red hair and a bloated face. The brothers had obviously gotten their looks from a far superior set of genes in their family DNA pool.

She pulled herself from thoughts of his dreamy eyes and gene pools and looked at him. The worry was all over his face, and she knew it was all over hers, too.

"I'm sorry," she repeated, knowing an apology wouldn't do much to help.

He nodded, repeated the words back to her and then mumbled, "I'm going to kick that doctor's ass."

Sighing, she dried her hands and followed him into the kitchen, where she found the usual stash of chips and orange soda that he always had for her at these noncelebrations. Odd, though, that for a couple of minutes, she'd actually forgotten about this unjoyous event. That was because the current unjoyous event of the plus sign had usurped it.

Temporarily, anyway.

Nola was certain it wouldn't be long before her mind managed to fix on both of the double whammies.

"Let's make another pact," Nola suggested as she popped the top on one of the sodas. "We won't talk about the positive sign until I've repeated the test. Since that won't happen until tomorrow, let's just eat our stash and do what we usually do every August 15."

What they usually did was not talk about the adoption or that other pregnancy. They talked around it, tripping and stumbling down memory lane while all the time mourning the loss of what they hadn't been able to hold on to. Off-limit topics included but weren't restricted to the current age of their DNA-only daughter, where she might be, what she could be doing. It made for depressing conversation. However, with the current plus sign off the table, it took the discussion possibilities into the depressing stratosphere.

Nola broached that stratosphere with something she was going to have to tell him sooner or later, so she went with the sooner option. "I haven't started the research for the Last Ride Society. I have three months to do it. But I'll need a photo of Griff's tombstone. I don't want you to come with me for that. I just wanted to let you know I'd be out at the cemetery."

That photo was one of the Last Ride Society's requirements, even though they'd recently updated the rules to include a picture of a cremation urn. Or even the location of where the ashes had been scattered, if there was no urn. Griff, though, had a tombstone, and Nola knew exactly where it was because she'd visited it over the years. So had others, because every time she went, there'd either been fresh flowers left there or the remnants of a bouquet.

And there was also the ring.

A simple gold band that someone had put on top of the tombstone. Perhaps a wedding band, but it'd been etched inside with little hearts, so it was possible that it'd been meant for nonmarriage purposes. It'd been too small for Griff's hands. She knew because she was familiar with Wyatt's hands, which were a genetic copy of his twin brother's.

Nola had first noticed the ring a couple of weeks after Griff's burial, and it'd been there ever since. Some people had even reported picking up the ring from the ground and replacing it on the tombstone after it'd been knocked off by a bad storm. In some towns or cities, a thief likely would have swiped it, but apparently that was too cruel or morbid to happen in Last Ride. Plus, there was the whole mystery of it. Who had put it there?

And why?

Wyatt certainly hadn't offered up any theories, so Nola hadn't pushed, but she had to wonder if Griff had given it to someone. Maybe someone he'd loved. And then the owner had "returned" it to him after his death.

The obvious choice was Lily, since she'd been involved with Griff up until several months before his death, but her sister had denied it was hers. Since the mere thought of it seemed to distress Lily, Nola stopped asking her about it.

With the research, though, it might be time to ask the question again to those who knew Griff but wouldn't go into a deep well of grief by discussing it. Of course, Wyatt was probably wishing she'd ditch the whole project and not discuss anything about Griff with anyone. Nola wanted that, too, but there was the whole deal about this assignment already stirring up gossip. Added to that, the town's founder, Hezzie Parkman, had left generous provisions in her will to donate money to various charities and causes for every completed research project.

Nola's phone dinged with a text while she was eating the chips she didn't want and drinking the soda she equally didn't want while Wyatt took a shot of whiskey that he did seem to want.

"It's Lorelei," she relayed with a sigh after she glanced at the screen. "She'll be worried that I'm in a pit of despair."

Which she was, but Nola frowned when she read the message.

Wyatt left his receipt in the self-checkout at the pharmacy, and the clerk gave it to me to give to him. The receipt that clearly shows what he bought. Do you want to talk?

Nola groaned and showed Wyatt the text so that he could groan, too. It also prompted him to toss back another shot of whiskey.

"Lorelei won't blab," she assured him, but it added yet another thing to her to-do list.

Buy pregnancy tests, pee on sticks, drink lots so ample pee was available, deal with what would no doubt be a trash basket filled with plus-sign pee sticks and talk to her sister. And if that wasn't enough to drop her into the deepest sludge of panic and despair, she had to visit the grave of her ex-lover's dead twin brother. Sometimes, life was just a big bucket of crap.

Will talk tomorrow, Nola texted Lorelei back, but she'd no sooner hit Send than her phone dinged again.

What the heck? People who knew her were well aware this wasn't a good night to text her. Especially this person whose name popped up. Evangeline knew not to call or text during the noncelebration because her mother was well aware this was the alone time Wyatt and she needed.

"My mother," she grumbled, and once again, she showed him the screen so he could read the message for himself.

Just checking to see if Wyatt and you got my earlier messages, her mother had texted. Bright Blessings.

It didn't seem appropriate to snarl "Screw you," but that was what Nola did. She wasn't in the mood for Evangeline's cheery optimism right now.

"Why does she want to talk to us?" Wyatt asked. "Does she know you might be pregnant?"

Nola quickly shook her head. She'd gotten the message from her mother when she'd still been getting dressed to come to Wyatt's. That was before Nola had even realized she was late.

"It's probably about the research," Nola guessed.

Heck, maybe even about the mystery ring on Griff's tombstone. That wasn't a long-shot kind of guess either since Evangeline was a counselor, and it was possible that someone had confessed to her about it in the past fourteen years. Her mother never ever spilled anything that was revealed to her in therapy, but maybe she intended to make an exception. Or it could be she just wanted to offer her help with the research so that Nola and Wyatt wouldn't have to get involved.

Nola didn't respond to the text. She'd tack on "Call my mother" to that mental list that was taking on the same dread as the Black Plague.

She nearly muttered another "I'm sorry" to Wyatt, and

he looked as if he wanted to do the same for her, but they both settled for more drinking. Whiskey for him. Orange soda for her, though it wasn't giving her a sugar high at all. Instead, it was making her feel queasy, and she hoped she didn't add to the night by barfing.

Nola saw the slash of headlights in the front windows and heard the car when it came to a stop in front of the house. She didn't bother to ask Wyatt if he was expecting anyone because she knew he wouldn't be. Again, this was their night and they didn't double-book it or invite anyone to share.

"That better not be anyone from the Sherlock's Snoops," she grumbled. "Or anyone in my gene pool."

Wyatt tossed back yet another shot and headed for the door just as someone knocked. Whoever it was, Nola was certain he'd tell them to go to hell and not come back anytime soon.

Since his house had an open floor plan, Nola could see the front door when he opened it, but she couldn't see the visitor. However, she did hear the barely audible murmur of a female voice. She also saw when Wyatt froze. Just froze. It was sort of like the reaction he'd had to the plus sign.

Wondering what had caused the repeat stiffening, Nola went to the door and peered around him at the young dark-haired woman wearing a yellow dress. A stranger.

Except she wasn't.

No, by God, she wasn't.

It only took Nola a glance to recognize those features. Her own eyes and mouth. Wyatt's hair and olive skin.

"Hi," she said, her cautious gaze flitting between Wyatt and Nola before it settled on Wyatt. "You're Wyatt Buchanan?" she asked.

Wyatt nodded.

The girl nodded as well as if it had only confirmed what she already knew. "I'm Marley Silva. I'm, uh, your daughter."

CHAPTER FIVE

WYATT THOUGHT HE might be hallucinating. That he'd gotten some bad whiskey or had already had so much to drink that his mind was playing tricks on him. But that doubt didn't last long when the girl threw herself into his arms.

Since he was in no way expecting a hug, and he sure as hell hadn't been expecting this visitor, he wasn't braced for it and staggered back a step before regaining his balance. It took another couple of seconds for him to slide his arms around her and return the hug. It felt...

He cut off any possible finish to that particular sentence. Right now, he didn't want to feel anything. Not until he'd sorted out what was going on.

When she, *Marley*, eased back from him, there were tears in her eyes, but since she was also smiling, he thought they might be of the happy variety. Well, good. That was better than the sad, overly pissed off sort.

"I can't believe it," Marley muttered. "I can't believe I'm finally seeing you."

On this point, Wyatt was right there on the same page with her. He'd never expected this moment and hadn't steeled himself for it. Then again, he wasn't sure he could have ever managed that.

He had to stuff down those feelings again.

"I didn't know you'd be here," Marley added, swallowing

hard and shifting her attention to Nola. "I hadn't prepared myself to meet you."

Marley certainly didn't say that with a smile nor any happy tears. There was some ice in her voice. Ice in her eyes, too.

Nola made a soft gasp, causing Wyatt to look down at her, and he saw she was experiencing the same level of shock as he was. Except there were tears in her eyes. Maybe happy ones.

Maybe.

But there was no way Nola could have missed the fact that Marley hadn't included her in that hug. Nor had she missed Marley's "prepared myself" remark. The girl had clearly done the preparation for coming to his house, knocking on his door and greeting him as if she were damn glad to see him. That hug hadn't felt forced or rehearsed but rather joyful.

"Marley Silva," Nola muttered. "I always wondered what you'd be named. And how you'd look." She motioned to Marley's face. "My eyes and mouth. My mother's nose, but you favor Wyatt and his brothers, too."

None of that knowledge seemed to impress Marley, who spared Nola the briefest glance before shifting back to settle her attention solely on Wyatt. "Can I come in so we can talk? Or is this a bad time?" she added with another cool glance at Nola.

Wyatt wasn't exactly in the right place to do good deeds and try to right whatever had caused Marley to act the way she was acting toward Nola, but he somehow managed to gather enough words to speak.

"Every year Nola and I get together for your, uh, birthday," he said, figuring that was better than noncelebration for the DNA-only child that they'd sworn never to see in the flesh. That part of their pact had obviously gone to hell in a handbasket, even though Nola and he hadn't been the ones to break it.

"Oh," Marley said. She fluttered her fingers toward her powder blue car, which was parked behind Nola's. "Then how about I come back—"

"Come in," Nola interrupted, and she stepped away from the door. She caught on to Wyatt's sleeve to move him, too. Something he appreciated, because someone had cemented his boots to the floor.

"I guess you're wondering why I'm here," Marley continued as she came into the foyer. "And why I didn't call or something first to give you a heads-up. I considered calling, but I figured it'd be better if I came in person." Her words were running together in a way that showed her nerves.

Wyatt was sure he had nerves, too, but he couldn't sort them out from the other stuff going on in his head. Mercy, a pregnancy test, too much whiskey and the arrival of a DNA-only daughter had put his brain on overload. Nola had to be experiencing something similar, but she managed to motion toward the living room sofa and then the kitchen.

"Would you like to sit down?" Nola asked. "And how about a soda or something to eat?"

Marley made a noncommittal sound, maybe declining the offer of food and drink, and she took slow, cautious steps toward the sofa while she gave them both the once-over again.

"You two aren't, like, together, are you?" she asked. "I mean, I didn't see anything about that being the case on social media."

Wyatt wasn't on social media, so that meant the lack of a mention had come from Nola. And that told him that Marley had not only discovered they were her biological parents but had also done some research to get ready for this visit.

"We're, uh, not together," Nola said.

Wyatt was thankful she'd been the one to respond. First, his tongue still felt all tied up, and second, because it might have sounded like a slam to Nola if it'd come from him. Because, technically, they had been together two weeks ago.

Oh, hell.

The pregnancy. Not that Wyatt had forgotten about it, but talk about seriously bad timing. In the span of less than a half hour, he'd come face-to-face with the reality, and the consequences, of his screwing around with Nola.

"How did you find out about us?" Nola asked, and she sat in one of the chairs across from Marley when she took the sofa.

Marley's mouth tightened, and she sighed. "Look, I really didn't know you'd be here, and I didn't expect to have to... well, deal with you."

Oh, yeah. The chill in her voice was even colder this time, and he figured it felt like a stab to the heart for Nola. Nola nodded but didn't get a chance to say anything because Marley continued.

"I mean, you gave me up for adoption, so I figured I was out of the picture for you. Out of your life," Marley added.

Nola stayed quiet for a moment. "You were never out of the picture, never out of my life. Nor Wyatt's." Her voice was a sure contrast to Marley's. Deep, deep emotions and equally deep hurt.

"And I agreed to the adoption," he couldn't point out fast enough.

Wyatt dropped down in the chair next to Nola and was well aware that his whiskey buzz was fading fast. That was both good and bad. Good because he could think clearer.

Bad because he could think clearer.

"Yes, you agreed," Marley repeated, not sounding at all

convinced of that, "but it wasn't really your decision. It was hers."

Hers, said in the same tone as if discussing some kind of fungus.

"Now, wait a minute," Wyatt started, and he would have said a whole lot more in Nola's defense if there hadn't been the sound of another vehicle pulling to a stop in front of the house.

Hell's bells. What now? Alien invaders? Another round of shocking, perhaps shitty news? But at the thought of that last part, some of the anger vanished, because he realized this could indeed be shitty news about one of his brothers. Dax had gotten hurt pretty badly while riding bulls and the worst could have happened.

He went to the door, threw it open, expecting to see his other brother, Jonas, or the local cops there to do some kind of notification. But it wasn't any of them. It was a man and woman who'd obviously arrived in the two vehicles that were now parked behind Marley's. A bright red Porsche and a white BMW. They appeared to be in their fifties and were dressed as upscale as their vehicles.

"We're looking for our daughter," the man immediately said. Not a greeting. Not a friendly one, anyway. He barked that out in such a way that made Wyatt think that barking was his usual style of communication.

Wyatt went through another round of *Hell's bells*. Because these were obviously Marley's adoptive parents, and his first impression of the father wasn't a good one. That impression probably wasn't going to add any positive moments to this meeting.

"Is Marley here?" the woman asked. Not a greeting either, but at least there was worry and concern in her voice and all over her face.

"She's here," Wyatt confirmed as he stepped back.

Wyatt didn't issue an invitation, but the man came inside anyway, walking right past him. He paused only long enough to glance around, and when he spotted Marley, he made a beeline toward her.

So did Wyatt.

He didn't know this man from Adam, and if the guy was going to get pushy or mean, Wyatt intended to mop the floor with the man's ass. He was not in the mood to take any crap from an asshole.

"Mom, Dad," Marley said, getting to her feet. So did Nola, and she might not have noticed that she sidestepped to move closer to Marley, taking a protective stance.

"Marley, you shouldn't be here," the man snarled, but the woman quickly moved in front of him, went to Marley and hugged her. She murmured something Wyatt didn't catch before she turned back to give Nola and Wyatt a nod, which appeared to be one of greeting that her husband had skipped.

"I'm Heather Silva," she said, "and this is my husband, Alec."

"Marley's parents," Alec added in a snap. "And our daughter shouldn't be here. I'm sorry she disturbed your evening."

Alec reached out as if to take hold of Marley's arm, but Heather saved him from that whole floor-ass-mopping by maneuvering herself in front of Marley again. Heather was about half the size of her husband, but it was obvious she wasn't going to take any of his BS tonight.

"I came because I wanted to meet him," Marley insisted, going to Heather's side. A position that put her right in front of Nola as if she'd forgotten she was even there.

"And I told you meeting him wasn't a good idea," Alec argued. "You don't even know him."

"That's why I'm here," Marley argued right back, "because I want to get to know him." Again, just *him*. No mention of Nola. If he got the chance, Wyatt was going to have to better explain the mutual adoption decision Nola and he had made.

Alec's mouth tightened. "He could be a criminal—"

"Don't finish that," Wyatt warned him, his tone proving he could bark and snarl when needed.

It was a skill that came in darn handy since he had over a dozen ranch hands working for him. Alec might be a boss and think he was in charge, but Wyatt was a boss, too, and the man was on his home turf.

Alec shot him one cold glance. But he didn't finish saying what he'd started. Instead, he turned back to Marley.

"It's time for you to come home," Alec insisted. "Let's go."

"No," Marley said, and she didn't stutter. However, she did march across the room and stood arm to arm with Wyatt. "If he says it's okay, I'm staying."

Marley paused, maybe to give Wyatt a chance to say that *okay*, but he didn't know what the right answer was. So, he went with one that was potentially the least wrong.

"I'm not going to make her leave," Wyatt spelled out. "And neither are you," he added to Alec.

Wyatt hoped he could back that up with something that didn't require the ass kicking and floor mopping. He didn't know the law when it came to such matters, but Marley was a minor. In fact, today was her seventeenth birthday. Still, Wyatt figured the law would give her at least some say in whether or not she wanted to leave the house with an asshole.

"She can stay," Heather interjected, causing Alec to aim a very nasty glare at her. She glared right back, and Wyatt was suddenly in Heather's cheering section. At least it didn't appear Marley had an asshole mother.

"She can't," Alec growled.

"I can," Marley growled back. "The only reason you want me home is so you can use me as a pawn." She looked at Wyatt then. "They're getting a divorce. Not a pretty one where everyone agrees to play nice with each other. My father is demanding full custody of me."

Well, that explained the separate vehicles and the vibe that there was no love lost between Alec and Heather. That didn't make Wyatt feel better about this situation. Nope. He'd been through family strife—aka shit—and it wasn't something he'd want his biological daughter to have to experience.

"Marley will decide with whom and where she wants to live," Heather pointed out. Alec started saying something, but Heather talked right over him. Quite an accomplishment, considering she didn't even raise her voice. "In Texas, a child over the age of twelve can tell the judge his or her wishes for custody, and they'll be taken into account."

"But those wishes aren't gospel," Alec finally managed to say loud enough to be heard. "It's still the decision of the judge, and once he hears how irresponsibly Marley has acted by coming here to see…" He stopped, and after noting Wyatt's steely glare, he obviously rethought that. "Once the judge has the whole picture, Marley will be living with me."

"You really want to force the issue when she's only a year away from being an adult?" Nola asked, but judging from the way her eyes widened, she hadn't intended to say that aloud.

Alec shifted toward her. "You're the birth mother, the so-called glass artist who gave up Marley for adoption."

Oh, there was way too much smugness and venom in his

voice, so Wyatt went ahead and clarified. "Nola and I were sixteen, and we weren't in any position to raise a child. We thought, hoped, we were giving her to people who'd do a better job than we could."

It was as if Wyatt had tossed gasoline onto Alec's simmering fire of a temper. The anger flared in his eyes. "You gave her up. Practically threw her away, and if you forget that, then maybe I can do something to remind you."

Well, hell, that was even more gasoline, this time on Wyatt's no-longer-simmering temper. It was at full flame, and he took one menacing step toward Alec. His expression must have been plenty fierce because it sent both Nola and Heather scurrying to get between them.

"Stop it!" Marley yelled when Alec tried to move around the women to do something that Wyatt would make sure he regretted. "See how unreasonable you are?" she snarled to Alec. "This is why I don't want to live with you."

That seemed to have Alec taking a mental step back. Oh, the anger was still there, but he was clueing in to the fact that agitating the daughter he was trying to get custody of probably wasn't a bright thing to do.

"Please let me stay," Marley said, shifting her attention back to Wyatt. "Please."

This was the very definition of a rock and a hard place, but he was just going to have to put up with the discomfort for a while. No way was Wyatt going to act like Alec and try to force her to do something.

"You can stay," Wyatt told her, and it caused Marley to launch herself at him for another hug. One that sent Alec's temper flaming again.

"This isn't over," Alec said, storming toward the front door. "I'll be back with a court order."

He left the door wide open when he left, and Heather

sighed as she watched him get into the red Porsche. "I'm sorry," she said, and it seemed to be a blanket apology to all of them. "Believe me when I say he wasn't always like this."

Wyatt figured she'd added that last part because of the sickening worry she'd seen in both Nola and him. But he hoped her words weren't hollow or an outright lie because it was gut twisting to think of that man trying to clamp that kind of steely control over Marley.

"You're sure it's okay if she stays?" Heather asked Wyatt.

He nodded, though "sure" wasn't anywhere in this scenario. A biological child whom he'd just met would apparently be under his roof.

"All right." Heather dragged in a long breath and looked at Marley. "Do you have money? Your phone charger? Your meds?"

Marley answered yes to each one, and Wyatt wondered exactly what meds Heather meant. It gave him another gut twist to know that Marley might have some medical problem, maybe even a serious one.

"I'll be all right, Mom," Marley assured her, and she kissed Heather's cheek. "I just want to spend some time here."

Heather's nod was sort of like the one Wyatt had just given, the one that'd lacked the "sure" factor. The woman obviously had plenty of doubts about this, and Wyatt couldn't blame her. But Heather and/or Alec had clearly done some kind of background check on him, because they'd known where he lived and who he was. Which meant Alec had also likely been aware that Wyatt wasn't a criminal.

And that gave Wyatt a weird feeling.

If he'd been in Alec's overly priced shoes, then maybe he wouldn't have been as trusting either of Marley staying with a man she had just met. It didn't sit well with Wyatt to know he had that in common with the hothead asshole.

"Thank you for allowing me to be Marley's mother all these years," Heather said, after giving Marley another hug. She looked at Nola. "You and Mr. Buchanan created a bright, beautiful baby, and it's been a privilege and honor to have raised her these seventeen years."

Now, this was what Wyatt had wanted for his child. What he wanted for the baby girl who had become Marley Silva.

"Good luck with the custody fight," Nola told the woman.

Heather managed a thin, watery smile. It blended with her watery eyes, which now threatened to spill the tears she was trying to hold back.

"Call me if you need anything," Heather murmured to Marley, and after another round of kisses and hugs, she went to the door and walked out. She gave Marley one last glance over her shoulder and then waved goodbye as she got in the white BMW.

Since it was mosquito heaven outside, Wyatt shut the door, smacked at one of the little bloodsuckers that had managed to fly in, and he turned back to Marley and Nola. That was when he realized he didn't have a clue what to say or do. Thankfully, Marley filled in the silence.

"I have an overnight bag in my car," she said. "Were you serious when you said I could stay here? If not, I can get a room at the inn in town."

"I was serious," Wyatt assured her. "I have a guest room. Actually, three. You can take your pick."

"The one that overlooks the stables has a pretty view," Nola remarked. "It's the last one at the end of the hall."

Marley made a noncommittal sound that could have meant anything, but Nola obviously took it as a "when are you going to leave?" because she said, "I should be going." Nola added to him, "You'll be all right?"

Wyatt had no idea. None. And he could say the same for Nola. "How about you?" he asked.

She managed a smile similar to the one Heather had doled out before her exit. "Fine. I'll call you in the morning after I've done those…errands."

The pregnancy tests. No, he hadn't forgotten about those. "Call me when you pick up the…supplies, and I'll try to come over."

He didn't want Nola to go through that alone, but he also didn't want to just ditch Marley here in an unfamiliar place. Maybe by morning, he could figure out a way to do both without screwing up both things.

"All right," Nola murmured. She picked up her purse but didn't leave. She stood there, looking at Marley. "Do you mind me asking how you found out about us?"

Good question, because as part of the pact Nola and he had made, the adoption had been private and the records were sealed.

"Oh, I thought you knew," Marley said, her tone almost matter-of-fact. "I thought your mother would have told you."

Nola's eyes widened, and Wyatt got a third round of gut tightening.

"Evangeline had something to do with this?" Wyatt asked.

Marley nodded. "She sure did. Nola's mother is the one who got in contact with me and told me who you were."

"Oh. She did," Nola remarked, and in those three words, there was a question, a reckoning and a snarl. "I guess I'll be having a conversation with my mother, then," Nola added, and she headed out the door.

CHAPTER SIX

NOLA BLEW INTO her Harry Potter tube, put her thumb over the hole and watched. And watched. Apparently, there was no magic today and she was making a misshapen glass blob that was eerily similar in every way but color to the other three misshapen blobs she'd already made this morning.

Considering she'd been at work for nearly two hours already, she didn't have a lot to show for her efforts. But then, it was barely seven in the morning, and with as little sleep as she'd managed, she was surprised she could even stay awake. Of course, it might take another decade or two for the adrenaline to settle down and for her nerves to quit doing a jangle.

The handful of minutes she'd managed to sleep had been filled with images of pregnancy tests, orange sodas and Marley. All reasonable since her thoughts had been filled with those things before she'd finally managed to drift off for what was basically a catnap. Her mother was also mixed into that flurry of images. Again reasonable because she'd yet to be able to speak to her after Marley had dropped the bombshell.

Nola's mother is the one who got in contact with me and told me who you were.

Since that had been the first Nola had heard about it, she'd tried to call Evangeline the moment she'd left Wyatt's, but her mom hadn't answered. That meant her mother was likely dodging her, and that riled Nola to the core. Riled her enough that she'd considered driving to her mom's and having it out with her. But in the end, Nola's drive had taken her out of Last Ride and to the first all-night pharmacy she could find on the outskirts of San Antonio.

The half-hour drive sure as heck hadn't soothed her. Neither had returning home with her purchases to drink gallons of water and orange soda so she could pee on each test. After that, she'd given in to the dark mood and just wallowed in self-pity.

Marley hated her.

The beautiful child Wyatt and she had made, the very one who'd been an honor and privilege for Heather Silva, hated her for giving her up for adoption. Nola couldn't blame her. There were plenty of times she hated herself for doing it, and all those "logical" reasons she'd had for signing the adoption papers no longer seemed logical at all. They just seemed selfish.

She tapped off the glass blob, figuring even though it was ugly that Lorelei could sell it as a paperweight or "affordable" objet d'art.

At the thought of her sister, she made a mental note to call Lorelei today and address the issue of Wyatt's receipt from the pharmacy. Nola would probably just fess up because at the moment it all seemed too much to try to come up with a lie.

And why bother?

Soon, there'd be enough gossip about Marley's arrival that it would overshadow any gossip that the clerk might start if he'd seen the items on that receipt before handing it off to Lorelei.

She took the blob to the annealer to let it cool and went back to the area where she kept her selection of glass to see if one stirred the magic. Or one that at least stirred a mild enough interest to make something that would keep her mind occupied. However, the mind-occupying attempt went south when her phone rang, and she saw Wyatt's name on the screen. Nola nearly knocked herself in the head with the pipe when she tried to hurriedly set it aside and answer.

"What happened after I left?" she immediately asked Wyatt. "And how's Marley this morning?" She stopped herself from adding a flurry of questions to that so Wyatt could get a word in edgewise.

"We talked some before she went to bed at ten. She didn't get into her parents' divorce or what was going on there, but she told me she wants to work with horses. Maybe train them or be a vet."

Horses. Well, maybe she'd gotten that through the DNA from Wyatt since that had always been his big dream. It would make the ranch even more appealing to Marley, even though Wyatt seemed to be the girl's main draw. She'd said several times that she wanted to get to know him.

"Did she ask anything about me?" Nola had to know.

"No. Sorry." He muttered another "sorry" and sighed. "I'm sure she will. Just give her some time, and I'll talk to her about you when she gets up. In the meantime, when are you getting the tests so—"

"It's already done," she interrupted. "I know I probably should have waited, but I couldn't. I had to know."

"And?" he pressed when she paused.

"Plus signs on all six tests I bought." She'd bought a dozen more, selections of every brand on the shelf, and she had no doubts that those twelve would have the same plus signs that the other seven completed tests had.

Wyatt sighed again, and she could clearly see the image

of him and his ruggedly handsome, frustrated face. "So, it's for sure."

Of course it was. Only an idiot would have any doubts at this point, but she was going to give Wyatt a little reprieve since he was dealing directly with Marley. "I'll make an appointment with my doctor in San Antonio and have a test done there."

She sometimes saw a doctor here in Last Ride as well, but she'd learned the hard way that a mere visit to a doctor when you weren't visibly sick with a cold or such would spur gossip. It was easier to make the half-hour drive and keep any ailments like a urinary tract infection to herself.

"Let me know the time of the appointment, and I'll go with you," he offered.

And she knew he truly would, but she didn't want to put him through that when the outcome was inevitable. Besides, she might take the time alone for a little meltdown and a cry. After that, though, she was going to have to woman up and deal with everything that was hitting her.

"She's beautiful, isn't she?" Nola murmured, and she didn't have to explain who she meant. She was talking about the child they'd made.

"Yeah, she is." His voice was a mix of emotions. Maybe some pride. Lots of worry, too. And more than a tinge of *What the hell are we going to do?*

Nola didn't have a clue, but it turned out she didn't have to come up with any possibilities because the workshop door opened, and Evangeline came in.

"I have to go," Nola told Wyatt. "My mother's here. I'll let you know what half-assed excuse she has for doing what she did," she added before ending the call.

Evangeline came in with two mugs of what Nola knew would be some kind of herbal tea concoction and that the mugs would be real glass that would have to be washed. Minimal carbon footprint for her mother, something that usually pleased Nola, but today she was reasonably sure that nothing about Evangeline was going to please her.

"You dodged me last night by not answering my call," Nola said the moment her mother had shut the door.

Evangeline nodded and went closer to hand her one of the mugs. It smelled of apples and cinnamon. "I didn't think it was a good idea to have that particular discussion over the phone. I take it Marley contacted you?"

"No, she came to Wyatt's house last night and asked to stay with him." Nola added a huff. "Mom, why would you find Marley and let her know that Wyatt and I are her bio-parents?"

Her mother did seem a little distressed at hearing what Nola had just tossed at her, but she didn't jump into an answer. She had a sip of tea first, then another.

"I've been keeping tabs on Marley for years," Evangeline eventually said.

Nola was certain she blinked. "Why? You knew Wyatt and I made a pact not to ever try to find out anything about her."

Another nod. "But that was your pact, not mine. She's my granddaughter," Evangeline added. "And I just wanted to be able to see pictures of her, to know she was all right. I would have never passed along anything to Wyatt and you."

Nola heard the *but* at the end of that, and she voiced it. "But?"

"Marley's active on social media, and like most girls her age, she tends not to keep things private. I read her posts about her parents' divorce, about the horrible custody suit they're going through, and I knew Marley was hurting. She was talking about running away or doing something to make her father back off."

"What do you mean by *something*?" Nola could barely speak the words. "You mean like harm herself?"

Evangeline lifted her shoulder. "She didn't say that directly, and I got the feeling she had something else in mind. Like maybe acting out or underage drinking. You know, all those things Lily and you used to do and you thought I didn't know."

"No underage drinking for me," Nola quickly argued. "That was Lily's deal." And she realized that she had just ratted out her sister.

Her mother gave a soft, knowing, motherly smile. "Anyway, I thought with everything Marley was going through that this might be a good time for a distraction."

Nola mentally worked through that explanation and found a flaw. "How'd you know she even wanted to meet her birth parents?"

Evangeline took out her phone, scrolled through some photos and showed her one of what looked to be a composite drawing. "Because Marley used a computer program to do artist renditions of what her biological parents might look like. She posted this one along with several others. I could practically feel her longing and pain jump right off the page."

The fit of anger that Nola had nursed and fed vanished. She likely would have done the same thing in her mother's shoes. "You should have still given us a heads-up."

"I tried. That's why I called you both last night. And I didn't know Marley would actually come to Last Ride. I figured she'd just try to contact Wyatt, and then you, and then you could both decide what to do from there."

"Contact Wyatt," Nola repeated. "Because she didn't want to talk to me."

"I'm sorry." Her mother hugged her and managed not to spill a drop of tea from either of the cups. "She seems to be angry about the adoption. It's a common reaction," she added. "It's not logical, but if there's hurt, it feels as if there should be blame for the hurt."

"And she blames me," Nola concluded.

"For now. But that'll change," Evangeline said like gospel. "Just give her time."

Wyatt had said something along those same soothing lines, but nothing about this felt soothing. Or gospel-like. It was more like BS that a mother would use to try to soothe her hurting child. And there was no doubt about it. Nola was indeed hurting.

"How did you find Marley?" Nola wanted to know "How did you even know her name?"

"I saw the adoption record before it was sealed. I might be good-natured, nonjudgmental and trusting, but I had the adoptive parents vetted."

That got Nola's attention. "And? Because Alec Silva's a dipstick."

"Yes, he is," Evangeline agreed. "But he wasn't that way in the beginning. I think he and his wife gave Marley a very good life before he started going through this midlife crisis thing. So cliché," she added.

"Is he dangerous, abusive?" Nola wanted to know.

"I don't think so, and I think his soon-to-be ex-wife can keep him in check. Heather runs a successful real-estate business in San Antonio that her parents own, and she has lots of old money to be able to afford good lawyers. I suspect if Marley tells the judge that she wants to live with her mother, then he or she will grant Heather custody."

Nola hoped that was the way it played out, but judges didn't always play fair or do the right thing. It was also possible that dipstick Alec could sway the decision in his favor.

Evangeline gave Nola's arm a loving pat. "I want Marley to have this time to get some space from her parents. And to also get to know Wyatt and you."

Well, she'd likely get to know Wyatt anyway unless Alec managed to force her to go back home.

Her mother opened her mouth to say something else, but she stopped when she glanced around the workshop and her attention landed on *the* art piece. The flame-red one that Nola still hadn't gotten a chance to hide.

As if it were a lure and she were a hungry, mesmerized fish, Evangeline went closer to study it. "It's incredible," she said.

Nola hadn't expected the sudden wash of pride she felt at hearing her mother's reaction. She might be considered successful in some circles, but like so many women, she also had regular battles with impostor syndrome. That feeling she was a fraud and sucked at what she loved, that she would never be a real artist worthy of the prices that some buyers paid for her pieces.

Her mother moved around, looking at the piece from different angles, and Nola braced herself for the *Wyatt and you had sex* accusation. She really did have to come up with a nonsexual name for it so that just saying it would get people's attention veering away from the notion of Wyatt's junk.

Evangeline abruptly turned to her. "You had sex with Wyatt and you're pregnant?"

Nola replaced her frown with a scowl, and that had her reexamining the piece. "How'd you come up with that really bad assumption by looking at a piece of glass?"

Her mother smiled again. "Well, the piece just exudes

sex, and you have a One-Step Pregnancy Test box in your back pocket."

Crap. These were the same jeans she'd worn to Wyatt's the night before, and she recalled putting the box in her back pocket because she hadn't wanted to leave it in his trash can. Why hadn't the darn thing fallen out when she'd taken off the jeans and then put them back on? Better yet, why hadn't she noticed it?

Nola did have an answer for the last one. She'd been too seriously preoccupied with the other tests and Marley to realize there was a box and a pee stick in her pocket.

"It doesn't take much to put two and two together," her mother went on, "and figure out that you had sex with Wyatt a little over two weeks ago when you went to tell him about the research on Griff. And now you're either pregnant or believe you are. Which is it? You believe you might be pregnant or you are?"

"Both," Nola admitted on a heavy sigh. "It's a mess, Mom. My whole life is a mess."

"No, it isn't. You created that." She pointed to the piece that could apparently lift the veil on any secret she wanted to keep. Before long, it would probably start telling people about those five pounds she was trying to forget she'd gained.

"I created a pretty piece of glass, that's all," Nola argued, sinking right into that dark abyss she'd been climbing in and out of for the past twelve hours. "I've made a mess of everything else."

Evangeline made a sound to indicate she didn't agree with that. "Have you just considered trying to test the waters with Wyatt again?" she asked.

"I tested waters with him," Nola grumbled. "That's why I'm having to pee on pregnancy test sticks."

"You had sex with him." Evangeline used her calm-as-a-lake voice. "That's not the same as a commitment."

Nola's frown-scowl deepened. "That's so unmotherly of you to say something like that."

"No, it's a very motherly thing to say and want for my child." She moved closer, looking Nola straight in the eyes. "You know you have commitment issues and involve yourself with men who can't give you what you need."

"When have I done that?" she asked a little quickly. Nola should have given it more thought because her mother certainly had.

"Well, off the top of my head, just last year when you were on that tour of the missions in San Antonio, you flirted with a priest," Evangeline reminded her.

"Hey, I'd just watched those old reruns of *The Thorn Birds*, and he was nice."

That earned her one of her mom's flattest of flat looks. "You got engaged to a man who still lived with his mother and had strung along his last girlfriend for six years."

"He was nice," Nola repeated.

"He was safe because you knew it wouldn't actually lead to marriage."

All right, so her mother had hit the nail on the head. The only man she actually wanted or had ever truly wanted was Wyatt. But the only other thing she'd wanted other than a place in the glass art world was a child.

"The bottom line is I can't have Wyatt and a child because he doesn't want to be a father," Nola admitted. "And I've come to terms with that." She thought that was true. "I've come to terms with it," she repeated, "and I want to raise a child by myself."

There. It was all spelled out. And, yes, it was definitely true. It was actually good for her to see and accept everything she just said because she could stop peeing on sticks, stop obsessing about everything that was ill-timed about the pregnancy and have that baby she'd always wanted. Her baby, one she didn't have to share or give up to anyone else.

"Thank you, Mom," Nola heard herself murmur.

Evangeline's smile was cut off, though, when the door opened, and Wyatt stuck his head in. "Am I, uh, interrupting anything?" he asked, glancing at Evangeline and then Nola.

"No," her mother assured him. "I was just leaving." She kissed Nola on the cheek and did the same to Wyatt as she passed him on her way out.

"I think she has ESP," Nola grumbled, and then she checked the time. "And you must have the ability to teleport. I just got off the phone with you like twenty minutes ago."

He nodded, stepped inside but didn't shut the door. When Wyatt looked back over his shoulder, Nola followed his line of sight and spotted Marley inside the TipTop Diner, which was adjacent to the workshop. She was standing near the front of the store in the to-go area.

"When Marley came into the kitchen, she was already dressed," he explained, "and she said she needed to come into town and get some breakfast. She's diabetic and needs to eat low-carb, high-protein meals. I didn't have anything fresh in the fridge, so I drove her here. I figured I could check on you while she picks up her omelet."

Nola felt several pangs, some of happiness over being able to get this glimpse of Marley, but the other was green-eyed jealousy that Wyatt had this kind of contact that Nola wouldn't. But there were more pangs about Marley's diabetes. Nola had no idea if Marley was managing to control that. Of course, the protein breakfast was a good start.

"I'm sorry I wasn't with you for the tests," he said, his gaze skimming over the workshop.

She shrugged. "You were better off staying with Marley. It wouldn't have been good for you to leave her alone her first night." Nola paused, wishing she could have been part of that *first night*. "Has she said how long she'll be staying?"

Wyatt shook his head. "She apparently finished her high school junior classes early so she doesn't have to go back to school. She's taking some college courses, but she says those are all online."

"So, she's smart," Nola remarked. That was good since Nola had never considered herself a particularly good student. Probably because her interest had been elsewhere back then. On Wyatt and the glass.

It was ironic that some things didn't change.

But they had, she supposed. The glass was still important. So was Wyatt, but after the conversation she'd just had with her mother, Nola knew she was going to have to have the talk with him. One to let him know that she already wanted and loved this baby she was carrying.

And that he wouldn't have to have any part of raising the child.

She was betting that talk would not go well because no matter what she said, he'd feel the obligation and the guilt. Eventually, the resentment would come. And it would be like balancing on a tightrope to have the life and baby she wanted while trying to hang on to her best friend. Because that was exactly what Wyatt was.

"Any more contact from the Silvas?" Nola asked just to push back on the worry of what she'd eventually have to tell him about her plans for the baby.

"Not from Alec, but Marley made a quick call to Heather on the drive over to let her know she was okay."

Good about the no contact from Alec. Good, too, that Marley had given her mother that assurance since it'd been obvious that Heather was worried about her. And that she loved Marley. This time, Nola didn't get one of those jealousy pangs. Well, not a huge one, anyway, and she was still standing by the decision she'd made all those years ago. Marley wasn't hers. For better or worse, Marley belonged to Heather and Alec since they'd been the ones to raise her.

Wyatt made another glance back at the diner before he continued looking around the workshop, and Nola saw the exact moment he'd spotted the red piece. He had a similar *holy smokes* reaction as had her sisters and mother.

"That's my junk?" he asked in a whisper.

"Apparently. Well, half of it is, anyway. The other half is probably my junk. It just happened," she went on, trying to explain it. "I kept blowing, kept jiggling it around, and that's what came out."

The corner of his mouth lifted in a dirty smile, and when she mentally replayed her words in her head, she poked his biceps with her index finger. "I didn't think anyone would associate it with sex because of the color. There's nothing sexual about fire-red genitalia."

"That's not genitalia," he disagreed. "That's sex. The color suits it just fine." Then he stopped and looked at her. "You're not going to sell it." It wasn't a question.

"No," she agreed. "I'll treat it like those R-rated pictures of us I found two weeks ago. I'll tuck it away."

And when she wanted the reminder of just how amazing fire-red Wyatt could be, she'd take a look at it. Maybe at the pictures of them, too.

She tipped her head up toward him just as he tipped his head down. Nola caught the scent of his breath. Coffee and Wyatt. She got lost in his eyes—oh, those eyes—for a moment before the sound of Marley's voice yanked her back out of the minifantasy she was weaving.

"I got my order," Marley called.

Nola looked out and saw that the girl wasn't coming toward them. While holding a white take-out container, she was standing by Wyatt's truck and clearly had no intention of coming inside. Probably because she'd already spotted the bio-mom she wanted nothing to do with.

"Go," Nola told him. "I'll let you know about any other tests and the doctor's appointment."

She nearly kissed him. Not one of those scorchers that was foreplay but the casual goodbye, good-luck kind. But she stopped herself because any sort of kiss with Wyatt suddenly seemed too intimate, and she didn't want him reading anything into the gesture. Such as her assuming they could be one happy family.

Nola watched him go to Marley. Watched Marley not give her so much as a second glance when she got back into the truck. Watched as Marley struck up a conversation, an apparently cheery one, with Wyatt as he drove away. She was still standing there, still watching, when her phone rang, and she saw Derwin's name on the screen. Since the president of the Sherlock's Snoops would likely visit in person if she didn't answer, Nola went back into the workshop, shut the door and took the call.

"I want you to know that I don't think the fundraiser to get Griff's car is a good idea," she said right off. "It'll dredge up old memories."

Since Derwin didn't say anything for several seconds, she'd obviously surprised him. It didn't take him long, though, to recover. "Or it could give us new facts about the investigation."

"There is no investigation," she reminded him.

"No, but the case is still technically open because the medical examiner wasn't able to determine if it was suicide or foul play or simply a tragic accident. The only thing the sheriff's office could verify was that there were no skid marks to indicate Griff had tried to stop before he crashed through that barrier. But that doesn't mean the car didn't malfunction in some way, making it impossible for Griff to apply the brakes."

Nola was betting the man and his snooping cronies knew every last detail about Griff's last moments. Well, every last detail except what Griff had taken to the grave with him, but she seriously doubted the Sherlock's Snoops could uncover anything the cops had missed.

"Examining that car could help you with your research," the man went on, obviously applying some pressure. "Think how much better your report would be if we could once and for all put an end to this."

Oh, if only. But answers, any answers, would restart the grieving process for Wyatt and the gossiping process for everyone else.

"We could possibly put an end to it, too, if Bennie Dalton would just cooperate and talk to us," Derwin added.

Bennie Dalton. Nola hadn't thought of him in ages, but he'd been Griff's best friend. And if what she'd heard was true, he was also the last person to have seen Griff alive.

"Bennie might talk to you, though," Derwin went on. "I mean, if you ask him to help with the research."

"I don't want his help," she muttered, but Nola immediately rethought that.

Maybe it wouldn't be a bad idea to speak to Bennie, not to ask him about Griff's death but to fill her in on some happier memories. Bennie probably had some fun stories she could include in her report, and that was what she wanted to focus on since Wyatt might eventually get around to reading it.

"Are you still there?" Derwin asked when her silence dragged on.

"I'm here. Don't do the fundraiser for Griff's car," Nola repeated, and she might have kept repeating it if the door hadn't opened and Lorelei came in. "And I don't need help with the research," she told Derwin instead. "I have that all under control." And with that new lie, Nola ended the call, ready to deal with Lorelei's questions about the receipt.

Obviously, Lorelei was ready, too. "I just left Stellie with the nanny and thought I'd see you before I went to the shop."

Nola checked the time. "The shop doesn't open until ten." That was two and a half hours from now. "And you usually take Stellie to the shop with you." Though Lorelei did sometimes leave the baby with her nanny, who almost certainly cared for Stellie far, far less than the average nanny because Lorelei preferred having the baby with her as much as possible.

Lorelei shrugged. "I have some paperwork to catch up on, and I need to order supplies for the items we ship. Plus, I wanted to come by and check on you, and I don't like bringing Stellie in here because of the heat."

Nola frowned and glanced around. She was so accustomed to being in the workshop, she didn't often notice the heat, but Lorelei was right. This wasn't a place for a baby, and it meant she'd need to come up with her own childcare arrangements. Unlike Lorelei, she wouldn't be able to bring her baby to work.

"Have I ever thanked you for setting up a shop to sell my pieces?" Nola asked.

Lorelei smiled. "Many times, and as you well know, those pieces have made us both a lot of money. Now that we've done the chitchat, are you going to confirm or deny if you're pregnant?"

"Confirm," she answered. No need to hesitate or draw this out with hemming and hawing.

Her sister just stood there for a second, her startled gaze combing over Nola's face. Maybe trying to figure out if it was true and how Nola felt about it. Nola managed a smile that caused Lorelei to squeal with obvious delight. She hauled Nola into a hug despite the fact she was wearing her nice work clothes and Nola was in her usual un-nice ones.

"Oh, this is so wonderful," Lorelei gushed. "I hope it's a girl because that'll mean all three of us have daughters." She paused, stopped gushing. "Daughters we can keep and raise," she amended with a grimace.

That was definitely something to gush about. So, why wasn't Nola doing that? The answer was obvious, and he'd just driven away in his truck with Marley.

"How's Wyatt dealing with the news?" Lorelei asked, obviously zooming right in on the reason for Nola's lack of glee.

"He's not yet, but when it finally hits him, I'm not expecting him to deal with it well," Nola said.

Lorelei sighed, hugged her again. She pushed wisps of Nola's hair from her face. "So much going on for you." She paused again. "Do you want to talk about Marley? Mom told me," she added.

"Uh, Marley's not handling this well, either. Not the pregnancy," Nola amended. "She doesn't know about that. What I meant is Marley's not dealing well with me."

That spurred a third hug, an even longer one than the others. "I'm so sorry. If there's anything I can do to help, let me know."

"I will," Nola assured her, and when the hug ended and she faced her sister, she tried to appear not to be the emotional wreck that she was. No need to drag Lorelei into the wreck with her.

"Do you have the research under control?" Lorelei asked, and it took Nola a second to remember that her sister had walked in on that last part of the phone conversation and had obviously overheard what she'd told Derwin.

"Uh, no," she admitted. "Haven't even started." But she could actually do something about that today. "I need to go to the cemetery and take a picture of Griff's tombstone."

"You have to do that today?" Lorelei pressed. "Because if it can wait until tomorrow after school, you could take Hayden with you."

"Hayden?" Nola couldn't figure out why her sister would want her to take their thirteen-year-old niece along for that.

"Yes, she's taking a weekend course on photography, and she's really into it. She'd probably love doing it, and she could use it for one of the projects she has to do for the course."

Nola wasn't convinced a teenager would enjoy going to a cemetery, but she understood being "really into" something. Her own love of blowing glass had started when she'd been fourteen.

"All right, I'll call Hayden tonight and see if and when she wants to do it."

Then after that, she'd make an appointment to have a chat with the last person to see Griff alive.

Bennie Dalton.

And maybe, just maybe, Bennie wouldn't tell her anything that Wyatt couldn't handle hearing.

CHAPTER SEVEN

WYATT WAS WAY out of his comfort zone here as he drove Marley into town for lunch. Of course, he'd been flung far, far away from any semblance of comfort, starting with Griff's name being yanked from a bowl at the Last Ride Society meeting. At the time, when Nola had ridden out on Honey Bee to tell him the news, he thought that would be the toughest thing he'd have to deal with for a while.

It was laughable in a nonhappy kind of way to realize just how wrong he had been about that.

That'd been the day Nola and he had had sex because he hadn't been able to keep his hands, and other parts of him, off her and because he'd stupidly thought a vasectomy was the safeguard he needed to prevent a repeat of what'd happened when they were teenagers.

But nope.

The repeat had happened, and because of karma, fate or whatever the hell was driving this, Marley had shown up on his doorstep two nights ago. That alone would have weighed down his things-to-deal with pile, but her parents had been right on her heels.

One pissed-off father who Wyatt still wanted to punch. And one decent, caring mother who Wyatt needed to thank for doing such a good job with Marley. He only hoped Heather was as decent and caring as she was on the surface, but what he didn't want in that things-to-deal-with pile was that his biological daughter had had less than a stellar childhood because Nola and he had handed her over to the wrong people.

He glanced at the passenger seat where Marley sat, taking in the sights. Such as they were. This was the Texas Hill Country, so it had some legendary things going for it if you were into green pastures, wildflowers and country stuff. He was, always had been, but Marley had been raised in the city, and he figured she would either tire of it really fast. Or fall in love with it as he had.

"After lunch can I hang out with Janie again?" she asked.

Janie Reagan was one of the horse trainers, and it hadn't taken Marley long to meet her and convince her to let her hang around while Janie worked with the new palominos that had just arrived at the ranch.

"Sure," Wyatt told her. "If that's what you want."

"It is," she assured him, and then paused. "You don't always have to agree to everything, you know. I mean, you don't have to worry about pissing me off and having me storm out." Another pause. "Unless you want me to storm out, that is."

That was a mixed bag kind of comment. No, he didn't want any storming, didn't want to do anything to add to the mess she was already going through with her parents' divorce. But having her here was making him feel a little like a tennis ball that was being slapped back and forth across a proverbial net.

Part of him wanted to hang on to whatever moments or days he could have with Marley. Another part of him wanted to find a time machine and go back two and a half weeks to the life that he had so carefully planned out.

A life where he believed his biological child had had the best possible love and parenting. A life where he hadn't knocked up the very woman whom he'd screwed over all those years ago.

"I want you here if that's what you want," he settled for saying.

"Good," Marley declared, but she repeated it under her breath in such a way that made him think she wasn't so sure of that.

"Will this cause any problems for you?" she asked when he turned into the parking lot of O'Riley's Café, their lunch destination. Of course, it was only one of three such destinations for lunch, and he figured Marley was already tired of the TipTop, and he wasn't taking her to the Three Sheets to the Wind bar for pub food. "Problems with people talking, I mean," Marley added.

That was less of a mixed bag question. "If people haven't already heard who you are, they soon will, and they'll talk. But it's okay."

Well, it was okay for him, but maybe not so much for Nola. While Wyatt expected folks to dole out congratulatory looks and smiles to him over the fact that he'd finally been able to reunite with Marley, it wouldn't take long for those same folks to realize that Marley hadn't included Nola in this reunion. Nola, in turn, would get all the sad *there, there* pity looks. Something she would hate. Of course, she probably disliked Marley's cold shoulder, too, and that was Wyatt's reminder to broach that particular subject again.

O'Riley's was a '50s-style café that had been around when poodle skirts and James Dean had been in fashion, and the menu hadn't changed much since then. It basically had the greasiest, best-tasting cheeseburgers for miles around, along with having some healthier protein options for Marley like grilled chicken salad or fish sandwiches.

What O'Riley's didn't have was a drive-through or indoor seating, and that meant Marley and he would be more or less on display where any and all would be able to see them. That was all right. He'd already steeled himself for the looks and smiles, but he figured no one would actually come over and speak to them. Too awkward. Most wouldn't want to dive into conversational waters like—*Hey, want to introduce me to the kid you gave up for adoption?*

Wyatt parked, and after they ordered at the window, he directed Marley to one of the unoccupied tables. Thankfully, all the seating areas were under the shade trees or had umbrellas to stave off the blistering sun, but the owner had also put out some huge fans, similar to those that Nola used in her glass workshop. It always felt a little like sitting in a breezeway.

"So, how long have you been diabetic?" he asked when she took out a little meter to prick her finger. He'd seen her use it several times already and knew it was so she could monitor her blood sugar.

"Since I was three. I collapsed and went into a coma when I was in a playgroup. I nearly died."

Wyatt hadn't meant to curse, but that was exactly what he did. Hell. He obviously hadn't prepared himself to hear that.

She shrugged. "It's okay. I don't remember it. In fact, I can't remember a time when I didn't have to do blood sugar checks and take insulin shots. Mom did that for me at first, but as I got older, I could manage it myself."

That put a hard knot in his stomach. Not the part about Heather taking care of her, but the realization of what Marley had been through. And what she might still have to go through. He needed to hit some internet sites and would no doubt get the crap scared out of him when he read about the pitfalls that she'd face. Still, he needed to know.

"I'm considering getting a pump," she went on. "That'll

monitor my blood sugar, and I won't have to stick myself so often. But there are pluses and minuses."

She went on to explain what those were but paused when the server, a teenage girl on roller skates, brought out their food. Instead of continuing about insulin pumps, Marley had a sip of her ice water and glanced around.

"People are watching us," she said. "Maybe even trying to read our lips to know what we're saying." She chuckled a little. "Are you sure you're okay with this?"

"I'm sure, and I like hearing about what you're going through. Well, not that whole coma and nearly dying, but I like hearing the rest of it."

She studied him as if trying to decide if that was true before she nodded and had a bite of her salad. "I'd like hearing about your life, too," she threw out there.

No, she wouldn't, but if she stayed in Last Ride long enough, she'd hear things, so Wyatt decided to give her some of it and add to the bits he'd already told her. "Well, you know I have, *had*, three brothers. My twin, Griff Jonas, who's four years older than me. He's a horse trainer and has a stepson named Eli, who's thirteen. Jonas's wife died a couple of years ago. And then there's Dax, my kid brother."

"He's the bull rider," Marley provided with a smile. "I checked out some things on Google and social media. Will I ever get to meet them?"

"Of course." In fact, Wyatt had already called both his brothers to let them know so he could get ahead of the gossip. "Jonas is on a business trip, delivering some horses, but he'll come over to River's End when he gets back. Not sure when Dax will come to town. Because he's always on the road, he doesn't visit a lot." Still, Wyatt was betting Dax would show sooner than later.

And speaking of folks showing up, Wyatt spotted Nola

coming up the sidewalk. She was wearing her work clothes and had likely walked over from her workshop. She didn't see them. Not at first, but the murmuring of other diners must have alerted her that something was up because her gaze zoomed around until it landed on them.

Even though Nola was a good twenty feet away, he could still see the happy surprise on her face. Then the unhappy follow-up when it must have occurred to her that Marley was not going to give her a cheerful welcome. Not that Nola hadn't already tried for that. She'd gotten Marley's number from him and had sent the girl a text, one that Wyatt knew Nola had agonized over because she'd called him to read him the various versions. She'd settled for a simple Just wanted to say hi, and had left it at that.

So had Marley. She hadn't responded, and he knew that the silence was stomping all over Nola's heart.

"And Griff is your brother who was killed in a car wreck," Marley supplied, pulling his attention back to her. "I googled him, too. Some people aren't sure how he died."

The bite of burger that Wyatt had just taken didn't lodge in his throat, but it was close. He'd heard the Sherlock's Snoops had a website and posted on lots of blogs with people with similar interests who also had serious nosy streaks. There had no doubt—no doubt—been plenty of blabbing and speculating about Griff.

Since he actually wanted to swallow his food, Wyatt went with a slight change of subject. "I'm guessing you did the Google thing on Nola, too, and that you know she has two sisters."

Marley's mouth tightened more than a little as if she'd tasted something bitter in her salad, but Wyatt knew the lettuce wasn't the source of that particular reaction.

"I wish you'd cut Nola a break," he added. "She's going through a tough time right now."

Judging from those still-tight lips, Marley had no intention of any break-cutting where Nola was concerned. "She gave me up for adoption so she could move to Italy."

Nope, definitely no break-cutting, and he heard both the anger and hurt in Marley's voice, with the anger leading the way. "No," Wyatt corrected. "Nola and I gave you up because we were sixteen and didn't have the means to raise you, and then she went to Italy."

"You didn't have the means, not then, but she did," Marley snapped. "She's a Parkman."

He would have clarified that she was a Parkman without funds, thanks to Evangeline giving away that silver-spoon wealth, but Marley's phone rang.

"It's Mom," she said. "I need to take this so I can let her know that I'm okay and that you're taking good care of me."

Wyatt wasn't so sure just how well he was taking care of her. Yeah, he was making sure she got what she needed to eat, and he'd even gone grocery shopping with her for that. But he was sorely lacking in one big area and that was convincing Marley that Nola wasn't the bogeyman in all of this.

Hard to do much convincing, though, since Marley glared when she spotted Nola ordering and studying them.

"Hold on a sec," Marley told Heather after she answered. "I'll just be over there," she added to Wyatt and she pointed to some shade trees where there were no tables or diners.

Nola sighed when she watched Marley move as far away as she could manage and still stay on the café grounds. Wyatt got up and went to Nola, even though he knew every eye within fixing distance was now fixed on the drama that was playing out. And Wyatt wasn't convinced that some of the eyers weren't actually capable of that lipreading that Marley had joked about.

He didn't ask Nola if she was okay. No way she could be, but he didn't want to add to her troubles by risking heatstroke, so he took her by the hand and led her to another unoccupied tree. He hadn't wanted to take her to the table because then he would have been risking that Marley might not come back over to finish her salad.

"I heard Marley and you went shopping for groceries," Nola said. "And that she's watching Janie train the horses. Gossip," she added, though he'd already figured that out. "Most people mean well, I think, but others just want to spill to see my reaction. I haven't thought about drop-kicking too many of them."

"Good. Because you look too tired to drop-kick a potato chip right now. Did you get the appointment to see your doctor?"

She nodded. "It's a week from today at one o'clock. That's the earliest I could get, but I did more of the pregnancy tests. I swear, I think the plus signs are getting bolder, kind of like they're saying, 'Yes, we're positive. Now give it a rest.'"

Despite that not being the news he wanted to hear, he smiled a little and wished he could pull her into his arms. Hell, he wished he could kiss her because that might get their minds off the stuff going on. But any public display of affection would boomerang back to her in the form of gossip. Nola had enough of that.

"I didn't manage to talk the Sherlock's Snoops into nixing the fundraiser for Griff's car," Nola went on, only waiting a couple of seconds in between the glances she was giving Marley.

Yeah, Wyatt had seen the collection jar just inside the

order window here at O'Riley's, and he'd chosen to ignore it. But he was betting other such jars were already positioned all around town.

"And on Saturday morning," Nola continued, "Hayden's going with me to the cemetery to take a picture of the headstone. That'll finally get me started on the research."

"Hayden?" he questioned. "Why take your niece?"

Nola shrugged. "She's into photography and wants to do it. In fact, she's all excited about it."

Good, because it meant Nola wouldn't have to go to the cemetery alone. Not that she would have an extreme reaction at seeing Griff's final resting place, but it didn't seem right for her to have to do that by herself.

"Your nachos are ready, Nola," someone called out from the pickup window.

Nola motioned that she'd heard, and she looked at Marley, who was still on the phone. "She's talking to Heather?"

"Yeah. Alec's texted her a couple of times, but Marley didn't answer." He groaned because that was the same treatment Marley had given Nola. "Sorry."

Nola waved that off, and he watched as she put on her brave-little-soldier face. It would fool some people. Not him, though.

"Let me know if anything changes with Marley," she said, adding a muttered goodbye, and she went to the window to collect her food.

He tried not to watch Nola walk away just in an effort to minimize the gossip, but failed. Folks obviously knew he hadn't just had a happy moment with her. On a heavy sigh, Wyatt went back to the table to finish the burger that he already knew was going to put up a protest in his stomach.

Marley looked over at him, and she seemed to be on the verge of finishing her conversation with Heather, but then

she froze a little when she saw Evangeline making her way
to Wyatt. Nola's mom gave Marley a cheery wave though
they hadn't officially met yet, but Marley had let him know
that Evangeline and she had had several chats on the phone.

"You just missed Nola," Wyatt told the woman.

Evangeline nodded. "I waited until she'd left so I could
have a quick word with you."

Wyatt groaned again, silently this time, and he motioned
the offer for her to take a seat. He was glad, though, when
Evangeline declined. Maybe that meant her bright-blessing
lecture and smothering positivity wouldn't take that long.
Sometimes, it was just better to go ahead and wallow in the
misery than try to embrace the rose-colored-glasses stuff.

"I'm worried about Nola," Evangeline said. So maybe
no bright blessings or positivity after all. "She's under a
lot of stress."

"I know," he admitted but wasn't sure how to fix that.

"Along with worrying about Marley, she's also stressed
about the possible pregnancy that you and I both know full
well isn't in the possible zone any longer. She's definitely
pregnant."

"I know," Wyatt repeated, and he didn't know how to
fix that, either.

"Added to that," Evangeline went on, "I'm also worried
about Nola talking to Bennie Dalton."

This was something Wyatt hadn't known. "Why is she
going to talk to Bennie?" But as soon as he heard the question, he remembered the Last Ride Society research, and
he cursed.

"Yes." Evangeline apparently agreed with his profanity
sentiment. "I'm worried because Nola is well aware that
dredging all of this up will bother you, and that in turn will
cause both of you more stress."

He wasn't sure *more* was possible. It seemed Nola and he were eyeballs deep in a swampy stress bath. But he immediately rethought that. Bennie could indeed add to it if he poured out his heart and said some things that he'd maybe been keeping to himself all these years.

"Yes," Evangeline said, obviously reading his *Oh, hell* expression. "Her appointment with Bennie isn't until Saturday after the photos at the cemetery, so you'll have some time to talk to her before then."

Evangeline hadn't made that sound like an option, and Wyatt wouldn't take it as one, either. As much as it would hurt to hear anything Bennie had to say, he'd ask Nola if he could go to that appointment with her.

"Anything else?" Wyatt asked her when Evangeline just continued to stand there and stare at him.

"Yes," she said for a three-peat. She leaned in and lowered her voice. "Nola wants this baby she's carrying."

Well, of course she did. Nola wanted kids. But he didn't think Evangeline was here to have him confirm the obvious.

"So?" Wyatt prompted when she didn't continue.

Evangeline looked him straight in the eyes, not hard to do now since she was only a few menacing inches from his face. "So, you should do the right thing and give her your blessing. And then you get on with your life, and she'll get on with hers."

CHAPTER EIGHT

NOLA MIGHT HAVE been willing to sacrifice a chicken or two for a single cup of coffee. The fully caffeinated kind that would clear up some of this thick London fog in her head. Unfortunately, the strength and amount of coffee—which was strong and gallons of it—wasn't allowed during pregnancy, so she was trying hard to wake up the old-fashioned way.

With a doughnut that she'd picked up from the bakery and by forcing herself to keep moving.

The doughnut was doing its job, sort of, but the moving was limited since she was following Hayden around as the girl seemingly studied, and dismissed, every possible angle for photographing Griff's headstone.

"Too bad it's not that one," Hayden said, glancing over at a black marble mausoleum. "The light's better there."

Nola couldn't see straight enough yet to be aware of lighting preferences, but at least Hayden hadn't been talking about the size of Griff's tombstone. It was one of the smaller ones in the cemetery, probably because it had been all Wyatt and his brothers could afford at the time. Still, it was simple and tasteful and had the heart-touching script above Griff's name.

Beloved Brother.

She didn't know who'd decided to go with that, but it was probably Jonas. Nola recalled hearing that Wyatt had been seriously messed up after losing his twin, so she doubted he'd been in any kind of mental state to come up with the wording on a tombstone. Dax would have only been fifteen at the time, so he might not have had any input, either.

Nola had been pretty messed up herself about Griff's death since she'd known him as long as she'd known Wyatt. But her grief had been a tiny drop in the bucket compared to Wyatt's and she hadn't even been able to personally offer him any condolences. At the time, he'd been living in Wrangler's Creek. He'd come home for the funeral, of course, but he'd also been seeing someone else, so she'd made sure their paths hadn't crossed.

Well, they had certainly crossed more than a time or two since then. Crossed, mingled and given in to things they should have resisted. The baby she was carrying was proof of that, and that reminder got her thinking about a weird text she'd gotten from Wyatt two days ago. A text he'd sent only a couple of hours after she'd seen Marley and him at O'Riley's.

I just want you to know I'll support you in any way I can, Wyatt had messaged.

That was okay, fine even, if it hadn't felt so, well, detached. It certainly hadn't been a declaration of how he'd had a change of heart and now wanted this baby. In fact, in some ways, including a kick-to-the-gut kind of way, it'd felt a little like a goodbye.

So, after some tears and hours of obsessing, Nola had decided to just give him some time and space, and that was why she hadn't poured out her heart to his puzzling text. She'd simply responded with a thumbs-up emoji and had given him that space by not calling or texting.

"What do you think?" Hayden asked, and for a moment Nola had no idea what she was talking about. Then her niece came closer with the massive camera she'd been using and went through some of the shots she'd taken of the tombstone.

Maybe it was Nola's artistic eye, but she could see the subtle differences in all of them. The different slants of light. The angle of the shots. The clarity of some and the intentional blurriness of others that made them take on a dreamy, otherworldly quality.

"These are all great," Nola said, studying them even more. "You're really good at this."

Hayden shrugged as if she didn't quite believe that, but Nola didn't miss the little smile of pride. Her niece had found a way to create magic. For better or worse, Hayden would likely spend her life trying to keep doing what she'd just managed while at the same time never being completely satisfied. Always hungry for more. That was the problem with magic. It wasn't easily sated.

"Thank you," Nola went on. "Which one do you think I should use for the research report?"

Another shrug from Hayden. "Maybe this one."

She scrolled back to one with the morning sun practically highlighting the *Beloved Brother* on the marble. And also emphasizing the gold ring perched on top of the marble. The angle of the sun had also managed to shield the death date. It was still visible, but the eye wouldn't catch that first. The focus was the inscription and the mystery ring.

"All right," Nola agreed. "Send it to me. Maybe the others, too, in case I decide to go with more than one photo. I can have a better look at all of them."

Hayden nodded, hit some buttons on the camera and then started packing up her equipment. "My mom used to love him, right?" she asked, tipping her head to Griff's tombstone. "He was her boyfriend."

Nola thought of all those hickeys Lily had had to conceal, and the nights she'd sneaked out to meet Griff. "Yes. But they broke up, and then she fell in love with your dad," she added, just to let Hayden know that her mother had moved on.

Of course, that marriage hadn't lasted, but Lily had gotten Hayden out of it. And unlike Alec Silva, Hayden's father hadn't been a butt-munch during the divorce. That was the good news. The bad news was that he hardly ever saw his daughter. Nola couldn't imagine doing that. But then again, she had chosen to give up Marley, so it was a little like the pot calling the kettle black to think badly of Hayden's father.

"So, what's the story behind the ring?" Hayden wanted to know. She didn't touch it, but she studied it as if wishing she could get more photos of it.

"I'm not sure. No one seems to know."

But unfortunately that might be one of those things she learned when she had her meeting with Bennie in… She checked the time. A half hour. Bennie had shifted their appointment so they could talk before he had to be at work. If anyone would know about a mystery ring, it would be Griff's best friend.

They started back toward Nola's car, but Hayden stopped at one of the other tombstones. Another simple one, but it carried a lot of emotion, too. For different reasons, though, than Griff's.

"That was Stellie's birth mom, right?" Hayden asked.

Yes. Dana Smith, and according to the dates, she was only twenty-three when she died. Giving birth to Stellie. Not exactly a settling thought for Nola, considering she was pregnant, but apparently everything that could go wrong in a delivery had, and Dana had died just minutes after giving birth to her daughter. Since no one in Last Ride had actually known Dana and no next of kin had come forward, Stellie had been placed in foster care with Lorelei, and now Lorelei was in the final stages of adopting her. All's well that ends well—except for Dana.

Hayden and she got moving again, but they were still a few yards from her car when Nola spotted Wyatt's truck come to a stop. He wasn't alone. Marley was with him, and they got out of the truck together before Marley spotted her and came to a standstill.

"That's Marley?" Hayden asked.

"Yes," Nola managed and wondered just how much more that vise was going to clamp around her heart.

"I finally get to meet her," Hayden said and headed in their direction. Marley continued to stay put, but while the first cousins were having their first face-to-face, Wyatt came to Nola.

"When you said you'd be here in the morning, I thought you meant later," he told her. "It's barely eight."

"Hayden was excited and couldn't wait to come. She called me at six, but it took me a while to get going since I can't have coffee. Why are you here?" And she asked that because she knew Wyatt didn't make a habit of coming to visit his brother's grave.

"Marley wanted to see Griff's tombstone."

She tried to gauge how he felt about that, and she saw the worry. But then, the worry might have been for the multitude of other things going on in his life. For instance, that message he'd sent her.

I just want you to know I'll support you in any way I can.

That "maybe a goodbye/see you sometime" message was still annoying her, but Wyatt spoke before she could make the mistake of voicing that annoyance.

"Do you want me to go with you to see Bennie?" he asked.

She didn't ask how he'd known about the appointment because it was possible Bennie had told folks and it had gotten around. While she wouldn't have minded having Wyatt there for support, Nola had to shake her head. It was best if she learned what she could under the guise of the research, and then she could put a soft spin on it when she put it in the report for the Last Ride Society.

And when she gave the recap of the meeting to Wyatt. Which she would do, despite that frustrating text.

"Don't cut this time short with Marley," Nola said. "I'm dropping off Hayden and then heading straight to Bennie's. I won't be long," she added, to make it sound as if it was in no way the big deal it could turn out to be.

He looked as if he might want to argue, but then he heard Hayden and Marley laughing about something, and he probably realized that he did indeed want to take some time with this trip to acquaint Marley with her kin.

"Nola," he said when she started to walk away.

She stopped, looked back at him, and she saw that argument/debate again. Maybe for a new subject this time. "We'll talk," he finally said.

Nola waited a couple more seconds to see if that was it. It apparently was, so she went to her car and tried not to notice Marley trying to ignore her. Nola finally gave up and saw Marley make her way to Wyatt just as Hayden came and got in the car.

Thankfully, Hayden didn't want to have a long, meaningful conversation on the drive back to Lily's ranch. In fact, the girl didn't want to have a conversation at all. She took out her camera and started fiddling with the pictures she'd taken.

Once she was home and getting out of the car, her niece

did add, "Marley's nice. Thanks for letting me take the pictures."

Nola wished Hayden had elaborated on the "nice," especially since she hadn't personally witnessed any niceness aimed at her from Marley, but Nola didn't push. Not when she had to save what little energy she had for this next meeting.

She left Lily's ranch and drove to town, meandering through the back streets until she reached Dalton's Auto Shop. It was a nice, clean building, and Bennie obviously did good business since there were only two auto shops in Last Ride, but she had to wonder what his family thought about his career choice. The Daltons were the other blue blood surname in town, and Bennie's dad was a doctor and his mom was a socialite who sat on seemingly every committee with other Parkmans and Daltons.

She spotted Bennie on the side of the shop, seated in one of the chairs that had probably been set up for customers beneath a cluster of shade trees. He was smoking, but he quickly snuffed out the cigarette as she made her way toward him.

Her first impression was that he was nervous. But then, so was she. He was also starting to show his age and no longer had the golden-boy looks that had made him popular in high school. As far as she could tell, the popularity and goldenness had continued until shortly after Griff's death, when Bennie had seemingly gone downhill.

"Hope it's okay to talk out here," Bennie said, extending his hand for her to shake and then pulling it back perhaps because he remembered the old rule about a man never offering his hand to a lady.

"This is fine." Nola decided to try to break the ice, so

she initiated the handshake and then sat in one of the chairs that he motioned for her to take.

"It's just one of my guys showed up for work earlier than I'd expected," Bennie went on. "And he can be a gossip. I didn't want him to hear us talking and think anything about it."

Yes, definitely nervous, and since she figured it might help to tamp down those nerves, she smiled at him and pulled out a small notebook from her purse. She hoped because it had Harry Potter's picture on the cover that it would make Bennie think this wasn't a totally serious deal.

Even though it was.

"So, like I said when I called, I drew Griff's name," she started, "and I was hoping you'd tell me about him for my research report. I mean, since you were his best friend," she added when he gave her a blank look.

Bennie dragged in a deep breath as if he still had that cigarette in his mouth. "This research stuff and the drawing are all bullshit," Bennie complained. "I mean, what the hell does it matter? And why not just let the dead stay dead?"

It sounded to her as if Bennie was just complaining rather than actually asking questions, but since she'd had the same thoughts, and was doing the research anyway, Nola spelled out her justification. Or rather, more of a justification than her just doing her civic duty as a Parkman.

"Well, there's money involved. Hezzie Parkman's foundation will give a nice donation to a charity of my choice. I'm going with improvements to the kids' section of the library."

She paused to give him a chance to respond to that. Instead, he gave her an *I'm not convinced* grunt.

"Maybe just tell me some fun stories I can write up," she suggested.

"Fun," he repeated in that same not-convinced tone as

his grunt. But he gathered his breath, lifted his eyes to the sky for a moment and apparently started a mental journey to revive the dead. "Like you said, Griff was my best friend. Of course, Wyatt and Griff were close, too, what with being twins and all, but they weren't much alike. Griff used to say that Wyatt was born old, and he was born young."

That was an apt summary of the differences between the two. Wyatt had still done plenty of irresponsible things, most of those with Nola participating right along with him, but Griff had always been the fun-loving party guy who had a penchant for getting into trouble.

"Do you have any clean stories about Griff I can add to the report?" Nola asked.

He gathered his breath again. "Well, there was the time he put a whole bunch of ducks in the principal's office. Griff did it on a Friday night, and by the time school started up on that Monday, the ducks had crapped everywhere."

Bennie chuckled at the memory, but his laughter and smile quickly faded. "Griff got up to the usual stuff. He streaked across the football field." He stopped. "Lily probably has a lot better stories to tell about him."

Nola acknowledged that with a nod. "But I'm trying to get a bunch of stories from different people. That way, I can use the best ones."

And maybe there'd be some that painted Griff as more than just that streaking, duck-pranking teenager. It made her regret that she hadn't known him better, but looking back, Nola realized she hadn't liked Griff that much. He'd been fine with Lily, but there'd been a daredevil edge to him that had put her off.

"Must have been weird for you," Bennie went on. "I mean, seeing Griff's face that was identical to your boyfriend's. Griff and Wyatt didn't ever try to trade places to fool you, did they?"

She shook her head, confident that hadn't happened because she would have known just by looking into their eyes. Genetically identical, yes, but Griff never looked at her with the same heat Wyatt had. Strange now that she thought about it because Griff had obviously been an attraction to her identical twin.

"What about things that happened closer to the time of Griff's death?" she asked, knowing that she was about to venture out into deep, murky waters.

The muscles stirred in Bennie's jaw, and he took more than a couple of moments, obviously trying to figure out what he was going to say about that. "It's all in the police report."

Not the soul pouring that she'd hoped for and worried about.

"Deputy Azzie Parkman took my statement back then," Bennie said, his voice clipped now.

Nola knew Azzie fairly well, and the woman was a distant cousin. Of course, so were plenty of people in Last Ride, but it occurred to her that Azzie might be a good source if she needed more for the research.

"Maybe you can go over what you told her," Nola suggested since it seemed as if the man wanted to jump to the end of Griff's life rather than more of the events that had led up to it.

"Well, yeah, I told Azzie that Griff and I had been friends. Had been," Bennie emphasized, "but we had a falling-out a day or two before he died."

Nola was betting the cops had looked at the timing of that falling-out. Since they had treated it as a suspicious death, Bennie had almost certainly been on their radar for having had some part in or at least some knowledge of what caused Griff's car to go off that bluff.

"What did you argue about?" She expected him to take a moment to recall it. But he didn't.

"My sister, Carlene," Bennie readily answered. "Griff had started seeing her, and I didn't like it. She was barely eighteen, and yeah, I know he was only a year older, but Carlene hadn't made her way around like Griff."

That was probably a polite way of saying Griff had a lot more sexual experience than Carlene had. "You thought your sister would get hurt?"

"Damn right I did. I mean, you remember what was going on then. Griff and your sister had just called it quits, and Griff was on the prowl, looking for a way to show everybody that he was over Lily. Whether he was or not."

Nola latched right on to those words. "Griff didn't want to end things with Lily?" Because in the version she'd heard from Lily, it was Griff who'd done the breaking up. She silently groaned. She so didn't want to have to ask Lily about all of this, but she just might have to.

"I don't know," Bennie answered, the strain and some old anger rising in his voice. "I don't know why Lily and him split, but Griff sure as hell wasn't happy about it. He was drinking too much, running around too much, and he put my kid sister right in that mix."

Nola could definitely understand Bennie feeling that way. "So, you argued with Griff and told him to leave your sister alone. Then what happened?" she asked.

Bennie certainly didn't jump to answer this time, and Nola got a really bad feeling in the pit of her stomach.

"Your sister died a couple of years later," Nola said gently. "She drowned while on a camping trip with friends." And here was the biggie that could maybe shut down this conversation. "Did she take her life because of Griff?"

"Yes," Bennie snapped, but then he shook his head, groaned. "I don't know. She was never the same, though, after Griff broke up with her, and she blamed me. She was so mad at me. *So mad*," he repeated under his breath, and he was obviously recalling those painful memories. "She believed I'd forced Griff to dump her."

Again, this was boggy ground, so she tried to carefully word her next question. "You didn't know your sister had such strong feelings for Griff?" Nola asked.

"No. I dismissed it as a crush, and I didn't know Griff was her first. Griff admitted to me that he didn't know she hadn't had sex either until after they'd done the deed."

Oh, crap. Nola could practically see all of that playing out as well. Griff on the rebound, looking for a way to ease his sorrow, and he'd ended up having sex with the virgin kid sister of his best friend. That meant it was possible that what Griff had done to and with Carlene had played into his decision to end his life.

If that was indeed what had happened.

Nola definitely hadn't wanted to go this route of focusing on the possibility that Griff might have died through suicide. No, it was best for her to have Bennie's and Griff's other friends fill her in on a boatload of happier memories that she could actually put in her report. No way could she mention any of this about Carlene.

"Neither Griff nor Carlene ever mentioned suicide," Bennie went on. "And I didn't talk to Griff again after we had it out that night. He seemed kind of sick to his stomach, you know, but not like he was ready to end things."

Well, that was good to hear. So, maybe it truly had been an accident. Being sick to his stomach, though, could have been enough of a distraction to cause him to accidentally lose control of his car.

"My sister, well, she never talked about it, but when I'd try to see her and tell her how sorry I was, I could tell she was down. And still pissed off at both Griff and me."

Nola opened her mouth to ask about that anger, but there was something in Bennie's body language that had her holding back. And just waiting. She didn't have to wait long.

"I think Carlene might have done something," he finally said. "Something to Griff's car."

It was as if a Mack truck had slammed into her. "What?" Nola managed to ask.

"I don't know," Bennie added, shaking his head. "I can't be sure. And I didn't say anything to Deputy Azzie about it because I didn't know then."

"Know what?" she pressed.

"Uh, I didn't know that right after Griff broke up with Carlene that she talked to one of our cousins. He's a mechanic and he lives in San Antonio. Anyway, Carlene asked him what the best way was to tamper with a car to make sure it wrecked."

Oh, mercy. "And the cousin didn't think to report this?"

"He's never lived in Last Ride and didn't know Griff. He mentioned it to me in passing at Carlene's funeral. He said she'd called him a couple of years back, saying she was doing some research for an essay she had to write for school. So, he told her a couple of ways it could be done."

Bennie stopped and lifted his head so their eyes met. "I didn't tell anyone because I thought, what good would it do? Griff and Carlene would still be dead, and if word got out about it, people would be calling my sister a killer."

Those people might have had good reason to.

Bennie abruptly stood, and when she looked at what had

gotten his attention, she saw Wyatt making his way toward them. He'd obviously done exactly what she had told him not to do and cut his time short with Marley.

But Nola had never been happier, or sadder, to see him.

"Bennie," Wyatt greeted him.

Bennie stuffed his hands in his pockets and nodded. "Wyatt. Man, it still gives me a jolt to see you. You look just like him. Like Griff." Bennie gathered his breath, waved that off and started toward the shop. "Gotta go. Gotta get to work."

"I'll bet it is a jolt," Wyatt muttered under his breath, and he turned to her. "I know you didn't want me here, but I had to come. I dropped Marley off at the ranch first, and she's hanging out with Janie. She'll be out there the rest of the morning."

Good. At least Marley wasn't waiting in his truck and watching her with cold disdain, but she also knew Wyatt wouldn't want to be away from the ranch too long in case Marley needed him. That fell into the good category, too, because Nola was glad that Marley had at least one of them she wanted to be around.

"You texted me a thumbs-up," Wyatt said like an accusation. One filled with anger that he'd been holding in.

It took her more than a couple of seconds to shift gears and zoom in on what he meant, and her anger came, too. "You gave me an *'I just want you to know I'll support you in any way I can.'* What a BS thing to say."

"Blame your mother. She thought it was something you needed to hear since you're under so much stress. I'm guessing you didn't."

"Nope." She wanted other things from him. Things he couldn't give her. So silence was the best way to go.

"Come on," she said, taking hold of his arm and walking toward their vehicles. "Since Marley's busy, let's go to your house and talk."

Nola had things to tell him. Stressful, painful things that she so wished would have stayed buried.

CHAPTER NINE

WITH NOLA PULLING to a stop right behind him in his driveway, Wyatt took a second to try to steady himself. Whatever she had to tell him was almost certainly something he didn't want to hear, and part of him wanted to tell her to just keep it to herself.

But he couldn't.

Because this was clearly eating away at her, too. Maybe because of the effect it would have on him, but it was also possible that it was something that had hit even closer to home. Maybe that meant Bennie had spilled something about Lily.

Nola came inside his house, her gaze sweeping around. She was obviously looking to see if Marley was there. She wasn't.

"Before I left to go to Bennie's, I texted Janie and asked her to let me know when Marley finished up watching her train the new horses," Wyatt explained.

He hadn't done that to keep tabs on Marley but rather because he was still uncomfortable leaving her alone. Yes, that was stupid. She was seventeen, not a baby, but the worry was still there for him. Plus, Wyatt hadn't wanted her to be by herself in the house in case Alec had come for a repeat visit so he could try to badger her into going back with him.

Wyatt wished he could ban the asshole from any and all future attempts at badgering, but he was in a precarious position when it came to Marley and her future. Legally, he'd surrendered any right to have a say in what she could or would do, but as long as she was here, then he could at least run interference for her.

"There's orange soda in the fridge," he offered.

But Nola shook her head and went to the huge window in the breakfast area. Still looking for Marley. And she spotted her. Marley was right where she'd been when Wyatt had left. In the corral with Janie while they worked together with the horses.

"Just go ahead and tell me what Bennie said," Wyatt insisted while they stood arm to arm in front of the window.

Nola gathered her breath. "Bennie said that he thinks his sister, Carlene, might have tampered with Griff's car."

Wyatt's head snapped toward her, and he didn't manage to even get out the bad curse words that were already flying through his thoughts. He'd figured that Nola would have tried to sugarcoat what she'd learned, but there was no sugar or coating on that. Just the raw accusation that plowed right into him.

His first instinct, not a particularly good one, was to go back to Bennie's and demand to know why the hell he'd kept something like this a secret. Why hadn't he told someone that his sister might have killed Griff?

"Might have tampered," Nola repeated, emphasizing each word, and that helped to yank him back a bit.

Oh, he wanted to make that *might* a thin, watery one. Wanted to turn it into a *slight possibility* that Carlene had done it. From there, it wouldn't have been much of a stretch to decide that the woman had had no part in it whatsoever. He still wanted to hang on to the belief that Griff had died because of an accident.

But the hope of that *slight possibility* and *no part* faded damn fast.

Even though Nola had gone quiet and was just watching him, he could practically hear what she wasn't saying. That the best way to find out if Bennie was right was to have the car examined.

Of course, doing that carried with it the possibility that there was no tampering, that Bennie had stirred all of this up for nothing. There was also the possibility that the car would somehow indicate that it hadn't been an accident. And then Wyatt would have the proof that Griff had indeed taken his life.

As long as the car stayed put, he didn't have to face that. But that cowardly thought sickened him. Always had.

"You didn't ask why Carlene might have done something like that," Nola commented.

No need for him to ask. "Griff told me he'd had sex with her and that he hadn't known she was a virgin," Wyatt explained. "He also said the only reason he slept with her was because he was messed up about his breakup with Lily. Don't tell your sister that," he added.

She took a moment, obviously following that through to what the possible conclusion of that might be if Lily realized she'd had some part in that potentially fatal chain of events. Lily could blame herself, and since Wyatt was intimately familiar with how guilt could eat away at you, he hoped to spare Lily from that. Besides, he was betting Lily already had enough doubts and memories about Griff and didn't need the addition of more.

However, Wyatt did have a question about Bennie's theory that he'd kept secret all this time. "How would Carlene have known how to do something like tampering with a car? Did Bennie tell her?"

"He says no, that she got the info from a cousin, claiming that she told the cousin it was for an essay for school. I suppose it wouldn't take much to confirm that with the cousin," Nola commented.

No, and the fact that Carlene hadn't gotten that particular information from her brother, who was already by then a mechanic, was probably proof that she was doing something she had wanted to keep hush-hush. Or at least keep from Bennie perhaps because he would have almost certainly tried to stop her.

Wyatt pulled up the image of Carlene, the quiet, shy kid sister of his brother's best friend. She'd been pretty in a wholesome kind of way, but she definitely hadn't been Griff's fun-loving type. Then again, maybe any woman had been his type since he was on the rebound.

"Did Griff ever tell you why Lily and he broke up?" Nola asked.

He had to shake his head on that one, and he continued to watch Marley. The girl seemed to have no fear of the horses, and she was obviously trying to pick up a few training techniques from Janie.

"Did Lily ever tell you why?" he countered.

Nola answered with a head shake as well. "They argued a lot. Lily had more than a bit of a temper in those days, and she'd get furious when Griff would flirt with another girl. I always assumed he'd done more than just flirt and that Lily found out about it and they broke up."

It could have easily played out that way, but it made Wyatt wonder why Griff hadn't just told him that. Then again, it was possible that Griff hadn't told him a lot of things.

Such as feeling the desperate need to end his own life.

Going back to Carlene's possible behavior about her potential tampering, maybe Griff hadn't broached the subject because Wyatt would have without question done something to stop it. Even if he'd had to hog-tie Griff and drag him to a counselor, Wyatt would have stopped it.

Marley switched her training to one of the other horses, and Wyatt knew Nola had her attention pinned to the girl's every move. Maybe to help ease some of the sting from the bad news Bennie had told her.

"If Bennie doesn't go to Azzie with this," Nola went on, "then I'll have to do it. It was her case, and she'll have to know."

Yeah, she would, but that would mean putting Nola through yet another emotional wringer. It would put him through it, too, but he didn't want to lay this on Nola's shoulders.

"I'll do that," Wyatt insisted, and because of her already-laden shoulders, he looked at her. "How are you feeling?"

"Well, I'm not feeling pregnant, if that's what you're asking. No morning sickness or fatigue like I had with Marley, but it's early."

She'd answered so easily, and it told him she'd already moved on from the shock of all those plus signs and had accepted that she was indeed going to have a baby. Wyatt wasn't there yet, but he'd soon have to be. Again, because of all that shoulder weight on Nola.

"I made this glass piece for her," Nola said, tipping her head to Marley.

He thought of the red sex one and frowned. "What kind of piece?"

"Nothing like *Wyatt's Junk*. It was a little yellow-and-blue bird I made when I first got to Italy. She would have only been like two months old then."

Wyatt thought back to what he'd been doing around that

time. It wasn't hard to remember. He'd been moping and throwing himself into work. That was the summer he'd started working on the sprawling Granger ranch over in Wrangler's Creek. He'd worked hard, long hours, hoping to forget Nola and their DNA-only.

He hadn't succeeded.

But the ranch owner, Lucian Granger, had been so impressed with his work that he'd offered him a full-time job. Wyatt had accepted it and had ended up finishing high school with online courses while he stayed in the Granger bunkhouse and socked away nearly all of his paychecks. That had given him the start to eventually buy River's End after Maude's death.

Of course, that "start" at the Granger Ranch had meant he'd been miles away from Griff, his other brothers and therefore Maude, so he might have missed something that could have ended up saving Griff.

There it was again. That guilt. And Wyatt might have stepped right into it and let it swallow him if the sound of Nola's voice hadn't stopped him.

"How's she doing?" she asked while Nola continued to keep her gaze on Marley.

"Good, as far as I can tell." But what the hell did he know about teenage girls? He didn't add that, though, to Nola. "She talks to Heather and some of her friends a couple of times a day."

"Does she seem to miss them?" Nola pressed.

"Can't tell, but I guess if she starts missing them too much, she'll go home. Or have them come here. I told her she could invite her friends." He paused and admitted the truth. "I still feel as if I'm walking on eggshells around her."

"I'd rather dodge eggshells than have her hate me. Marley

didn't choose the guest room with the view that I suggested, did she?" Nola tacked on to that before Wyatt could respond.

He sighed, shook his head. "But that doesn't mean she hates you."

"Really?" Nola questioned, looking him straight in the eye.

He realized it would take a lie to give her any kind of reassurance, and he was too raw from what he'd just learned about Griff to come up with a lie.

"Marley blames you for giving her up," he admitted. "It doesn't matter that I told her I agreed to it, that it was what I thought was necessary."

Realization went through her eyes and they widened. "She thinks I gave her up so I could go to Italy and focus on my glass?"

Wyatt couldn't lie about that, either. "I tried to set her straight, but I think her emotions are a hot mess right now."

Much as Nola's and his were.

"I love her," Nola muttered. "I mean, I always did, even before she was born. I loved her, and that hasn't gone away. In fact, it's stronger now that I've seen her and know her name."

Wyatt had tried his damnedest not to feel that same level of love. It'd been a way of guarding his heart since he'd known practically right from the start that they'd have to give her up. He still wanted some heart guarding because he wasn't sure how long Marley would be in his life.

She could change her mind and just leave.

Or Alec could pull some judicial strings and try to force her to go back home with him.

Since either of those things could happen, it was logical for Wyatt to try to tamp down his feelings, but there was nothing logical about any of this. Seeing Marley had moved her out the safe, pigeonholed DNA-only category and right into the daughter mode. However, she wasn't his daughter to have. No. Because he'd given up that right to the people who'd raised her.

"Who is that?" Nola asked.

Wyatt yanked himself out of his thoughts and looked out at the corral. Janie and Marley were still there, but they weren't alone. There was a lanky boy leaning on the corral fence, and Wyatt was familiar enough with the body language. The boy was chatting up Marley.

"Charlie Lambert's son, Trey," Wyatt grumbled. "He's working here part-time on weekends. Or rather, he's supposed to be working." He damn sure shouldn't have been chatting up Marley, and Wyatt intended to have a little chat with—

He stopped when he heard himself, and he regrouped. He couldn't have this reaction over Marley talking to a kid who was probably her own age, and he got the sucker-punch reminder that by the time he'd turned seventeen, he'd already gotten Nola pregnant—

Wyatt stopped again. Cursed again. There were plenty of things he put on the emotional back burner, and the idea of Marley having sex was going to stay as far back on that stove top as possible. Better yet, he didn't even want that particular stewpot of worry anywhere in his house.

To get his mind off, well, a whole bunch of things, Wyatt decided to fill Nola in on what he'd been doing. It wouldn't lift her mood, would probably only make her worry more, but he didn't want to keep her in the dark on this.

"I'm having background checks done on both her parents," he said. "I hired a PI in San Antonio to do it."

He'd expected for that to put some alarm in her eyes, and it did. "What are you looking for?"

"Nothing specific, and no, I don't think they were physically or sexually abusive. No sign of it whatsoever." He could at least relieve her mind of that. "And from what both Marley and Heather have said, Alec didn't start this bully routine until recently."

"Bully," she repeated. "Yes, that's exactly what he is." Nola stared at him. "Has he tried to put pressure on you?"

"He tried," Wyatt admitted. "And failed. Not personally, but he had his lawyer call me to tell me they're trying to get an earlier date for the custody hearing and that I should be doing everything in my power to get Marley back to San Antonio so she can prepare for that. I asked her if there were any such preparations she needed to make, and she said no."

But the looming custody hearing was troubling. If Marley got to live with Heather, then Wyatt would consider that a good outcome. Marley would be with the parent she clearly loved, the parent who'd raised her and seemingly had her heart in the right place. But just in case Heather's heart was elsewhere, Wyatt wanted to know. That started with background checks.

"The adoption agency would have vetted the Silvas," Nola reminded him. "I know because I just went through the vetting process. It's not easy—" She stopped, muttered, "Monkey balls. I'll need to let the agency know I'm pregnant." She paused again. "But I can wait a few weeks on that."

He certainly hadn't forgotten about her plans to adopt. "How soon did they say it'd be before you got offered a baby?" he asked.

"Within the year, maybe sooner."

With the way their luck was running, the agency would call her in the next hour and tell her she had to go pick up the baby then and there. And that it wouldn't be just one baby but quadruplets. Then Nola would go from not being an actual parent to having five kids and another on the way.

He continued to mentally snarl at the way Trey Lambert was going on and on to Marley, and while Wyatt hadn't perfected the lipreading that he suspected others had, Trey was laying on the charm. Charm that he'd better not think was going to get him into Marley's—

For a third time he stopped himself and regrouped. Hell, this fatherhood deal of a teenage girl was not fun and games. Especially since he'd once been a teenage boy.

Scowling and mentally snarling, Wyatt decided to go ahead and get one last thing off his mind. Not Trey and his slimy charm but rather something else he knew he had to man up and do now that he was aware of Bennie's "confession."

"I'm going to make arrangements to have Griff's car brought up from the bluff," he threw out there and waited for her reaction.

He didn't have to wait long, and it shouldn't have surprised him that she wasn't shocked. No wide eyes, no quick sucking in of her breath. Nola just sighed and pulled him into her arms.

Wyatt hadn't thought anything would help the decision settle any better in his gut, but the hug came close.

"A crew might not even be able to recover the car," he added, judging from what the cops had told him shortly after the wreck. A recovery would be an expensive, perhaps long process and could result in the car dislodging and falling even farther, all the way to the bottom of the bluff.

Of course, if that happened, the investigators could at least use some of the many trails around there to get down into the bluff to examine the vehicle. Or rather, what was left of it, anyway, since the drop itself would likely break the old car into heaven knew how many pieces. Even if by some miracle they did manage to get enough of what was left of it to a lab, there was no guarantee of answers. In other words, he could be right back where he'd started.

But no, it'd be worse than that since he'd then have to box up everything in his mind. Again. He'd have to learn how to live with this. Again. He'd have to feel things he preferred not to feel. Because at the heart of all of this, Wyatt had one big-assed fear. That he would end up in that same cold, dark pit that could have caused Griff to drive off that cliff.

He didn't voice any of that to Nola, but he was betting she knew the gist of it. They hadn't been close at the time of Griff's death, so he hadn't poured out his heart to her about that, but they'd had plenty of noncelebration birthdays over the years, which had involved all sorts of ill-advised confessions.

Like the time Nola had told him she'd never been able to have an orgasm with another man.

Like the notion of Marley having sex, Wyatt hadn't wanted the image in his head of Nola being with another man. It didn't matter if they weren't together. It was just something he hadn't wanted to know. But like the strongest superglue ever, it had stuck in his mind and always came up at the worst time.

Like now, for instance.

"Before that day in the pasture two weeks ago, had it really been seventeen-plus years since you'd had an orgasm?" Wyatt asked when she eased back from the hug to face him.

Clearly, that question shouldn't have come out of his mouth, but as bad as it was, and it was *bad*, it caused her to laugh. Well, maybe not laugh—not at first, anyway—but a surprised burst of air left her mouth that was close to laughter. And afterward, she smiled.

"With another person present, yes," she admitted, "but I've managed some on my own."

That admission shouldn't have grabbed him by the throat. Or any other part of him. But it did. Oh, man. He got some too-clear images of Nola doing just that. Too clear. Because even after all this time, he knew that look she got when she came. Not a dreamy kind of slack relief. It was more like a warrior who'd claimed a once-in-a-lifetime prize.

He suddenly wished he could see that look right here, right now.

That would certainly chase away this dark mood. Of course, to get that look, she'd have to get the climax. Again, his body volunteered to do the job.

"You know there's a market for handblown glass dildos," she threw out there, giving him a sneaky, sly, sexy look that told him she knew exactly what this conversation was doing to him.

"You're making that up," he managed to say.

"Nope. They can be done in all shapes and sizes, and they really aren't that hard to…wait for it," she teased, "…blow." She pursed her lips and mimicked that in a very sneaky, sly, sexy way.

Now she really did laugh, and mercy, it was good to hear. It made Wyatt think of all those sappy metaphors about the sound of it chasing off the blues. And it did. But more than that, much more, it just reminded him of how much he'd missed it. There often wasn't much laughing at their noncelebrations, and lately their time together had been filled with pregnancy tests, Marley's arrival and Griff.

Wyatt didn't want to think of any of those things right now. He just focused on her laugh, on the smile that followed, and before he could even try to talk himself out of it, he lowered his head and tasted that smile.

Nice.

Even nicer was the slide of need it gave him. Definitely not one of those punch-to-the-gut feelings that had been dominating his life. This was a much-wanted yank right into some serious heat.

Her lips were slightly chapped from the temps in her workshop, but she tasted like a doughnut. And like Nola, of course. No amount of glazed sugar would ever cover that up, and it took him exactly where he wanted to go. To another time and place when they'd kissed like this often. When the kisses had started off slow and easy and then had deepened.

Like now.

Wyatt slid his tongue over her lips and into her mouth. Oh, yeah. More of that taste, and he got another familiar reminder of the past. The sound that purred in Nola's throat to let him know she was just fine with this. He'd heard it only two and a half weeks ago in the pasture. Not long. But he realized he was starved for that sound. Starved for Nola.

The heat fired up some, and Nola slid her arms around him, pulling him closer until his chest landed against her breasts. Somewhere in the back of his mind, he realized he should put a stop to this, but before that thought could take hold, Nola pressed him even harder against her. Harder and in just the right spot.

And the dance began.

The kiss got deeper, and the gnawing hunger came. A hunger that he'd had for her right from the start. From the first time he'd kissed her when she'd been fifteen. The kisses had gradually gotten longer and hotter. Had gradually led to touching. Which in turn had gradually led to sex about four months later.

Since they were each other's firsts, neither of them had done even a half-assed job of dealing with that heat. She'd climaxed the first time he'd touched the front of her panties, and he'd nearly done the same because that'd been the first time he'd seen her warrior face. Her mouth slightly open in victory. Her eyes gleaming, again in victory. Her breath hot and rough.

Thankfully, he'd held off just long enough to get on a condom that he'd snagged from Jonas and held off even longer so that Nola and he had left the truck, which had also belonged to Jonas, with their virginities lost. In that moment, Wyatt had been sure he'd died and gone to heaven.

Which was something similar to what he was feeling now.

That had a lot to do with Nola moving her hands from his back and to his butt. She had never been shy about positioning him exactly where she wanted, and she wasn't holding back now. She came up on her toes, aligning her body with his. Jeans zipper to jeans zipper. And that meant with his quickly forming erection he was already wondering just how fast those jeans could be peeled off her.

He managed to get his hand between them, because, hey, he'd never been shy about this sort of thing either, and he cupped her right breast, flicking his thumb over her puckered nipple. The next step would be to hike up her top and replace his thumb with his mouth, but it occurred to him that maybe they shouldn't be doing this since she was pregnant.

"Don't you dare stop," Nola insisted. It was her warrior's voice. "I need this. I need you."

All right, then. That was the reassurance Wyatt needed, and he decided it was time to move this to the bedroom. He started in that direction.

But then two things happened at the same time.

And neither of those things was Nola's climax.

His phone dinged with a text, and he groaned because he instantly knew that it was probably from Janie to let him know that Marley was finished in the corral. But Wyatt would have preferred that heads-up just a couple of seconds earlier so he could disentangle himself from Nola.

He hadn't had those extra seconds, though.

Because at the exact moment of the text ding, Marley walked in. And her gaze zoomed right to him in midgrope of Nola's breast.

CHAPTER TEN

BECAUSE HER PULSE had kicked into high gear and because her body was on fire, Nola didn't actually hear the front door open, but she had no trouble feeling Wyatt's body stiffen. And she wasn't talking about the manly stiffening behind the zipper of his jeans, either.

Nope.

Every muscle in his body went rigid, and before she even followed his gaze to see what had caused that reaction, she knew that Marley had just walked in on them.

She had, Nola confirmed with a glance. Marley had strolled into the house, obviously seen what was going on and had come to a complete standstill. Her mouth wasn't open in shock, but there was plenty of shock in her eyes. It seemed to Nola there was some disgust, too.

"I, uh," Marley said just as Nola muttered something similar. Wyatt dropped an f-bomb under his breath.

Wyatt and she darted away from each other as if they'd just been scalded, but this was a textbook definition of closing the barn door after the horses, cows, pigs, sheep, etc. had already gotten out. No way could Marley unsee what she'd just seen.

Since Nola's father had died before she was born, she hadn't ever had the awful experience of witnessing anything like this. And maybe that wouldn't be an accurate comparison anyway since Wyatt and she weren't the ones who'd raised Marley. Still, they were adults, and in the mind of a teenager, they were probably too old to be carrying on like this. If Marley had known such a carrying-on had left Nola pregnant, it almost certainly would have disgusted her even more.

Maybe disgust her enough so that she'd run out the door and never come back.

Nola held her breath, waiting to see if that was what was going to happen, but Marley didn't say anything. Nor did she run out to her car, which was still in Wyatt's driveway. Instead, she mumbled something Nola didn't catch and headed down the hall to the guest room that she'd chosen over Nola's recommendation.

Wyatt cursed again, and he looked as if he wanted to hit himself on the head with a rock. Since Nola was feeling the same thing, she was ready to go locate a rock for both of them.

The heat was gone, vanishing in a blink, but all the kissing and touching had left her feeling antsy and irritable. Having Marley witness the heat had only added to the irritability.

"I should go," Nola said, "and you should try to talk to her." She glanced down at the front of his jeans. "Well, talk to her in a few minutes. You can tell her I lost my head and went after you."

"I'll tell her no such thing. That was my tongue in your mouth, and I'm the one that put it there."

"No doubts about that." It was a very familiar tongue. "But I'm already her bad guy in this, and she needs a good guy. So, let's keep your rep clean." That way, Marley might not head straight for San Antonio.

Of course, in a big-picture kind of way, that was probably what should happen. Marley should go home and try to work out a reasonable agreement with her parents for her custody. But Nola wasn't feeling reasonable, not with the antsy pants and irritability, and she didn't want her daughter to leave before said daughter had even gotten a chance to know her.

Or forgive her.

Then again, maybe forgiveness would never happen. Still, Nola didn't want to deprive Wyatt of this chance to be with Marley. That meant at least one of them would get a half-assed semi-do-over. For at least a little while, anyway.

Because Wyatt looked as irritable as she was, Nola brushed a quick kiss on his mouth and held back on any attempt to lighten his mood by telling him that one day he could watch her blow—ha ha—a glass dildo. The joke would register off the lame meter, and besides, they didn't need even the hint of anything sexual between them.

"I'm going to the workshop to get some stuff done," she told him and headed for the door. She heard him mutter another f-bomb. Then a goodbye. But Nola didn't look back.

Since Nola didn't especially want to spend the ten-minute drive mulling over what had just happened or speculating about the consequences of it, she used her handsfree to call Lily to set up a time when she could make her sister's mood utterly miserable by telling her about Bennie's confession. But the miserable-mood scheduling was apparently going to have to wait since the call went straight to voice mail.

Still trying to stave off thinking about Marley or the sexual-frustration ache Wyatt had left her with, Nola made the next call on her mental list. To Simon Waterstone, owner of the Waterstone Gallery in San Antonio, where Lorelei sent the best of her best glass pieces. Unlike her sister, Simon answered right away, and he'd obviously seen her name on the screen.

"Nola," he immediately greeted her. "Tell me you have something exciting and wonderful."

Well, her life had been exciting lately, but in an out-of-control roller-coaster kind of way. Best not to mention that. Best not to mention the pregnancy outright either until she'd broken the news to Lily. So, that was going to make this conversation a little like walking on eggshells, to borrow a phrase from Wyatt.

"I just wanted to let you know that I might be taking a little time off," she said. "I'll still be working, but I might be cutting back," Nola amended when he made a sound of horror.

She wasn't sure what her doctor would say about her working in a hot space for the endless hours that she now put in. As a minimum, she'd likely need to take frequent breaks, get fresh air and follow other such rules that would keep her away from working. Then, once she got megapregnant, she might not be able to lift a glass-loaded Harry Potter at all.

"I wanted you to know in case you'd like to start buying from another artist," she added.

"There is no artist like you, Nola," he assured her. "You produce magic."

She was dead certain he said that to every one of the artists whose work he commissioned. After all, a delusional artist was a happy, productive one.

"Thanks for that," she told him, despite the BS. "I also won't be doing any commissioned pieces for a while. I'll finish the request you sent me last week." An abstract blue waterfall, she recalled.

"Oh, good. Dodo will be so happy about that."

"Dodo?" she asked. "That's the name of the customer?"

"Actually, I'm not sure. It's an alias, you see," he added in a whisper as if divulging a secret. "I'm not even sure if it's a man or a woman because a courier service always picks up the pieces."

"So, how does Dodo—" she winced a little at saying it aloud "—see the pieces?"

"Oh, from the pictures I put on my web page. Dodo obviously knows quality art, and that's why he or she also commissioned you to do specific pieces. Dodo also snaps up nearly all your art that comes into the gallery."

Nola frowned. Then she huffed. "How many is *nearly all*?"

"All but two," Simon finally admitted.

All but two? Good grief, Lorelei had sent Simon dozens and dozens of pieces since they'd started doing business with the Waterstone Gallery.

"Like I said, Dodo obviously loves your work and appreciates you for the talented artist you are," Simon added.

That sounded like more BS, and it was smelly and suspicious enough for the impostor syndrome to swoop in and make her mood even worse. Because she knew that Dodo could be her mother. Or some other family member with thousands of extra dollars to spend so she'd think she had earned that talented-artist label that Simon had just laid on her.

"How do I get in touch with this Dodo?" she asked.

"Oh, dear. You can't. He or she said that in the first email contact, that the sales had to remain anonymous. He's probably worried someone might try to steal them. Or maybe he or she wants to keep the artistic treasure trove for his or her eyes only."

Nola could think of another *or*—that her mother or family members didn't want her to know they were feeding her artist delusions and keeping her happy.

"Give me the email address, then," Nola insisted.

"Well, there's a problem with that. Each time Dodo makes a purchase or requests a commission, he or she uses a different email. Again, probably because of privacy concerns." Simon huffed. "Nola, I'm sure it's nothing to be concerned about. Just know that someone values your talent for what it is."

Yeah, and what it was might all be a fraud. Monkey balls. She didn't want to yell out a rhetorical question of how much worse could this day get because Nola was afraid the universe would take that as a challenge and dump something else on her.

She ended the call with Simon to cut off any more of his ego-soothing gushing, and she went to her workshop even though she wasn't that interested now in losing herself in her *art*. In fact, she had the urge to make six hundred glass dildos and send them to Simon so he could arrange for Dodo to pick them up. Her gift to the person who "valued her art." Then she could go to her mother's house and see where Evangeline had stashed the dildos and the other pieces.

Nola frowned, though, rethinking that. Evangeline's house wasn't that big. She'd moved into a cottage smaller than Nola's and had given Lorelei the big house that their father had inherited from his father shortly after Evangeline and he had married. Lorelei had plenty of room to store glass.

But that required more rethinking, too.

Lorelei had a trust fund. They all did. Nola had used hers to build the workshop and buy the cottage. Lily had put hers into the ranch. So, maybe Lorelei was Dodo, and she'd tapped into her inheritance to bolster her kid sister's career and therefore ensure she could run the shop. But that seemed like a lot of hoops to jump through, considering that Lorelei could have bought and run other shops.

Obviously, she would need to ask some questions and do more snooping. For now, though, Nola had just enough temper brewing that she went in the workshop and fired up the equipment to get started on the first dildo. It would be big and green and have some warty bumps on it, so she gathered the right color and got to work.

Nola had just gotten started with the first blow when the door opened. "Shut it," she snarled, "or you'll let the heat out."

She waited for the usual "God, it's hot in here," but when her visitor didn't whine that out, she turned and saw someone she definitely hadn't been expecting.

Alec Silva.

For a couple of stunned, horrifying moments, Nola thought that maybe he was there because Marley had called him and told him about the lip-lock and other stuff she'd seen Wyatt and her doing, but Alec lived in San Antonio, a half hour away. That meant he would have had to have gotten in his car right away and sped here. And if he'd done any hasty trips to console his daughter, Alec would have almost certainly gone to Wyatt's and not here.

Unless Marley wasn't at Wyatt's.

Nola nearly blurted out an *is Marley all right?* question, but she held back. If something was indeed wrong, she was sure he was here to tell her all about it. And if Marley hadn't called him, if this was just some random visit, then asking something like that would alarm him. Or rather, give him reason to try to twist Marley's arm to do what he wanted.

So, Nola stayed quiet and waited and watched as Alec glanced around the workshop. Some prowling followed the glancing, and he went to the shelves to look at the pieces she'd made over the past couple of days. He didn't seem impressed.

Nola could have told him the feeling was mutual.

Marley's father was wearing a suit, complete with a tie that looked as if it was choking him, which she was counting on to help make this visit a short one. She had the glory hole going full blast now, and even though the fans were on, he'd be a sweat ball in no time flat. She hoped it was the stinky kind of perspiration that would make people turn up their noses at him since that was what he did to her when he finally graced her with his attention.

"Interesting," he said, not addressing anything in particular. Some people could say that about spiderwebs, dust patterns or fungus. Maybe even an ugly baby when you didn't want to insult the parents.

"Why are you here?" she came out and asked, and she moved directly in front of the fan nearest him. Not only because she wanted to keep cool but also to deprive him of the air.

"Marley, of course," he said, and he gave that neck-choking tie a little wiggle to loosen it. "I'm hoping you're a reasonable woman. After all, you were reasonable enough to give up Marley because you knew you couldn't give her what she needed. You wanted her to have a family who could raise her the way she should be raised."

"Yeah, I'm rethinking that whole thing," Nola grumbled, and she reminded herself to tamp down the anger she felt for this man. It could backfire and hurt Marley. "Why are you here, Mr. Silva?" she repeated, but this time she softened her tone as much as she could manage.

"Because I believe you still want what's best for Marley."

Well, there was no way she could argue with that. Nola did want what was best for her. She just wasn't sure the *best* was this man in front of her with sweat already popping out on his forehead.

"Why are you here?" she said again and hoped this would be a third-time's-a-charm kind of deal.

He looked at her in such a way that she thought he was trying to intimidate her. Or maybe the heat had sucked up all the fluid in his eyeballs. She was willing to give him the snarky benefit of the doubt on that.

"I want you to talk to Marley and try to convince her to come home," he finally said.

Nola gave him a flat look and nearly blurted out that she was the last person Marley would listen to, but she held back on that, too. Her instincts told her the less she said to Alec Silva, the better.

"Your partner," he said in a tone of disdain, "has chosen not to do that. Perhaps you can convince him otherwise."

Nola didn't feel threatened, not exactly, and she certainly didn't feel as if she were in danger. After all, she was still holding a carbon steel pipe that she could use to defend herself if it came down to it. Of course, it wouldn't. If Alec had any violent tendencies, Heather or Marley would have said something by now. Then again, maybe he'd never aimed those tendencies at them.

Before Nola could tell the a-hole to get out, the door opened, and it was one of the rare times when she was glad to lose the heat. Another form of heat walked in.

Deputy Azzie Parkman.

She wasn't your typical deputy. For one thing, she was in her early seventies and had no plans to retire, ever. For another thing, she was six feet tall and had managed to keep her body toned and muscled. She didn't just look capable of kicking ass. She could do it.

Azzie took one look at Nola, her gaze skirting over the somewhat defensive way she was holding the pipe. Then she turned her stony cop's gaze on Alec.

"You a customer?" Azzie asked him in the same tone she would use to interrogate a serial killer had there been such a thing in Last Ride.

Alec tried to match her stare. He failed big-time. "Not exactly."

"Then why don't you move that penis-mobile of a car out of the no-parking zone before I write you up a ticket." Azzie hiked her thumb in the direction of the street.

Oh, Alec did not like being dismissed, and he gave Nola an angry glance with a *This isn't over* chaser before he walked out.

"Do I need to apologize for running him off?" Azzie asked the moment the door closed.

"No, but I need to thank you for getting rid of him," Nola countered. "That was Marley's father."

"Yeah, I know. I was in the diner when he pulled up and ran the license plates. I didn't like the way he swaggered in here, so I figured I'd check on you."

"Thanks again." Nola paused. "So, you know all about Marley and her parents?"

Azzie didn't hedge or dodge. She nodded. "Pretty much everybody in town knows. Marley's apparently had some phone conversations with her mother when she's been around the ranch hands. Gossips, every last one of them."

She thought of Trey and wondered if he fell into that loose-lips category, but Nola went with a different question. "When you ran Alec's plates, did anything come up?"

"You mean like an arrest warrant, piles of unpaid speeding tickets? Naw," she added. "He's clean. Well, clean by law enforcement standards, anyway. Is he giving you some trouble?"

Nola definitely didn't want Azzie getting in on this because, again, any blowback from Azzie harassing him and such could hurt Marley, and that was why Nola shook her head.

"I think he just wants to make sure Marley is okay," she settled for saying.

Azzie made a sound of agreement as she strolled over to look at the glass pieces on the shelves. Thank God, Nola hadn't added any glass dildos to the stock yet. "Yeah, it's got to be unnerving for Marley to have come to her birth parents," Azzie said. "That would fire up a whole bunch of insecurities in some people."

Nola had intimate knowledge of insecurities. That didn't mean she sympathized with Alec, but at least she could understand.

Azzie walked to the other side of the workshop, where her attention would soon fall on the fire-red glass piece. It did, but she didn't have the same wow reaction as others had. She merely gave it the once-over and looked back at Nola.

"I'm here about Bennie," Azzie explained.

Oh. That. Nola had obviously let Alec's visit throw her, because Bennie was already off her radar. She moved it right back on, front and center.

"Bennie came by the office to talk to me," Azzie went on, "and he told me his suspicions about his sister. He said he told you, too."

Nola nodded. "He did, and I passed along the info to Wyatt."

Azzie sighed. "Well, that'll sure mess with his head."

"It already has," Nola admitted. "Of course, other things have, too."

"Your daughter. That'll do it." Azzie paused a heartbeat. "Does Lily know about what Bennie told you?"

"Not yet. I'm still trying to arrange a visit with her since I want to do it in person, but she's tied up with business stuff right now. I just hope no one tells her before I get the chance."

"Well, right now only four people know. Bennie, Wyatt, you and me. I'm sure as heck-fire not telling anybody other than Sheriff Corbin, and he won't be blabbing. As for anyone getting wind of or a peek at it, I can hold off putting it in an official report for at least a couple of days. If that's not enough time, let me know. I'm sure the sheriff will agree to stretch that out a bit."

There were some disadvantages to living in a small town—for example, the gossip and practically living in a fishbowl—but there were huge advantages, too, and this was one of them.

"Thank you," Nola told her. She nearly left it at that, but she knew Azzie was someone who'd give it to her straight. "Do you think Carlene could have actually tampered with Griff's car?"

Azzie lifted her shoulder. "Could have done. A woman scorned and all that, and maybe in a twisted kind of way, she thought having sex with a guy meant they were as good as married. If that was the case, there'd be a whole lot of early marriages and some bigamies."

Nola immediately latched on to that. Not the bigamies but something else. "Maybe it was Carlene who left the wedding ring on Griff's tombstone. You know, because she had been expecting him to marry her, and that was the ring she intended to give him."

Azzie nodded in such a way that Nola realized the deputy had already considered it. "I'll make some calls and see if anybody remembers Carlene buying a ring like that. It looks kinda small for a man's hand, but Carlene could have bought it for herself, I guess. For sure there won't be any usable DNA on it after all this time, and even if there was any trace evidence, it wouldn't necessarily point to who put it there. I suspect a lot of people have touched that ring over the years."

Nola was certain Azzie was right. She hadn't touched it because it would have felt like a violation of Griff's grave, but others might not have felt that way. Added to that, there'd been those who'd replaced the ring on the occasions when it'd fallen off.

Azzie sighed, turned toward the door, but then hitched her thumb to the fire-red glass piece. "That's real pretty, but what exactly is it supposed to be?"

Apparently, Azzie didn't see sex and genitalia when she looked at it, and Nola wasn't going to fill her in on it. "It's supposed to be whatever people see in it."

Azzie nodded. "That's what I figured." She paused. "You think Wyatt knows that's his pecker you've re-created there?"

But she didn't wait for any answer. Good thing, too, because Nola didn't have one. Azzie just tipped the brim of her Stetson, muttered something about her having a good day, and she strolled out.

That was the other downside to living in a small town. No secrets. None. Because there were too many people who could see right through you. That was a strong reminder that she needed to have that talk with Lily and that she needed to tell the rest of her family she was pregnant. Most women waited a couple of months to do that, until the threat of miscarriage had passed, but Nola knew she was already on borrowed time in that department. She couldn't wait days, much less months, or her family would all hear it from someone else.

Nola stood there several moments longer, letting the fan cool her, and glanced around the workshop as both Alec and Azzie had done. So many changes on the horizon, and some of those changes weren't all happy.

Wyatt would be a big part of that unhappy deal because he'd have to come to terms with being a father. Not that Nola would expect him to dive right into a daddy role. No way.

But he would help because he was a decent guy.

And that help could quickly turn to resentment if she wasn't careful. That meant no more making-out sessions in his kitchen, or anywhere else, for that matter. Best not to add this heat between them into the mix with the pregnancy or Wyatt would be offering her a marriage proposal that he didn't want. Nola had no desire to get on that resentment train. She cared too much about him for that.

This workshop would give her some sadness, too. Or rather, the sadness would come from the time she wouldn't be able to spend here. It was one of the reasons she'd wanted to adopt, so there wouldn't be any workshop downtime from a pregnancy. But that was only a tiny part of why she'd chosen adoption.

Having a baby at sixteen, especially a baby she'd known wouldn't be hers for long, had been the worst form of hell. She'd gone through a hard pregnancy with lots of morning sickness that'd lasted the entire nine months. The gossip had been nonstop, and girls she'd thought had been her friends had fueled a lot of that talk. Added to that, the labor and delivery had been traumatizing.

So much pain.

So much fear when the cord had been wrapped around the baby's neck. In that moment when she'd been pushing with every bit of her breath and energy to save the baby, Nola had made the decision that the pregnancy would be her last. She hadn't done anything like Wyatt's vasectomy, but she'd been very careful not to have a repeat.

Careful until that day in the pasture with Wyatt.

Now she would have to go through a pregnancy that brought on the flashbacks. The fear. The worry. The complete change of her life. She figured the only thing that was stopping her from full-blown panic was that she already loved this child and wanted it more than her next breath. More than the glass. More than the nonpanic she'd have if she weren't carrying this baby.

She was still standing there lost in her thoughts when the door opened again, and she practically came to attention when Marley walked in. Nola's heart gave a little leap, and for just a second, she thought that maybe Marley was here to tell her that she was letting the past go.

But no.

One look at Marley's face, and she knew this wasn't an *I forgive you, Mom* kind of visit.

"Was my father just here?" Marley asked.

Nola nodded. And left it at that.

Marley huffed. "I'd hoped Trey was wrong about the car. One of his friends spotted the Porsche in front of your workshop and called Trey. He told me. Why did my father come here to see you?" she tacked on to that explanation.

Nola considered just blurting out the ugly truth, that Alec had tried to apply some pressure, but it was obvious that Marley was already agitated, and she didn't need more fuel to that particular fire.

"He wanted to know how you were," Nola said.

Not a lie. Not exactly. In a roundabout way, it was possible that Alec's snarliness was because he was worried about his daughter. Nola would have been had their positions been reversed. However, in such a role reversal, she wouldn't have been a butthole.

"Did he want you to talk me into going back to San Antonio?" Marley pressed.

"He did." And again, Nola tried to soothe rather than lay out every word of the truth about her butthole father. "He doesn't know Wyatt or me, and he probably just wants to make sure you're safe."

Marley huffed. "He wants to make sure I'm under his thumb."

Yeah, that was Nola's take, too. Under his thumb and in his custody. Maybe because custody was control for him. And a way to score a win against the woman he was divorcing. And that was Nola's reminder to push this a little.

"Has your relationship with your dad always been a little—" oh, to find the right word "—strained?"

Marley's laugh wasn't one of humor, but then she stopped and seemed to rethink that. "I know why you're asking. You don't want to feel guilty if you gave me up to someone who could...*strain* my life."

There was some truth in that snark. "You're right. I don't want to feel guilty, but that ship's sailed." And had taken her straight to guilt island. "But I also want to—" again, she had to search for the right way to finish that "—make sure you're okay."

Not her best effort at pouring out her heart, but sadly, it wasn't her worst, either.

"Oh, I'm just fine and dandy," Marley said.

More snark. And, dragging in a deep breath, she glanced around the workshop. She didn't even look in the direction of *the* glass piece, so that was a small blessing.

"So, was it worth it?" Marley asked. "Was it worth giving me up so you could have all of this?"

If Marley had stabbed her in the heart, it couldn't have hurt more. "No, it wouldn't have been worth it," Nola managed to say around the lump in her throat. "If that's why I had given you up. It wasn't. It was because I was too young to be a real mother to you."

Marley made a sound that could have meant anything or nothing, and it seemed to be a precursor to her leaving.

"Wait," Nola said before she could walk out. "I have something for you."

Nola paused a moment to see if Marley was indeed going to stay put, and since she wasn't moving toward the door, maybe that meant she would. Nola hurried back into the small office, such that it was. She didn't actually do any office work in there, but she used it to store stuff for future projects.

And other things.

Nola went straight to the bottom drawer of the desk and took out the small box that had been there for years. Before that, it'd been in her room in Italy and then her bedroom at her mom's. It'd even spent a little time in her cottage before Nola had brought it here for safekeeping.

Since the box had seen better days, Nola carefully opened it and took out the little glass bird. The window allowed in a spear of light that caught the glass just right, causing it to come to life in its own way. The blue shimmered like wings ready to take flight, and there was just a slight hint of red in the yellow chest, and as corny as it sounded, it looked as if she'd managed to capture the little bird's heartbeat.

So many memories were in that little figurine. Both good and bad ones. But she'd known from the moment she'd blown that first breath into the pipe that this was her daughter's.

So were the other birds that had followed.

There were seventeen of them now. Each a different size, shape and color that she'd made with her breath. And tears.

Literally. She'd cried while choosing the colors of the glass gathers, cried when blowing and shaping each piece, cried some more when she'd taken each one from the cooling oven and packed them away. Those other sixteen were in a large box beneath her desk.

Out of sight but never out of mind.

Just like Marley.

Nola gave this particular bird, the first one, a quick polish that it didn't actually need, and she went back into the main part of the workshop. She halfway expected Marley to be gone, but she'd waited. Though not necessarily with patience and eager anticipation, because she had her arms folded over her chest, and her mouth was set in a flat line.

"I made this for you," Nola said, speaking around the lump in her throat, which was not only still there but was growing by leaps and bounds. She held out the bird for Marley.

Marley studied it, not with snark or the disdain she usually aimed at Nola. "It's a bluebird," she remarked.

Nola nodded. "Apparently it's an eastern bluebird. I didn't know that's what it was going to be, though, until I blew and shaped it. I made it for you," she repeated when Marley didn't say anything.

Marley looked at her, and Nola was shocked and unbelievably touched when she saw the tears watering Marley's eyes. "It's beautiful," she said. "Even back then, you obviously had talent."

Nola thought that was the highest compliment she'd ever heard or would ever hear again. Her hopes soared.

Then crashed.

Because with her eyes filled with tears and without a smidge of snark on her face, Marley turned and walked out.

Leaving Nola and the heart-beating bluebird behind.

CHAPTER ELEVEN

WYATT FINISHED HIS call with Mike Gonzales, the owner of one of the biggest towing services in the county, and then he sat back at his desk and tried to process, well, the process he'd just put into motion.

Recovering Griff's car.

It'd taken Wyatt hours of research and a lot of calls to find someone who thought they could do the job, and Mike apparently believed he could. The man had a big crane he was convinced would work in tandem with a helicopter that he used for some of the more complex removals. Like this one.

Wyatt would have to sign a whole bunch of waivers and disclaimers, not holding the company liable if they damaged the car more than it already was. He'd also have to write a very large check to cover the cost. Then they'd have to wait for the property owner to give them permission, which in turn would mean signing more waivers and disclaimers. Because the owner wasn't local and lived in Houston, Mike was going to take care of that as well.

At least the sheriff's office hadn't given Wyatt any argument on agreeing that he and his brothers were Griff's next of kin and therefore had permission to try to recover the car. He'd been worried that with Bennie's confession the cops would now consider the area a crime scene or something. But instead, Sheriff Corbin and Azzie had given him the green light. Even with Bennie's confession, the sheriff had admitted it could be months before they got the funding approval for the recovery.

If they got it at all, that was.

Because, after all, even if the lab could prove there had been actual tampering, there was no one to charge with a crime since Carlene was dead. It'd be a waste of the taxpayers' money to try for a conviction of a dead woman after all these years.

Added to that, there was no proof that the mechanic cousin had knowingly aided and abetted her, though apparently the guy had admitted in a phone call with the sheriff that he had spoken to Carlene during that time frame. He'd also admitted to giving Carlene instructions on how to cut a brake line and muck up the fuel line by adding something to the gas tank.

Of course, it was possible that Carlene had done absolutely nothing with the information she'd gotten. And that was what Wyatt was going to hang on to until someone proved otherwise. No tampering. No suicide. Just an accident.

He heard the knock at the door and wondered if Marley had forgotten her key. The key he'd given her, making her the only person other than him and his brothers who had a copy. Wyatt had pointed out that locking up wasn't necessary, but Marley had been raised in the city, where something like that was second nature. She might have locked up when she'd left to go into town to get some grocery items and then realized she didn't have her key.

But it wasn't Marley.

It was Nola at the door. Nola looking her usual disheveled, amazing self.

He'd been trying not to think of all the kissing they'd

done the day before, but he was failing big-time. He'd been doing plenty of thinking about her, and that thinking included a really bad urge to kiss her again. Yeah, even after all the trouble that last make-out session had caused when Marley had walked in on them.

Marley hadn't brought it up to him, and he sure as hell wasn't going to bring it up to her. He didn't especially want to know what she'd thought of the goings-on of her birth parents that she probably thought were old enough to know better. Apparently, that kind of wisdom hadn't come with age. In fact, Wyatt's need for Nola was growing by leaps and bounds.

Before they'd had sex in the pasture, it had been well over seventeen years since he'd had sex with her. That hadn't cooled the heat, but it had been long enough that touching her would have felt awkward.

Or rather, it should have.

But nope, one leaned-in kiss of what had likely been comfort for her had turned into a scalding-hot frenzy where common sense and awkwardness didn't even enter his mind. He'd just gone with it, going at her clothes, and his, as if there'd been no possibility whatsoever of consequences or one of the hands riding up and spotting them. It'd been the starving teenage hormones all over again. Now Nola and he were going to have to pay the piper.

Unfortunately, this piper situation would put more of the paying on Nola.

She'd be the one to carry this baby, and seventeen years hadn't dulled his memories of the hell she'd gone through with the last pregnancy. They might have been too young to raise a kid, but both of them had been well aware of just how close they'd come to losing that baby. Ironically, a baby they had already lost in a different sense of the word.

Feeling the sting of those too-clear memories, he nearly reached for her, but Nola spoke before he could make that particular mistake.

"Have you been buying all my glass pieces?" Nola asked.

Wyatt frowned and realized he'd been wishing she was there to throw herself into his arms and have her way with him.

"No, and hello to you, too," he said. "Why would you think that?"

She studied his eyes as if looking for the lie. Which wasn't there. He'd never bought any of her work, though she had given him a couple of pieces over the years during their noncelebration get-togethers. A little horse and a red heart paperweight that he kept on his desk.

"Have you ever or do you now use the name Dodo?" she pressed.

He was certain he gave her a weird, puzzling look because these questions both fell into those particular categories.

"No," he assured her. "If I were going to use an alias, it wouldn't be an extinct bird or one that would make me sound like an idiot. Why?" Wyatt repeated.

She didn't explain, and apparently, after more of that long eye study, Nola became convinced he was telling the truth, because she sighed and waved it off. Wyatt would have pressed for an explanation, but he saw her gaze drift out to the vacant spot in his driveway where Marley was usually parked.

"Marley's not here," he told her.

"I know. She's in town at the bookstore, and soon she'll be picking up an order at By the Slice for a black-olive, anchovy and pineapple pizza." Nola made a face to indicate that sounded disgusting to her. It did to Wyatt, too. "She's getting a double-cheese meat lovers one for you."

His favorite, and possibly info Marley would have gotten from whoever was working the pizza place today. It was a takeout-only kind of pizzeria, but the same handful of people worked there. "And you know this how?" Wyatt asked.

"Because when I went into the diner to order some lunch, Matilda Farmer was on the register, and she gave me Marley's itinerary." Nola huffed, and when he stepped back from the door, she came inside. "She was fishing for dirt and more gossip because she saw Alec and then Marley both leave my workshop yesterday."

Everything inside Wyatt tightened. He apparently wasn't in the gossip loop, because this was the first he was hearing about that. "What the hell was Alec doing there?"

"Trying to convince me to pressure Marley to bend to his will. He didn't stay long, and I was about to give him the boot—or rather, a poke with my pipe—when Azzie showed up and threatened him with a parking ticket."

As threats went, that sounded on the tame side, but Wyatt knew Azzie could make a hello sound lethal when she was in the cop mode. Which was pretty much a hundred percent of the time.

"Did he upset you?" Wyatt pressed.

She waved that off as she'd done the puzzling *did you buy all my glass or go by the name Dodo?* questions. "No, but I am interested in reading that background check on him when it's finished. Azzie said his record was clean. Hard to believe that his temper had never gotten him in trouble."

Wyatt heard the low growl in his throat. If Nola was aware of the man's temper, then that meant Alec had likely acted like the dick he was.

"I'll call him and tell him to back off," Wyatt snarled.

Nola patted his arm. "It's okay. I made him sweat. Or rather, the heat in the workshop did. He left glistening, and not in a good way. He no doubt stunk up his penis-mobile and had to breathe his own stench for the drive back to San Antonio."

Glistening and breathing in stench weren't nearly enough punishment. Wyatt would make that phone call after Nola had left. For now, though, he wanted to hear more about the other thing she'd said.

"Marley came to your workshop?" he asked.

Nola nodded, went to his fridge and reached for a can of orange soda. She froze, seemed to change her mind, her hand hovering by the carton of milk before she took a bottle of water instead. Sighing, she also poured herself a glass of milk. He didn't have to guess that the pregnancy had played into that choice, because Nola wasn't a milk drinker.

"Marley came to see me shortly after Alec left," she explained, and she drank down some of the milk like medicine. Fast and while grimacing. Then she chased it with some water. "Someone told her he'd been there, and she wanted to know what he'd said."

Wyatt thought back to the day before. He'd known Marley had driven into town because he kept close tabs on her. Not in a hovering-over-her kind of way, but more because she always told him before she left to do an errand and then she gave him an estimate of when she'd be back. She had told him about that particular trip into town, but in hindsight, she hadn't mentioned why.

Doing more hindsight, Wyatt figured she'd probably known that he wouldn't like hearing about Alec pestering Nola. Or Marley trying to apologize for her father's pestering.

If that was what she'd done.

He wasn't so sure it was, because if Marley had gone to the workshop to smooth over any kind of ruffled feelings, Nola would have clutched on to that like a victory. So, no. Something else had gone on.

"Want to tell me what happened when Marley came to see you?" he came out and asked.

She shrugged, set her milk and water on the counter, and that was when Wyatt saw something that had him cursing. The hurt in her eyes. Hell.

What now?

And better yet, how could he fix it? He didn't expect an answer to that last question anytime soon, because so far, he'd made zero headway convincing Marley not to put all the blame for the adoption onto Nola.

"I tried to give Marley the glass bird, the one I made for her two months after she was born, and she wouldn't take it." Nola ended that with a long sigh, and she closed her eyes a moment as if trying to shut out the pain.

Wyatt knew from plenty of experience that shutting eyes did nothing to ward off anything like pain. He also knew just how much Nola was hurting right now. He hadn't known about the bird, not until recently, but it had to be important to her since she'd kept it all this time.

Even though the sliver of logic in his head shouted that what he was about to do was a bad idea, he did it anyway. He pulled Nola into his arms. Yep, in the very spot where they'd gone at each other the day before. And just like the day before, he didn't keep his mouth to himself. He brushed a kiss on her forehead.

She looked up at him. The hurt was still there in her eyes, but there was something else. A question.

"Should we be doing this?" she asked.

"No," he readily admitted, but he kept holding her.

Thankfully, he did have the sense left not to let his mouth slide down in the direction of hers. Because as primed as his body still was, that would be all it took to do a whole lot more.

He wanted to think that Nola would put the brakes on anything that would involve a "whole lot more," but she was even worse of an emotional mess than he was. So, if anyone was going to be the adult here, it had to be him.

"Do you know one good thing about us having sex again?" she came out and asked.

"Only one?" Wyatt countered. "I'd like to think that two things could come out of it. You and me." Yeah, both lame and stupid, but that was what happened whenever he touched Nola.

She smiled, and he was glad the lameness and stupidity had chased away some of the sadness. "All right, three things could come out of it. Ha ha," she added, acknowledging his juvenile humor. "If we had sex, at least you wouldn't be able to get me pregnant."

He didn't laugh. Though it was true. And he was sort of glad that Nola could see the bright side of this. If they'd intended to have sex, that was.

But they weren't.

Were they?

Of course, his dick tried to get in on this, but again from experience talking, he knew that part of him wasn't known for its wise decision-making skills when it came to matters of sex with Nola.

"Sometimes, I just think what would it hurt, why would it matter?" Nola went on, and she was probably just shifting her position, but the shifting sent the front of her jeans brushing against his. "Then I come to my senses because it would complicate things."

"I'm right there with you," he admitted, and he forced himself to focus not on the incredible sensations of sex with her but on those complications.

Wyatt wasn't sure he'd get the worst of it there.

This wasn't a case of once sated, always satisfied. After the sex haze wore off, a new need would just move in to take its place, and along with that need, both of them would start thinking about the future sex.

And the future itself.

Nola would wonder if he was changing his mind about being a father, and he would wonder just how much that would hurt her if his notion about that stayed firm. First, he'd have to get through all those memories—which in this case was just another word for *trauma*. He'd have to get past that he had been the one who had gotten Nola pregnant and that had ended in their baby nearly dying.

Maybe he'd be better able to process such a thing now that he was thirty-three, but those memories and the trauma weren't those of an adult. They were big-assed baggage created by a kid that a therapist would say was still there, still dealing with the guilt.

A therapist would be right.

"I made two dildos," she said, snapping his attention back to her. "I'm going to make a box of them and send them to this Dodo person. You're sure it's not you?"

Now he was able to smile just a little. "No, it's not me, and I'd very much appreciate *not* getting a box like that." He paused, studied her. "Are you going to tell me what this is all about?"

She huffed, her breath hitting him right on a very vulnerable spot on his neck, but he didn't back away from her, and Nola didn't leave his arms.

"I called the owner of the gallery where Lorelei sends

my better pieces, and he told me that one person, aka Dodo, had bought the bulk of them."

Wyatt forgot all about her breath and that spot on his neck, and he frowned. "How many pieces are we talking about?" he asked.

"Dozens," she muttered.

It took Wyatt a couple of seconds to see where this was going. Or rather, where it could be going. "You're not thinking you have a creepy fan on your hands, are you?"

"No, I'm thinking I have someone trying to protect my ego and make me believe I'm a whole lot better than I am."

Well, hell. He obviously hadn't followed through with that notion. And he immediately dismissed it. "That's a lot of money and glass for an ego boost that you in no way need because you're a talented artist. Besides, who the hell would do something like that?"

The moment the question left his mouth, he came up with an answer. Evangeline. He didn't voice it, but Nola did.

"I figured if it wasn't you, then it was my mother. Trust me, I'll ask her about it," Nola added in a snarl.

Now he was certain he'd gotten the gist of what was going on in her head, and he took hold of her shoulders, making sure they had eye contact. "You're a talented artist." He repeated it three times, and then went on to spell out some proof of that. "Every time I walk by your shop here in Last Ride, there's new stuff in the window, and it's all sold by the next time I go by there."

"That's not art. That's just glass stuff. The whims of Harry Potter and my breath." She dismissed it with a scowl. "An unexpected muscle cramp in my arm can turn a wine goblet into a paperweight that someone thinks might look cute on their desk."

"No, you turn those things into whatever they're sup-

posed to be, and people want to buy them. Just like you turn
the better pieces into art and someone wants to buy those."

But Wyatt made a mental note to check up on this Dodo.
He could add it to the PI's to-do list since the guy was already running the background checks on the Silvas. Because
even though Nola had dismissed it, she might indeed have
a stalker-buyer who was obsessed with her.

Wyatt was obsessed with her, too, but no way would he
have gone to such lengths even if he'd thought about it. That
was because he was dead sure Nola didn't need anyone to
obsessively buy her art.

But this had smacked her upside the head with doubts.

Wyatt could see that now, along with all the other stuff
troubling her. He wished he had the knack like she did for
pulling him out of the cold, dark place, but he didn't. So,
he went with what had worked before.

He kissed her.

He didn't go French, though he did think about it. Nope,
he kept it PG-rated since it wasn't possible to go just G-rated
with Nola. Too much lingering heat for that. But he behaved
himself, acted like an adult and kept it short and sweet, just
the right amount—he hoped—to improve her mood.

She did smile just a little. And kissed him back. However, she went a notch deeper and played dirty by flicking
her tongue over his bottom lip.

"I'd promised myself I wouldn't do that again," she confessed.

"Yeah, me too. Let's just face it. We're weak-minded
when it comes to each other."

Now he got a real smile and even a little chuckle. It didn't
last because her phone dinged with a text. Wyatt scowled,
thinking it might be Alec trying to pester her again, but it
wasn't.

"It's an automated message from my doctor's office," she said, reading it. "To remind me about my appointment on Tuesday. Do you still want to go to that?" she asked and then immediately added, "If you want to stay here with Marley, I'll totally understand."

"I want to go," he insisted, not sure if that was true. Well, he was sure he wanted to support Nola, but this might turn into a moment of reckoning. A very uncomfortable, hard-to-face one.

"Right now, the baby is sort of an abstract deal for me," Wyatt tried to explain. "I mean, I know you're pregnant. I get that. Believe me, I get that. But I don't think it's fully hit me yet that in a little over eight months, you'll be going into labor and bringing this baby into the world."

Wyatt had been on a roll with that attempted explanation, mentally absorbed in every word of it, and that was probably why he had continued to talk even after the front door had opened. Even after his brain had registered that someone had come into the house.

That someone was Marley.

And this was a déjà vu all over again. She hadn't walked in on Nola and him kissing, but she had heard what he'd just said. Wyatt had no doubts about that after taking one look at the girl's face.

"You're pregnant?" Marley asked, looking at Nola, and her gaze slid down to Wyatt's arms—which were still firmly around Nola.

"Yes," Nola confirmed after she swallowed hard.

Nola moved away from him, no doubt to go closer to Marley so she could perhaps attempt some explaining herself. Wyatt would need to be in on that as well. In fact, he would need to make it clear to Marley that he was the one at fault here.

But neither Nola nor he got the chance.

"I need to call my mom," Marley murmured, and already taking out her phone, she hurried down the hall to the guest room.

CHAPTER TWELVE

DO YOU WANT TO TALK? Marley read when the text popped up on her phone.

It was from Wyatt, and she didn't have to think about her answer. No. She didn't want to talk to him right now. Nor Nola. *Especially Nola.* Despite what she'd told them about having to call her mother, she didn't want to talk to her, either. She just needed some time to deal with what she'd just heard.

Nola was pregnant.

Again.

And it didn't require a rocket-scientist IQ to know the baby was Wyatt's. Not after what she had seen when she'd walked in on them. They were obviously still lovers, which carried an ick factor that she didn't want to dwell on. They weren't her parents, not really, but they still fell into the whole parent-sex deal, and it wasn't anything she wanted clogging up her head.

So, after she had gone to the guest room—where up until now Wyatt hadn't made her feel like a guest at all but rather, well, sort of like family—she'd slipped out through the patio doors and had come to the stables. Her favorite one where there were newborn colts and fillies on their wobbly legs and with their fresh newborn smells. It was usually hard to feel pissy and rotten around them, but even they weren't lightening her mood.

Because Nola was pregnant.

She ran her hand over the silky golden coat of one of the fillies whose mother was giving Marley a watchful *Don't you dare hurt my little girl* stare. A look that Nola had certainly never given for her, and it made her wonder if she would give that kind of care and caution to this new baby.

Probably.

And Marley knew it was selfish and unfair to feel jealous about that. But she did. God, she did.

She hated that she felt that way. Hated that she couldn't force herself to get over it and move on. Heck, she even hated that she hadn't taken the blasted bird from Nola. It would have maybe stopped some of the hurt she'd seen in Nola's eyes, but it would have been like a lie, too. A lie that could cause her to want more from Marley.

More than Marley could give her.

It wasn't as if she hadn't had that kind of love and attention from her parents. She had. They'd adopted her, loved her, raised her. Even though her dad had been acting like an ass lately, that didn't undo the love that she knew they had for her. Just like these few days around Nola didn't undo the resentment. Because the bottom line was that Nola would have been the one to hand Marley over to whatever nurse or doctor who would have then taken her away.

Sure, Wyatt had said it was his decision, too, and maybe it had been, but Marley figured he had just been going along with Nola. That he hadn't wanted to stand in the way of her almighty glass art career. Added to that, he wasn't an ass, so he had probably thought his wishes didn't have the same weight as Nola's since she had been the one who'd actually had to endure the pregnancy.

Marley moved back from the filly, making her way down the stalls while she fingered the little purple glass heart charm that dangled from her phone. Just touching it always made her a little mad, but it grounded her, too, by helping her remember why Nola had given her up. So she could create stuff like this that people could ooh and aah over.

Marley had ordered the charm online from the Glass Hatter. The shop that Nola's sister owned to sell Nola's pieces. It'd cost her less than twenty dollars with shipping, and while it wasn't actually one of Nola's art pieces that she'd seen in the gallery in San Antonio, it was something she'd touched with her own hands. A symbol of her work and who she was. And what she'd given up to get there.

She looked up at the sound of footsteps and expected to see Wyatt come in to check on her. He definitely would want to try to smooth out things with her because it obviously bothered him when she was down.

But it wasn't Wyatt.

However, it was someone that she recognized from pictures she'd seen when she had researched Nola and Wyatt. This was Wyatt's brother Dax, the bull rider. He was slightly shorter than Wyatt and not quite as muscled. He was leaner and rangier, and his smile was a lot quicker than Wyatt's, too.

"You must be Marley," he said, his boots thudding on the stable floor as he made his way to her. "I'm your uncle Dax."

It was the first time anyone here in Last Ride had used a "family" label to her. Wyatt had always been careful not to call her his daughter, probably because he figured he didn't have that right. But Marley didn't think she minded Dax playing the uncle card.

"Are you in here hiding out or because of this little guy?" he asked, leaning over to give a head nudge to the mare who had a colt nearby. A colt who'd obviously found his legs and was now trying to trot. The ranch hands would likely be moving them out of the stables and into the front pasture.

"Both," Marley admitted. "I overheard something I probably shouldn't have."

"Yeah, Nola's knocked up. She told me right before she left."

So, Nola wasn't still inside the house. That was good because, sooner or later, Marley would have to go back in and face Wyatt. She was dreading that but not nearly as much as she would have dreaded it had Nola still been around.

"I take it you're not happy about having a DNA sibling?" Dax added.

Marley shrugged and decided to keep her opinions to herself. "Does this mean Wyatt will be marrying her?"

Dax shrugged. "Couldn't say. Maybe. Those two have had an on, off, on, off thing for years."

Off when Wyatt had been briefly married. Marley had read about that, too, but it had taken lots of Google searches. Nola had had at least one engagement as well, so that would have been an *off* time for them. But they'd obviously gotten *on* for Nola to be pregnant.

"You got any questions about, well, anything?" Dax asked. "Not the sex stuff. Please, God, not that. But something along the lines of family skeletons or tips for staying on a bull long enough to impress people."

She smiled in spite of her mood. And she did have a question that might dredge up a family skeleton or two.

"What was it like when Nola got pregnant with me? Was your family upset?" She hoped that would lead to him telling her how Wyatt had dealt with the news.

He pushed back his cowboy hat a little and scratched his head. "Well, I was thirteen and therefore all wrapped up in myself. They were sixteen, and I remember thinking they should keep you because I thought it'd be cool to have a kid around. Then I stayed with a friend who had triplet sisters, and I changed my mind like any good self-absorbed thirteen-year-old would."

Marley allowed herself to imagine what it would have been like to be raised around uncles, aunts and cousins. So many cousins, because half the people she'd met in Last Ride had been Parkmans and therefore related to Nola. Her parents had been only children, so she'd had none of that.

"But as for the families getting mad," Dax went on. "There was some of that, sure. Not, though, from Evangeline, Nola's mom. Have you met her?"

Marley shook her head. "But I've talked to her on the phone."

"Then you probably know she's not the getting-mad type. She's more of the showers-of-sunshine kind of person."

"Bright Blessings," Marley muttered, recalling what the woman had said.

He chuckled. "Yep, that's Evangeline. If you're going to knock up somebody's teenage daughter, then that's a good choice. No threats to do bodily harm or cut off parts of Wyatt so he couldn't knock up anybody else."

Yes, she could believe that about the woman. "And what about your family? Were they upset?"

"My cousin Maude was," he readily admitted. "She was our guardian at the time and was none too happy about it, but you could say that about pretty much everything when it came to Maude. She liked to drag people into the misery wallowing with her."

So, their guardian had likely given Wyatt a hard time and probably wouldn't have offered to help him if he'd chosen to keep her. Unlike Evangeline. She couldn't imagine anyone who spouted *Bright Blessings* not offering help to her pregnant teenage daughter. Added to that, Evangeline wouldn't have been that old at the time she'd been born.

"If you need to blame someone about the adoption, blame me," Dax said out of the blue.

"Why? You didn't get pregnant with me and then give me up," Marley quickly pointed out.

"No, but I was a pain in the ass…butt when I was little." He stopped. "Let's just call it what I was. A pain in the ass, and my brothers had to deal with that. Had to raise me," he admitted. "Things weren't good at home."

Even if he hadn't just told her about Maude's love of misery wallowing, Marley had guessed that was the case when she'd read about their parents being killed when Wyatt and his brothers were all just children.

"Anyway, Wyatt had had a full dose and then some of daddy duty by the time Nola got pregnant. Then he felt like shit because he thought he'd messed up Nola's life."

"But he didn't," Marley pointed out. "Because she went to Italy as planned."

He looked at her, not frowning, not even really judging that. "Yeah, she did. Hard to say, though, what was going through her sixteen-year-old mind, but maybe you should ask her about that."

Now Marley shrugged. She'd rather eat that glass charm than do that. But she could talk to Wyatt about it. Of course, he'd defend Nola—that was his default setting—but Marley didn't mind that. It just proved to her that he was a decent guy who was willing to accept more than his fair share of the blame for what'd happened.

Far more.

"I saw you in the hospital right after you were born," Dax said, snagging her attention again. "Wyatt and Nola couldn't. They were both emotional train wrecks. But I sneaked in, borrowed a set of scrubs and skulked around until they brought you out of the delivery room and into the nursery. By the way, I wasn't fooling anybody with the sneaking stuff. Easy to recognize a thirteen-year-old kid in scrubs a couple of sizes too big for him." He paused. "But nobody told me to get lost because I guess they figured I had a right to see you."

Marley wasn't sure what to make of that. "And?" she pressed.

"And you were really pissed off. I mean, crying with your little hands balled up into fists." He chuckled. "I probably should have said you were cute and looked like a little angel, huh?"

She shook her head. "I like hearing the truth. I like knowing that someone wanted to see me."

"Ouch." He exaggerated a wince. "Well, then hear this truth." Dax looked her straight in the eyes. "A lot of people, especially Wyatt and Nola, wanted to see you. They wanted to see you more than they'd ever wanted anything."

"Then why didn't they?" she snapped.

"Because sometimes what you want more than anything is the exact thing you can't handle. They couldn't have handled it," he assured her with absolutely no snap in his voice. "Hell, I was only thirteen, and I knew that."

Even though Marley didn't especially want to see that moment with Wyatt and Nola handing her off, she saw it anyway. Worse, she felt it.

The silence came, settling between them. Not in a bad way. It felt comfortable. Like family.

"Anything else you want to know?" Dax asked.

She thought about it a second and decided to shift this conversation in a much lighter direction. "Does it hurt your butt and other parts of you when a bull tries to buck you off?"

"Oh, yeah," he admitted with that quick smile. "It hurts like hell for about eight seconds, but it's what I'm good at, so it's what I do."

He was good at it. She'd seen his rankings, and even though he'd just downplayed it a little, she suspected he was good at it because he also loved it.

They both turned at the sound of more footsteps, and it was a speak-of-the-devil kind of moment. Or rather, speak of Bright Blessings. Because Nola's mother came in.

"Dax," she greeted him, and they exchanged hugs and smiles before the woman looked at Marley and extended her hand. "I'm Evangeline Parkman. It's good to finally meet you."

"Good to meet you, too," Marley said, thinking that might actually be true.

Awkward but true. After all, it was Evangeline who'd contacted her to tell her about Nola and Wyatt. If she hadn't done that, Marley had already made up her mind to try to find them when she turned eighteen, so Nola's mom had just sped things up a little.

"Did I interrupt anything?" Evangeline asked. "Would you rather I wait in the house until you're done talking?"

"It's okay." Dax spoke up. "I need to be going anyway. I'm riding tonight and just stopped by on my way to Austin to meet my niece." He gave Marley a playful jab with his elbow, followed it with a hug, and he headed out.

"Oh, I hope he didn't feel as if he had to leave because of me," Evangeline muttered. "I could have waited."

"It's okay," Dax called out. He was obviously still in earshot, and that was maybe why Evangeline stayed quiet a few seconds.

Or maybe it was because she was feeling the awkwardness, too.

She clearly wasn't at home here in the stables. Not that her pale gray pants and white shirt were dressy, but they were clearly designed for office work. Ditto for her sensible flats, which Marley was betting were vegan leather. The woman could have been wearing an I'm Environmentally Responsible sign.

Even though it wasn't obvious, Evangeline brushed at her nose as if to wipe away the smells. Marley didn't mind it, but she walked a short distance away to the end of the stable so she could open the doors and let the fresh, but hot, air in.

"Wyatt's done well for himself," Evangeline remarked, looking out at the other horses in the nearby pasture.

Yes, he had, and Marley had fallen in love with nearly everything about River's End Ranch. Too bad she had no idea how long she'd be able to stay. Her father was pushing to move up the custody hearing, and it was possible a judge would force her to go live with him.

She would.

Not without a fight, but she would if that was what it came down to. She wouldn't break the law and get a smudge on her record since that might hurt her if she ended up applying to vet school. But if her father did force this, if she had to go back to him, she would leave at eighteen and never speak to him again. Actions had consequences, and he would soon learn that.

"How are you getting along with Wyatt?" Evangeline asked.

"Good. He's a terrible cook, but other than that, things are fine."

"Good," Evangeline repeated. "Any problems monitoring your blood sugar?"

"No. It's good." Marley didn't mind the small talk, but she figured sooner or later they were going to grow tired of using the word *good*.

That sooner came very soon.

"Bright Blessings," Evangeline muttered, and this time it sounded as if she'd cursed it. "I'm just going to come out and say this. If you need to blame someone for your adoption, then blame me."

"There's a lot of blame sharing going around today," Marley muttered. But she'd bite. "Why do you think you're to blame? Did you pressure your daughter into giving me up?"

"No." There seemed to be an unspoken *of course not* tacked on to the end of that. "But I waited too long to talk to Nola about safe sex. I mean, I talked to her, but I guess I didn't emphasize the precautions enough. Then, after she got pregnant, I didn't have the kind of money on hand for Wyatt and her to have the option of trying to raise you themselves."

"Because you fund a lot of charities," Marley supplied.

"Yes, and the girls all had trust funds from their Parkman grandparents, but they couldn't touch a penny of that until they were twenty-one." Her words were running together. "Anyway, I really need you to know that Nola and Wyatt did want you, but they just couldn't keep you."

Marley thought about that for a couple of seconds. "Are you ever going to put any of this blame and guilt on your daughter?" She heard the anger in her voice and tried to soften it. She certainly didn't feel any anger toward this woman. "Because you're not the one who gave me up. Nola did."

"And it broke her heart," Evangeline said, her voice cracking a little. "I went in her room one morning to check on her, and her pillowcase was wet from all her crying."

"Touching," Marley grumbled before she could stop herself.

"It is," Evangeline assured her. "She loves you, Marley. Always did."

Marley shrugged and didn't say what was on the tip of her tongue.

That now Nola would have another baby to love, and this time she might love it enough to keep it.

CHAPTER THIRTEEN

NOLA SAT IN the workshop in the center of the massive fans that she had arranged in a circle around her, and she drank a cup of milk. Pretending it was coffee. She even had a pretend doughnut to go with it, even though her actual breakfast was a healthier egg-and-veggie burrito.

She hadn't fired up the furnace and couldn't remember the last time it hadn't been shooting out heat when she was there, but she hadn't wanted to work and get all sweaty since her doctor's appointment was later that day. In fact, she wasn't even sure why she'd come to the workshop after she'd gotten there. Her body and mind had just been on autopilot.

Well, with the exception of her thoughts about Marley.

Nola hadn't heard a peep from the girl since she'd walked in on the news about the pregnancy. And Nola hadn't expected to, either. However, she'd hoped, and maybe that was why she'd come here after all. Marley knew the location of the workshop, but she'd never been to the cottage.

Her phone rang, and she answered it right away when she saw Lily's name on the screen. They'd been playing phone tag for days now, and she had to talk to her about so many things.

"I know you're pregnant," Lily said right off. "Mom told me, and I'm sorry you weren't able to tell me yourself. Are you okay?"

"Somewhat," Nola answered and then had to shout it

over the roar of the fans. She hit the off switch on a couple of them, and dragging the single chair in the place, she moved to the other side of the workshop. Unfortunately, that put her right next to the sex art, which she hadn't gotten around to moving.

"Somewhat," Lily repeated on a sigh. "God, I'm so sorry. I should have made time to go over and see you. Want to come out to the ranch, and we can have lunch? We'll be able to talk because Hayden's at school."

"I do want to talk, but I can't today. I have a doctor's appointment. Just a checkup kind of deal, and Wyatt's supposed to go with me."

"Are you okay with that?" Lily asked after a long pause.

"Somewhat," Nola repeated. "He insisted."

"Oh," her sister said, and she was probably mulling over what that meant. Nola didn't give her any possibilities because she wasn't sure what it meant, either. "Well, good, I guess. How about us getting together tomorrow, then, and you can tell me all about the pregnancy? How it happened, if you're happy about it or ready to scream. I'm guessing that's why you've been so anxious for us to talk?"

In part. But Nola kept the other *in part* to herself. She needed to tell Lily what she'd learned from Bennie before it became a tasty bit of gossip that Lily overheard at the Quik Stop.

"Lunch tomorrow, then," Nola told her. "See you." And she ended the call before Lily clued in that something other than the pregnancy was worrying her.

Nola stood when the door opened, a little surprised that Wyatt had shown up so early. But it was not Wyatt. Apparently, everyone in Marley's immediate adoptive family knew the location of her workshop, because Heather came in.

The woman looked around, probably allowing her eyes

to adjust to the dim light, and she smiled when she spotted Nola. It was tentative—how could it not be?—but Nola definitely didn't feel cornered as she had when Alec had visited.

"I'm glad you're here," Heather said. "I wasn't sure you would be, but the waitress at the diner next door says you work every day—" She stopped and pressed her hand to her heart when she saw the glass piece. Of course, she couldn't have missed it. "Oh, it's beautiful. Wow. You have so much talent."

That gave Nola a nice little jolt of pride, but it didn't last. "Hey, you've never used the name Dodo, have you?"

Clearly, she hadn't, because Heather gave her the blankest look in the history of blank looks. "No. I don't have a nickname." She glanced around again, maybe this time in search of a chair. There wasn't any, other than the stool that Nola sat on when she was working with the glass. "Do you have some time so we can talk?"

Nola checked the time. "I have a couple of minutes." Forty-five of them, to be exact, because that was when Wyatt was supposed to show so they could drive into San Antonio together. "Come on. Let's go in my office. There are chairs in there. And I use that term loosely. There are places to sit, but I can't promise it'll be comfortable."

Before Nola headed in that direction, though, she took an old jacket that she kept on a peg for those winter mornings when she came in and was waiting for the oven to warm the place. She tossed the jacket over the art piece, something she should have done from the get-go. Not that she was tired of seeing Wyatt and her wound around each other like that, but she was tired of other people seeing it.

Heather followed her past the tables of equipment and shelves of glass into the small office. However, before they even got to the sitting part, the woman jumped right into the reason for this visit.

"Marley called me and told me you were pregnant," she said.

Since Evangeline and her sisters now knew the news, Nola didn't hold back confirming it with a nod. Besides, she doubted Heather was going to blab something like that around town, and even if she did let it slip, the news would get around sooner or later. In Last Ride, *sooner* was usually the default.

"I am," Nola confirmed. "Did Marley say anything as to what she thought of that?"

Of course, she already knew what Marley thought. Or rather, she knew how the girl had reacted by walking away. Nola could guess she hadn't been overjoyed about it. Or any kind of joyous, for that matter. But what Nola didn't know was how Marley would have framed that news to her mother.

"Marley didn't come out and say it, but I think she's worried," Heather admitted. "I believe she thinks maybe Wyatt might want her to go home so he can deal with the news of him being a father. Again," she added like a skipped heartbeat.

"Wyatt wouldn't do that. Send Marley home, I mean," Nola clarified.

She didn't even try to speculate, though, how Wyatt was going to handle that whole *deal with the news* process. *Again.* Nola had had over a week of trying to wrap her mind around it, and she was still struggling. Wyatt, too. And while they'd done some of that struggling together by talking, and kissing—he'd yet to spell out any kind of acceptance that he'd be able to cope with fatherhood on any level.

This baby wasn't Marley. Their firstborn, the child they'd

been without all this time. She was practically an adult who wouldn't stir the old memories of his own rotten childhood. But this unborn baby would perhaps do that and more because Wyatt had had seventeen-plus years to decide fatherhood wasn't for him, and here he was, having it thrust on him, again, by the very woman who'd caused it the first time.

"I didn't figure Wyatt would ask Marley to leave," Heather said, but her forehead bunched up, making Nola think the woman wasn't pleased about the reassurance she'd just tried to get from her about Wyatt not sending Marley home.

"I also know that Alec came to see you," Heather went on a moment later. She sat in one of the chairs that was more suitable for a lawn than an office and winced a little, then squirmed trying to find a spot that probably didn't feel as if it were cutting into her butt. "He tried to pressure you into telling Marley to go to him."

It wasn't a question, but Nola confirmed it with a nod. "He's intense and persistent." Neither of those were compliments. Better, though, than spelling out that she considered those synonyms for an asshole and a jerk.

"Alec is indeed that and more," Heather said in the tone to indicate she, too, had applied those same synonyms. "I'm guessing you didn't mention anything to him about the pregnancy?"

"No way." Nola paused but sat, too, behind her desk. Her chair caused the same squirming attempt as Heather's. "Did Marley tell him?"

"No," Heather quickly assured her. "And she won't. Right now, Alec is looking for any- and everything he can use to force Marley back home. He might try to use this pregnancy as a way to convince the custody judge that Marley isn't in…an appropriate environment."

Nola didn't bother to stop herself from huffing, but she supposed some, maybe even a judge, would see this as a concern. That it might not appear to be an appropriate environment because Wyatt and she were having yet another child without being married.

"I want you to know that I don't see things that way," Heather continued. "It's obvious that Wyatt is doing a decent job watching out for Marley and making her feel welcome."

Yes, he was. A surprise since he'd never had sisters. But then, Marley hadn't exactly presented him with any serious challenges. Yes, the girl was plenty angry about Nola giving her up and her parents' divorce, but she hadn't acted out, and it seemed to Nola that the girl had put Wyatt in the can't-do-a-damn-thing-wrong category.

"A decent job," Heather repeated, and she met Nola's gaze, "but I'm her mother, so of course, I want to be the one who's caring for her and making sure she's truly all right."

Nola gave a slow, cautious nod and stayed quiet to let the woman finish what she'd obviously come here to say.

"I would like Marley back home with me," Heather spelled out. "I won't use Alec's heavy-handed approach to try to make that happen, but I'm appealing to you now. Mother to mother. Please try to encourage Marley to come home. If she's with me, then maybe that's where the judge will decide she belongs."

Until Heather had added that last part, Nola had been about to say that she had no influence whatsoever over Marley. But Wyatt did. And Heather could be right about that judge. Encouraging the girl to go home might prevent Alec from getting custody of her.

But it would also mean Marley leaving.

That tightened Nola's chest and clamped a fist around her heart. She wanted Marley here so she could see her because maybe, just maybe, Marley would forgive her and let go of some of her resentment and anger. Of course, Marley could do that away from Last Ride, but it felt better having her nearby.

Mother to mother, Heather had said, and Nola considered that a moment. Heather wasn't asking her to intervene for selfish reasons. Nola truly believed the woman had Marley's best interest at heart and wanted custody of her because that was in Marley's best interest. That was what good mothers did. Even when it tightened her chest and crushed her heart.

"I'll talk to Wyatt," Nola told her, and she saw Heather's face instantly brighten. "I can't make any promises, though, that he'll agree to give Marley any kind of advice about what to do." But he perhaps would if Nola pushed that best-interest-of-the-child angle. "There's also no guarantee that even if Wyatt does talk to her, that Marley will go, and Wyatt won't force it."

"I understand." But Heather was obviously breathing a little easier at the prospect of finally getting her daughter home—and staving off the takeover that Alec was trying to stage like a military coup.

Heather smiled. It was on the thin side and still loaded with worry, but she got to her feet. "Thank you," she muttered. However, she stopped when she spotted the little blue-and-yellow bird on the desk.

The bird she'd made for Marley.

Nola silently cursed that she hadn't packed it back away so it would be out of sight, out of mind. Well, as much out of mind as anything associated with Marley could be.

"Oh, it's beautiful," Heather said. Her eyes brightened as they'd done when she'd seen the other, larger piece out in the workshop. "Is it for sale?"

"Uh, no. It's a personal piece." As personal as personal could get.

Heather nodded as if she understood that, but she picked it up, holding it up to the light. "It's like a little heartbeat inside," she added.

"Yes," Nola murmured, but she made sure that she didn't blurt out the history behind it. That she'd blown it at one of the lowest points in her life. When her own heartbeat had stabbed like a pain in her chest for the child she'd given up.

Given her up to this woman.

Who had obviously taken care of her and done all the things for her that Nola hadn't done.

"I can make you a glass bird," Nola heard herself offer, and then she took this impromptu sharing one step further.

She dragged out the box from beneath her desk, opened it and set it in the chair so Heather could see the other birds. One for each year of Marley's life. The most recent one, a sleek cardinal, was on top where Nola had added it the day her life had turned upside down. Again—there was that word *again*. She'd made it the day she'd learned she was pregnant and Marley had arrived at Wyatt's ranch.

"These are, uh, personal mementos, too," Nola went on, "but if you'd like, I could make you a set. A gift," she added.

Heather muttered a "Thank you" that was heartfelt— another repeated sentiment going on in this conversation. She reached in, gently touching and clearly admiring each one.

Silently counting the number of them, too.

Seventeen total with the one on her desk.

"I see," Heather said. And she obviously did because her eyes watered with tears. So had Nola's. "I'd love a set of them. Thank you. Uh, maybe you could also write down which years these original ones were made. That way, they can be personal mementos for me, too."

They shared another long glance. "I will," Nola assured

her. "But there'll be some differences in them. I can't blow an identical piece."

Now Heather's smile was not as thin. Those tears, though, were still threatening to spill. "Like a mother's love for her child. Slightly different, but at the heart of it, the same. Yes, I know that sounds sentimental, and if Marley heard it, she would certainly give me an eye roll."

Nola wasn't doing any eye rolling, but she was having to battle some tears of her own. Heather got it. She understood.

"I know you love Marley," Heather spelled out. "I can see it on your face and hear it every time her name comes up. Even if it comes up when we're talking about something difficult like the custody."

Oh, yeah. Heather got it all right.

"What made you decide to adopt?" Nola heard herself ask.

Heather made a slight sound, not of pain, but more like from her remembering something that seemed a lifetime ago. Which it more or less was. "Infertility issues. Basically, my body didn't produce viable eggs. I tried every treatment, including some that probably I shouldn't have tried. I even did one attempt that included a donor egg, but that didn't work, either. It just wasn't in the cards for me to get pregnant and carry a child."

The heartbreak of that was still there, and here was where there was no common ground with Heather. Nola had had the exact opposite of infertility. She was what some called a Fertile Myrtle. A condition that many women, maybe even Heather, had wished they'd had.

"Nola?" she heard Wyatt call out.

Nola quickly pressed her eyes to do away with any lingering tears, and Heather did the same. "I'm sorry, but I have to go," Nola told the woman.

"I understand," she said as they made their way out of the office and back into the workshop. "Thank you for taking the time to talk to me. Thank you for sharing those beautiful glass birds with me."

She nodded, and even though it seemed as if Heather was ready to hug her, Nola didn't move closer to make that happen. She felt too fragile right now. Like the too-thin glass that she sometimes made. As if one wrong flick, and she would shatter. She couldn't do that. Not with Wyatt here. She couldn't dump all that on him, especially since it wouldn't make anything better.

"Wyatt," Heather greeted him. "It's good to see you. Is Marley with you?"

He shook his head and eyed both of them. Even though Nola wasn't crying or shattering, he almost certainly knew this visit from Heather had tangled up her nerves some.

"I'm okay," Nola mouthed to him.

He seemed to consider that a moment before he turned to Heather to answer her question. "No, Marley's at the ranch. She's hanging out with Janie today." Since he didn't spell out who Janie was, that meant Marley or he had already told Heather about the trainer. "If you want to drive out and see her, she'll be in either one of the stables or the corral. Maybe the pasture, if she takes out one of the horses for a ride."

"Thank you, but no. I need to get back to work, and Marley and I have already talked on the phone this morning. She said she had a full day planned. She sounded happy," Heather added but didn't wait for Wyatt to confirm that. "She loves being around all those horses."

"I think the horses love being around her, too," Wyatt said, still giving Nola that questioning look. Obviously, her mouthed *I'm okay* hadn't tamped down his worry.

They said their goodbyes to Heather, and the moment

the woman was out the door, Wyatt looked at her. "Did she upset you?"

"No," she quickly assured him. Heather had done some upsetting but in a way that was mostly positive. Well, positive except for what she needed to bring up to Wyatt. "She's concerned if Alec hears about my pregnancy, that he'll try to use it some way in the custody fight."

Wyatt cursed, and because he looked ready to hunt Alec down and punch him, Nola caught on to his arm. "It's a really long long shot that something like that could play into the judge's decision, but Heather thought it might help her case if Marley came home."

"You mean like possession-being-nine-tenths-of-the-law kind of thing?" he snarled.

Obviously, she had some temper soothing to do. "No, more like if Marley's chosen to be there with Heather, then the judge might be inclined to keep her where she wants to be."

He cursed again, but this time it smacked more of frustration than anger. "Heather wants me to try to talk Marley into doing this?"

"Yes, but I told her that'd be a really long long shot, too. And I'm not telling you to do it. I'm just saying, you should give it some thought and decide if Heather has the right worries about this."

The muscles started tightening in his jaw, and she could see the mental debate he was having with himself. "We can talk about it on the drive to the appointment," she suggested and checked the time.

They still had nearly a half hour before they were due to leave, and Nola had padded the estimated time to get to the doctor's office in case there was a problem with traffic or parking. Still, it wouldn't hurt for them to get there early. But Wyatt didn't budge when she gave his arm a little tug.

"I need to get some things out of the way before I get behind the wheel," he said, and judging from his somber expression, these weren't going to be fun, happy things.

"The owner of the bluff and canyon called me this morning," Wyatt explained. "He gave permission for the excavation crew to go onto the property." He paused. "That was the last step needed for work to start." Another pause. "They'll start day after tomorrow."

Oh, mercy. Yeah, that would cause that somber expression all right, along with giving Wyatt a hard slam of the worst of memories.

"I'll go out to the site," he went on. "Not sure how long I'll be out there."

"I'll go with you," she insisted.

But he shook his head. "It'll be hotter than hell, and there's no need to put yourself through that. Besides, the crew might get down to those rocks and decide they can't get the car out. It's something I'd rather handle myself," he added, which he probably thought was an ultimatum that would cause her to stay away.

It wouldn't.

Just like it wouldn't stop her now from giving him a hug. She was still teetering on that whole shattering ledge, but Wyatt looked as if he wasn't that far behind her. So, she hugged him and risked a kiss.

Of course, kissing him never felt like a risk. Probably because each time their mouths met, the heat took over and flung aside reality. This was indeed playing with fire and would complicate emotions. That was why she kept the kiss short so as to lessen the effect of those complications and maybe help Wyatt get his mind on something else.

It worked.

He looked at her and even smiled a little. "What glass birds was Heather talking about?" he asked.

So, obviously he hadn't missed that. Nola crooked her finger for him to follow her and they went back into her office. Since she'd left the box open on her desk, Wyatt saw the glass figurines right away.

As Heather had done, he looked at them. Touched them. Counted them. "These are Marley's birds."

She nodded. "The ones I made each year for her. I'm going to make Heather a set, too. It only seems right," she added.

He didn't object to that, and he didn't squirm as if he'd attempted sitting in one of the chairs, but Wyatt was, well, antsy. And she thought there was more to his mood than learning about the work starting on Griff's car.

"Look," she said, "if you're worried about going with me to this doctor's appointment—"

"It's not that," Wyatt interrupted. But then he didn't explain what it was that was troubling him. "It's not that," he repeated on a heavy sigh.

He reached in his jeans pocket and came out with a little box. Since she had the glass birds on her mind, for a second Nola thought he'd bought her one. Or some other similar keepsake. But then Wyatt flipped it open.

No bird.

No keepsake.

It was a diamond ring, and there was no mistaking the type of ring it was.

He cleared his throat and looked totally uncomfortable, as if he'd sat on a dozen of the butt-hurting chairs. "Nola, will you marry me?" he asked.

It seemed as if time stopped. Just stopped. And the only

thing moving was her mind, where the thoughts suddenly seemed to be wading through a syrupy swamp.

Like the birds, the sunlight caught the diamond, causing the prism of colors to dance around the room. Those colors made it through to her syrup-covered thoughts.

Mercy, did they.

"Well?" Wyatt prompted, holding out the ring for her to take.

She still couldn't read the expression on his face. But that wasn't necessary because she was well aware of her own expression, and it didn't take quick thoughts or a clear head to know how to answer his "Well?"

"No," Nola muttered, dropping a kiss on his mouth, a scalding-hot one, before she shut the lid on the little box.

CHAPTER FOURTEEN

WYATT HAD BEEN right about the heat. Even though it was barely eight in the morning, it was already blistering hot as he stood back and watched the two men rappel down the gorge toward Griff's car.

He couldn't actually see the car, and that wasn't because there were no optimal angles for Wyatt to get a look at it. It was because he'd purposely positioned himself so the only things he could see were the descending men, their supervisor, a guy named Leroy Mercer, who was looming on the ledge above them, and the other side of the canyon.

Of course, just because Wyatt couldn't physically see the old car didn't mean he had a blank image of it in his head. It was there all right, keeping company with the other things that were eating away at him.

He stood there and wondered just how the hell everything had come at him at once. Come at him and might not be resolved anytime soon. Because even if he got answers about Griff's car, that didn't put an end to it. Not to anything.

Wyatt groaned when one of his unresolved issues drove up and got out of her car. Nola. She'd come despite his telling her to stay away.

Despite her having turned down his marriage proposal.

Despite her not having come to see him or Marley in the two days since he'd gone to the doctor's appointment with her.

Hell's bells. He'd just wanted one thing in his life that wasn't cluttered with uncertainty, and Nola hadn't gone along with it.

He groaned again after hearing his mental tirade and admitted—because, hey, he didn't like lying to himself—that her acceptance of his marriage proposal wouldn't have fixed much. It might have even added more problems. But at least he would have felt less like a deadbeat asshole who'd knocked up a woman for the second time and had caused her life to turn upside down.

Yes, he would have felt less of that.

Maybe.

But he'd latched on to that *maybe* and run with it as if it'd been a sure thing. Now there'd be some awkwardness between Nola and him. Just what he didn't need. What he needed was his best friend, and she was firmly in that category, but here he'd gone and blown it perhaps for good. She might never be able to look at him again and not think of how she'd turned him down.

He watched as she made her way to him, but the angle he'd chosen wasn't especially good for seeing her face. The light was glaring right at her, so he had to wait until she got closer. Like numbers ticking down on a bomb. But he could see the shape of her. A shape that even now jacked up his testosterone and made him want her despite her having tossed his proposal back in his face.

"Yes, I came," Nola said like a challenge. She had two bottles of water that were clearly cold and beaded with moisture, and she offered him one while she drank from the other.

Wyatt took the bottle and looked at her as she stepped beneath the meager shade of a scrawny mesquite tree. "It's dusty and hot out here. There's really nothing to see," he grumbled.

"There's you," Nola argued. She nudged him with her elbow, and while it wasn't a kiss, which could often be as hot as it was confusing, the nudge made him feel a little better. It felt, well, like something a best friend might do.

She tipped her head to the supervisor, who was observing the team below him. "Any progress?"

"Not yet. It might take a while for them to do this initial assessment. The heat isn't good for you," he tacked on to that.

That wasn't something he was pulling out of thin air, either. At the appointment when Nola had told the doctor about her glassblowing, the doctor had said she'd have to research it, but for now, until they had some clearer answers, Nola should cut back. Of course, that was advice for her avoiding the blistering-hot oven in the workshop, but heat was heat, and the temps out here would just keep on climbing.

"I won't stay long," she said. "I'm heading out to Lily's. She needed to move our lunch date yesterday to brunch today since she had some business come up." Nola glanced around again. "I'm surprised your brothers aren't out here with you for this."

"They listened when I told them to stay away," he griped.

But in Dax's case, it was because he wasn't even in town but rather at a rodeo somewhere. Jonas would have been here had Wyatt pressed, but he'd needed to drive his son to an appointment for a physical so he could do summer training for the middle school football team. Wyatt hadn't wanted them to have to adjust their plans to come out and watch this. Especially since *this* might end in the next couple of minutes if the crew decided they couldn't retrieve the car after all.

"Well, I didn't listen because I wanted to see you," Nola said, her tone matching his. "And because I wanted to tell you that I got back the results from the blood test I did at my doctor's appointment."

The blood test that'd been taken to determine if she was indeed pregnant. "And?" he asked when she didn't jump to volunteer the results.

"Another positive," she said after a big sip of water. "I think that makes the thirteenth confirmation without a single negative in the mix to allow us any wiggle room for doubts."

Yeah, he hadn't needed the last one. There was one hundred percent certainty of the pregnancy on his part.

"Anyway," she went on, "they set me up with an appointment to have an ultrasound. It's hardly more than a speck at this point, but by the time of the appointment, they might be able to hear a heartbeat."

A heartbeat. He'd remembered Nola telling him about that when she'd been pregnant with Marley. He hadn't gone with her to that appointment because Wyatt had figured there would be some kind of exam that she wouldn't want him to see, but she'd come back from it looking the happiest, and the saddest, he'd ever seen her look. It had been a moment of reckoning for her. She'd seen their child and had known it couldn't be their child after all. DNA-only.

"Will I be able to go to the ultrasound with you?" he asked.

"Sure. If that's what you want."

"It is." But he noted the slight grimace she made. "Why? Is there a reason you wouldn't want me there?"

"Well, it's the goop-on-the-belly deal, but the doctor will

have to move the wand really, really low. I'm talking below my panty line."

"I'll keep my eyes closed for the parts I'm not supposed to see." It didn't matter that he'd seen those particular parts of her, either. There were just some things he'd rather not personally witness when it wasn't sex play.

"There's good news, though," she went on. "The blood test measured something called hCG, which is the abbreviation for some hard-to-pronounce words. The levels of hCG are right where they should be, and they aren't high to indicate I'm carrying twins." She paused, gave a dry laugh. "With the way our luck's been going, I thought there might be more than one in there."

He'd had that same thought, too. Good to know that it was just one and that she had the right levels of that hard-to-pronounce stuff.

Wyatt looked up when the crew called up something to the supervisor. Not a shout of success but rather a comment about the boulder appearing to be stable. He thought that might be good when it came to their chances of retrieving the car. After all, if the boulder gave way, so would the car.

Nola had obviously stopped to listen to the chatter, too, and she must have held her breath because she finally let it out, making a sound that was part sigh, part huff.

"I can't believe you asked me to marry you," she said, tacking it on to the end of that sound.

Finally. She was going to talk about it. Or rather, lecture him about it, if her tone was any indication.

"What was I thinking?" he snarled with a Texas-sized amount of sarcasm.

"You were thinking with your emotions, that's what," Nola declared.

Wyatt looked at her as if she'd sprouted an extra head.

"And what should a man be thinking with when he asks a woman to marry him?"

She obviously didn't have a quick answer for that, and Wyatt wasn't sure he wanted any answer at all, whether it be speculation or the truth. In fact, he wasn't sure he was pleased now that she'd even decided to discuss it.

All of this had been impulse for him. Impulse that had started when he'd made a quick trip into San Antonio the day before her doctor's appointment so he could meet a buyer's lawyer to sign some routine papers. That was when Wyatt had spotted the jewelry across the street from the attorney's office. He wasn't sure what had prompted his feet to start moving in that direction, but they had. They'd prompted him to go inside, too, and fifteen minutes later, he'd come out with what the jewelry clerk had called a classic round-cut two-carat diamond set in traditional yellow gold. The clerk had congratulated him and put the ring in a pretty box.

A box that Nola had snapped shut after delivering her "No." A "no" that sure as hell hadn't been accompanied by any explanation whatsoever. Now she apparently had an explanation. A stupid one.

Because his emotions had made him do it?

Hell yeah, there'd been emotions and some gut-tightening fear. He could add a *hell yeah* for that, too. It hadn't been easy getting out the words to that simple question because he had known the proposal would forever change both of their lives. For better or worse, that was the deal, what some people said with their vows. For better for worse, which included but was in no way limited to raising a child he wasn't sure he was fit to raise.

Still, he'd been directing that life-altering question at Nola, and his "emotions" had reminded him that he hadn't wanted her to go through another pregnancy alone. Not that he would be absent, but still, he'd believed it would make things easier in some ways if she was married to him.

"You should have been thinking with this," she said, tapping her head. "Or even with your junk." She motioned toward his zipper.

The best response Wyatt could manage for the next couple of seconds was keeping his gaze leveled on hers. "I get the head part. Which, by the way, I was thinking with."

In his own roundabout way, he had been. Thinking and worrying about Nola facing another pregnancy without a commitment from the baby's father.

Wyatt leaned in closer to her and lowered his voice to a whisper. He definitely didn't want the crew eavesdropping. "But there's no way sex should have played into this," he insisted.

"Sex would have been a better reason to ask me rather than doing it out of obligation," she insisted right back.

"That still doesn't make sense. We can and have had sex without us being married."

She sure had a quick response to that. "And we can and have made a child together without being married."

Wyatt was certain there was a reasonable argument to put an end to this very confusing discussion. But he couldn't think of exactly what that argument point should be. However, he could clarify something.

"I didn't ask you to marry me out of obligation," he started, but he came to a quick halt when her leveled gaze outdid his. "All right, maybe I did it because of some obligation since I care about you and don't want you to have to go through this alone."

"*Some obligation* is like being a little bit pregnant," she concluded. "It can take hold and grow and grow and grow."

She turned, got closer but not in a right-in-his-face kind of way. In fact, her expression actually softened. "And because I care for you, I don't want that. I don't want it for either of us or for this baby."

He didn't want any of that to make sense. But it did. It made sense because Nola knew him down to the marrow. Wyatt would have liked to assure her that the resentment over that *some obligation* wouldn't fester and grow, but he couldn't do that without issuing what would possibly be a lie. And that made him feel like an idiot for buying that ring and proposing.

Especially since he knew her to the marrow, too.

In his gut, Wyatt had known that she would turn him down. All he'd managed to accomplish was an argument and to make them both feel even lousier about a situation that in no way needed anything else lousy added to it.

He was ready to eat his mistake and tell her he was sorry, but the supervisor, Leroy Mercer, started toward them. One look at the man's craggy face, and Wyatt knew the apology would have to wait.

"My crew just looked around down there," Leroy said, "and they tell me the car's pretty rusted out and falling apart. That's to be expected, considering how long it's been exposed to the elements."

Wyatt didn't have to guess about the emotions he was feeling now. It was relief. So much of it that it made him feel ashamed. But learning the truth wasn't going to make Griff rest any easier. It wouldn't for Wyatt, either.

"So, the car stays put," Wyatt concluded.

"Oh, no." Leroy grinned around the wad of gum he was chewing. "My crew says they believe they should be able to stabilize it enough to bring it out in one piece. Good news, huh?" He gave Wyatt a congratulatory slap on the back.

"Won't be long now before we can get that baby on the way to the lab for you."

Yeah, Wyatt silently repeated to himself. It wouldn't be long now at all.

NOLA TOOK THE turn to the Wild Springs Ranch and tried to forget that she'd just left Wyatt to have to deal with the news that his brother's car would be retrieved.

Of course, she couldn't actually forget that, especially erase that look on his face from her mind, but he'd insisted that she come ahead to her brunch with Lily. Nola had finally agreed only because she knew that Wyatt needed some time to work this through. Work it through alone. That was the way he handled things. The way she had to let him handle things, though it'd been darn hard to walk away from him.

Later, she could go to him and try to pick up the pieces.

For now, though, he had to do some shattering and picking up pieces here. It was possible that Lily would easily handle what Nola had to tell her about Griff and Carlene. After all, all of that had happened years ago. Years in which Lily had gotten married, had a daughter, bought the Wild Springs Ranch and gotten a divorce. Maybe it wouldn't matter to her sister that Griff's accident might not have been an accident after all.

Yes, and maybe pigs would fly, too.

No matter how much time had passed, there'd be no *easily* handling of the news. News that would stir up so many memories that her sister almost certainly wouldn't want stirred.

With that dismal thought hanging over her, Nola parked in the driveway and made her way to the house. The Wild Springs Ranch wasn't as big as Wyatt's—few were in the area—but it was nearly a hundred acres of prime pastures dotted with small ponds and three barns.

Where Wyatt had gone the route of supplying volumes of horses to his buyers, Lily had chosen to provide the highest-quality breed stock for selective buyers—aka people with money to burn who wanted a horse with championship bloodlines.

Along with her ranch manager, Jonas, they'd built an impressive reputation that clearly translated to profits since everything on the grounds looked well-kept. Loved, even. The reputation, though, also translated to her sister working long hours while also managing the role as a single parent. That had been especially hard when Hayden had been younger, but at least now her niece didn't require baby-sitters and such.

Nola went up the steps of the three-story Victorian that Lily had restored from top to bottom. It was big and sprawling but still felt like a well-loved, well-lived-in home. Probably because Hayden's bike, skateboard and some baseball equipment were on the porch. Hayden clearly had a lot of interests, but judging from her recent emails with the girl, photography was her current passion. Hayden had gone back to the cemetery twice to get more pictures for Nola's research.

The research Nola hoped that Lily could fill in for her after she heard the bad news about Carlene, of course.

As usual, the door was unlocked, but Nola gave a quick knock before she went in and called out, "It's me."

"I'm in the kitchen," Lily called back.

Nola stood there for a moment, letting the cool AC spill over her and giving her nerves time to settle. She heard Lily puttering around in the kitchen. Heard, too, the music Lily had turned on while she worked. Not anything current. Lily had always listened to the older stuff even when she'd been a kid. Back then, it'd been the Beatles' and the Rolling Stones' more upbeat songs. Over the years, though, her tunes choice had mellowed some. Had become somewhat sad, even. Nola recognized the voice on this one because Lily played it a lot. Rod Stewart, singing about how he didn't want to talk about it.

On this point, Nola could agree with Rod. But she put on her big-girl panties and followed her nose into the kitchen. Lily had cooked something with bacon because the scent was still in the air, but Lily was now filling amazing-looking scones with whipped cream and strawberries.

"I hope none of these smells make you queasy," Lily said, leaning out from her task to kiss Nola's cheek.

"Not yet." But she figured that would come soon if things ran the same course as when she'd been carrying Marley.

Nola helped herself to some juice and one of those scones. She wanted to eat before she ruined the mood. She took a bite and then went to the window over the sink to look out.

And she certainly got an eyeful.

Wyatt's brother Jonas was by one of the barns. He'd ditched his shirt, and he was holding the hose over his head, letting the water slide down his bare chest and stomach.

"Holy moly," Nola remarked, not in a lustful way. This was more in the manner of admiration, look-at-those-biceps ogling, the way she'd look at one of those hot guys in a calendar picture.

Lily looked out, following her gaze, and made a noncommittal sound.

"I can't believe you've never tested the waters with him," Nola commented.

"I'm his boss," Lily reminded her. "And he's Griff's brother. Added to that, he's busy with his stepson."

Nola knew all about that. Knew, too, that Jonas was still grieving for his late wife.

"I'm busy with my daughter," Lily went on, obviously continuing to spell out the reasons why she couldn't and wouldn't test those particular waters. "And Jonas and I are both busy with the ranch."

"All valid points," Nola agreed, "but he's still hot."

"Yes, he is," Lily quietly agreed, and the tiny smile lingered on her mouth for a moment. "You should see him when he lifts feed sacks." But then she gave herself a little cheek slap as if to punish herself for the thought. "Go ahead. Sit down and eat and get your mind off rippling muscles."

That made Nola think of Wyatt's own rippling muscles. Muscles that she had a strong urge to touch, unlike his brother's. But thoughts of Wyatt and his superior body would have to wait.

Nola sat, but she caught on to Lily's hand and had her sit, too. However, before Nola could launch into a little chitchat, catch-up lead-in, she spotted something else that caught her attention. Not a shirtless ranch manager this time.

But the pale lavender glass teapot on the table.

"That's one of my pieces," Nola said.

Lily looked at it and smiled. "It is. Hayden and I went by the shop a couple of weeks ago to pick up Stellie because she was fussy, and her nanny couldn't come and get her since she was at a doctor's appointment. Anyway, I saw the teapot and bought it. Hayden bought one of those little glass charms for her phone."

Nola didn't remind her sister that she didn't have to pay for stuff like that. Instead, she went with the possibility that popped right into her head.

"Have you ever used the name Dodo and did you buy a whole bunch of pieces of my glass?" Nola demanded.

"Uh, no," Lily answered with her eyebrows lifted practically to her hairline. "Does this have something to do with you being pregnant? Like hormones, maybe?"

Despite the little jab Lily had just doled out—hormones!—Nola searched her sister's face to try to see if she wasn't lying. She wasn't. Or if she was, Lily had gotten a whole lot better at deception.

Lily reached into a warming tray, took out some perfectly crisp bacon strips and some little quiches, and she set them on the table. "Are you going to tell me about a glass buyer and Dodo?"

"No." Nola sighed. She had way too many important things to discuss, but she added the disclaimer first. "Just don't buy any of my pieces. If you want something, I'll give it to you."

"Even the *Wyatt's Junk* one?" Lily smiled around the piece of bacon she'd just eaten.

"No, definitely not that one, but if you tell me whose junk you want me to blow, I'll see what I can do."

They laughed at the dirty joke, as Nola had hoped they would. Mercy, she needed this even if it would be a short reprieve.

"Seriously, though," Nola emphasized. "Don't buy my glass. The same for Hayden. I'll give her all the phone charms she wants." She paused. "But it does surprise me that she's into that sort of thing." Her niece was more of a tomboy.

Lily lifted her shoulder. "She's not, but she happened to see one on Marley's phone when they ran into each other at the diner, and Hayden decided she wanted one, too."

Nola's hand froze just as she'd been about to bite into the bacon. "Marley had a glass phone charm?"

Her sister nodded and then gave her a *what's this all*

about? look. "I'm pretty sure it was one of yours. You know how you usually do the little curlicue at the bottom of the charms. Well, apparently Marley's had that, so Hayden was pretty sure it was one of yours."

"It wasn't," Nola assured her, but she rethought that.

Maybe Marley had bought it. Or someone had given it to her as a gift. Yes, that had to be it. No way would Marley have plunked down money for anything Nola had made. In fact, if Hayden had mentioned that it was likely her aunt Nola's work, then Marley likely would have removed it then and there and stomped on it until it was nothing but glass dust.

"Things still not going well with Marley and you?" Lily asked, sliding her hand over Nola's for a moment.

"No." Nola didn't want to pull any punches here because it could backfire.

If she happened to say, for instance, that she desperately wanted Marley to forgive her, then that might prompt Lily to pay the girl a visit, just to see if she could try to smooth things over. Because Lily was her identical twin and therefore shared her face, that likely wouldn't turn out well. Marley might transfer some of her resentment to Lily.

"I'm actually here to talk about something I learned," Nola started. "Something about Griff."

Lily nodded, drank a huge gulp of tea and nodded again. "I heard about Wyatt hiring someone to take a look at the wrecked car to see if it can be taken out of those rocks."

Nola wasn't the least bit surprised that news had made it back to Lily. Unlike Bennie's confession, which was still under wraps, people would have seen the crew in town.

"The car can be taken out," Nola told her. "Or at least it probably can be. Wyatt got that news right before I came over."

"Oh." There was a lot of emotion dripping from that one

word. "And you didn't cancel with me to stay with him?" Lily asked.

"I'll be heading back over there after we've talked."

Nola could tell from her sister's expression that she now knew just how important this chat was. She cleared her throat before she began laying it out there.

"I talked to Bennie Dalton, figuring I'd get some stuff for the research report on Griff I had to do. And I got something." She met Lily's gaze, which was already going guarded and wary. "Bennie believes his sister, Carlene, might have tampered with Griff's car and caused him to crash."

Lily didn't move. Didn't speak. But the tears immediately began to well up in her eyes.

"Bennie's not sure she actually did the tampering or if that's what caused Griff to go off that cliff," Nola went on. "And now I should tell you why Carlene would do something like that." She took a deep breath for that, but it wasn't necessary because Lily spoke before Nola could add anything else.

"Because Griff had sex with Carlene and didn't carry that through to a relationship," Lily provided in a voice that was barely louder than a whisper, but it was plenty loud enough for Nola to hear that her sister hadn't been guessing about that.

"Griff told you?" Nola asked.

Lily nodded. Then, on a loud groan, she got up, went to the sink and looked out again through the large window at the pastures. "Griff told me," she verified, but she stopped, shook her head. "Are you up to hearing a sad story?"

"Of course." Nola wasn't sure she was, but that didn't matter.

She'd listen even if this was something she was already

positive she didn't want to hear. However, she hoped with all the hope inside her that Lily wasn't about to confess to some car tampering of her own. Or that she'd said or done something to Griff that caused him to consider ending his life.

"You know how this sad story begins," Lily started. "Because you were starting up with Wyatt about that time. Griff and I began dating. Kisses led to touching, yada yada." She paused, keeping her focus out the window. "Trust me, though. We got a lot more careful with birth control after you got pregnant. I went on the pill, and Griff doubled up on the condoms."

Nola was glad she'd become that cautionary tale. The gossip would have still been going strong if twin teenage brothers had managed to knock up teenage twin sisters. Added to that, Griff and Lily would have had to have gone through the same gut-wrenching experience as Wyatt and her since they wouldn't have had the means to support a child, either. Nola didn't wish that on anyone.

"As you know, Griff and I were together for a couple of years after you left for Italy," Lily added several moments later. "But then he broke up with me. You know that, too, because I sobbed my eyes out during one very expensive phone call to you."

Yes, to the sobbing and the expense of the call. The phone bill had been over a thousand dollars, and Nola was sure their mother hadn't been happy about that. Still, that talk had been necessary, and if Nola had been able to tap into her trust fund then, she would have gotten on the first flight available to the States so Lily could cry it out on her shoulder.

"Griff broke up with you because he said you deserved something better," Nola supplied. She didn't have to ask if she was remembering that right. Lily had emphasized that a lot in her phone call.

Lily's laugh was hollow. "Yes. Because he was from the wrong side of the tracks. He actually used those words. It made me want to slap him. I always figured he said that because he couldn't tell me the truth. That he was tired of me and wanted someone different in his bed."

"Was that really the reason?" Nola asked, hoping it wasn't the wrong button to push.

"Maybe. He certainly didn't waste any time going after Carlene and some others that gossips made sure I heard about. The talk got so bad and I was crying so much that Mom finally tried to soothe me by telling me I could go to Italy to be with you for a while."

Now, this was one thing that hadn't come up in their phone conversations or emails. "You never mentioned that."

"No." That was all Lily said for several moments, and she repeated it before she continued. "You were within a month or two of coming home by then, and I knew it would cost a lot for me to go, so I just stayed put and dealt with the gossip."

That gossip had still been around when Nola had returned, but her mere presence took some of the gossipy heat off Lily. After all, it'd only been two years by then since Nola had given up her child for adoption, and Griff's catting around couldn't hold a candle to that.

"You moved on with your life," Nola reminded her. She was about to launch into some stating the obvious about that. The obvious being that while Lily hadn't gone the catting-around route, she had eventually gotten involved with Hayden's father, Cam Dalton.

"Yes, I moved on with my life, but not by choice." Lily stopped and groaned in such a way that had Nola springing from the table to go to her. However, when she tried to pull her into a hug, Lily waved her off. "Just let me get this out. Let me say it."

Oh, mercy. Was Lily about to make an awful confession that she'd played some part in Griff's death? She prayed not, and Nola had some hope to hold on to in that particular arena. Lily wouldn't have had a clue how to tamper with a car. Still, that left the other possibility that Lily had perhaps *influenced* Griff in some way to do what he'd done. Nola knew plenty about a guilt-trip expression when she saw it.

And she was seeing it on Lily's face.

"I saw Griff two weeks before he died," Lily went on, going full speed ahead. "I'd gone out with Cam a few times by then, but we hadn't even kissed. But Griff showed up and he asked me to take a ride with him. He looked so upset that I forgot about the way he'd broken up with me, and I went with him."

"He was upset because of Carlene?" Nola asked when Lily fell silent again.

Lily shook her head. Then shrugged. "Maybe. I'm not sure. He said he'd just gotten back from an appointment, so maybe that was code for a confrontation with Carlene or Bennie."

Nola heard the change in her sister's voice, and she saw how this had likely played out. "You had sex with Griff?"

"Yes," Lily admitted, turning to face her now. The tears were spilling down her cheeks. "We had sex, and seconds later, Griff decided it was a mistake. A huge mistake," she said. "So, he left, and two weeks later, he was dead."

Oh, God. Even though Nola had known the finale of this sad story, it still hit her hard. Was obviously hitting Lily harder.

"His dying wasn't your fault," Nola insisted. "Wyatt believes the crash was an accident, so maybe that's all it was. And even if it happened because of Carlene's tampering, then it still wasn't your fault."

Lily nodded, but there was nothing about the gesture or look in her eyes that suggested she believed it. If Nola hadn't been pregnant, she would have broken out the wine and ice cream and had a sister talk, pity party until Lily had cried out some of this sadness. Instead of wine, though, the scones and some ice cream would have to do.

Nola was already headed to the freezer to retrieve whatever flavor was there, but Lily stopped her with two words.

"There's more," her sister said.

Nola slowly turned back around to face her. "What?" she managed to ask, and the wild thoughts began to fly. Sweet merciful heaven. Lily didn't know squat about the mechanics of a car, but had Lily run Griff off the road? She couldn't even ask the question aloud.

"About two weeks after I had sex with Griff, I realized my period was late," Lily explained.

"Shit," Nola said before she could clamp her teeth over her lip. She immediately pulled up a mental picture of her niece. Of Hayden. She looked nothing like Griff, but then, she was the spitting image of Lily and her.

"Hayden is Griff's child," Lily confirmed. "I went to Griff to tell him, and he, well, he just looked sick. I mean, ready-to-throw-up sick. He told me he'd fix it, and he left. A couple of hours later, he was dead."

Nola squeezed her eyes shut, mentally scrambling to try to figure out if there was anything she could say that would help. Nothing, absolutely nothing came to mind. She couldn't even console Lily with the possibility the wreck had been an accident because that in turn would lead Lily to point out that the accident had likely happened because Griff had been so worked up about the pregnancy.

"I broke down and told Cam after Griff's funeral that I was pregnant with Griff's child, and when he insisted on marrying me anyway, I accepted. We eloped that same day. I know that was a terrible thing to do—"

"No," Nola interrupted. "You didn't deceive Cam. He knew the child you were carrying wasn't his."

"No, there was no deception with Cam. Just with everyone else. Sometimes, even with myself. I was only a little over two weeks pregnant, and Hayden was overdue. People thought she came right on time, exactly nine months after my so-called honeymoon, but she was two weeks late."

So, the timing had worked to help Lily conceal her secret, and it twisted at Nola to realize she hadn't suspected the truth. She hadn't seen what had been right in front of her own eyes.

Lily finally wiped away some of the tears, and she turned to face Nola. "And now you have to do something that I've been doing for thirteen years."

"What?" Nola asked. Though she knew. Mercy, she knew.

"You have to swear to never tell anyone, especially Hayden, a single word of this. Carry it to the grave, Nola." Lily took hold of Nola's hands and looked her straight in the eyes. "Promise me."

And with plenty of reservation about what she was doing, Nola made that promise then and there.

CHAPTER FIFTEEN

WYATT HAD BEEN sure what the crew supervisor was about to tell him before he even answered Leroy Mercer's call. He'd been keeping an eye on the weather report for the past twenty-four hours and knew the storm that was supposed to have passed them by wasn't cooperating and was going to dump a ton of rain on them. The pastures could always use a good soaking, but Leroy's work crew probably wouldn't appreciate it.

And he was right.

"Just wanted you to know that we're nearly there, that the cables on the car are in place, and we're within a half hour, maybe less, of being able to pull it out," Leroy said right after he'd issued a quick hello. "But I can't keep the crew down there if it starts lightning or if the rain makes it too slippery. The helicopter won't be able to get in, either. We'll try, but I can't promise you that we'll have the car out today."

"Understood. Keep me posted." Which, of course, the man would.

By now, Leroy and his crew no doubt knew the whole story behind the lodged car. The story and the speculation to go along with it. They knew this was a big deal and important to Wyatt.

Wyatt ended the call with Leroy and texted Nola to let her know he needed to come see her later so he could update her on a few things. Things she wouldn't especially want to hear, but it was possible she had some info for him that fell into that same category. After all, he knew she'd gone to see Lily the day before, and afterward when she'd texted Wyatt, she'd been sketchy about the details of how Lily had taken the news about Carlene.

Wyatt hadn't pressed for those details because he'd figured Nola had left her sister's house and dived straight into work. For Nola, blowing her glass was the cure for a lot of things, and that would include trying to deal with sending Lily into a dark pit of old, painful memories.

When Nola didn't respond right away to his message, Wyatt continued with his to-do list and texted his ranch manager, Jace Davidson, to make sure he'd already started battening down things and bringing in the horses that needed shelter. Jace was, of course, already on that, leaving Wyatt to deal with the paperwork he should be doing. Instead, though, he went to the window and looked out at the brewing storm.

There were already some angry-looking dark purple clouds, towering up like bruises, and they appeared to be just minutes away from opening up. Definitely not a time to be out and about, but apparently Trey didn't feel that way because Wyatt spotted the boy coming across the yard and toward the back of the house. And Wyatt hoped Trey wasn't heading to the patio doors that led into Marley's room, but it sure as heck looked as if that was his intention.

Wyatt put a monkey wrench in Trey's plan.

Scowling the meanest scowl he could conjure up, Wyatt went to the back door, threw it open and took a couple of menacing steps onto the porch. Steps that were apparently loud enough for Trey to hear because he stopped, whirled and looked ready to piss his pants when he saw Wyatt.

"Mr. Buchanan," he said. He glanced at the patio doors and wisely changed his course toward the porch. He didn't go close to Wyatt, though, probably because he was still scowling. Trey stayed on the steps and looked up at him.

"Marley's working on her online classes all morning," Wyatt informed him. "She can't get behind."

Trey nodded, and even though a few raindrops started to splatter on him like fat bird droppings, he stayed put and didn't move under cover of the porch roof. "I was just going to ask her a quick question."

"Ask me instead," Wyatt snarled, and in the back of his mind it occurred to him that he was acting like a father.

That wasn't exactly a comforting thought.

But he had a damn good reason for it in this case. No way did Wyatt want to give Alec any fodder to force Marley to go back home, and that was what could happen if Marley did indeed get behind in her schoolwork. Of course, there were zero indications that Marley could or would get behind. She seemed diligent about her online courses, but there was no need for Wyatt to pass along that info to Trey.

Trey bobbed his head again in a nod. "I just wanted to know if she'd like to go to O'Riley's with me later. I've got my dad's truck."

"It's about to storm," Wyatt pointed out. "I don't want Marley out in this." And again, that sounded like a dad thing, but Wyatt could blame that on Alec, too, on the fit the man would pitch if he learned that Wyatt had allowed Marley to take that kind of risk.

"Yes, sir, but it's supposed to clear up in a couple of hours, and I figured Marley would be done with her homework by then. I was just going to ask her," he added in a mumble with his words trailing off.

Wyatt stared at the boy and got a flashback of himself

showing up at Evangeline's door to pick up Nola for a date. Evangeline wasn't six-two and not especially good at scowls, but she'd still intimidated the hell out of him, and it was because of that flashback that Wyatt decided to cut the kid a break.

A small one with strings attached.

"Wait until the storm passes and then text Marley," Wyatt said. "If she wants to go to O'Riley's with you, then she can, but since the roads will be wet, no driving around. Just there and back. Keep your speed down, too, especially around that curve right before you get to town."

Judging from Trey's wide grin, he would have agreed to pretty much anything. Wyatt was familiar with that particular feeling as well, but he still might have added a few more warnings and conditions if he hadn't heard the vehicle approach the house. Thinking that it might be Nola, which would have explained why she hadn't answered his text, he snarled a goodbye to Trey and went back through the house to the front door. But it wasn't Nola.

It was Bennie.

Bennie climbed out of his truck, and while he didn't have that *ready to wet my pants* look the way Trey had, he didn't come onto the porch, either. However, he did have enough sense to come in out of the rain because Bennie went half-way up the steps so the porch roof would cover him.

"I was just out at the canyon," Bennie immediately said. "They're close to getting Griff's car out."

Wyatt nodded. "It might be out any minute now. If not, it'll be a day or two until things dry out."

Bennie shook his head. "I want you to call this off," he snapped. "I don't want my sister's name ruined, and that's what'll happen if you find out the car had been tampered with. I mean, what good would it do to learn something like that all these years later?"

It would do worlds of good because then Wyatt wouldn't have to keep being smothered with the guilt that he hadn't stopped Griff from taking his life. Hell, that he hadn't even been aware that his twin brother was anywhere low enough to do something like that.

"I need to know," Wyatt settled for saying. "I'd think you'd want to know, too."

"Well, I don't," Bennie said, snapping it out again. "I don't want anyone to know. Carlene was my sister," he added, as if that would cause Wyatt to change his mind.

It wouldn't. "And Griff was my brother."

"Yeah, a brother who had sex with my sister and then broke up with her," Bennie fired back.

Wyatt saw the temper flare in the man's eyes. Saw the grief, too, and since Wyatt knew what it was like to lose a sibling, he didn't give Bennie the go-to-hell scowl that he wanted to give him. However, that temper did get Wyatt thinking. Maybe Bennie was dealing with a mix of both grief and guilt. Guilt because Carlene hadn't been the one to tamper with Griff's car.

That Bennie had done the tampering himself.

Hell. Wyatt didn't know why that hadn't occurred to him already, and wondered if something like fingerprints could survive after all this time. It was as if fate decided to give Wyatt some help to see if such a thing was possible, because at that moment Wyatt got a text from Leroy.

We got it, Leroy messaged. Pulled it up in one piece. Once we get it loaded on the tow truck, we can take it to the lab. Unless you want to see it first.

Wyatt sent a quick reply. Good job. No, I don't want to see it, and then he looked up at Bennie.

"They got the car out," Bennie said, obviously not needing Wyatt to fill him in. Spitting out a string of curse words, Bennie stepped out into the rain and stormed back to his truck.

Oh, yeah. Wyatt would definitely be pushing the lab guys to see if they could find prints. Not Carlene's, though, but Bennie's.

He stood there, watching Bennie speed off, while he let all of this sink in. Fourteen years was a long time to go without answers, and it twisted at him to know that by burying his head in the sand on this, he might have buried any chance for Griff to get justice. If Bennie or Carlene had indeed tampered with the car, that was. Then again, learning the truth even after all this time would still be justice.

Wyatt was still mulling that over when another vehicle turned into his driveway. It was Nola, and he was sure he'd never been so glad to see anyone. He needed her. Needed for her to work her magic on him so he could get through this sickening fresh wave of guilt and dread.

She hopped out of her car, popping up a perky pink umbrella over her head, and she ran to the porch. She wasn't smiling, didn't especially look as glad to see him as he was to see her, but she came up the steps to toss the umbrella and pull him into her arms.

"I didn't answer your text because I was already on the road. And then I saw Bennie driving away from here in what I think I've accurately interpreted as a bat-out-of-hell speed," she said. "I'm guessing he's the reason you've got that gloomy look on your face?"

"In part," Wyatt admitted, and he kept her in the hug a little longer before he pulled back to meet her eyes. "The crew got out Griff's car, and I think Bennie might have been the one to tamper with it."

Her eyes widened, and she yanked him back to her for another hug. "I'm sorry. What can I do?"

He wanted to say *You're doing it*, but Nola probably didn't need to hear that she was his emotional support. Especially since she might be the one who needed some supporting.

"Where's Marley?" she asked just as Wyatt asked, "How'd your talk go with Lily?"

He went ahead and filled her in on Marley. "She's in her room doing her online classes."

But Nola didn't jump to answer. She stood there a moment, doing her visual exam of his expression, no doubt to see just how much this news about Bennie and the car was getting to him. She knew the answer to that was *a lot*, but she was obviously also aware that part of his mood was because he was worried about her.

"The talk went fine," she said. "I told Lily about the Bennie-Carlene stuff. I obviously didn't tell her that Bennie might have done some tampering to Griff's car because I didn't know that at the time."

He waited for more details of how Lily had reacted, but she didn't give them. However, judging from the sadness he saw in her eyes, Lily likely hadn't taken the news well.

"Did Lily cry?" he came out and asked.

Nola nodded.

"Did you cry?" Wyatt pressed.

"Yeah, and I saw Jonas without his shirt," she added. Just like he clued in to her sad eyes, he knew a Nola deflection when he heard it. And he welcomed it.

"Ogling my brother?" he teased and even managed to flash her a brief smile. "It'll make him feel so cheap if he knew."

"Well, you weren't there to ogle, so I have to get my cheap thrills where I can find them."

Oh, he needed this. Needed the quick, chaste kiss, too, that she dropped on his mouth. That was why Wyatt just stood there, looking at her, while Mother Nature threw a temper tantrum. The thunder rumbled, angry and mean, and those bruised clouds hurled down the lashes of rain so fast that it was only a couple of seconds before the water started to sheet off the metal roof. It curtained them on three sides, making a little cocoon around them.

"Are you going to tell me what's bothering you?" he asked, sliding his index finger over the part of her forehead that was bunched up.

"Nothing specific. Well, you know the specifics," she amended.

Yeah, he did, but Wyatt thought there was at least one specific she was keeping to herself. "Did Lily get into why Griff and she broke up?"

For a moment he thought she would deflect again or just shake her head. She didn't. "Two weeks before Griff died, he saw Lily and told her he'd just come from an appointment. She said he was very down. Do you know anything about that?"

There was a lot of information packed into her brief recount, but for the moment Wyatt focused on the question. "No," he said after riffling through his memory. "What kind of appointment?"

"Lily didn't know, but I wondered if maybe…well, if it maybe had something to do with what happened."

"You mean, maybe Griff got some bad news?" If so, Griff hadn't shared that with him. Griff hadn't shared anything in the days before he died.

Nola nodded. "I'm not sure this is a good idea, but I wanted to run it past you first. Maybe this is something—" she stopped, grimaced "—that the Sherlock's Snoops could maybe try to track down. They have a lot of time on their hands and ways to get info on stuff like this. Or at least that's what Derwin claims, anyway. What do you think?" she pressed when he didn't say anything.

Wyatt had never in his wildest dreams thought he would consider going to that group of weirdos for anything, but maybe they could indeed help. Of course, then there might be the problem of them maybe helping so much that they would uncover something that Wyatt might not want to get around. Still, this was a possible lead that should be checked out.

"You can ask the Snoops," he finally agreed. "If they don't get anywhere with it, let me know, and I can ask the PI to do some digging."

Nola glanced away when he continued to stare at her. Yeah, she was dodging, and Wyatt went back to her statement. Specifically, the part about Griff having paid Lily a visit two weeks before his death.

"Was that visit the last time Lily saw Griff?" Wyatt wanted to know.

She hesitated. "No, he paid her a visit right before he died. A couple of hours before."

Wyatt was positive this was the first he'd heard about that. There'd been a lot of grief and chaos in those days following his brother's death, but he was certain he would have latched on to learning anything about those last hours before the car had gone off the bluff.

"Why did Griff and Lily see each other that night?" Wyatt insisted. "Were they getting back together?"

Nola looked about as uncomfortable as a steer's ass would be on a heated-up branding iron. "I think they were just talking."

If so, then Lily would have likely said what they'd talked

about. After all, it would have been her last conversation with Griff, and she would have committed every word of it to memory.

And that was when it hit him.

Thankfully, he was good at math, but he obviously wasn't any good at putting things together until it hit him right upside the head. Hell's bells.

"Hayden is Griff's daughter," he concluded, causing Nola to huff. That huff gave him the confirmation he needed.

"I wasn't supposed to tell you." She huffed again. Groaned. Cursed. "Lily made me promise." Her voice came out like a whine.

"You didn't tell me. I guessed." And in hindsight, he should have guessed it years ago. "So, how did Griff take the news when she told him she was carrying his child?"

"Apparently he didn't take it well," she finally answered after a long pause, more groaning and more cursing. "He gave her some BS about her being too good for him, and he left."

Well, that painted a shitty picture of his brother, but Wyatt wanted to hold on to the hope that Griff had said that out of shock, that had he lived, he would have come to his senses and gone back for another, more reasonable talk with Lily.

But there was another possibility.

That the news had caused Griff to break. Like the camel who just couldn't deal with another piece of straw on its back. For plenty of reasons, Wyatt hoped like the devil that wasn't true, because if so, it was going to put Lily on that guilt train right along with him.

Mother Nature got busy again, and a bolt of lightning slashed through the sky, and he could feel the crackle in the air. That was Wyatt's cue to leave their rain cocoon and get Nola inside.

Where this catch-up, tell-all conversation could continue.

Nola had just doled out some shocking news, and he would eventually have to process that Hayden was his niece, but for now, he had some surprises of his own to tell her. He started with the easiest one first.

"The PI finished the backgrounds on the Silvas," he said, keeping his voice low. Marley used headphones for her classes, but he definitely didn't want her overhearing this. "Alec is having an affair with his twenty-eight-year-old assistant."

That obviously got Nola's mind off her sister, and she huffed. "Not very original. Middle-aged man, much younger woman. Wonder if it was lust at first sight."

Wyatt shared her smirk. "Well, he has been discreet. Probably because he doesn't want to give Heather the power to take him to the cleaners in the divorce. But if Alec shows up again at your workshop, don't try to take a jab at him about this. If it pisses him off enough, he might try to take that out on you, and then I'd have to kill him."

That last bit was only partly in jest. Wyatt wouldn't actually kill him, but he'd beat the shit out of Alec if he laid one finger on Nola.

"No taking jabs at him," she agreed. "But if he comes back and I'm holding a hot pipe, he won't touch me. Harry Potter could mess him up." She huffed again when Wyatt gave her a hard stare. "I won't take a jab at him no matter what I'm holding."

"Good." He'd do more pressing on that point, but for now, he went with the surprise news behind door number three. "Evangeline knew Heather. They were roommates their first two years of college and apparently stayed friends until seventeen years ago, when they seemingly broke off all contact with each other."

He watched Nola process that. Watched the surprise morph into enough anger to give those pissed-off storm clouds some competition. "Oh, did she now?" Nola asked none too pleasantly, and he stopped her from reaching for her phone. No doubt to call Evangeline and have it out with her.

"Yeah, and I suspect Evangeline helped things along so that the Silvas could adopt Marley. That explains why your mother felt so worried—and guilty— when she saw Marley posting about Alec and Heather's divorce."

"Yes, it does," Nola said, turning away from him to pace. "She chose her good friend Heather for motherhood and then regretted it when Heather's marriage went south."

With that recap, Nola's pacing picked up some speed. Her expression gathered some anger, too. He knew the anger was fueling her right now, knew as well that Lily's news was playing into this thundercloud of emotions, but beneath all that, Nola was…antsy, he decided. He could feel the restlessness coming off her in waves.

He gave her a couple of minutes, hoping the pacing would burn off the urge for her to do something she might regret. Like calling her mother and yelling her lungs off at what Evangeline had kept secret.

"Are you going to give your mother grief about this?" Wyatt finally asked.

She paused, obviously thinking about that. "No." Her answer came on a sigh, a sag of her shoulders and with some of the sting obviously gone. However, the restlessness continued, and Nola glanced around while she rubbed her hands down the sides of her jeans.

"Are you still coming to the ultrasound appointment with me?" she asked.

He nodded. "I'll be there." He kept studying her, wondering if that was what was bothering her, but he didn't think it was. "Other than the obvious, what's the matter?" he came out and asked.

"I haven't blown any glass for the past forty-eight hours."

Wyatt blinked, pleased that this surprise news wasn't of the gut-wrenching variety. It was obviously a huge deal, though, to Nola, and it explained this nervy energy.

"I'm cutting back until I hear from my doctor," she explained. This time, she did the rubbing on her arms. "I didn't know blowing was this much of an addiction."

"Really? You work like eighty hours a week."

And that made him feel like crap. Because she didn't work those hours because she needed the money. She did it for the love of her art. The pregnancy—yes, the very one he was responsible for—had put the pause button on what she loved.

"Earlier, I tried to shape some candle wax," she admitted. "I gathered it up on a metal shish kebab skewer and started turning it like a minipipe. Reheating it with the flame and shaping it with a piece of leftover pizza crust. That's sick, I know, but I managed to make a pretty interesting-looking turtle."

Wyatt had to smile. Had to go to her and pull her to him for what he promised himself would be a quick hug. But when Wyatt went to move back, she held on.

"Oh, if only I could think of a way to burn off all this energy," she said, looking up at him. Smiling. Inviting.

Wyatt groaned, reined in his nether regions. "Marley's in her room" was all he had to say.

Nola made a face, groaned in disappointment. He didn't

dare suggest taking any burning-off-energy attempts to his bedroom and locking the door, because he seriously doubted they could fool around with Marley just up the hall.

But he rethought that.

Okay, they probably could fool around, but the point was, they *shouldn't* be doing that. And he didn't want to remove any obstacles to what wouldn't stay at just fooling around or burning off energy. Nope, with a locked door, they'd have sex, and while that would please his nether regions, and hers, it was a supremely lousy idea.

"All right," Nola grumbled. "So dance with me, then," she said, and she used her free hand to take out her phone and hit Play on her music. "Lily was listening to this yesterday when I went to talk to her, and it got stuck in my head, so I downloaded it."

Rod Stewart's raspy voice began to play through the room, and Wyatt actually recognized the song because Griff had played it when he'd been in a moping mood. Lily and his brother had shared the same taste in vintage music.

Along with a child.

Soon, he'd need to fit that info into a neat little box in his mind after he figured out how to deal with it. For now, though, he wanted to focus on Nola in case this dance got carried away.

"It's a sad song," he pointed out, easing her closer while they swayed into a pseudo–slow dance.

"It is. I've practically memorized the words by now. I think it'd be interesting to blow glass with it blaring in the workshop. I could probably re-create that storm if I did that."

She was creating some pretty interesting things with him, too. Well, not interesting, but there was heat. As often as it was there between them, Wyatt was always surprised at how new, and intense, it felt. Always surprised, too, at how easily he could forget what'd happened in the past. Both the way back past and the more recent one.

"I am not making out with you or having a sensitive conversation so that Marley can walk in on it," he said.

But as proof that he was one twisted SOB who didn't need a locked door to act out, he leaned down and kissed her just as Rod whined on about someone listening to his heart. Wyatt was reasonably sure that Nola didn't have to listen to the ins and outs of his heart. They'd been on the same page there for a long, long time.

Still were.

Because the look she gave him was smoking hot.

"I've taken way too many cold showers in the last few weeks," he said on a groan.

"That should make me feel guilty, but it doesn't." She skimmed her finger down his back. "We could make a pact with each other like we did when we decided to give up Marley for adoption."

He wondered if she'd realized that was the first time she'd used Marley's name when talking about the adoption. She'd always said "the baby" before. He wasn't sure if that was good or bad, but things were definitely changing, and he wasn't talking about the hardening of his dick now.

"What kind of pact?" he asked.

"One that involves sex where you wouldn't feel obligated to propose to me or be involved in this pregnancy in any way you don't want to be involved."

Well, hell. Now he knew how Adam had felt when Eve had supposedly offered him a bite of the big juicy apple. It was many, many degrees past merely being tempting.

But it was also impossible.

Wyatt shook his head. "I wouldn't be able to climb out of bed with you and then forget you're carrying my child."

The moment he said the words, he regretted them, because that was more or less what Griff had done. It had likely crushed both his brother and Lily, and Wyatt didn't know why it'd had to be that way. Griff and Lily had been young but they'd been more or less adults. And even if Griff had decided he didn't want to be a father, he could have still stayed in Lily's life and helped her through the pregnancy.

He stopped that dismal train of thought when Nola kissed him. She renewed his old train of thought when she used her tongue.

She'd kiss him to get that look off his face.

When she'd finished, she pulled back, studied her work. "I want that look on your face instead of the one you had." And she kept him off balance by adding, "You remember the first time we had sex?"

"Every minute of it," he admitted. Not that there'd been a lot of minutes to remember. "That first time was Quick Draw McGraw for me."

She winked at him. "You held out long enough, though, for me to get off."

"Yeah, only because I already had you at the brink with my fingers."

"Hey, fingers work. So do mouths." She kissed him. "We could test that out if you agree to the pact."

But she didn't give him a chance to agree to anything. Not verbally, anyway. That was because she occupied his mouth with another kiss. A kiss that quickly ended, though, when they heard someone clear their throat.

"It's me," Marley called out. She even added a knock on the wall. Obviously, she knew Nola was there and hadn't wanted to walk in on another scene. Good thing, too, because Nola and he had been moving right along with something the girl shouldn't have had to witness.

"We're in the kitchen," Wyatt told her after Nola turned off the music.

Marley still gave them a couple of seconds, no doubt in case they needed to disentangle themselves, before she finally came in.

"Sorry to disturb you," she said, "but you didn't answer my text, and Trey's waiting for an answer."

Wyatt felt his scowl automatically shift into place, making sure not to aim it at Marley, and he pulled out his phone. Yep, her text was there, and he hadn't heard the ding over Rob Stewart's crooning and the throbbing heartbeat in his ears.

He read the message where Marley had asked him if it was okay if she had lunch with Trey and that she needed to let Trey know so he could in turn tell his dad that he'd be using the truck for a while after his shift ended.

"The storm," Wyatt reminded her, but the rest of what he'd been about to say trailed off when he realized the storm was already moving off, and the rain had slowed to a drizzle. "Sure, you can go to lunch with him. If that's what you want."

It obviously was since Marley smiled and lifted her phone to send that text reply. The gesture didn't seem out of the ordinary to Wyatt, but he looked at Nola when she made a little gasp.

Marley looked, too, and then noticed what Nola was staring at. The little blue heart charm on her phone.

Marley finished the text, her mood changing in a snap. She definitely wasn't smiling now. "Yes, it's one of yours," she said, flicking the heart with her finger. "I just liked it, that's all."

With that, Marley turned on her heels and went back toward her room.

Wyatt figured Nola had to be stinging from Marley's hasty exit, but she wasn't. Now she was the one smiling a little, and he thought he knew why. The fact that Marley had kept something of Nola's so close, right on the phone that she almost always had in her hand, gave Nola hope.

Hope that Marley could let go of the anger.

Of course, it was just as likely that Marley would keep on being pissed off, but it gave him hope, too.

Nola was still smiling when she kissed him again. No tongue this time, but it was obvious she was in a much better mood than she had been when she'd arrived.

"I need to go see my mother," she said, adding a second smiling kiss. "But think about that sex pact and get back to me."

That yanked him right back into the heat. Oh, he would indeed think about it, and once his erection had softened, he might be able to walk to his bathroom for that cold shower that was waiting for him.

CHAPTER SIXTEEN

NOLA TOOK THE exit toward the doctor's office and wondered how many times she'd make this journey in the coming months. Correction—how many times *they* would make the journey, since she figured Wyatt would insist on coming along with her for future appointments. She wished he was doing that because he genuinely wanted to be involved in this pregnancy, but she knew obligation when she saw it.

Knew worry, too.

Some of that had been spurred by the call Wyatt had gotten shortly after they'd started the drive to San Antonio. A call from Leroy Mercer, the crew supervisor who'd told Wyatt that the lab had started work on Griff's car and they might have answers soon. Of course, Leroy had also added they might not get answers at all, and Nola wasn't sure what bothered Wyatt the most.

The knowing or not knowing.

She was going with both on this because either way posed its own set of problems. If Bennie or Carlene had been at fault, that would come to light and stir up the past. If there was no definitive proof whatsoever, then a stirred-up past was still on the proverbial table.

"By the way, have you given any more thought to the sex pact I offered you?" Nola threw out there.

As she'd known it would, that yanked Wyatt right out of his current, clearly dismal thoughts. "What do you think?"

he asked with just the right amount of sexual frustration in his voice.

Good, because she was experiencing some sexual frustration of her own. And she kept dreaming about a shirtless Wyatt pouring water from a hose over his head.

"You've thought about my offer and decided it's a great idea," she spelled out. She noted his flat expression. "Or you've thought about it and decided it would complicate things. Mercy, I hate that word." She hated even more that it was true. "Past, present and future complications."

"We could manage to ball them all up into one set with a sex pact," Wyatt grumbled.

"Yes, but at least I'd temporarily stop lusting over you." She stopped, sighed. "No, I wouldn't. Well, except for those minutes when you could render me thoughtless, speechless and incapable of considering the aftereffects."

Though she didn't think Wyatt would go along with that whole eat the cake and have it, too, because of the consequences. There was another word she hated. *Consequences.* Wyatt and she had plenty of past, present and future of those, too. Because this baby wouldn't stay an embryo.

If all went well with the pregnancy, she would give birth and be the best mother possible. Wyatt would attempt the best-father deal, but in those future consequences, she could already feel him drifting away from her. It wouldn't be intentional or something he wanted—just the opposite. She had seen this sort of thing happen with Lily and her husband, Cam.

Of course, at the time of their divorce, Nola hadn't known about Hayden not being Cam's bio-daughter, but Nola recalled Lily mentioning that Cam had regretted being a father. In hindsight, that could have meant he regretted taking on another man's child, but the regret and resentment had stewed until Cam had left. Now Hayden had to go through the hurt of believing her father had abandoned her.

Which had actually happened, if Griff had ended his own life.

Either way, Hayden was caught up in the emotions of it all, and Nola didn't want to put her child through that. Didn't want to put Wyatt through it, either. So in her mind their best bet was a sex pact. A sort of friends with really great benefits. And co-parenting in a way that put no pressure on Wyatt but still made their child feel loved and wanted. Now, if she could just figure out how to make sure all of that happened while not getting her heart crushed.

Her phone rang, and Nola's eyes narrowed when she saw it was her mom.

"Have you talked to her yet about what the PI learned?" Wyatt asked, obviously seeing Evangeline's name on the car dash screen.

"No. I tried to talk to her for the past couple of days, but she said it'd have to wait, that she had meetings stacked up. It's her classic dodging ploy, so she likely knows I'm mad at her."

That probably had something to do with the snarly tone Nola had used in the voice mails she'd left. Yes, she had told Wyatt she wouldn't have a go at her mom for keeping secrets, but she'd earned the right to give Evangeline a little mental thump upside the head.

"Mom," Nola greeted her when she hit the button to accept the call. She jumped right into it. "How long has it been since you've talked to your old friend Heather Silva?"

Evangeline's answer was some poking-along moments of silence.

"I've got you on speaker," Nola went on, "and Wyatt is listening. FYI, Wyatt had a PI do a background check on the Silvas, and that's how I knew about your friendship with your old college roommate. It would have been nice to have heard about your connection with Heather from you instead of learning about it through a stranger."

"I didn't know if it'd help or hurt if I told you," her mother finally said.

Wyatt gave her a scolding look, a reminder to play nice. And she would, now that she'd gotten in that little thump.

"I don't know if it would have helped or hurt, either," Nola admitted on a sigh.

That was the gospel truth, and she spent a lot of time mulling it over, and it seemed to be the right thing to say because she heard Evangeline's own not-so-soft sigh of relief.

"I think it's safe to say that you did the right thing by keeping it to yourself," Nola continued after her own long pause. "If I'd known Marley's name, I would have been tempted to break the pact Wyatt and I had made about not trying to find out anything about her." She sighed. "But you probably kept up with what she was doing over the years."

"I did," her mother admitted. "Heather and I didn't talk much, but I'd call her every year on Marley's birthday and catch up."

Nola glanced at Wyatt and knew he was thinking those calls would have happened on the same dates as their non-celebrations.

"Alec doesn't know that Heather and I stayed in touch," Evangeline went on. "In fact, he didn't want her to have any contact with me at all. He was worried that I'd start to regret the adoption and that I might try to encourage Wyatt and you to fight for custody. That was especially true after Wyatt and you became successful with your chosen professions."

As much as Nola disliked Alec, she could understand him worrying about something like that. Because from accounts, he hadn't been a butthole back then. He'd just wanted to make sure he didn't lose his daughter.

"Uh, there's something else," Evangeline went on. "In fact, I thought it was the reason you were so anxious to talk to me. I was hoping I'd be able to put a stop to it before you heard anything."

Good grief. Not another surprise. Nola wasn't sure she could handle it. "What happened?"

"There's been some talk…about Marley and Trey Palmer. Apparently, folks saw them together at O'Riley's a couple of days ago."

Nola sucked in her breath so hard that she coughed. "What do you mean *talk*?" Wyatt snapped, taking the question right out of Nola's mouth.

"It's just gossip. You know how people are." Her mother punctuated that short and inadequate response with a couple of huffs.

Nola was huffing, too, and working her way to a growl. "What are the idiots saying?" But she knew. Mercy, she already knew. It was the blasted past, present and future colliding to mess with Marley.

"That Marley will probably get pregnant like her mom," Evangeline spelled out. "Nola and Wyatt, I'm so sorry."

Wyatt wasn't growling, but Nola wouldn't have been surprised to see steam coming out of his ears. "Who's saying those things?" he demanded. "Because I'm in a taking-names, kicking-ass kind of mood."

"I know you are, and it might surprise you to hear that I am, too. I might be a peace-loving woman, but it riles me to the core to hear someone speak like that about my granddaughter."

"I want names," Wyatt insisted.

Her mother did some more sighing. "It's teenagers, and you can't kick that many asses."

"Wanna bet?" Wyatt's voice was low and dangerous.

"You can't," her mother said in spite of all that danger. "Because it would only add to the gossip along with adding talk of your arrest, which is something that would happen if you assaulted a bunch of teenagers. And don't consider forbidding Marley to see Trey," she added.

Judging from Wyatt's fresh growl, he'd been thinking of doing just that.

"From what I can see," her mother went on, "Trey has been nothing but a gentleman around Marley. Probably because he's terrified of you. Maybe because he doesn't want her to get in trouble with her folks."

Oh, God. Nola hadn't even gone there yet, but she made the quick journey to that conclusion now. If Alec found out about this, he could use it to force Marley home. His home. And that ninth-tenths-of-the-law deal might kick in, and the judge could grant him custody.

"I haven't found out who started the rumor, but I'll keep digging," Evangeline continued. "From what I can tell from the more reliable sources, Trey and Marley did kiss at O'Riley's. Just that, a kiss. Trust me, I got much more detailed reports about Wyatt and you back in the day."

Nola was certain she had, and now she knew how mortified, and hurt, Evangeline must have felt when she heard those things.

"When did this talk start?" Nola asked.

"I got wind of it yesterday afternoon," her mother answered without even having to think about it.

So, Marley had likely heard. Wyatt must have had the same thought because he couldn't get out his phone fast enough. She saw the quick debate he had with himself over whether to call or text. He finally went with a text, but he clearly debated what to say because it took him a while to compose a single sentence. He showed it to Nola when he had sent it.

Just checking to make sure you're okay.

"Hold on a second, Mom," Nola told Evangeline while the little dots below Wyatt's text taunted them. "I might need you to go out to Wyatt's and check on Marley."

"Of course I will," her mother assured her just as the dots went away and Marley's reply came.

I'm fine. Working with Janie in the east pasture.

Nola could practically feel some of the tension fade in the car. *Some.*

Good, Wyatt answered back. I'll be home in a couple of hours. He paused, added, Text me if anything comes up.

Marley responded with the okay emoji.

"No need for you to go to Wyatt's," Nola relayed to her mother as she pulled into the parking lot of the doctor's office. "In the meantime, find out who's behind the talk."

Nola wasn't sure it was a good idea for Wyatt to have actual names, but if they found out who was spreading rumors, then she could maybe quietly talk to them. Quietly and in such a way that involved no yelling or cursing.

Speaking of yelling and cursing, that was what Nola wanted to do after she ended the call with her mother. She settled for banging her hands on the steering wheel. It actually helped some, but she doubted that would work with Wyatt. Doubted even dirty talk or the mention of the sex pact would defuse the anger, so she went with a different approach. The direct, honest one.

"Let's just get through this appointment, and then you can get back to Marley and talk to her about this. I'd like to be there for that, but I doubt she'd appreciate it."

Wyatt didn't argue with any of that, and he didn't look happy that this would fall to him. But he knew the score, Marley resented her, and if Nola was there, that resentment would bubble over into anything Wyatt tried to tell her.

She gave the steering wheel one last hit with the palm of her hand, and they went into the appointment. At least they didn't have to wait, which would have given them time to mull over and rehash what had just happened. The nurse ushered them into an exam room and gave Nola a green gown to put on for the exam.

Wyatt sank down into a chair, anchored his elbows on his knees and covered his face with his hands. No doubt trying to put his anger in check. Definitely not the mood setter Nola had wanted for what would hopefully be their first glimpse of the baby.

He kept his face covered until after she'd stripped and put on the gown, and he finally looked at her once she was on the table. A dozen unspoken questions went through his eyes, which still managed to be dreamy despite all the worry and stress.

"I'm okay," she assured him, answering one of his top questions. "And you?"

"Okay," he lied.

Now she went with the distraction. "You'd be better than okay if you agreed to my sex pact."

He looked her straight in the eyes. "Marry me first and I'll agree."

Maybe that was his own attempt at a distraction, and it

worked. Nola was too shocked to say anything before Dr. Alice Darby came in. Not Nola's usual doctor but the OB that her regular doctor had recommended. The petite brunette smiled at Nola but then did an almost comical double take when her attention landed on Wyatt.

"Oh," the doctor said, flushing a little. "Oh," she repeated. "You don't remember me?"

Oh, monkey balls. Nola hoped this wasn't one of Wyatt's old girlfriends.

Wyatt shook his head. "No, I'm sorry I don't."

The doctor dismissed it with the wave of her hand. "I dated your brother Dax for a while. Briefly dated," she added.

The *briefly* hadn't been necessary since all of Dax's relationships fell into that category.

"Anyway, Dax took me to your ranch once so I could see the horses. He introduced us, but you didn't stay and chat because you were tied up with a mare who was having a hard delivery."

Wyatt again had to shake his head, and when he added a second "I'm sorry," the doctor waved it off again and turned a bright smile to Nola. "All right. Let's see if we can get a peek of this baby. Are you hoping for a boy or a girl?" she asked, washing up and then putting on gloves before she got in position at the bottom of the table.

Wyatt did a third head shake as if the baby's gender wasn't something he'd even considered, and Nola just shrugged. She had considered it, but it didn't matter.

"I just want him or her to be healthy," Nola settled for saying.

"Well, that's what I want, too. I read through the notes on your first delivery," the doctor went on in between murmuring instructions to Nola about what she was about to experience. "You delivered vaginally, but there were some complications with the baby itself. That doesn't mean there'll be a repeat, but we'll keep a close watch on you. Now, remember, even if we don't see the heartbeat today, that doesn't mean anything's wrong. It could just mean it's still a little too early."

Nola saw the image come onto the screen and she could no longer hear what the doctor was saying. That was because in the middle of all those snowstorm images, she saw the speck, and thanks to the magnification of the equipment, she saw something else.

The heartbeat.

The little thump, thump, thump of life.

And just like that, her bad mood vanished, and it seemed as if everything shifted into place. Of course, it hadn't. Her problems would still be there after she got up from this exam table, but for now, she could see the baby.

She'd had ultrasounds with Marley, but she'd dreaded those because they'd been a slap-in-the-face reminder that she was a pregnant teenager who had no means to support a child. But there was no dread here. Only the love. Only the hope that this time she'd get it right.

Nola risked looking at Wyatt, and while he wasn't smiling, he was studying the little heartbeat, but then he stepped back. Maybe because he'd realized he might get a glimpse of what was going on with the position of the wand.

At least, that was what Nola chose to believe.

She stayed in her little euphoria cave while the doctor finished and degloved to help Nola to a sitting position.

"All looks good," she told Nola. She looked at the tablet she picked up from a table. "I understand you had a question as to whether or not you could continue to work as a glass artist." She smiled again. "I actually own one of your pieces."

Nola automatically frowned. "Have you ever used the name Dodo?" she couldn't help but ask.

"Uh, no," Dr. Darby said, clearly confused. "Why?" She shifted her attention to Wyatt, maybe thinking that was something Dax had called her.

"No reason," Nola muttered. "Sorry. You were going to tell me something about if I could work or not."

The doctor nodded. "Yes, you can, but I'll need you to cut back on how long you're in an overly heated room. Take frequent breaks and hydrate well."

Nola had prepared herself to hear the heart-squeezing news that she'd be out of the workshop for the next eight months or so, but she wouldn't be. She could have that cake and eat it, too. Well, with the breaks and hydration, anyway.

The doctor printed out something and handed it to her. A photo of the little heartbeat, and once again, all seemed right with the world.

Well, almost right.

That was when Nola knew she had a call to make. After the doctor left and she got dressed, Nola took out her phone and called the adoption agency.

To take her name off the list for a baby.

CHAPTER SEVENTEEN

WYATT THOUGHT IF he had to sign one more contract or take one more call about a problem with a shipment or order, he was going to stomp on his phone and every pen in his office. Normally, he loved working all aspects of the ranch.

But not today.

Not for the past three days, actually.

Not since he'd gone to the appointment with Nola and had gotten his first glimpse of the child she was carrying. It had been so moving for her that she'd decided not to adopt. Not a bad decision in his mind since it would be hard enough dealing with a newborn without adding another baby to the mix.

But that wasn't the only thing that'd gone on that day. Nope. Wyatt had had to come home and talk to Marley about son-of-a-bitching gossip. She thankfully hadn't had a clue about the talk, which was somewhat of a miracle, but that was possibly because she didn't go to school in Last Ride and not many people had her phone number. Still, he'd figured she would have picked up at least some snippets at the diner or grocery store where she occasionally went.

Marley had been alarmed by the gossip, but she probably would have been even more bothered had Wyatt not softpedaled it some. Actually, he'd downplayed it big-time once he became aware she didn't know, and in the end, Marley thought this was just a pseudofatherly, roundabout way of lecturing her about safe sex.

She hadn't smirked, hadn't mentioned that he wasn't one to give out such advice even in a roundabout way. She'd simply hugged him. Yes, hugged him and hurried off to the stables, where she spent more time than she did in the guest room. If Alec truly wanted custody of Marley, then the man should buy a horse ranch. But Wyatt wasn't going to help Alec out in that particular arena.

During the past three days, there were some things that hadn't happened, too. Evangeline hadn't been able to find out the names of the gossip spreaders. The lab hadn't come back yet with any results on Griff's car.

And Wyatt hadn't seen Nola.

They'd texted, had even had one hot, teasing phone call where she'd joked and asked him to send her nude photos so she could make another glass piece. He'd sent her a picture of a banana that had made her laugh. He liked to make her laugh. But he'd stayed away to give her, well, whatever the hell it was she might need. Space, time to think, time to blow glass and ease some of that fireball of tension he'd seen in her eyes.

But he'd wanted to give himself those things, too.

Not with glass, of course, but by throwing himself into his work and hanging out with Marley. Both had been satisfying enough, but now it was time he went to Nola so he could check on her. Despite her two-time refusal to marry him, he didn't want her to think she was alone in this.

With Marley settled into her room for four hours of her classes and with Trey nowhere on the grounds, Wyatt ignored an incoming phone call from a buyer, letting it go to voice mail, where he'd deal with it later. He headed to the door with plans to go straight for his truck. Or rather, it would have been straight had he not practically run into Jonas. His brother was already on the porch, his hand lifted to knock on the door. Since it was the middle of a workday, and Jonas put in as many hours as he did, Wyatt had an immediate question.

"What's wrong?"

Jonas shrugged, and Wyatt stepped back so they could both get out of the heat. "Maybe nothing, but I wanted to tell you in person Eli was at O'Riley's a couple of days ago, and he saw Marley and Trey Palmer."

Wyatt groaned. "Did Eli also happen to see someone who started ugly rumors about Marley?"

That caused Jonas to pause a moment. "Maybe. He saw a man across the street looking at Marley."

That went through Wyatt like a ball of ice. "What man?"

"Eli had never seen him before, and he said the guy didn't get out of his car, but that he thought he might be taking pictures of Marley. Or maybe of Trey."

WTF? "Are you talking some kind of kidnapper here? Pervert?"

Jonas shook his head to both. "Don't know. Eli didn't even mention it to me until this morning, and it came up when I asked if he'd gotten a chance to meet Marley. I mean, since it seems as if she might be staying awhile."

Wyatt had no idea if that was true, but because she'd been there almost three weeks now, he guessed that qualified for *a while*. "Tell me about this man," he pressed.

"I don't have much. It was a white guy in a dark blue Honda with tinted windows. I pressed Eli for more, but he only got a glimpse of the guy and told me he drove off after just a couple of seconds."

Well, this was yet something else to eat away at him,

and it prompted Wyatt to send Marley a text even though she might not even read it until she'd finished her classes.

If you head into town today, let me know, he messaged and hoped it sounded as if he wanted her to pick up something rather than him wanting to know her every move. He sent another text to his ranch manager for him and the other hands to be on the lookout for any strangers that might show up.

That was probably the very definition of overkill, but he couldn't take any chances with Marley.

"You're on your way out," Jonas said, glancing down at the truck keys Wyatt had in his hand.

"I'm going to see Nola."

Jonas scratched his chin, and because he didn't budge, Wyatt figured he had something else on his mind. "Are you going to marry her?" Jonas asked.

"It appears not. Nola's choice, not mine," he added because he knew Jonas wouldn't tell anyone. Wyatt also thought of something else. "Is Lily okay?"

He probably should have kept that question to himself or Nola because Jonas stared at him. "Why wouldn't she be?"

Wyatt went with the dodge. "I asked first."

That earned him a scowl, but then Jonas shook his head. "I think she's been a little down lately. You know the reason why?"

He did. Or rather, he knew Lily's secret, but Wyatt also suspected her down mood had just as much to do with having the past brought to the surface so it could give her a hard slap in the face.

"Griff's car is at the lab," Wyatt finally settled for saying since that wouldn't be a lie. Lily had to be as concerned about what the lab guys found as he was.

"Yeah," Jonas agreed. "I figured the research Nola was doing for the Last Ride Society was playing into it, too."

Wyatt didn't want to put any of the blame for this on Nola, but people were definitely talking about Griff because of the tombstone drawing and the car, and that talk had to be affecting Lily and dragging her back to the memories of that fateful night.

Which caused Wyatt to think of yet something else he'd been meaning to ask his brothers.

"Did Griff mention anything to you about an appointment he had a couple of weeks before he died?" Wyatt asked.

Jonas gave that some thought, shook his head. "But we weren't seeing much of each other back then. I was already the manager of Sunset Creek Ranch, but Lily hadn't bought it yet. I was working for Otis Jenner then. Still trying to figure out a way to buy the place from him," his brother added in a mumble.

A reminder that Jonas hadn't gotten that chance because before he'd scraped together the cash that Otis was demanding, Lily had come into her inheritance and had bought it. Sometimes, Wyatt wondered why his brother hadn't just quit and moved on, but by then he'd been married to Maddie, and they'd been raising her toddler son from her ex. Besides, maybe Jonas just liked working for Lily. She'd certainly taken Jonas's vision for the ranch and run with it.

"If you talk to Dax anytime soon, ask him about the appointment," Wyatt said. Dax would have been only fifteen at the time and had been living with Maddie and Jonas, but maybe Griff had mentioned something to him.

Then Wyatt considered something else. Something bad. Maybe the appointment had been with Bennie. Griff was always working or needing work on his old car, so maybe he'd gone to Bennie, and that could have been when either

Bennie or his sister had tampered with it. Yeah, that was a long shot, but so was everything else that could maybe finally lead him to the truth.

He said his goodbye to Jonas, walked him out and then went to his truck. Wyatt had to ignore two more work calls on the short drive to get into town, but he couldn't tamp down the urgency to get to Nola. And no, it didn't have anything to do with her dirty phone conversation or sex pact talk.

Well, not much, anyway.

It was hard to think of Nola and not also think of that heat she fired up inside him, but his priority was to make sure she was okay.

He went to the workshop first and didn't see her car, but since she walked most days, he tested the workshop door and found it unlocked. He stepped into the heat that nearly knocked him back a step. So did the blare of Rod Stewart. The same song she'd played in his kitchen.

"Hey," Nola greeted him, looking back at him and flashing him a grin. "I'm nearly finished and will need to take a break."

Doctor's orders, and since Nola wasn't drenched in sweat as she was sometimes when she worked, that told him she was sticking to those orders. On the hydrating, too, since there was a jug of water next to the stool where she was sitting. Thankfully, she had a bathroom just a few yards away.

He shut the door and walked closer to see what she was doing and stepped into the wind tunnel she'd set up with the fans. That explained the lack of sweat.

"It's harder to work with the glass this way because the fans keep cooling it down too fast, but at least I can get stuff done without me overheating."

She was indeed getting stuff done. He looked at the end

of the rod and saw a wave of all sorts of shades of blue swirling and threading around clear streaks. He had no idea what it was or how she could create something out of glass, but there it was. And it was beautiful.

Nola hauled the project to the table where she did the shaping, rolling and even some snipping before she hurried back to the oven to fire up the glass again. He watched as she freed the piece from the pipe, and she stood back and looked at it.

He looked, too, and while it wasn't fire red like the other one, the fluid shape and colors were as sexual as they came.

"I didn't make the storm," she said, using her phone app to cut off the music. "I can call it *Slow Dance.*"

"Or *Foreplay,*" he muttered, causing her to laugh.

"Let me get this in the annealer before it shatters." She slipped on gloves for that and hauled the piece away. Wyatt actually held his breath, hoping it stayed together, and he watched as she eased the piece into the cooling oven with all the care and gentleness that one would use with a newborn baby.

Nola did a little happy dance as she made her way back to him, and before he realized what she was going to do, she took hold of him, her still-gloved hands moving to his back. She whirled him around and kissed him.

"It feels so good to make something like that." She was gushing. Giddy, even, and it made him smile. She hadn't been moping or sad after all. "I've cut way back my hours and my time in front of the furnace." She led him back to the fans. "But I'm working enough to take off the edge."

He wondered exactly what edge she was talking about. She wasn't rubbing her hands on her jeans or asking him to dance, and that kiss and hug she'd given him were more

244 MORNINGS AT RIVER'S END RANCH

of the celebration sort than, well, the start of anything that could lead to smoothing out edges.

She checked her watch. "I can spend about fifteen more minutes in front of the furnace. Let me show you what it feels like."

Again, he wasn't sure what she was talking about, and Wyatt was a little disappointed when she didn't kiss him again. Instead, she heated up the pipe and went to her crushed glass stash.

"You know I have no artistic skill whatsoever. I'll suck at this," he complained.

"No, you won't suck. You'll blow." Nola chuckled. "What color do you want to play with?"

"Surprise me," he answered. Considering all the surprises they'd gotten over the past month, that was probably tempting fate, but so what if he ended up with a puke-green ball?

She gathered several colors, hurried back to him and handed him the pipe. "Now, stick it in there, and yes, you can snicker like a randy teenage boy that it's called a glory hole."

Wyatt didn't snicker, but he did react when Nola moved behind him to adjust his arms the way a golf or tennis instructor would do to a student. She probably hadn't meant to graze the front of his jeans with her hands. Probably.

She used her phone app again to play some music. Something low, bluesy and as sexual as that piece she'd just put in the cooling oven.

He refused to say the name of the fire-churning furnace, but he shoved the pipe in and, letting Nola's nudges and shifts lead him, he pulled it out when she saw it was at the right temperature.

"Now blow into the pipe, slide your thumb over it to trap your breath," she instructed, "and see what happens."

"Is this foreplay?" he asked, and then he blew.

"I sure hope so. I've been fantasizing about getting you naked in here."

He laughed and probably screwed up the placement of his thumb because Nola slid her arms underneath his to add some cover to the pipe hole. She moved with him, her breasts pressing into his back. He had no idea what he was making and didn't care.

"See, you don't suck. Blow again," she murmured, and blew, in his ear.

Hell. Enough was enough. Wyatt practically threw the pipe on the metal table, turned on the stool and took hold of Nola, pulling her down for the kiss he wanted a hell of a lot more than the breath he'd just put in that pipe. She could do this to him. Set him on fire and drive him crazy.

And he intended to do it right back to her.

She was laughing when he pulled her onto his lap, and he sank right into the kiss. Long, deep and exactly what he needed from her. A kiss that told him this wasn't going to end with a slow dance or with someone walking in on them.

"Lock the door," he managed to say.

She pulled back, looking at him with eyes already glazed with heat, and she took out her phone, using the apps to not only lock up but to shut off the furnace. To turn on the AC, too, because he could feel the cool air fall down on them from the overhead vents. He hoped that added some time to the minutes she was supposed to be in here. Because he very much wanted those minutes with her.

Her mouth came back to his while she fumbled to put her phone away. She dropped it on the floor and didn't go after it. Nola went after him instead, straddling him and pulling him against her. Wyatt had already started in that direction, so they were of a like mind. They usually were when it came to sex.

Except this wouldn't be sex.

Something that displeased his dick immensely, but he didn't want to roll around with her on a floor covered with bits of glass and equipment that looked as if it could do some serious damage. Besides, this wasn't about him. This was about going a couple of steps past a slow dance and making her come. That would definitely take off the edge, and after all, he was supposed to be good at this.

With her, anyway.

And being good with her was really the only thing that mattered.

Nola was certainly good. With her hands and with her mouth. All that blowing with glass had obviously honed her mouth to torture him in the best kind of way. He tortured her right back, going after her neck, that spot just at the base of her throat. From there, it was only a short trip to her breasts.

He kissed her through her top, and she made a sound of both pleasure and protest when he stopped her from going after his zipper.

"Just let me do the touching," he whispered.

She balked at that, too, and blew it off by opening a few buttons on his shirt and sliding her hand through the sweat on his chest. That required him to latch on to his self-control and threaten it within an inch of its life if it didn't hold strong.

"You don't even know if it's okay for you to have sex," he reminded her. Of course, it was. If not, pregnant couples would be in a constant state of horniness, but at least it caused her to slow down.

And give him a dirty look. That was dirty in both a sexy

and slightly mean way. "We're not walking out of here without orgasms," she insisted.

Well, she was partly right. She wouldn't be walking out without one, and Wyatt had to move things along faster than he wanted because she licked his chest and then used her tongue, lowering her head all the way to his stomach.

Nola knew his hot spots, too.

And there was that clever breath thing, too. His dick rather liked the idea of a blow job, but that would cause him to lose focus. This was the pleasure-Nola show, not time for a BJ.

Wyatt put a halt to her licking by flicking open the button on her jeans, yanking down the zipper and sliding his hand in her panties.

Then into her.

Nola stopped all right, and in the same breath she cursed him and gasped in pleasure.

She caught on to his shoulders, anchoring herself though Wyatt had hold of her because he'd already hooked an arm around her, and he kept her occupied with the strokes of his fingers. Sliding in and out of her. While he kissed her. While she gasped, moaned and cursed it.

He wanted all of this. The feel of her slick muscles already trembling against his finger. The moans. The gasps. The curses. But what he wanted most was when her eyes met his.

This was why he'd stayed focused.

This was why he could ignore the throbbing ache in his own body.

Because he wanted that look. Her crystal-blue eyes burning for him. Pleading with him to give her that release. Her eyes taking him in as if he was the only thing in the world that mattered.

Wyatt kept her on that ledge so he could hold on to it just a little longer. Until Nola could take, or give, no more. Then he finished her and sent her flying.

CHAPTER EIGHTEEN

NOLA DID A little dance across the floor of her workshop and admitted that she was way too happy, considering all the unresolved stuff in her life. But one thing was resolved.

Well, confirmed, anyway.

Wyatt still had the magic touch, and he had proved it big-time the day before when he'd been in here with her. Too bad he hadn't let her attempt a magic touch on him, but when she'd tried, Wyatt had just kissed her and said they could save that for another time.

Hopefully, that time would come tonight, though Nola was still trying to work out the logistics of it. It probably wouldn't happen at the ranch because it would be hard to attempt that kind of magic with a teenager around. But Nola could invite Wyatt over to the cottage for takeout, where she could ask him if he was ready to accept that sex pact. He'd certainly gotten a good start on accepting it, and she thought it might be time to take it to the next level.

Of course, that next level was probably a bad idea because of that whole deal of sex muddying already-muddy waters, but she wasn't ready to give up Wyatt or the magic he created because of what-ifs.

She was about to fire up the furnace so she could blow a piece or two, but she'd just opened the app when her phone rang, and she saw Derwin's name pop up. Nola certainly hadn't forgotten about texting him less than an hour earlier about digging into Griff's mystery appointment. With way too much enthusiasm and giddiness, Derwin had agreed to do it and said he'd get back to her.

Since Nola doubted he could have accomplished much in—she checked the time—forty-five minutes, he was probably calling to get more info about it. Info she didn't have because no one seemingly knew squat about it.

"Nola," Derwin greeted her when she answered. That way too much enthusiasm and giddiness was still there. "The Sherlock's Snoops came through, and we think we have it. I'm guessing you want this to include in the Last Ride Society research?"

"Yeah." Whatever. But for now, she just wanted some clarification. "What do you mean you *have it*? Did you actually find out what appointment Griff had?"

"Sure did." He paused and lowered his voice as if sharing a secret. "I'd rather not tell you how we came by it, though. We have friends and helpers in all areas, and we wouldn't want their covers blown."

"You have snitches," she spelled out. "Now, tell me what you learned." No giddiness in her voice. She wanted to know now, and she hoped whatever Derwin was about to tell her was 1) actually relevant, 2) accurate and 3) something that wasn't going to send Wyatt into an emotional tailspin.

"Well, we figured out that Griff had two doctor's appointments. The first one happened two weeks before and the other was the morning of the *incident*." He put a lot of emphasis on that last word and probably thought it sounded kinder than the alternatives. It was. "The appointments were with a Dr. Michael Sanchez in San Antonio."

Good grief. She certainly hadn't expected Sherlock's Snoops to come up with that kind of specific info. At best, Nola had expected Derwin to relay some vague gossip.

"Dr. Sanchez is retired now," Derwin went on, "and he didn't answer my call. I did leave him a voice mail, though, and told him I was president of Sherlock's Snoops and that I urgently needed to talk to him."

Nola rolled her eyes. The odds were extremely high that a doctor wouldn't return a call to anyone claiming to be a Sherlock's Snoop. But he might return a call to Nola if she didn't make herself sound like a giddy pest with a weird hobby.

"What kind of doctor is Sanchez?" Nola asked.

"Internal medicine," Derwin quickly supplied.

In other words, he could have been seeing Griff about a whole bunch of things. "You're sure Griff actually had two appointments with this doctor?" Nola asked before she went on a wild-goose chase.

"We're sure. But as I said earlier, we'd rather keep our sources confidential." He'd lowered his voice again for that part.

But Nola gave it some thought and saw how this could have played out. "Margaret Dayton is a Sherlock's Snoop, and she's a retired nurse who used to work at the Last Ride Hospital. I'm guessing Margaret had a peek at Griff's old medical records and saw that Griff's doctor here referred him to Sanchez."

Derwin's silence confirmed that. Confirmed, too, that they'd likely bent the privacy laws to get info like this. She doubted, though, that Margaret would have the access to do more bending and get into Dr. Sanchez's records, so if the doctor didn't respond to her call, she'd need to try to arrange a trip to pay him a visit.

"I need the doctor's phone number," she said, and Nola jotted it down when Derwin rattled it off to her.

"You'll tell us what he says, right?" Derwin asked. "Because this might help us close the case on Griff."

Yes, it might, but it might just open another can of worms. Or not be relevant at all. She thought of Wyatt having a vasectomy when he'd been twenty-one, so it was possible Griff had wanted to go that same route, especially if he had some inkling that Lily was pregnant with his child.

She ended the call with Derwin and had some gulps from the carton of milk she didn't want before she tried the doctor's number. It was almost ten in the morning, so not too early, but as expected, he didn't answer. After a couple of rings, the call went to voice mail, and she wished she'd practiced what she wanted to say.

"Uh," she started and added a few more of them before she found her words. "I'm Nola Parkman, and I was a close personal friend of one of your former patients, Griffin Buchanan. Griff died fourteen years ago, and I, uh, need to talk to you about him. To get some medical history," she added. "For his daughter."

She wanted to smack herself for adding that last part, but hey, in a really roundabout kind of way, that history would be nice to have since Hayden was Griff's daughter.

"Anyway," she went on after some more *uh*s, "if you could call me back, I'd appreciate it—"

"This is Dr. Sanchez," a man interrupted as he obviously cut off her voice mail. "I got a call earlier from some group called Sherlock's Snoops. Are you one of them?"

"Not a chance," she quickly assured him. And here was where she did some more word stumbling. "Griff had a twin brother, Wyatt, and he and I are…partners," she settled for saying. "We're expecting a child." Best not to mention the other child they'd already had since this conversation was already complicated enough.

"I see," the doctor murmured. "You mentioned you needed medical information for Griffin's daughter?"

Again, she wanted to smack herself. "Yes, a daughter he didn't know about when he died. I'd like to keep it that way, with others not knowing about it," she clarified and silently groaned. So much for her promising Lily that she'd carry this secret to the grave. She'd already spilled to Wyatt and now to this doctor.

"Is the daughter ill or experiencing any kind of medical problems?" he asked, sounding very much like the skeptical doctor that he no doubt was.

"No, but it seemed like a good idea to have Griff's medical history in case anything comes up," she said.

Silence. For a long time.

"Griff might have taken his own life," Nola added. "He died in a car wreck, but we're not sure if the wreck was intentional or if what happened was because he was sick. Or maybe severely depressed."

She expected him to ask if there was a reason for Griff to be depressed, and Nola so didn't want to get into Carlene's threat and the fact that Griff had just found out he was going to be a father.

The silence continued and continued, but Nola didn't try to fill it in with more of her babbling out things she clearly wasn't going to take to the grave.

"I'll take your request under consideration," he finally said. "And if I can confirm that Mr. Buchanan died in the manner you just described, then I'll decide if and what I might be able to share with you. Good day, Miss Parkman."

Nola didn't mind the doctor's chilly tone and instead considered this conversation somewhat of a miracle. When she'd contacted the Snoops, she hadn't thought they'd get this far, this fast.

Of course, it might still lead to nothing.

Dr. Sanchez might decide to share nothing whatsoever with her, but the fact he hadn't denied that Griff had had the appointments with him meant there was some reason for Griff having gone to see him. That reason probably wouldn't end up in the research report, but this might be the start of some answers.

Answers that she probably wouldn't share with the Sherlock's Snoops, either. In fact, it was entirely possible Nola might have to make them do some swearing to take this to their graves, too.

And she hoped they were a lot better at keeping quiet than she'd been.

Nola didn't put her phone away. She pressed Wyatt's number to relay what she'd just learned, but she'd barely managed to get out a hello when he answered. That was because the door opened, and Alec came in.

"Wyatt, I'll have to call you back," Nola told him. "Mr. Silva is here."

That caused Wyatt to let out a string of profanity. "What the hell does he want?"

"I'm not sure." But considering he was already glaring, she doubted it'd be good. "I'll get rid of him," she assured Wyatt.

She ended the call and picked up her pipe. Not because Alec was stalking toward her or anything, but because she just wanted him to know she was willing to use the tools of her art to give him a jab if he did try anything. She had backup as well since Alec had left the door wide open. If things got ugly, she'd just let out a yell and any- and everyone in the vicinity would come running.

"I'm here because of my daughter," Alec said, as if that were some kind of revelation. "I've heard what she's been getting up to since she's been here in this town with her so-called birth parents."

"Oh, yeah? And what exactly has she been getting up to?" Nola challenged.

She'd let the *so-called* snark slide for now, though she wanted to tell him he was acting like a so-called jerk of a father. But she didn't toss that at him since it would likely come back on Marley somehow. In fact, anything she said or did could become fodder for Alec's custody fight.

"My daughter has been running around with young men and ruining her reputation," Alec snarled.

Oh, to heck with letting the remarks slide.

"You arrogant, misinformed asshole," she started. "I don't know your source." Though Nola suspected it had to do with the gossip mill. "But Marley has not been *running around*. Whatever the heck that means," she added in a grumble. "Thankfully, we don't live in olden times when a young woman couldn't be seen in public with a young man who has not only not soiled her reputation but has a decent reputation of his own. You arrogant, misinformed asshole," she repeated.

Clearly, Alec didn't like being called exactly what he was. Twice. "I'm not misinformed. I got it from a reliable source."

"Who? The clerk at the gas station? Or maybe the tooth fairy told you."

Alec's eyes narrowed, but there was smugness in them, too. "No, I got it in a report from a private investigator that I hired to keep an eye on my daughter."

A private investigator, and Nola immediately connected the dots. "This was the guy who was taking pictures of Marley outside O'Riley's?"

"It is," Alec verified.

Wyatt had told her about that incident, but he had also assured her it was probably nothing. No doubt so she wouldn't worry. However, Nola had worried, and it had apparently been something after all. Not a perv or stalker as she'd speculated but the result of an arrogant asshole who apparently knew no boundaries when it came to violating Marley's privacy.

"I hired the PI because I knew I couldn't trust you and that so-called rancher to make sure my beautiful, innocent daughter stayed safe," Alec added.

Oh, he was really racking up the insult points, and Nola wondered if she could wipe away some of that smugness and *so-called* crap if she *accidentally* hit him in the balls with the pipe.

Putting a choke hold on her temper, and the pipe, Nola went with an alternative plan. "I'm betting Marley doesn't know that you hired someone to spy on her."

"She knows I'd do whatever it takes to look out for her," he argued. "Whatever it takes." That last part came out like a threat.

"So, that's a no. You haven't told her. And how do you think she'll take that news, huh? Do you believe she'll be pleased or pissed off? I'm going with option number two on this."

That tightened his jaw. "My daughter will understand that I love her and want to keep her from suffering any consequences for being here with—"

"If you say *so-called* anything, your balls are going to be hurting," Nola warned him.

He didn't finish the sentence that he'd started and sure as heck didn't use that insult again. However, he did give her some serious stink eye.

"My daughter knows that I love her," he finally replied.

"How do you think she'd feel if she knew you just threatened me?"

Nola didn't have a clue, but she doubted Marley would jump to defend her no matter what this jerk-wad said.

"You don't deserve custody of her," Nola said.

"But I'll get it." Alec aimed his index finger at her.

She aimed the pipe at him. "Mine's bigger than yours," Nola reminded him. "And it's made of steel."

"Another threat." His laugh was hollow. "Yes, I think this is something my daughter should hear. But in the meantime, you hear this. I will ruin you and that rancher if you get in my way of me getting custody of Marley. Ruin you both," Alec repeated in a snarl.

At that exact moment, Wyatt came rushing in. Not alone. Marley was right behind him. Nola had no idea how they'd gotten there that fast. And she didn't have to be a member of Sherlock's Snoops to know they'd just overheard the threat Alec had made.

WYATT HAD NEVER before wanted to punch someone so badly. In fact, he wanted to rearrange the features on Alec Silva's face and maybe shove his ass where his mouth was. Nola obviously knew he was considering doing just that because she stepped in front of him and Marley.

No way would he let Nola take any more heat, so Wyatt moved in front of her. And then Marley moved in front of both of them, meeting her father's glare head-on.

Of course, Alec's glare softened considerably when he went face-to-face with Marley, and Wyatt could practically see him trying to figure out how to worm himself out of that "ruin you and that rancher" and the other stuff he'd said right before that.

"I'm sorry," Alec said, taking a step back. Wise move

because if he'd tried to go to Marley, he might not have gotten the fatherly reception he wanted.

"You're sorry?" Marley snapped. "You came here to try to threaten Nola into doing what, exactly? Bribing me to go running to you? Frightening her so she'd do that?"

Wyatt could have told her that Nola didn't frighten easily, and she would have been more likely to bust Alec's balls than to let him ride roughshod over her. But what made Wyatt want to spit bullets was that Nola sure as hell shouldn't have had to go through this. When she was pregnant, no less.

He thought of that little speck of a beating heart he'd seen on the ultrasound, and he hoped and prayed none of this stress was making its way down to him or her.

"I'm sorry," Alec repeated, probably because he knew he didn't have a comeback that would fix this. He scrubbed his hand over his face. "I'm just so worried about you. Worried about the gossip I heard about you fooling around with that ranch hand."

Wyatt moved next to Marley so he could see her face and response to that. It was not a good response. Her face went tight in a way that reminded Wyatt of himself. Her jaw was set. Yep, his was like that, too. But Wyatt doubted even he could match the cold, hard glare Marley aimed at the man who'd raised her.

Because no way was Wyatt going to refer to this moron as her father.

Not ever again. Alec had just lost that right, as far as Wyatt was concerned.

"Gossip," Marley repeated. "Lies," she clarified. "And how is it you knew about those lies?"

Alec swallowed hard. "I hired a PI to follow you. He got pictures of you kissing that boy."

"Kissing him. Yes, I did that," Marley verified. "Would you like to know what else I did with him?" she snapped.

Wyatt shook his head, hoping she wouldn't go there because it wasn't anything he wanted to hear. Alec shook his head, too, but that didn't stop Marley.

"Nothing," she practically yelled. "I did nothing else with Trey because we're still getting to know each other. If and when I *fool around* with him, maybe your PI can get some pictures of that, too."

"Marley," Alec said on a broken breath, and he made the mistake of going toward her.

"No." She aimed her finger at him. "You don't touch me. You don't come near me, and sure as heck better not judge me. Not after what you've been doing."

Alec's shoulders went back. "What I've been doing is trying to get my daughter to come home, where she belongs."

"I'm not talking about that," Marley informed him. "I'm talking about you sleeping with your assistant. Yes, I know about that."

Deer caught in headlights had had less of a reaction than the one Alec did. "I don't know what you're talking about—"

"Your affair with your assistant," she spelled out for him. "I went by your office after hours about a month ago, and I saw you with your hand up her skirt."

Nola made a soft gasp, no doubt because she'd worked out the timing and knew that would have been when Marley had shown up at the ranch.

Wyatt silently cursed, hating that Marley had had to witness something like that. Hating, too, that he couldn't help but think that Alec had done him a favor. Marley might have never come to Last Ride had Alec kept his dick in his pants. Or hand away from his assistant's skirt.

"Does your mother know?" Alec asked.

"No." Marley groaned and spun around as if she was trying to stop herself from yelling again. "And I won't tell her because it'll hurt her. She'll start thinking it was her fault because she's just like that. You don't get to put her on that guilt train."

Despite Marley's harsh words, Alec looked relieved. "Thank you for that."

"I'm not doing it for you," Marley assured him.

Alec nodded. "I've made a lot of mistakes," he admitted. "But I want you to know the mistakes I've made with you were done out of love. Have I been perfect? No," he answered for her. "But the bottom line is I'm the one who raised you. The one who was there for you for seventeen years. And I still believe I'm a better parent than either of them would have been." He shot a look at both Wyatt and Nola. "Just remember they're the ones who put you up for adoption. They're the ones who didn't want you."

"That's not true," Nola said before Wyatt could make a move. "We did want you very much," she said to Marley. "We loved you and thought we were doing the right thing."

"The right thing for you," Alec interjected, getting that holier-than-thou look on his face, which took another swipe at Wyatt's temper.

"The right thing for them was the right thing for me, too," Marley tossed right back at Alec.

Wyatt didn't know who was more stunned by that, but after a quick look, he thought Nola was going to take that particular prize. Her mouth had dropped open, and the tears had already sprung to her eyes.

No way were these tears of sadness or anger.

Marley had just given her a huge olive branch. Maybe

that didn't mean all was forgiven, but he hoped that was the start of it.

"Marley," Alec repeated, reaching out his hand to her. "I'm sorry."

But Marley didn't reach back. Nor did she tell him where to shove that apology. "I'm going for a walk. And don't you follow me," she added in a warning to Alec, right before she went out the door.

"Go after her," Nola whispered to Wyatt.

"No way. I'm not leaving you here with him." Though Wyatt didn't especially want Marley out there alone. Upset and maybe crying. "You go check on her," he told Nola.

She debated that and probably knew Marley would take consoling a lot better from him than her. But Wyatt figured he'd just offered Nola something she couldn't resist— a chance to add to that olive branch and spend a little time with her daughter.

"If I leave, you'll punch him," Nola muttered.

"No. I won't. I promise," Wyatt added since that was the only way she would go. Of course, he hadn't promised not to do other bodily harm, but he wouldn't punch the sack of shit. "Go ahead. Check on Marley."

Nola had a quick debate about that, giving both Alec and him a few long looks before she nodded, handed him the pipe and hurried out.

Alec smirked some at the pipe. Maybe because he thought it was a threat with no bite to it. But Wyatt kept his hard stare on the man while he laid the pipe on the floor and faced the asshole head-on. Alec quit smirking.

"Something you want to say to me?" Wyatt challenged. "Maybe a repeat of some of the threats you made to my woman."

He actually hadn't intended to put that cringeworthy

"my woman" label on Nola, but it had just flown out of his mouth. And it was more or less true. After all, he'd had his hand in Nola's pants right here in this very space not too long ago, and she was carrying and had carried his babies.

The staring match continued for a couple of seconds, and then Alec gave another of those apologetic shakes of his head. "I'm under a lot of pressure," he finally said.

"So, that's your excuse for acting like a dick?"

Alec flinched, but his eyes didn't flare up with anger this time. The breath that left his mouth was long and sounded weary. "I'm under a lot of pressure," he repeated. "From Heather's parents."

Wyatt sure hadn't expected him to say that, and he quickly thought back through the background he'd had run on the man and his wife. Heather's folks had money, lots of it, and they owned the real-estate business that Heather ran for them. However, her parents also owned a good chunk of Alec's investment company.

"Her parents are old-school," Alec went on, "and they don't believe in divorce."

"Do they believe in their daughter staying with a husband who cheats on her?" Wyatt threw at him.

"No," Alec said, and this time there was a smidge of temper. "They wouldn't approve," he admitted. "Nor would they approve of me losing custody of my own daughter."

Wyatt didn't think "approve" was the right way to phrase that, but he could see what Alec was trying not to spell out. So Wyatt spelled it out for him. "As long as you have custody of Marley, your in-laws won't kick your cheating ass out on the street."

Now the anger went from smidge to epic proportions. "I love my daughter. I love her," he repeated through clenched teeth. "And I started that investment company. I built it from the ground up, and I won't stand by and have it and my daughter snatched from me."

Well, there it was. All laid out, exposing Alec's jerk-wad motive. "And how do you plan to stop this shit train that you've already set into motion?"

Alec didn't give him the reaction Wyatt had expected. The man lifted his hand, fanning it around Nola's workshop.

Wyatt saw red, and the color wasn't coming from any of the glass. "Is that a threat to try to ruin her business?"

"A promise. And before you say I can't do that, there's something you should know. For the past decade, I've been buying the bulk of this so-called art that Nola makes. Me," he emphasized, tapping his finger to his chest.

Hell's bells, and Wyatt added a lot more unspoken profanity to that. "You're Dodo?"

"I am. That was the name of our cat at the time, so I borrowed it. I figured if I bought her glass so she could earn a decent living and gloat over talent she thinks she has, then she wouldn't be tempted to go looking for the child that she gave up to me." Alec's voice got a lot louder with those last two words.

Wyatt did some silent cursing and wondered if he stood a snowball's chance in hell of keeping this from Nola.

Alec fanned his hand over the workshop again. "And what do you think it'll do to your woman's reputation when I tell everyone that she's a hack? No talent whatsoever. When I tell them that the only reason she's stayed in business is because I chose to buy this crap that she believes is art?"

Wyatt heard the sound, the soft gasp, and he whirled around to see Nola in the doorway. Well, shit. That snowball's chance in hell was nil because Nola hadn't missed what the jerk-wad had just said.

CHAPTER NINETEEN

NOLA CONTINUED TO do what she'd been doing for the past twenty-four hours. She stayed in bed and groaned at the text she got asking if she was all right. This latest one was from Lorelei, but she'd gotten multiple texts and calls from Wyatt—so many from him—and every member of her gene pool.

Including Marley.

Hers had been a simple I'm sorry, to which Nola had texted, No need to apologize. It's not your fault.

That brief exchange had lightened Nola's mood a little, but it hadn't made her forget where the fault was in this. It belonged to Alec for doing what was basically a con, but the blame fell on her, too. Because if she'd created actual art instead of just crap, then someone else would have snatched up the pieces before Dodo/Alec could get his grubby conning hands on them.

Nola had wondered where he'd stored all the pieces he'd bought, but she'd quickly pushed that thought aside. It didn't matter if they were stuffed away in storage or if he'd trashed every last one of them. Her heart was crushed and knowing the fate of the pieces wouldn't help.

Her phone dinged with another text. Wyatt again. I want to see you, it said.

He'd sent similar messages, had even left flowers at her door, but he hadn't tried to come in. Probably because she'd clearly spelled out that she needed some time alone. That was the truth. She didn't want to face anyone yet, and she definitely didn't want anyone seeing her tear-reddened face.

There was something else she didn't want to do. Nola didn't want to go anywhere near her pipe or glass, and this was the longest she'd ever been away from her workshop since she'd renovated it and started using it a dozen years ago. The hundred-year-old building had once been used for storage for feed and ranching supplies, and in her mind, that was how she was choosing to imagine it now.

As it was before she'd tried to put her mark on it.

When she'd thought she was something other than a hack.

Yes, some of that was pity-thinking, but the seeds of doubt had always been there, lurking, waiting. Apparently, Alec had tossed some water and fertilizer on those seeds because they'd taken root and were blooming like crazy.

Another text. Lorelei again. If you need anything, please let me know.

I will, Nola texted back, knowing there was nothing that would fix this. Knowing that she'd dragged Lorelei down with her.

Without a supply of glass pieces, there'd be nothing for Lorelei to sell in the shop. Of course, Nola could break down and make enough commercial stuff to keep it going, but she'd wonder if every purchase was because the buyer felt sorry for her. *Poor Nola. All that mess during her teenage years and now this. Let me show my support by buying this ugly, unimaginative paperweight.*

Despite all the gloom and doom she was feeling, there was something good that had come out of it. Well, two goods. Marley was actually communicating with her, had even stood up for her. The second good thing was Nola had gotten to tell Alec to shove his threat to ruin her. Specifically, she'd told him to shove it up his tight ass and then had ordered him out of the workshop.

Of course, Alec had already been heading out anyway because Wyatt was about to have a go at him and rip off his arms. Nola had managed to hold Wyatt back. Or probably the shell-shocked look on her face had accomplished that. Then she'd locked up and had him take her home so she could have that alone time.

And have those long crying jags, too.

Thankfully, Alec hadn't tried to contact her while she'd been in seclusion, and if he'd made an announcement of her hack talent, Nola hadn't caught wind of that, either. It would get around, though. She had told her family, and there was the likelihood that folks who'd been walking past the workshop would have heard the gist of the commotion as well.

Nola groaned when the doorbell rang, and she would have ignored it and stayed in bed, but she heard the familiar voice call out.

"It's me, Marley. I know you want to be left alone, but could we talk for a few minutes?"

Nola nearly pulled a muscle dashing out of the bed. Marley was here. Here. To see her.

"Just a second," Nola called back, and she scrambled toward the front door only to scramble back to the bathroom.

Monkey balls, she looked bad. Probably smelled bad, too, so she quickly brushed her teeth, combed her hair and changed into a clean shirt to go over the questionably clean jeans. The jeans would have to do, though, because she remembered she'd yet to do laundry.

Nola tried to slow down, tried not to look overly eager when she opened the door, and she settled some and went still when Marley gave her a tentative smile.

"I hope I'm not bothering you," Marley said as Nola

stepped back to motion for her to come inside. That was when Nola remembered she hadn't cleaned either, and the living room was a cluttered mess.

"No. No bother at all," Nola assured her as she cleared off a place on the sofa for her. "Sorry, I'm not the neatest person, but I'm usually a lot neater than this."

"It's okay," Marley assured her, and she glanced around, her attention landing on the mantel. At the family pictures there. Specifically the picture in the center.

"My father," Nola explained. "He died of Hodgkin's before Lily and I were born."

"Yes, my mom told me that." Marley glanced at her. "Recently told me," she amended. "After Wyatt and you found out about her friendship with your mother, she told me that Evangeline and your sister Lorelei had stayed with her when your father was going through treatment at a hospital there. Then, after he...passed, my mom came to Last Ride to be with Evangeline when she was giving birth to Lily and you."

Even though it stung a little that Evangeline hadn't mentioned that, it only confirmed why her mother had made sure her good friend Heather had gotten Marley.

"My mom said she'd been a little worried that folks here might recognize her from that other visit," Marley went on. "Worried because she knew Evangeline hadn't filled you in on their friendship. But if anyone here made the connection, they didn't say anything."

Probably because the connection hadn't been made. After all, there'd been thirty-three years in between Heather's visits to Last Ride. Some of the gossips had memories like elephants, but they probably wouldn't have been storing anything about Heather in their nosy little memory banks.

Marley continued to peruse the pictures until her attention landed on what was on the end of each side of the mantel.

The watery green glass candlesticks.

"Those are your pieces," Marley said, going closer to look at them, but she must have remembered that was a sore subject, because she turned back around to face Nola. "I'm so sorry for what my father did to you. Your work is beautiful."

Nola smiled but silently dismissed that as pity praise. Marley obviously felt bad for what Alec had done, and she was trying to make up for it in some way.

"Would you like something to drink?" Nola asked and was going through her limited choices when Marley shook her head.

"No, thank you. I won't stay long. I just wanted to come by and check on you. Then I can let Wyatt know I've seen you and that you're okay. You are okay, aren't you?" Marley asked, taking a seat on the sofa.

Nola thought about her answer while she sat across from her. "Tell him I'm all right." That was a lame dodge, but she didn't want anyone worrying about her. Especially Wyatt and Marley.

Marley made a sound as if she didn't buy that at all, but she didn't push. "I haven't talked to my father. Not sure when I'll be able to do that without yelling. Maybe when I'm thirty." She added a little smile that didn't reach her eyes.

"How about your mother?" Nola asked. "Will you tell her any of this?" And by *any*, Nola meant not just Alec's scam and threats, not just the PI he'd hired, but also the affair.

Marley shook her head. "I don't want to hurt her. And I've already done that just by coming here to Last Ride. I love her."

"I know you do, and she loves you." Nola nearly added her own name to the list of those who loved Marley, but she held back. Best to shift the conversation to steadier ground. "How are you getting along with Wyatt?"

This time her smile did reach her eyes, but it didn't last long. "Fine. He's a good listener, and he tries to make things right. Well, that isn't news to you. You've known him a long time."

Nola made a sound of agreement. Yeah, Wyatt was a fixer all right, and she had indeed known him a long time. Twenty-three years.

"Wyatt and his brothers moved to Last Ride when he and Griff were ten," Nola explained. "Fifth grade. And the first time I saw him, I think my heart did a little dance." She patted her chest and did a mock thump, thump with her finger, but there was nothing mock about that particular memory. "He was on the monkey bars, perched on top with Griff and him playing some kind of king of the mountain where they were shoving at each other, and I thought, *This is the one. I'll never want another boy as much as I want him.*"

Marley blinked. "You were ten."

"It wasn't sexual, not then. Later," she admitted and then decided to leave it at that. That was boggy ground, too.

"But you said Griff was there, and he was Wyatt's identical twin," Marley pointed out. "Why didn't your heart dance for him?"

"They never looked identical to me." She motioned toward her eyes. "There was always something different about Wyatt, and even though Griff tried to play switcheroo as a joke, it didn't work. I knew exactly who he was when he asked for my Little Debbie Snack Cake. I only saved that goodie for Wyatt."

Marley started to laugh but clamped it off. Maybe because she thought it would be an uncertain path for her if she started feeling too comfortable around the woman who'd given her up for adoption.

"Jonas told Hayden about that switcheroo fail," Marley remarked.

"Hayden?" Nola asked.

Marley nodded. "She and I have been talking, and she's come out to the ranch a couple of times to take pictures of the horses. She showed me the ones she took of Griff's tombstone. That apparently got her interested in doing some research that she's going to give you for your report."

This was the first Nola was hearing about this, and she wondered if Lily knew. And how Lily would feel about Hayden doing research on the man the girl didn't even know was her father. Nola would need to call her sister, which would mean getting through the *are you all right?* stuff before moving on to Griff.

"Now that she's finished with school, Hayden's going to ask her mom to take her to the bluff where Griff died," Marley went on. She was paying a lot of attention to Nola's expression. "Is that a bad idea? I mean, from what Hayden's learned, Griff and her mom were together when they were teenagers."

"Yes, they were," Nola verified. "And it might not be a good idea for Lily to go out there. If you talk to Hayden, tell her I can take her." Of course, that meant she'd have to push aside her alone time, but she could put the pause button on it. It wasn't as if it'd go away anytime soon.

"I'll tell her." Marley stood, obviously signaling an end to this visit. Nola wanted her to stay, wanted her to keep talking as if she didn't resent her. And maybe some of that resentment had faded, but the distance was there in spades.

Marley headed to the door just as someone knocked on it, and that someone called out as Marley had done.

"It's me," Wyatt said. "I brought food. Open up so I can feed you."

Nola hurried to the door before he added something sexual to that, and when she threw it open, she could tell he was surprised to see Marley there. While he stood there with a plastic grocery bag in each hand, Wyatt immediately shifted his attention, no doubt checking to make sure she wasn't crying. She wasn't, and she hoped her red face and eyes had cleared up enough so he couldn't tell that the dried tears were a very recent occurrence.

"I didn't see your car," Wyatt told Marley.

"It's at O'Riley's. I parked there and walked down. I'm not good at street parking and didn't want to hit anything."

That sounded logical. Truthful, even. But since Nola wasn't in the most positive frame of mind, she wondered if Marley had done that so that no one would know she was there. Like maybe that PI creep that Alec had hired.

"Uh, did you two have a good visit?" Wyatt asked. "Because if you need more time, I can put up these groceries and head out."

Marley shook her head. "I should be getting back. Homework. But yes, we had a good visit. Nola was just telling me about the first time she saw you. On the monkey bars."

Wyatt volleyed looks again at both of them, probably wondering how the heck they'd gotten on that subject. Maybe Marley wouldn't mention the whole heart-dancing thing. It'd sound sappy, and maybe a little creepy, when taken out of the context of the conversation.

"Nola was on the swings, giggling with her friends," Wyatt said, meeting Nola's eyes so that she knew he remembered that day, too.

They held that gaze for a moment, and then Wyatt set down the bags so he could reach in his pocket. He handed

Marley a piece of paper. "That's the license plate number of the PI that Alec hired. If you see him following you, I want you to call me and then the sheriff so he can arrest him for stalking you. The charges probably won't stick, but it'll mess with his day."

Marley took the paper, nodded. "Thanks." She brushed a quick kiss on Wyatt's cheek and headed out.

Wyatt closed the door, but they watched Marley from the front window. She wasn't storming off this time. Okay, she wasn't smiling either, but for once Nola didn't think she was the cause of the girl's unhappiness.

"She's beautiful," Nola heard herself say in the same tone that a mother likely would have for a newborn. "We made her," she added in a mumble.

"Yeah." Wyatt mumbled, too, but his voice didn't sound as wistful as hers, and with just that one word, Nola heard something else.

That "we made her" brought back some of the not-so-great memories as well. Of the shock of the pregnancy. A shock so embedded in him that he had never planned to go through it again.

Nola moved away from the window when Marley was no longer in sight, and she looked up at Wyatt.

He looked down at her. "I thought I'd find you crying in bed."

"I was," Nola admitted, "and then Marley came. She wanted to apologize for what Alec did."

"Yeah, she's taking it hard. Torn," he added, "because she's worried her mother will find out and fall apart. Apparently, Heather had a minibreakdown a couple of years back when her best friend was killed."

Marley hadn't mentioned that, but Nola understood better why the girl wouldn't want to heap more stress onto

Heather. Especially since Alec was heaping enough stress for the lot of them.

Wyatt took out a banana, an apple, a small carton of chocolate milk and a bag of her favorite chips, and he handed the stash to her. "I'll put the other milk and the rest in your fridge, but I thought you could use a treat."

She could, but Nola hadn't realized just how hungry she was until she drank some of the milk. Marley had been right about Wyatt always trying to fix things. He was trying to fix her with sugar and carbs. All in all, not a bad way to deal with it.

"Did you know you have three different kinds of old pizza in your fridge?" he called out from the kitchen.

"Four," she corrected. "You probably missed the one I crammed in the produce drawer."

"Four," Wyatt verified after she heard him slide open said drawer. "Are any of them still edible?"

"All of them probably are. People kept sending them over." She managed to smile at him when he came back into the living room. "But you're the only one who's bought me potato chips and chocolate milk."

He sighed as if admitting that wasn't an especially good thing for him to do, and he sank down on the sofa. Wyatt frowned, though, when his attention landed on the side table.

"What the heck is this?" he asked, picking up a bumpy blob of multicolored glass. It looked like an octopus that had imploded.

"That's the piece you made in the workshop," she informed him. "It fell a little flat, probably because we got distracted."

And that yanked her back to a dark mood, just remembering there wouldn't be more times like that. Well, she supposed they could go there just to use the glassblowing as foreplay, but there were more comfortable spots for that.

Like here, for instance.

"Are you going to agree to that sex pact?" Nola asked, figuring that if it was a yes, both of their moods would soon improve.

Wyatt sighed, took hold of her hand and eased her down on the sofa beside him. Not for a scalding kiss, though. He merely snuggled her against him.

"I'll agree to the sex pact if you agree to marry me," he said.

Nola rolled her eyes. In theory, a marriage would be a sex pact, but it would in no way be the no-strings, no-commitment arrangement she wanted for him. She was still convinced that was the only way to minimize Wyatt having a future mountain-sized amount of regret. There'd still be some of that, of course, some that would pick at those painful memories of her pregnancy with Marley. But at least with a sex pact, Wyatt would feel as if he had the freedom to walk away.

No way could she spell that out to him.

It would rile him to hear that he could, or would, walk away. He wouldn't be able to do that, not easily, but it'd be a heck of a lot harder if she went through the whole "I do" deal with him.

He kissed the top of her head. "We could fool around like we did in the workshop."

She looked up at him. "You mean where you do all the work, I get all the pleasure and you have to take a cold shower."

"Yes, that," he confirmed with a straight face. "But you got one part of that wrong. You don't get all the pleasure. I get some, too, just by watching you."

That shouldn't have made her start to melt like hot candle wax, but it did. Or maybe she would have started melting had Wyatt not said anything. The man still made her heart dance even when he was on her sofa and not on the monkey bars.

"Maybe I like to watch, too," she said, leaning in to kiss him.

Nola felt herself melting some more. Felt the zing of heat slide through her. She was pretty sure the heat zinged through Wyatt, too, because he slipped his hand around the back of her neck and eased her closer. If what he wanted was sex with no actual full-blown sex, then that was what they'd have.

Or not.

The *or not* came when the sound of his phone ringing speared through the room. "Don't answer it," she insisted, keeping his mouth occupied.

Somehow, he kept up the kiss and managed to check his phone screen. Nola eased back from him when she felt him go stiff. And that wasn't stiff in a good way, either.

"It's the lab," he said.

Even though her mind had already gone fuzzy, that came through loud and clear. This was a call from the lab that was processing Griff's car. "They've been calling you with updates?" she asked.

Wyatt shook his head. "They said they wouldn't call until they had results."

Results. That was a tame word for something that could crush Wyatt. Lily, too. And hearing it wasn't something Wyatt could put off.

He answered it, and even though he didn't put it on speaker, Nola still heard the caller's voice. "Mr. Buchanan," a woman said. "I'm Amelia Sweeny. The techs have finished examining your brother's vehicle. I'll email you the full report, but I thought maybe you'd want to know what we found."

"I do," Wyatt assured her, though Nola could see him quickly trying to steel himself.

"I probably should have said you'd want to know what it was we didn't find," the woman amended. "There's no evidence of tampering, and we couldn't find any signs that the car had malfunctioned in any way. There was nothing wrong with the steering mechanism or the brakes that would have caused an accident. Even the tires had good tread on them, and judging from the impact points, we don't believe the vehicle was traveling at a high speed."

The woman didn't add something like she hoped that news helped. Because she knew it hadn't. Yes, it meant Carlene hadn't done something that had caused Griff to lose control and plow off that cliff. That was both the good and the bad news.

Because it also meant Griff had been the one to end his life.

CHAPTER TWENTY

SOMETIMES, ANSWERS SUCKED, and guilt was like those teenage hormones that had gotten Nola and him in trouble. Because guilt was the gift that kept on giving, too.

Wyatt hadn't been able to work off that guilt over not having saved his brother. Though he'd given it one hell of a try. Over the past twenty-four hours, he'd fixed fences, moved horses into a better grazing pasture and had helped deliver two fillies. What he hadn't done was any of the paperwork required to keep the ranch running, and he hadn't acted much like a good boss, what with snapping and snarling at anyone who'd dared to approach him.

Later, he'd have to make amends for that, but for now he just preferred not to talk about why he was in this shithole of a mood.

Wyatt was dripping with sweat as he rode Moonlight back toward the barn after finishing his latest round of chores in the pasture. This time, he'd gone out to pick up rocks that had surfaced after the night's rain. A necessary chore since the rocks could hurt equipment and anyone riding a horse who happened to step on one.

It was normally something he delegated to the newbies or to the young workers like Trey, but Wyatt had needed something mindless since there wasn't room in his head for anything else other than grief.

And worry.

Oh, yeah, it was there, too, yanking every chain inside him that could be yanked. He wanted to bust Alec's balls for the crap he'd done with buying Nola's glass. It had left her thinking she was a hack. Added to that, the douchebag still wasn't backing off on the custody fight, probably because he knew Marley wasn't going to rat him out to Heather and risk the woman having another of those breakdown episodes.

That made Wyatt want to bust this man's balls a dozen times because he wasn't doing any of this solely because he loved Marley. No, this was about hanging on to family money.

Since the thought of that and the heat were probably sky-rocketing his blood pressure and filling his gut with acid, Wyatt tried to ram it all aside as he reined in Moonlight. With his muscles yelling at him for lifting those rocks, he climbed out of the saddle. He also spotted movement in the barn and saw Trey.

The boy approached Wyatt as if he were a coiled rattler ready to strike. "Uh, you want me to give Moonlight a good brushing and some water?" Trey asked.

Wyatt didn't snap, snarl or strike. He nodded and added a grumbled "thanks" that he'd maybe said loud enough for the kid to hear. But he did appreciate the offer. Moonlight was probably as tired of his surliness as Wyatt himself was. Best to spare the horse from any more of it.

Since Wyatt didn't want to carry his sweat and stench into the house, he pulled off his shirt, turned on the hose and leaned over to let the cold water pour over his face and head. He had a long drink of it, too, but had moved back to the improvised shower when he heard Nola call out.

"'Be still my heart,'" she said, giving him a smile and an exaggerated pat on her chest. "And other parts of me," she added in a mutter as she got closer. Obviously, a dirty joke meant for his ears only, which was good, considering he had ranch hands milling around.

"Well, you did ask me to re-create what you'd seen Jonas do." He heard his tone, and he was apparently back to snapping. Why, he didn't know, because Nola sure as hell hadn't done anything to cause this.

"I'll bet I can improve your mood if I kiss you," she said, just slightly louder this time.

"I'm too sweaty and too riled for a kiss," he informed her.

"No such thing." She took the hose from him, had a drink and let the water spill down her chin and over her breasts.

Man, she could play dirty.

"Why is your mood so good?" he asked, because last he'd checked, her life was in the same hell-in-a-handbasket stage as his.

"Because Marley called. She's hanging out with Hayden today, but she'll be back in about two hours and wanted to know if the three of us can have lunch. Together," Nola emphasized.

Well, that was a bright spot in an otherwise dark mess, and he was glad for Nola's sake that it'd happened. It was another step in building... Well, he didn't know what the hell they were building with Marley, but it felt right. One less thing on his guilt platter if Marley no longer blamed Nola for the adoption.

"Come on," she said, turning off the hose and hooking her arm around his waist. "Let's take a peek in your fridge and see if there's enough in there to fix a meal or if we'll have to order some takeout from the diner."

"There's plenty," he assured her.

That was mainly because of Marley's daily trips to the grocery store. At first, she'd done that to stock items she needed to eat to keep her blood sugar stable, but lately Wyatt had been finding plenty of his favorite deli meats and cheeses. So many of them, in fact, that he'd set up an account for Marley to use at the grocer's so she wouldn't be spending her own money on food—for either him or herself.

Nola kept her arm around him as they walked up the back porch and into the house, where he immediately wanted to set up a trust fund for the person who'd created air-conditioning. Even with his wet head and chest, it felt damn good.

Nola went to the fridge and poked through the contents. "There's a large spinach salad and this fresh salmon that we can throw on your stove grill."

Though he would have preferred a steak or those deli meats for sandwiches, Wyatt could go with the fish option, and there was indeed a fancy grill insert on his stove that he hadn't used nearly enough. It would save him from having to go back out into the heat to fire up the barbecue pit.

She pulled out her phone, and he realized she had googled cooking instructions for salmon. "It says three to five minutes on each side." Nola smiled and slid her phone into her back pocket, a maneuver that caused her wet shirt to tighten against her breasts. "Oh, what will we think of to do for the next one hour and forty-five minutes before Marley gets back?"

He went rock-hard. And then Wyatt cursed his reaction. He had no willpower and was clearly crazy-assed stupid when it came to Nola.

"Hey, maybe we can re-create the hose scene again," she said, opening the top button of her shirt. "You know, like maybe in the shower with the water sliding all over us." She opened another button, pushed aside the fabric and gave him a very tantalizing glimpse of the top of her right breast. "And to save water, we could even shower together."

"My shower's not that big," he lied.

"Even better," she purred. "Less space means we'll be sliding all over each other. Bumping around in there, touching each other—"

Wyatt made it across the room to her before she could finish that, and he hauled her into his arms. To hell with lack of willpower and hanging back so as to not blur any more lines. He wanted Nola, and he wanted her now.

She let out a delighted squeal that he caught with his mouth when he kissed her. And just like that, the playfulness was gone, and his pulse started to throb with that need she always fueled inside him. No way, though, did he want that need to play out on the kitchen floor in case Marley came back earlier, so Wyatt scooped Nola up. He didn't stop kissing her, and she hooked her legs around his waist as he headed for the bedroom.

And the shower.

It was big all right, fifteen feet square and with glass on all sides. The glass on the exterior, though, was a special reflective type that allowed no one to see in but it had an amazing view of the pastures. When he'd designed it, Wyatt had imagined standing there with the dozen sprays and jets on him while he looked out at what he'd built, what he loved.

"Wow," she said, lifting her head to look around. "It's like walking into one of my glass pieces."

It was, and he hoped that didn't remind her of what Alec had done to her. Apparently not, though, because she went after his mouth again. The kiss was Nola at her best. Needy, deep, and the greedy assault lasted until they finally had to break for air.

"You'd better not just give me a hand job this time," she managed to say. She sucked in a long breath and dived back in for more kisses.

Thankfully, the shower was automatic, so all Wyatt had

to do was hit a single button to get all the shower heads and jets turned on at just the right temperature. He added the steam function, not because Nola and he needed to generate more heat but because he thought it would be like taking her in a cloud. Of course, it was probably overkill, because she slid her hand down his bare chest.

And into his jeans.

With just that touch—or rather, the grip she put on his erection—he forgot all about clouds and such. This was going to happen, and he didn't want a hand job, either. She made a whimper of protest, probably because he'd stopped the sweet torture of her hands in his jeans, but he figured soon she'd be making an entirely different sound.

To ensure she didn't get him off with her hand, or that their phones didn't get ruined, he took them out of their pockets—which involved him groping Nola's butt— and he tossed them onto the vanity.

"Better strip off out here," he said. "I've got extra clothes, but you don't, and they'd be soaked for lunch with Marley."

"Good idea," she agreed in that purr again. "Why don't you strip me?" She issued it like a challenge.

Challenge accepted, and Wyatt got started, moving her top and bra. And he'd been right about the sound she made. It was a long moan of pleasure when he tongue-kissed every inch of her skin that he bared.

Starting with her breasts.

As always, they were perfect and apparently still a hot spot for her, because when he took her nipple into his mouth, she pulled his hair and called him a dirty name. He hadn't needed the dirty name to fire him up even more, but it was a nice bonus.

So was the taste of her stomach as he shimmied off her

panties and jeans. So was the sweet heat he found between her legs.

The steam rose up around them while the water hit them from every angle, and Wyatt might have lingered there, might have gotten lost in the moment, if she hadn't yanked his hair harder.

"No tongue job, either," she insisted.

Nola dragged him back up and went after his clothes. He could have called her a copycat, if she hadn't robbed him of speech, that was, by playing the *let's tongue-kiss what I uncover* game. She started with his chest. Then, after some torturing long moments, she managed to get off his shirt and get her mouth on his stomach.

Things went down from there.

Literally.

Not with his dick—that sucker stayed hard and ready—but Nola got off his jeans and boxers. Clothes, boots and maybe some car keys went flying, but all of that faded to background when she took him into her mouth.

Oh, she was so good at this, and he always wondered if she'd honed the talent for blowing glass with all the blowing she'd done on him. If so, then he was glad to have contributed to that particular skill set.

Unfortunately, though, the problem with good, well, blowing, was that he didn't want things to climax this way. Nope. He was all in on this and didn't care squat if he was later going to regret it. Boundaries be damned.

Scooping her up, he stepped into the streams and sprays of water, pinned her against the glass and pushed into her. And realized what he always did whenever he was inside Nola.

That nothing, nothing, had ever felt this good.

It was because of that *good* feeling that he wanted to hang on to this, wanted to make it last until they'd either pruned from the water or until it was time to fix lunch. But apparently, he'd honed his own skill set with Nola, because he only got a couple of minutes of that pleasure before he felt her muscles clamp on to his erection.

She looked at him. His warrior. His woman. And she came for him.

"Now, you," she muttered like a promise. She moved into him, letting the ripples from her climax finish him off.

NOLA DIDN'T WANT to move. Wasn't sure she could move, she mentally amended. Every muscle in her body had gone slack, her bones might have dissolved, and the only thing that prevented her from dropping butt first onto the shower floor was their still-intimate connection and Wyatt's body pressing against hers.

He didn't seem capable of moving, either. His breath was gusting, his heart pounding against hers. They were wet, warm and sated, and she was more relaxed than she had been... Well, she couldn't remember. A hand job from Wyatt was amazing, but full-blown shower and steam sex took *amazing* right out of the stratosphere.

"I really hope this glass is reflective like you said," she muttered. "If not, your ranch hands will be able to see my butt cheeks pressed against it."

Wyatt chuckled, kissed her. "They can't see in," he assured her.

He eased her to a standing position, kissed her and gave her one of those long, melting looks that made her want to have him all over again.

"Is this a good time for me to ask you again if you'll marry me?" he said.

Nola hadn't seen that coming, even though it certainly

wasn't the first time he'd proposed. She'd just thought the climaxes had been too great for him to think of anything else. Apparently not.

"Think of all the shower sex we could have if you married me and moved in here with me," he added.

So, his mind had still been on climaxes and such. Which was good. But there was something missing. Not with the finishes they'd just had against the shower glass. Something else wasn't there.

"You know what I haven't heard in any of these proposals?" she asked. Nola waited. Waited some more.

"I don't think you're talking about the ring," he finally said. "If so, it's on my dresser."

She scowled at him. "Not the ring. The *L* word, and don't you dare start naming off things like *lust* or *libido*."

He met her gaze head-on. "You're the love of my life. And an occasional pain in my ass," he added. "Always have been, and I'd like to think you always will be."

That was sweet, sort of, but it wasn't the same as Wyatt being in love with her. And it was something he'd never come out and said.

I love you, Nola.

Nope. Never said it. If he had, she would have definitely remembered. So, Nola tried to give this a jump start.

"I'm in love with you, Wyatt." And that seemed to prime the pump for her saying a whole lot more. "I've never loved anyone or anything more than you…and the baby we gave up. It nearly broke me to give her up, but it would break every part of me for good if I lost you."

Wyatt kept staring at her, but his mouth had dropped open a little. Probably because she'd never said anything like that to him.

Every word of it was the truth.

Her stomach braced when he started to speak, but whatever he'd been about to say was drowned out with the sound of her phone ringing. The bathroom must have had weird acoustics, because it sounded as if it were blaring.

"It could be Marley," Wyatt muttered.

That was one of the few things he could have said that would cause her to move so fast. She hurried out of the shower, coiling a big bath towel around her before she saw the name on the screen. Not Marley.

"It's Dr. Sanchez," Nola said.

Wyatt stepped out, too, and grabbed a towel, but his attention was focused on her face. On how she was handling contact from the doctor that Griff had seen shortly before his death. Nola had filled him in on that, but Wyatt had probably figured nothing would ever come of it.

And it might not.

Still, she braced herself when she answered and put the call on speaker. "Dr. Sanchez," she greeted him. "Thank you for getting back to me."

"Well, I debated if getting back to you was something I should do," he readily admitted, "but after thinking it over, I decided this is something Griff's family should know. I need the contact of his next of kin—"

"I'm right here." Wyatt spoke up. "I'm Wyatt, Griff's twin brother. He wasn't married and our folks are dead, so I'm his next of kin."

Maybe the doctor wanted to verify that, because he asked Wyatt his birth date, and when Wyatt told him, that was obviously Sanchez's green light to continue.

"Griff came to see me after a referral from his doctor in Last Ride. He was having some symptoms. Muscle twitches, some trouble swallowing. So, I ran a lot of tests and unfortunately discovered that your brother had the early stages of ALS, also known as Lou Gehrig's disease. His wasn't genetic," the doctor quickly added. "Some cases are, but not Griff's."

Nola tried to speak, and the only thing that came out was "Oh, God."

"Yes," Dr. Sanchez agreed. "I unfortunately had to tell Griff that his life expectancy was only about two to five years and that things wouldn't be easy for him, that he would likely soon be bedridden and would need a lot of care. I advised him to let his family know immediately so that plans could start being arranged for his future needs."

Nola took Wyatt's hand. It was stiff, and he was staring out. Stunned. It didn't matter that all of this had happened years ago. This brought on a fresh slam of grief.

"It was crushing news, of course," the doctor continued. "And Griff was still trying to absorb it when he left my office. I'd set up an appointment for Griff with a therapist, but Griff never showed. I now know that's because he was killed."

"Yes," Nola managed, and she asked one very hard question. "When exactly did Griff learn he had ALS?"

She heard the doctor drag in a long breath. "According to the information I found about his car wreck, he got the news several hours before he died."

Hours. Time enough for Griff to absorb the news. Or at least for him to see what the months ahead would hold for him.

"Thank you for this call, for telling us," Nola tacked on to that, and the moment she hit the end-call button for her conversation with the doctor, she caught on to Wyatt and pulled him to her.

"I'm so sorry," she said, not knowing if this news would help or make things worse.

Combined with the report from the lab and Lily's account of her last conversation with Griff, the odds were that he had indeed ended his own life. But not because he was upset about Lily's pregnancy. And not because Wyatt hadn't been there for someone to lean on. Maybe Griff just hadn't wanted to face going through all of that.

"I'm sorry," Nola repeated, and she knew there was nothing she could say or do to make this better for Wyatt. He was going to have to grieve his brother's death all over again.

Nola muttered some profanity when her phone rang again, and she was about to let it go to voice mail when she saw it was from Evangeline. Her mother was a counselor, after all, and while Wyatt might not want her help, Nola was going to ask for it.

She answered the call, but Evangeline spoke before she could get out a single word.

"It's Marley and Hayden," Evangeline blurted out. "They've been in a car accident out by the bluff where Griff died. Nola, you and Wyatt need to get to the hospital right now."

CHAPTER TWENTY-ONE

WYATT HAD TO tamp down a whole lot of worry, fear and adrenaline as he drove to the hospital. He figured Nola was doing the same while she also tried to get updates from her mother about what'd happened.

So far, she was striking out on that since the only thing Evangeline had been able to tell her was that Lily had called her in a panic with news of the car accident. Now Lily wasn't answering her phone. Neither was Hayden or Marley, and Wyatt figured that wasn't a good sign.

Hell.

He didn't want to think the worst, but thoughts of the worst came anyway. He'd already lost his brother on that bluff, and he couldn't stomach the thought of losing his daughter. Or Griff's daughter.

"Why the hell were Marley and Hayden anywhere near that bluff?" Wyatt asked, taking the turns way too fast and then fighting to keep the truck from going into the ditch.

"For the damn Last Ride Society research," Nola muttered. "Marley mentioned that Hayden wanted to get a picture since she's been gathering some info for the report. I guess Marley drove them out there."

Wyatt cursed again. That would have been an unfamiliar road for Marley, and it wasn't the easiest surface, what with the potholes, tight curves.

And the bluff.

He prayed the car hadn't gone over the bluff.

"I told Marley that I'd drive Hayden," Nola went on, "but I should have pushed on that. I should have insisted they not go there."

Wyatt heard the guilt in her voice. Felt it in the tightening of his chest. Because he should have issued a warning, too. He'd had a lot of practice trying to deal with his guilt over Griff, but this was so much worse. He couldn't lose Marley. He just couldn't.

Nola got out of the truck before Wyatt had even managed to bring it to a complete stop, and she ran toward the ER doors. He was right behind her and caught up with her before she hurried in.

Their frantic gazes slashed around the waiting room, and Wyatt spotted Evangeline, Lily and Jonas. Judging from the looks on their faces, the *so much worse* had happened.

"Nola, Wyatt," Evangeline said, rushing toward them. She gathered them into a hug. "We just got word that Hayden's injuries don't appear to be that serious. Just some cuts and bruises from the airbag deploying. Once they've done the X-rays, they're going to let Lily see her."

"What about Marley?" Nola asked, taking the question right out of Wyatt's mouth.

Evangeline kept her arms around them. "She's in surgery."

Oh, God. Wyatt didn't bother to try to choke down the groan of pain. "How bad?"

The woman shook her head. "I'm not sure. Because of privacy laws, they won't tell us, but they got permission for the surgery by phone from Heather. Alec and she are on the way. It shouldn't take them long to get here because they were already on the west side of San Antonio meeting with the arbitrator on their custody dispute."

Wyatt could see how that was going to play out. Terrified to the bone, they'd rush in and blame Nola and him for this. For not being able to keep their daughter safe. But Wyatt would take that blame and every crap threat and insult that came with it if Marley turned out to be okay.

"If Marley needs blood, I can donate some," he said, trying to focus on what he could do rather than all the other things that were now out of his control. "I seem to remember after she was born, they did her blood type, and it matched mine." That detail had stuck in his mind because it was one of the few things the medical staff had let slip about her.

Evangeline pressed her hand to his cheek a moment. "I'll let one of the nurses know that." She led them to where Jonas and Lily were standing before heading to the nurses' station. That was when Wyatt spotted Sheriff Matt Corbin, already talking to one of the nurses.

"What do you know about the wreck?" Wyatt asked, glancing at both Lily and Jonas.

Lily was as pale as notebook paper, and she tried to speak, but when the words didn't come, she reached for Nola and practically dissolved into her arms. Lily started to cry, and Wyatt didn't think Nola was too far behind with the tears. They were already pooling in her eyes.

Wyatt turned to his brother for answers. "Hayden is the one who called Lily. Lily said she was dazed and maybe in shock, so Lily called 911 to get an ambulance out to the site. I saw Lily running to her car, but I could tell she wasn't in any shape to drive, so I brought her here. I'm not sure what caused the wreck because Hayden was too upset to make much sense."

With each word he heard, Wyatt's stomach twisted even harder. "Were you here when the ambulance brought the girls in?"

Jonas shook his head. "No, but they hadn't been here long." He tipped his head to the sheriff. "Matt was, though. He's the one who's been getting us the few updates we've gotten."

Good. Wyatt trusted Matt and had known the man for years. If there was any info available, Matt would get it.

"The car didn't go over the bluff," Jonas added, looking Wyatt straight in the eyes. "This isn't like what happened to Griff."

Maybe not, but it many ways, it felt like it. The big difference was this had been an accident and not intentional. And that was a reminder for Wyatt that he was going to have to tell his brothers about Griff's ALS diagnosis. He wasn't sure it would help once they knew because he was still trying to sort it all out.

Sheriff Corbin moved away from the nurses' station and made a beeline toward them. "Wyatt, Nola," he said as a greeting. "Here's what I know. Neither girl is critical, and even though Marley's in surgery, her condition is stable." He shifted his attention to Lily. "In just a couple of minutes, you'll be able to go back with Hayden. She's fine but scared that she's in trouble because she didn't ask permission to go out to the bluff."

"I wouldn't have given permission," Lily muttered, but Wyatt could see the relief wash over her at hearing her daughter was okay.

Matt nodded. "I'll need to take her statement as to what happened," he went on, "but I was at the scene, and it looks as if Marley lost control of the car and slammed into one of those big piles of rocks. Not head-on. The car appears to have gone into a skid, and the impact was on the driver's side."

Nola's gasp was soft but plenty loud enough for Wyatt to hear, and he pulled her into his arms.

"Both airbags deployed," Matt went on, "but one of the EMTs said Marley had her purse in her lap and that the airbag might have jammed it into her midsection. I'm not sure if that's why she's in surgery…"

Matt's words trailed off when the ER doors opened, and Alec and Heather came rushing in. Heather's face was similar to Lily's and Nola's, and it was obvious the woman had already been crying. But Alec was, well, Alec. The anger was coming off him in waves.

"How the hell did you let this happen?" Alec demanded just as Heather blurted, "How's Marley? Where is she?"

Both Lily and Nola started to fill her in, but Alec didn't even seem to listen. He kept his icy glare on Wyatt, and Wyatt couldn't blame the man. He deserved some glares. And worse.

"How the hell did you let this happen?" Alec repeated. He cursed. "I knew it was a mistake for her to be here. You were irresponsible when you knocked up your teenage girlfriend, and you're still irresponsible. It's because of you that my daughter is here."

"Stop it," Heather demanded before Wyatt could even try to come up with a response. She moved between Alec and Wyatt, and she got right in her husband's face. "Maybe you're the reason it happened, what with all the stress you've been putting her through. Or maybe there was no reason at all other than it was an accident."

Alec opened his mouth, no doubt to return verbal fire, but Heather cut him off. "Just shut up and remember this. Our daughter is in surgery. Even if you had the right to blame Wyatt or Nola, which you don't, this isn't the time."

That didn't cool Alec's anger one bit, and he didn't shut up. "I'm calling my lawyer," he said, whipping out his phone.

Wyatt ignored him and turned to Heather. "The nurses might give you an update since you're Marley's next of kin."

Heather looked at the nurses' station and took hold of both Nola's and Wyatt's arms. She motioned with her head for Evangeline to follow as well. "You're all next of kin, too. Come with me."

That put some fresh tears in Nola's eyes, but Wyatt was sure these were of gratitude. They started toward the nurses' station but hadn't gotten far when a nurse came walking out into the waiting area.

"You can see Hayden now, but she's fine," he heard the nurse tell Lily. "Nothing's broken, but she's just getting a couple of stitches and an ice pack on her elbow."

Lily practically ran to get to her daughter, and Wyatt prayed they'd soon be able to see Marley as well.

"Marley's still in surgery," the nurse on duty, Esther Watkins, explained after Heather showed her ID. "But the doctor will be out as soon as possible to give you an update."

"What are her injuries?" Heather pressed.

He could see the debate Esther had about that since it was probably protocol for info like that to come from the doctor. But she must have seen the stark worry on their faces because she leaned in.

"They did X-rays," Esther explained in a whisper. "We only have one machine, so they did Marley's first because her injuries seemed a little worse than Hayden's. That's why Hayden had to wait and why Lily had to wait, too. Visitors aren't allowed in the radiology area. Anyway, Marley has a cracked rib and has some bruising on her chest and stomach."

"Internal injuries?" Wyatt managed to ask, and the worst-case scenarios were flying through his head. If necessary, he'd offer up a kidney or any other of his organs to save her.

Esther shook her head. "Just the cracked rib. She's in surgery because of her broken arm. A compound fracture."

Because of all those worst-case scenarios that had taken root, Wyatt didn't immediately process that. *Compound fracture*. That meant it was a bad break that had torn through the skin.

"Don't worry," Esther added. "Dr. Milbrath is doing the surgery, and he's good. He's the one who fixed your brother's arm that time he was here for the town festival, and he broke his arm riding that mean bull."

Yes, Wyatt recalled that, and Dax had needed surgery. And he also recalled Dax had been in a lot of pain. So, while this wasn't an injury requiring any of his organs, it would take Marley a while to recover.

"Just try to relax if you can," Esther went on when her gaze flickered over to Alec, who was now pacing and snarling into his phone. Wyatt couldn't and didn't want to hear what the man was saying. "Marley and Hayden should be fine."

Wyatt did breathe a little easier, but he wanted to see Marley for himself. Of course, that might not happen, because even though Heather had included Nola and him in the next-of-kin conversation, Alec sure as hell wouldn't, and the man might have a bigger say in this than Wyatt wanted.

Wyatt could make a stink about that and demand to see her. That might work. But Marley, Nola and Heather didn't need the added stress of that. Marley might be Nola's and his daughter, but in the eyes of the law, she still fell firmly into the DNA-only category.

When they stepped away from the nurses' station, Alec was still on his phone. So was Jonas, who was talking to his stepson, obviously filling him in on what was happening. Eli was thirteen and old enough to be left alone, but if the surgery dragged on, Wyatt would try to talk his brother into going home. Also, if Hayden was released and they needed a ride home, Evangeline would probably insist on driving.

"Well, I guess we should try to relax," Heather muttered, not sounding at all convinced that was possible.

It wasn't. No way could Wyatt turn off the worry tap just because of what the nurse had told them. True, it wasn't the worst of news, but it sure as heck wasn't the best, either.

"I'm glad she could get the surgery done right away," Heather went on. "I'm thankful, too, all of you are here." She cast a wary eye at her husband. "I'm not sure what Alec will try to do with this, but if I look as if I'm about to punch him, please stop me. I'll do the same for any of you."

Evangeline mustered up a smile and hugged Heather. Wyatt and Nola certainly didn't smile, and Wyatt doubted anyone would be able to hold him back if Alec played the dick card. Then again, plenty of the man's anger was justified.

"I should have talked to Marley about going out to that bluff," Wyatt said. "I should have warned her."

"You didn't even know she was going," Nola argued. "I'm the one at fault here. I knew Hayden wanted someone to take her out there to get pictures. If I'd offered to do that sooner, she wouldn't have asked Marley."

"I'm at fault, too," Evangeline admitted. "Hayden talked to me about getting those pictures, and I didn't discourage her. In fact, I just went on praising how good she's gotten at photography."

"All of you need to stop this," Heather insisted. "We're all worried sick, but Marley will be out of surgery soon. She'll be fine. I refuse to believe otherwise." She took a deep breath and turned to Wyatt. "Marley told me you'd let her give names to some of the horses."

Small talk. He didn't want it, but he couldn't bite Heather's head off for trying not to dwell on what was going on in surgery. So Wyatt nodded. "Usually I just go with whatever name the ranch hands end up calling them, but Marley came up with some better ones."

"Yes, she's especially fond of one she calls Buttercup."

"Buttercup's fond of Marley," he said but didn't mention to Heather that he'd planned on giving Marley the sweet-natured mare as a belated birthday gift.

Heather eked out a smile as well and turned to Nola as if she'd just remembered something she had to tell her. "I was going to call you today to let you know I found where Alec had been keeping your glass pieces. It's a storage facility that he rented in my name."

"Oh," Nola replied with seemingly no interest whatsoever in that. She kept her focus on the hall where she no doubt hoped the doctor would soon appear with news about Marley.

"I also learned Alec used money from one of my investment funds to buy the pieces," Heather went on, shooting a scowl across the room to her husband. "Since he did that without my knowledge or permission, my lawyer says the pieces are mine. There are nearly two hundred of them, so I obviously can't keep them all, but I would like a couple of the pieces. I can return the rest to you."

Nola waved that off, shook her head. "No, keep what you want and trash the rest."

Heather looked horrified. Evangeline gasped. "I will not trash art," Heather assured her. "If you don't want them, I'll contact the Waterstone Gallery and offer them the pieces. They can sell them again, and you can do whatever you want with the money. A charity foundation or maybe the start of trust funds for Marley and your baby."

Wyatt could see Nola dismissing everything Heather said. Until the woman had added that last part, that was. Marley no doubt already had a trust fund or two from Heather's rich family, but she'd likely known Nola might want to do something for Marley's future. For this new baby, too.

"Thank you," Nola said. She opened her mouth to say more, but Dr. Milbrath came walking toward them.

"Marley came through surgery just fine," he immediately said. "I anticipate a full recovery."

The relief came, a hard jolt that was nearly as much of a punch as the fear and adrenaline. The worst-case scenarios faded, replaced by the *just fine* and *full recovery.* Apparently, Heather, Nola and Evangeline were feeling some relief of their own, because they grabbed each other in a group hug. Wyatt got pulled into that, too.

"Marley will probably need some physical therapy," the doctor continued. "But we can get into that later. For now, Marley's awake and wants to see you." He aimed that invitation at Heather. Then he looked over at Alec. "And you."

That had Alec issuing a terse "I'll have to call you back" to the person on the other end of the phone line, and the man shot Nola and Wyatt another glare before he followed Heather and the doctor toward the recovery room.

Wyatt refused to let it sting that Marley had wanted to see Heather and Alec but not Nola and him. Of course, Marley would want that because the Silvas were her parents, and the month she'd spent in Last Ride was a drop in the bucket compared to the seventeen years she'd had with them.

Because he knew Nola was having the same thoughts as he was, Wyatt pulled her into his arms. "It'll be okay," Nola murmured, and it sounded as if she was trying to convince herself of that.

They stood there several moments, just holding each

other. Just giving each other what they could, something Nola and he had done so many times. Past, present and hopefully the future, he had always had Nola, and once again they could grieve the loss of a child they'd had to lose seventeen years ago.

The sound of footsteps had Wyatt and her looking up, and they spotted Lily coming out of the exam room with Hayden. The girl had plenty of nicks on her face, but she was walking on her own. Well, Lily did have her arm snuggled around her daughter, though that didn't seem to be because she physically needed it.

"I'm sorry," Hayden said, wiping away tears. "I shouldn't have asked Marley to drive me out to the bluff. Is she okay?"

"She's fine," Nola assured her and gave her niece a gentle hug. "Her arm is broken, but the doctor said everything is okay."

Nola had obviously left out the part about Marley maybe needing physical therapy. Wyatt was glad of that because it appeared if Hayden got any more bad news, she was going to crumble.

Sheriff Corbin, who'd been hanging back, came closer now. "If you're feeling up to it, I'll come out to the ranch tomorrow to take your statement. It's routine," he quickly assured Lily and Hayden. "No big deal at all. I'll just ask you how the accident happened so I can write it down for the report. Marley's insurance company will likely need it before they'll pay out for car repairs."

Hayden nodded and seemed to relax a little. "There's not much to tell," she said. "Marley was coming around that curve at the top of the bluff, and she hit a pothole. The car kinda bounced and started going toward the bluff. She jerked the steering wheel toward the rocks, and the car hit them."

So, Marley had stopped them from going the other direction—which would have been off the bluff. She'd saved both Hayden and herself.

Hayden's account of the accident caused Lily to go pale again. Wyatt was right there with her. They'd come damn close to losing both their children.

The sheriff sighed. "I've been trying to get the county to repair that road, but this should get them moving faster on that. We need better barriers out there, too. Metal ones instead of the old wooden planks that don't get replaced nearly often enough."

"I can work on pushing that," Evangeline volunteered. "If the county won't pay for it, the Last Ride Society has some funds we can tap into."

Wyatt figured a lot of people, including him, would breathe easier knowing that road was safer. It didn't get a ton of traffic, but a lot of teenagers did go out there since it was one of the town's make-out spots.

"We'll talk later," Lily said to her mother and Nola, and she gave them both kisses on the cheeks before Jonas and she helped Hayden toward the exit doors.

"Jonas will make sure they're okay," Wyatt reminded her. That might relieve some of the stress Nola was feeling right now.

There were more footsteps, this time from the hall, and Wyatt saw Heather and Alec walking toward them. Well, Heather was doing that, anyway, but Alec was on his phone and gave them a wide berth.

And a smirky smile.

A smile that nearly knocked the breath right out of Wyatt. Because he didn't think that was merely relief he saw on the man's face.

Heather came closer. "Marley wants to see both of you,"

she said. "She's a little drowsy still but awake. She's, uh, going to be okay."

That gave Wyatt no reassurance whatsoever. Not because he believed Marley's medical condition was worse than the doctor had said but because of Heather's hesitation and Alec's smirk.

Wyatt didn't ask Heather to explain either of those things. Nola and he just got down the hall fast, following the sign to the recovery room. Since the hospital was small, it wasn't hard to find, and there was a nurse outside the door waiting to usher them in.

"Keep the visit short," the nurse instructed.

Wyatt dragged in a long breath, which he was certain he'd need, and they went in. He got another gut punch when he saw the nicks and bruising on Marley's face. Her arm was bandaged and being held in some kind of stabilizer, and her eyes were slightly unfocused. Still, she managed a thin smile. A smile that didn't last, though.

"I wanted to be the one to tell you that once I'm released from the hospital, I'll be going back to San Antonio," she said.

Wyatt tried not to react to that, but inside there was a whole lot of reaction. Hell. This was ripping at his heart, though he should have expected it. She was hurt and wanted to be home. Except which home?

"You'll be going back with your mom?" Nola asked.

Marley paused. A long time. And Wyatt got another of those *oh, hell no* punches. "With my father. For now," she amended. "But he's agreed to work out a reasonable custody arrangement with my mom."

Wyatt's jaw went so tight that it was hard to speak. "What brought this on?" And he tried to steel himself to hear a truth he might not want to hear.

A truth that the accident had caused her to see that it'd been a huge mistake for her to come to Last Ride and spend time with them.

Marley made eye contact with both Nola and him. "My father will back off if I live with him," she finally said. "He'll stop trying to make things hard for my mom and both of you."

Nola was shaking her head before Marley even finished. "You don't have to do this. Wyatt and I can deal with anything your father throws at us."

Marley nodded. "I believe you. You're both strong people." She sighed. "But my mother isn't."

"Heather didn't ask you to do this," Wyatt said. No way. Heather might have had that breakdown in the past, but she was steady as a rock when it came to Marley.

"No, she didn't," Marley quickly assured him. "She's against it, but I've made up my mind." She shifted her attention to Nola. "But I would like one thing before I go. The glass bird you made for me. If you're still willing to give it to me, that is."

"It's yours," Nola said around what had to be a lump in her throat. Wyatt sure had a lump in his.

"No hurry about bringing it by," Marley went on. "The doctor said the anesthesia would make me sleep most of the day." Since she yawned and her eyes looked ready to close, Wyatt knew that wasn't lip service, so they'd give her some space. "I should be discharged in a couple of days, so anytime before then is fine. If you can't make it back here for some reason, please mail it to me."

"I'll make it back here," Nola assured her. She opened her mouth, closed it and seemed to have a debate as to what to say. She finally sighed. "We can figure out a way to deal with your father—"

"No," Marley interrupted. "I know what I have to do, and what I have to do is leave Last Ride so that all of us can get back to normal."

Normal.

That wasn't a word that usually caused Wyatt's heart to feel as if it were being crushed, but that was exactly what it did now. Because normal meant Nola and he wouldn't have Marley in their lives.

Their daughter was saying goodbye.

CHAPTER TWENTY-TWO

NOLA DIDN'T CRY as she hauled out the box of glass birds from beneath her desk. Probably because she had no tears left thanks to nonstop sobbing that'd started the moment she'd left Marley in recovery and had continued throughout the rest of the day, night and into the following morning.

Wyatt had held her all that time, and while he hadn't actually broken down, she knew this was crushing him. Crushing even more than it had seventeen years ago. Because they hadn't known Marley then. They hadn't had these precious weeks with her in Last Ride with them.

Nola had spent the night in Wyatt's bed. In his arms. She'd even gone through the motions of eating the breakfast he'd cooked for her. Well, cooked in the sense that he'd toasted her a bagel, cut up an apple and poured her a glass of milk. She'd eaten it not because she was hungry but because she hadn't wanted to add to his crushing by having to worry about her. Besides, she needed food. She couldn't just let Marley's goodbye gnaw away at her and risk harming the baby she was carrying.

After the breakfast, Wyatt had gone out to the stables to check on some mares, and that was when Nola had left. Since her car was still at Wyatt's from the day before, when they'd had shower sex, she hadn't needed to ask him for a ride or call Lily. Hayden was fine—Nola had made several calls to check on her—but she hadn't wanted Lily to have to leave her. So, Nola had written Wyatt a note.

Well, four of them, actually.

She'd scribbled out so many words on the first three that they were messy scrawls. So, she'd kept the fourth one simple. "I'm getting the glass birds from the workshop. Be back soon and then we can take them to Marley."

Of course, he'd still be riled that she had decided to make this trip without him, but this wasn't just about the birds. This was a sort of farewell to her workshop. It was probably a good thing she had no more tears left or that would have sent her into a paralyzing sob.

Cradling the bird box, she stepped out into the main area of the workshop and glanced around. Everything was cool and still now. Quiet. And she spotted the spiderweb that was already on one of the beams of the high exposed ceiling. The heat and activity usually kept the critters away, but apparently it sensed there'd be some quiet time in here.

Mercy, she was going to miss this.

But missing the glass was better than feeling the emptiness that would almost certainly be there if she picked up the pipe.

Nola didn't prolong the torture. She took out her phone to pull up the security app as she headed to the door, but it opened before she even reached it.

"Wyatt," she muttered, expecting him to ignore her instructions on the note. But it wasn't Wyatt who came in.

It was Simon Waterstone from the gallery in San Antonio.

The man looked positively giddy, and he hurried to her. "I'm so glad I caught you here because I wasn't sure how to get to your house." He took the box of birds from her, made a sound of approval and set the box on the floor so he could take hold of her shoulders. The giddiness had soared by leaps and bounds. "Thank you, thank you, thank you."

"For what? For what? For what?" She knew she sounded glib and didn't care. Right now, she just wanted to pick up the birds and get the heck out of there.

"For all the money we're making. Well, I understand from Heather Silva, aka Dodo, that your profits will be going into a foundation. I'll be donating part of my twenty percent commission to that, too, but that leaves so very much left over. So very, very much," he emphasized.

Nola gave him a flat look. "What are you talking about?"

"Oh, I just assumed Heather had told you. We've worked it all out." He was speaking a mile a minute, and Nola was having trouble catching all the words. "Heather's arranged to have your glass art pieces packed up and brought back to the gallery. They'll be there later today." He stopped and clapped his hands. The man looked ready to burst. "Nola, I already have buyers for every single piece."

She rolled her eyes. "Let me guess. My mother or Wyatt Buchanan bought them."

Now Simon was the one to give a flat look. "No. Though they're certainly welcome to place an offer. That's how I decided to sell them. I already had pictures of all the pieces, and as soon as I got pictures posted on the web page, I put out the word that I'd have dozens of your pieces available. And the offers started pouring in. You know that one you called *Motion in the Shades of Blue*, well, the last bid I got on it was for twenty thousand."

No eye roll this time, but she considered sniffing Simon's breath to see if he was drunk. But he wasn't. He was sober, giddy and having bursts of clapping his hands.

"Twenty thousand?" she questioned. "Dollars?" she clarified, wondering if it was some currency that would translate to enough to buy a cup of coffee.

"Dollars," he confirmed. He took hold of her shoulders again. "Buyers are hungry for your work, and they actually get a chance to, well, buy, now that Dodo isn't scooping them all up. I can see now I was wrong to let that happen. I could have been making you a lot more money if I'd just put the pieces on display and let the bidding wars start."

His phone dinged and he gave a delighted squeal when he saw the text. "The bid on *Motion* is now twenty-five thousand."

Nola tried to figure out if Simon was duping her. Or if Wyatt or her mother had put him up to duping her, but Simon lifted his phone to show her the offer.

And the dozens of offers on pieces before that.

Not one buyer/bidder. But dozens of them, maybe hundreds.

"They want the pieces," she muttered.

Simon stared at her as if she'd stated the most obvious of statements. "Yes." He let go of her and fanned his hand over the pieces on the shelf. Then at the birds in the box. "How could you not see how good all of this is?"

Nola felt as if she had a moment of reckoning. One interrupted when Simon got another text and squealed. "Twenty-seven-thousand bid for *Motion*."

She thought of that piece. Thought of others that she had thought were equally good or better, and she, too, looked down at the birds.

And Nola saw it then.

Just as Wyatt came rushing in. "You left me a note," he snarled. "I wanted to come here with you…" He trailed off when he saw Simon.

"Simon Waterstone," the gallery owner greeted him, grinning like a loon and giggling with every text ding.

"Wyatt Buchanan," he said, but it wasn't a greeting. He was still snarling.

Simon, however, didn't seem to notice the sharp tone. "I was just telling Nola how much money she's making."

Wyatt looked at her, obviously waiting for an explanation.

"Heather gave the pieces back to the gallery, and they're selling," Nola supplied.

"Like hotcakes," Simon gushed. "Better than hotcakes," he amended. "Multiple buyers, multiple offers. Dollar signs everywhere." He gave her an enthusiastic hug. "I have to get back to the gallery." He glanced at Wyatt. "Tell her to get back to creating all this wonderful art. Buyers are waiting."

Simon hurried out, taking all that nervous chatter with him. Leaving Wyatt and her in the still hush that fell over the workshop. Wyatt seemed to be processing everything Simon had just prattled on about.

And he didn't seem to be surprised.

"Well, have you accepted that you're a gifted, talented artist?" he asked. He didn't snarl, but there was definitely a challenge in his voice. He was clearly ready to argue with her if she said no.

But Nola didn't say no.

"Yes," she simply agreed.

He blinked. Then smiled. "Good. Because there's no way I want you to give any of this up."

"No way I want to give it up," she assured him, and she went to him to kiss him. It was long, deep, satisfying, and it added a whole new meaning to *sealed with a kiss*. It certainly felt as if she'd sealed some kind of deal here.

With Wyatt.

And herself.

She might have gone for a second kiss, just for the pure pleasure of it this time, but she saw Wyatt glance down at the box of birds that was ready to be taken to Marley.

"You'll go with me to the hospital," she said. Not a question. Wyatt would be there, just as he always was. "Let's get this done in case my body decides it can make more tears."

Because she was definitely on the verge of crying again. A mix of both happy and very, very sad.

She had regained her art. But not her daughter.

Wyatt didn't hug or kiss her. Maybe because he knew just how close she was to the edge. However, he did continue to study her while he lifted the box, and they started to his truck. Twenty minutes ago, she might not have even bothered to lock up, since she hadn't been sure she would ever want to see the workshop again. But feeling at peace with her art, she hit the lock app, knowing that she'd be back soon.

Maybe today, even.

After all, she was no doubt going to need help fighting off the lows after this visit with Marley. It would be a good time for her to make something dark. Smears of storm gray and smoky blue with a tiny ember somewhere in the mix. An ember to represent the baby she was carrying. The hope and reminder that Wyatt and she would get through this. Somehow.

Somehow.

And maybe if she repeated it enough, it might come true.

Nola was thankful that she didn't see Alec's Porsche in the hospital parking lot. Heather's car was there, though. And Evangeline's. Wyatt and she made their way through the hospital and spotted the women in the hall outside Marley's room. They both looked up, not with weariness and tears but rather... She couldn't tell exactly what, and then she got it when her mother spoke.

"Heather told me about all your glass pieces," Evangeline said with a giddiness that would give Simon a run for his money. "How wonderful."

"I don't want you buying any of it," Nola warned her.

"Oh, I can't afford it." Her mother chuckled. "But I'm really hoping you make me a vase like this." She lifted her phone screen, and Nola realized they'd been looking at the pictures of the pieces Simon had posted on the gallery's site.

Nola remembered—for the most part, anyway—how she'd made that daisy abstract piece, and she'd re-create it as best she could. For a lot less than the latest bid, too. Nola goggled a bit when she saw the price for it was nearly twelve grand. Good grief.

"How's Marley?" Nola asked.

"Great," Heather answered. "The nurse is in there with her right now, helping her take a shower, so Evangeline and I decided to step out and have a little chat. About Marley. The art. And the foundation I'm setting up with the proceeds from the gallery sales."

Nola was really only interested in one of those topics. Marley. But Heather didn't go there.

"Evangeline and I were just talking about how to use the money," Heather went on. She looked at Wyatt. "What do you think about having that bluff road and area redone? Maybe buying it and turning it into a park. It has amazing views, and we could even use some of the funds to make the bluff road safer for visitors."

"And we could maybe call it the Griff Buchanan Memorial Park," Evangeline quickly added. "What do you think?"

Nola thought Wyatt was stunned, that was what, but he

managed a nod. He had to blow out a breath, though, before he could add words to that nod. "I think that's a great idea."

So did Nola. Score one for her mom and Heather for coming up with the perfect way to pay a tribute to Griff. It would also be something uplifting to add to the end of her Last Ride Society research report. Maybe, just maybe, this would give Wyatt and his brothers some peace.

Well, peace about Griff, anyway.

The nurse came out and glanced at them. "She's showered and dressed, so y'all can go back in now."

Nola knew this pleasant interlude was up, and that Wyatt and she were about to pay the piper, so to speak.

"Marley wanted us to bring by the glass birds," Nola told Heather after the nurse had walked away.

Heather smiled just a little when she looked in the box. "Oh, she's going to love them. Go ahead and take them in. I know Marley's anxious to talk to both of you, and Evangeline and I will be in soon."

Heather was giving them time to say goodbye, and Nola muttered a heartfelt "thank you" before Wyatt and she went in.

Wow, what a difference a day could make. Marley was no longer drowsy, and she even conjured up a smile for them.

"I'm glad you came by," she said.

Nola nodded, and they went closer so Wyatt could set the box on the bed.

"Thank you." Marley ran her fingers over the ones on top and plucked out the first one Nola had made. The one she'd refused to take when Nola had offered it, but she didn't refuse now. Smiling, she held it up to the light. "I'll put this on my desk in my bedroom. There's a big window next to it, and I can watch the sunlight play with it. I'll find just the right place for the others."

Not trusting her voice, Nola made a sound of approval. A genuine one. She liked the idea of knowing that Marley would be so close to the glass that Nola had created for the baby who'd never truly been hers.

Marley was still smiling, still holding the bird in her un-injured hand, when she looked back up at them. "You don't look as if you had a good night," she muttered in a *welcome to the club* kind of way.

"No," Nola and Wyatt admitted in unison.

"How was your night?" he asked. "Are you in pain?"

"The meds kept the pain under control, and I can already tell it's getting better." She paused. "But my night was lousy. Not my morning, though. That got a whole lot better."

"Because you heard about the glass pieces selling?" Nola suggested.

Marley started shaking her head, stopped. "Oh, I'm happy about that. My mother made things right. But we made some other things right, too." She paused, gathered her breath. "I'm still going back to San Antonio," she finally finished.

The sunlight did its magic and created some rainbows all around Marley. For just a moment, Nola watched the dance. Focused on it. She didn't want to cry in front of Marley.

"I'm still going back to San Antonio," Marley repeated, "but I'm not moving in with my father. I'm going home with my mother, and he won't be there."

From the corner of her eye, Nola saw Wyatt's head whip up, and she heard the huge breath of relief he took. "Good. Because Nola and I don't care what he tries to do to hurt our businesses—"

"He won't try that," Marley said with absolute confidence. "He dropped the custody suit."

Nola couldn't have been more shocked had Simon told her that the bid on *Motion* was up to a billion dollars.

"Why?" Wyatt asked.

Marley smiled just a little. "Well, it wasn't exactly his choice. He dropped the suit when Mom sent his lawyers proof that he'd been taking money from her account. I think it also helped when I told him if he didn't back off, I'd tell his and Mom's lawyers about his affair."

The relief washed over Nola. Short-lived, though. Because she saw in Marley's eyes what this had cost her, and she quickly, and gently, gathered Marley into her arms.

"I'm so sorry you had to do that," Nola muttered.

Marley shook her head, blinked back tears. "He's my dad, and I thought that meant I owed him…many things, but then I looked at the way you've been with me." She glanced at Nola, then Wyatt. "You haven't tried to bend me to your will. You haven't tried to use me to save face with your family. I think that maybe that's what good dads do. And moms."

Marley's gaze settled on Nola for several moments. Several teary-eyed, heart-filling moments.

"So, I'm going with the theory that I can have two dads," Marley added, switching her attention back to Wyatt. "One who will hopefully come to his senses and quit acting like an ass. And another who'd hurt himself before he would ever hurt me. FYI, I meant that second one for you."

"Yeah, got that. It's true," Wyatt said, leaning in to brush a kiss on the top of Marley's head. "You name it, and I'll do it. Walk through fire and all those other things that fathers do for their daughters."

Marley's smile was wider now. The sadness lifted from her face when she turned to Nola.

"I think I can use that theory with two mothers, too,"

Marley said. "Heather will always be my mom. Always. But she wouldn't have me if you hadn't had me first. Those nine months count for something. And so does the love you've shown me since I've been here. And, yes, I know you loved me despite the way I acted toward you."

Nola lost her battle with tears and one—all right, two— slid down her cheeks. She didn't care. She didn't care if she cried buckets because these weren't the tears of that dark, stormy glass she'd planned. These were daffodils, birds and rainbow prisms.

"I'd like to spend time here in Last Ride with both of you," Marley added. "Maybe time with the baby after you have it. The nice thing is I won't have to go through being torn about who the baby is and how he or she fits into my life. He or she will be my brother or sister."

And that was when Nola lost it. The tears came flooding. So did the hugs, though she was mindful of Marley's arm. Despite the injury, they somehow managed a group hug.

No, it was a family hug.

One that Evangeline and Heather got in on when they came into the room. It was obvious that Heather had known exactly what their daughter had been going to tell them. Obvious, too, that the woman approved.

Later, when her voice wouldn't crack and some of the tears had dried up, Nola would tell Heather just how thankful she was that she'd been the one to adopt Marley. That she'd been the best mother possible to her.

For now, though, Wyatt and Nola just kissed their shared daughter and asked her to call them, and visit soon, before they went into the hall. Even though it was far from private, what with nurses milling back and forth, Nola went ahead and let herself finish falling apart. But this was falling apart in a really good way.

Like freeing a piece of glass from the pipe after she'd gotten it exactly the way she wanted it.

How many times in life was that going to happen? Nola had thought the answer was—not very often—and then she looked up at Wyatt.

"I've broken you off the pipe too many times to count," Nola murmured. "And each time, you just come back better and better."

He stared at her. A long time. "Excuse me?"

"It's a glass metaphor." One that she didn't want to explain because she had something seriously important to tell him. "I'm in love with you, and I don't want to lose you."

Wyatt relaxed because that obviously made more sense than the metaphor. "You're not going to lose me, and I'll fix any breaks—past, present or future ones. Going with a glass metaphor, I can reheat any cracks or breaks and make them all right again. Might even make them better than the way they started out."

That was a darn good glass metaphor. And he kissed her as if to prove that, but she also considered he might have done so to skirt around saying the *L* word. Because, after all, his kisses made her senseless and this one topped the heap in that particular department. It was dreamy and hot and all Wyatt. He didn't pull back until she was breathless and stepping over the mere foreplay line.

"I'm in love with you, Nola," he said.

She smiled. Then laughed. So, no skirting after all. "I've waited nearly two decades to hear you say that. You're going to have to repeat it a lot."

He nipped her bottom lip. Kissed her again. Made her senseless and breathless again. "You're the love of my life," he told her.

"And sometimes the pain in your ass?" she questioned.

Wyatt nodded. "Wouldn't have it any other way. And that's why I want you to marry me."

This time, it required no thought whatsoever. "Yes. I'll marry you." She watched him grin, and then her vision went blurry when he kissed her again.

From up the hall, one of the nurses snarled something about them getting a room. They would—they'd get his bedroom, or hers—and that was why Nola slipped her arm around Wyatt and got them started toward the exit.

"You'll marry me soon?" he asked.

"Soon," she verified. "We'll set a date that works for Marley and Heather and then have the *I do*s done before I start showing."

He stopped just outside the hospital and looked down at her. "I might suck at being a husband. And a dad."

"Don't worry," Nola assured him. "I'll help with that." Now she kissed him, and she put everything she had into it. When she stopped to breathe, she had one last thing to get off her chest. "I might suck at being a wife and a mom."

Wyatt grinned. It was *that* grin. The one that told her she was so about to get very lucky. "Nola, you don't suck at anything," he drawled. "You blow."

From somewhere in the parking lot, someone called out for them to get a room, the voice blending with Nola's laugh. Again, they would soon get that room. Nola would strip Wyatt naked and have her way with him.

Multiple ways, actually.

And, yes, there might indeed be some blowing involved as they got started on the amazing future part of their past and present.

* * * * *

Now, turn the page for Second Chance at Silver Springs,
a bonus novella from USA TODAY *bestselling author
Delores Fossen!*

SECOND CHANCE
AT SILVER SPRINGS

CHAPTER ONE

ROSALIE PARKMAN FIGURED in most towns that it wasn't a common occurrence to see a bunch of people dressed like Sherlock Holmes squaring off with another group of Hogwarts wannabes. But this was Last Ride, Texas, where folks took their favorite books seriously.

Or rather, they took their book-club meetings seriously.

It appeared the two groups were about to have a smackdown over a scheduling screwup at the library where they held their monthly meetings, and they had taken their fight to the steps of the Last Ride Police Department. Rosalie put her money on the Hogwarts fans because they looked capable of kicking some butt.

She threaded her way through them, bumping into a couple of deerstalker hats and crooked wizard wands before making it to the center of the group, where her cousin, Deputy Azzie Parkman, was in the process of dispersing the arguing, accusations-flinging crowd. Rosalie mentally amended her prediction as to who would win this literary squabble.

Azzie would, no doubts about that.

Even though her cousin was in her early seventies, Azzie could have taken on both groups, along with a horde of vampires and zombies. In any postapocalyptic world, Rosalie would want Azzie on her side.

Rosalie finally managed to get inside the police department, where both her feet and her heart immediately skittered to a stumbling stop. So did her eyes as they landed on yet another deputy. Not a cousin this time. But the only man she'd ever told the three-word sentence, the one that started with *I*, ended with *you* and had the *L* word in the middle.

Gabriel McCloud.

Or rather, *Deputy* Gabriel McCloud, though he hadn't been a lawman back when she'd bared her soul to him. He'd been a star of the Last Ride High School football team and her boyfriend. She had muttered those three words to him while they'd been slow dancing at their high school graduation party. Not only had he not muttered them back, two days later he'd sent her a breakup letter and left Last Ride.

Now, fifteen years later, he was back, looking far better than she wanted him to look and apparently still capable of making her knees weak and her stomach flutter. Even her heart got in on the reaction. It was racing and jumping, reminding her of an overzealous puppy greeting its owner.

Gabriel was talking to someone on the phone, but he obviously spotted her from across the desk-cluttered open room where the town's dozen or so deputies worked. Though today all the desks were unoccupied except for his. Probably because it was lunchtime and Azzie was outside.

Their gazes collided, his deep brown eyes meeting her blue ones, and Rosalie cursed when she felt herself go warm in all the wrong places. Really? After all this time he could still do that to her as well?

Apparently so.

But Rosalie had no intention of rushing into his arms like that overzealous puppy to tell him how glad she was to see him. Did she?

No, she assured herself. She didn't.

"Rosalie," Gabriel said in that drawl that sounded like

foreplay—something they'd done plenty of back in the day. But never the actual deed. No, Gabriel hadn't even given her that pinnacle of memories, and Rosalie had never been able to figure out if that was good or bad.

Most times, like now, she leaned toward it being bad.

Yes, she had plenty of memories of Gabriel, specifically of them steaming up his truck windows during their make-out sessions, but he hadn't given her the ultimate memory of being her first lover. Nope. He'd skirted around that by giving her a couple of orgasms during their five months of dating. And then he'd sent her that goodbye letter and left Last Ride to join the military.

He hadn't asked her to go with him. Or wait for him. Or do anything else to secure a commitment that he clearly hadn't been ready to make. That was probably the reason he hadn't had sex with her when he'd had plenty of opportunities to do so.

"Gabriel," she greeted him back. She took a couple of deep breaths to steel herself up and hoped he hadn't noticed the effect he still had on her.

He'd noticed.

It was subtle, but she heard the almost silent sigh, and was that dread she saw in his eyes? Maybe. Perhaps he thought she'd come here to have it out with him on his first week on the job. She hadn't. In fact, Rosalie likely would have just tried to avoid him—not actually possible in such a small town—but she certainly wouldn't have shown up in the very place where he was sure to be unless she'd had to.

"I heard you'd moved back," she said, trying to keep her voice pleasant. Trying not to snarl over him having broken her heart.

He nodded. Just nodded. What he didn't do was get into an explanation for his return, but it wasn't possible to avoid hearing gossip here either, so Rosalie had gotten the gist of it. Gabriel had been an Air Force security policeman and had been injured. He'd spent a long time in a hospital in Germany before someone, maybe Gabriel himself, had decided that it was time for him to get out of the military. He'd then accepted the deputy job that his good pal Sheriff Matt Corbin had offered him.

Gabriel glanced out through the large window at Azzie, and he sighed again. "She didn't want help," he muttered.

"She doesn't need help," Rosalie assured him. "Trust me on that."

Gabriel didn't dispute it, and even though he was a newbie here in the Last Ride PD, he likely knew all about Azzie's supercop skill set. Of course, Gabriel probably fit into that supercop category himself, but unlike Azzie, he wasn't wearing a uniform. Like some of the other deputies, he'd gone with nice jeans and cowboy boots. He was also wearing a shirt that fit his still-amazing chest to a T.

Rosalie swallowed hard and shook her head to clear it. Getting on with business, which didn't include any more lustful thoughts about Gabriel, she peered past him and into the sheriff's office.

"The sheriff went home for lunch," Gabriel supplied, obviously following her gaze. "Something I can help you with?"

She nodded, cleared her throat. "I need to report a missing person."

Gabriel blinked, clearly not expecting her to say that. Then again, this was Last Ride, where the usual crimes were escaped longhorns, pranks by bored teenagers and book-club squabbles.

Rosalie could practically see Gabriel mentally working this out. Because he'd no doubt already heard gossip about her, too. He likely knew the gist of her broken engagement the year before from her cheating ex, Reggie Dalton, who was making outrageous gestures to win her back.

"The person's been missing a while," she went on, "so I guess it's probably not urgent or anything."

"Who's missing and just how long is *a while*?" Gabriel asked, sounding all cop now.

Rosalie decided to answer the second part of that first. "Just a guess but I'd say he's been missing for fourteen years, eleven months and fifteen days."

Gabriel did another of those blinking double takes. Judging from his dumbfounded expression, he didn't know what the heck was going on. *Welcome to the club.* Neither did she.

"Let me start from the beginning," she said, regrouping. "You might remember the Last Ride Society drawing." But when she got a blank/*what does this have to do with a missing person* look from him, Rosalie backed up even further with her explanation. "The founder of the town, Hezzie Parkman, set up the Last Ride Society so that future generations of Parkmans would research the tombstones in the local area. Every quarter, a Parkman heir's name is drawn, and the heir in turn draws the name of a tombstone to research." She paused. "I'm the heir this quarter, and I drew your great-uncle's name."

Hamish Clyde McCloud.

He'd been Gabriel's grandfather's brother, along with being a mean-as-a-snake failed rancher who had undoubtedly also failed to tell anyone "I love you," and that included his wife/Gabriel's great-aunt, Carmen. In fact, gossip had it that Carmen and Hamish had spent five decades of marital misery before Hamish had passed away at the age of seventy-two.

"In addition to needing to do a research report on your great-uncle, I'm required to take a photo of his tombstone," Rosalie went on, pulling her phone from her pocket. "I drove out to the cemetery and found this. I'm guessing the grave caved in from those bad storms we had a couple of nights ago."

She showed him the photo and wished she'd done a little more of a lead-in to this jaw-dropping news. Because the grave was nearly empty. No coffin, no trace of a coffin, nothing except a small metal box the size of a deck of cards.

"I wasn't at your great-uncle's funeral," she went on. Rosalie figured not many were. "But I'm pretty sure he wasn't cremated." Few people in Last Ride were because there was no crematorium, and that would mean sending the remains into San Antonio or some other city.

Making a sound of agreement about the noncremation, Gabriel took her phone, using his fingers to enlarge the photo, and she stepped to his side as he zoomed in on the box. Something she'd already done, but because of the dirt, it was impossible to tell what kind of box it was.

"Is it possible Hamish was buried elsewhere? Or for some reason the body was moved later?" she asked, knowing that was a long shot.

"No. I went to the funeral, and I saw the coffin being lowered into the ground. It was to be Hamish's final resting place," he verified. "I went to the service for Aunt Carmen's sake," he added. "She only had me and my folks."

Bingo. Rosalie had been right about so few people attending the service to say their last goodbyes to Hamish. Gabriel and she had still been together then, and the funeral had happened just a couple of weeks before graduation—and their breakup. But Gabriel had insisted she not go with him to the graveside service because she'd been studying for finals. Probably had insisted, too, because he'd already been trying to put some distance between them.

Gabriel glanced up when the door opened, and Azzie came in. She was still scowling and snarling at the last of the "protesters," but she issued a friendly nod when her attention landed on Rosalie.

"You're here about Hamish's grave?" Azzie asked. "Derwin got a call about it when I was out there trying to settle the squabble," she explained after Rosalie raised an eyebrow to question how she'd already learned that.

Rosalie checked the time. It was barely a half hour since she'd discovered the empty grave and taken the photo, and there'd been no one else at the cemetery then. Obviously, though, someone else had seen it and had blabbed about it to Derwin Parkman—another distant cousin—who'd then reported it to Azzie.

Blabbing about the grave to Derwin wasn't as far out in left field as it seemed, though, since he was the current president of Sherlock's Snoops, a group of people with too much time on their hands who fancied themselves as crime solvers. This wasn't a crime. Probably. But it was a mystery.

"If you and Rosalie want to go back out to the cemetery to have a look, I can hold down the office," Azzie suggested, and she slid a glance from Rosalie to Gabriel.

A glance accompanied by a sliver of a smile.

Crud. This was matchmaking. A weird attempt at that, considering the destination. But it gave Rosalie some insight into things to come. Plenty of folks would just assume that Gabriel and she would hook up again. And those plenty of folks would be wrong.

Probably.

Gabriel was a hot cowboy cop, but she was still dealing with Reggie's attempts at a reconciliation. There was no *probably* for that. A reconciliation wasn't going to happen. Ever. But talk about a rekindling between Gabriel and her would only cause Reggie to escalate his efforts. After threatening him with a restraining order, he'd quit his dozen-plus calls and texts a day, but she was still trying to get him to stop sending her flowers and candy.

"I can go alone," Gabriel told Rosalie. "No need for you to go back out there and see it."

"I need to see it," she insisted. "I was so shocked when I saw the grave that I forgot to take a picture of the headstone."

Gabriel made a suit-yourself sound, told Azzie he'd be right back, and he motioned for Rosalie to follow him out the back exit and to his truck. No way to miss his limp. Not super pronounced, but it was there and was a reminder of why he'd likely come back to Last Ride. He probably wouldn't have qualified for duty in the military or a big-city police force.

And that made her ache for him.

Not in a lustful way, but because she knew that being a cop had been his dream, and while that dream hadn't exactly been taken away from him, he'd had to settle for something less than he'd planned.

She got into the passenger's seat and immediately caught Gabriel's scent. Hard not to catch it, considering they were only a few inches apart, but it caused more of that unwanted warmth. Warmth that she blamed on the Texas summer temps, which were just plain hot by anyone's standards.

"Word about this will get back to your great-aunt Carmen," she pointed out as he pulled out of the parking lot.

"Probably, but she doesn't always answer her phone, so that'll mean Derwin or whoever else might have to make a trip out to her place."

Oh, Derwin would do it even though it was miles outside of town. Carmen lived on the Silver Springs Ranch that she'd bought with her trust fund when she'd been twenty-one. A ranch that Hamish had insisted she buy and then had failed to make work. But the woman was apparently doing financially okay with her teacher's retirement pay and money she got from leasing the land.

"I'll go see her later," Gabriel said, glancing over at her. A glance that he seemed to cut so short that it barely qualified as a glance, and she couldn't help but think that was because he was feeling some warmth, too. "And I'll call my folks in case someone gets in touch with them."

"Are they still traveling around in their RV?" she asked.

He nodded. "They split time between my two brothers and sister, but they'll add Last Ride to their route now that I'm back here."

Rosalie knew his siblings, of course, even though they were all older than Gabriel and her. One by one, they'd moved away from Last Ride as they'd graduated from high school.

They drove up Main Street and past the elementary school where Rosalie was a pre-K teacher during the school year. A job that was both a blessing and a curse. She loved the work, loved the kids and loved having the summers off to travel and such, but her chosen profession meant listening to her parents remind her that she should be a lawyer. Or maybe a doctor like her brother. Or a dentist like her ex-fiancé.

Great expectations came with the Parkman surname, and her folks couldn't see that teaching was a calling for her. One with lousy pay, of course, but she had adjusted, and on the rare occasions when she wanted to travel somewhere that exceeded her budget, she'd been lucky enough to be able to tap into yet something else that came with the Parkman surname. A trust fund. It wasn't a massive one, but it had come in handy a couple of times.

"FYI, I'm not going to the reunion next weekend," Gabriel said when they drove past the high school.

She didn't have to ask what he was talking about. Rosalie knew their fifteen-year reunion was coming up.

She also knew why Gabriel wouldn't want to go.

The reunion committee had a habit of doing life-size cutouts of key moments from their graduating year. One of those such moments would be of Gabriel and her as the prom king and queen. Rosalie figured the committee would choose the photo of her starry-eyed eighteen-year-old self gazing up at the dreamy Gabriel. Her arms locked around his neck. His arms locked low around her back. Their mouths a breath apart, on the verge of a kiss.

And as if the picture wouldn't be enough, Gabriel and she would be expected to re-create the moment. The starry eyes. The dance. The near kiss. That, in turn, would accelerate the rumors of them reuniting.

Rosalie wouldn't be going, either.

It only took them a couple of minutes to reach the cemetery, and Rosalie immediately spotted the other vehicles. Eight of them, she counted, and she wasn't surprised when she saw the crowd now huddled around Hamish's grave. At least half of them were wearing the Sherlock outfits, and there was even one wizard in the group who'd come along for the nosy ride. They parted like the Red Sea, though, when Gabriel and she reached the grave.

No one said anything, though she figured before their arrival there'd been plenty of chatter and speculation. But while no one who knew Hamish believed Gabriel would be in mourning over this, they appeared to be respectful since he was Hamish's great-nephew.

Gabriel went closer, peering into the grave and seeing exactly what she'd seen. The empty space and the tiny box.

"You think somebody dug up the coffin?" Derwin asked.

Gabriel glanced around. "No heap of dirt or fresh dig marks," he said as if talking to himself.

"You might have been able to check for shoe prints," Derwin went on, "but everybody insisted on having a look, so any prints would have been walked over." He aimed narrowed eyes at some in the group, apparently ignoring the fact that he was there and had obviously done some walking over possible evidence to get in the position right next to the tombstone.

"Let me use that," Gabriel insisted when his attention landed on the selfie stick Derwin was holding.

It only took a second for the excitement to light in Derwin's eyes, and he quickly handed it over. Since Derwin's phone was already secured on the device, Gabriel lowered it into the grave, and he hit the button on the grip of the stick. He took several pictures from various angles and then had a look. So did Rosalie.

So did everybody else.

At least, the group attempted to cram in closer, but one hard look from Gabriel had them backing away. Rosalie stayed close, though, watching as Gabriel studied each photo. He zoomed in on one shot of the box, and she saw the writing.

"Something's engraved on it," she murmured.

"Yeah," Gabriel agreed. He kept enlarging it until the engraving got a whole lot more visible. Then she frowned. Reread it and frowned again.

Ha Ha, Carmen. I got the last laugh.

Unless her eyes were playing tricks on her, that was what was on the box, but what the heck did it mean? Judging from Gabriel's puzzled, suddenly riled expression, he didn't know, either.

"Come on," Gabriel said to her. "I need to go see my great-aunt Carmen right now."

CHAPTER TWO

WHEN GABRIEL HAD accepted the job as a deputy in his home-town of Last Ride, he hadn't expected to be dealing with a missing body his first week. Then again, he hadn't expected to have Rosalie doing a ride-along with him, either.

Rosalie, who looked every bit as good as she had back in high school when he hadn't been able to keep his hands and mouth off her. She was still curvy, and with her blond hair and blue eyes, she'd always reminded him of a young Marilyn Monroe. A brainy one without the breathy baby-doll voice.

A body, brain and a smooth, smoky voice that still got to him.

Yeah, he hadn't expected that, either. Or for her to be so close to him when he hadn't had the time to put up a mental barrier or two to make sure he didn't have the very reaction to her that he was having right now.

Of course, he'd known he would run into her sooner or later. He'd hoped for later. Had also hoped this blasted heat between them had cooled to bearable temps, but *sooner* had beat out the *later* as for his running into her, and the heat was still there. Heat that Gabriel figured shouldn't even be on his radar.

Not after what'd happened between them.

But that didn't seem to matter. He could feel the fire on his part. On hers as well. Strange, considering that at least one of them should be wary of having their hearts stomped on again. Strange, too, because she believed he'd done the stomping, and for a long time, he'd believed the fault had been all hers.

Should he clear that up for her? Should he tell her what he suspected?

He was considering it. Not that it would likely do any good to set a record straight after all these years. Also, if he played out the notion of the record straightening, where would it lead, anyway? Would Rosalie be relieved, pissed off or somewhere in between? Gabriel just didn't know, but in this case, he was pretty sure the truth wasn't going to set anybody free. It would just dredge up the past and wouldn't undo anything that'd happened.

He was mulling that over as he made the drive to his great-aunt Carmen's ranch. Rosalie and he hadn't discussed what they'd seen engraved on the silver box that had been in Hamish's grave. Probably because there wasn't a whole lot to say. The box and inscription gave them no answers and created a whole lot of questions. Well, one question in particular. Why had Hamish left such a message?

Ha Ha, Carmen. I got the last laugh.

Not exactly a traditional epitaph engraved on the little silver box. Then again, this hadn't been left on the tombstone or even the top of the grave, where Carmen could have seen it. It'd been buried in a grave that'd been meant for Hamish.

Yeah, a whole lot of questions.

Since his boss would likely have those same questions, too, Gabriel used the handsfree to send a text to Sheriff Matt Corbin. Of course, Deputy Azzie Parkman would fill him in on what was going on with Hamish's grave, but Gabriel wanted to make sure the "filling in" was correct.

Well, as correct as he knew it, anyway. Right now, all he knew was that Rosalie and he were headed to his great-aunt's Silver Springs Ranch to try to clear all of this up, and he'd keep Matt posted.

"How long has it been since you've seen Carmen?" Gabriel asked her after he'd sent the text.

Rosalie's forehead bunched up. "A while. She doesn't come to the Last Ride Society meetings very often, but she was there about two years ago."

Gabriel wasn't surprised by Carmen's occasional attendance at the quarterly meetings. Carmen was a Parkman, which made her a distant cousin of Rosalie's, and like Rosalie, she'd been born into money.

Lots and lots of money.

But Carmen hadn't had her family's blessing to go along with that money. Her relatives, both close and distant ones, had vehemently objected when she'd married Hamish, someone they had deemed unsuitable, and it hadn't helped that Carmen had used the bulk of her trust fund to buy the ranch that they later dubbed Hamish's miserable failure.

Carmen probably hadn't felt the need to mingle much with her family after that, and there would have been plenty of family mingling at those meetings.

When he pulled into the driveway of his great-aunt's Silver Springs Ranch, he spotted her on the porch. Carmen was in her eighties now, but she still looked healthy and strong. The woman definitely defied the image of a traditional little old lady. She was nearly six feet tall, lean, with thick gray hair scooped up in a sloppy bun.

The ranch wasn't sloppy, though, and looked a whole lot better than it had when Hamish had been trying to manage the place. The two-story pale yellow Victorian house had a fresh coat of paint. Ditto for the red barn and the white fences that surrounded the couple of acres that Carmen hadn't leased out. There were two horses grazing in a pasture dotted with wildflowers. It looked like a scene from a "wish you were here" postcard.

His great-aunt was beneath the overhang of the roof, sitting on the porch steps, where she sipped a beer and waited for them. Waited, because she'd obviously prepared for their visit. Gabriel saw the tray with the other two glasses, already filled with what appeared to be iced lemonade. Next to the glasses were two beers, no doubt to give them an option of beverages.

"Gabe, Rosalie," Carmen greeted them when they got out and approached the porch. Smiling, she stood and gathered them into her arms for a hug. "It's so good to see both of you."

"Who called you and told you we were coming?" Gabriel asked after he'd pulled back from the hug.

"Who didn't call me," she said with a chuckle. "Word is already all over. Sit, have a beer," she invited just as her phone dinged with a text. "Or lemonade if you're on duty."

Rosalie helped herself to a beer, adding a thank-you. Because he was indeed on duty, Gabriel had to settle for the lemonade and was about to launch into his questions, but Carmen spoke first.

"Are you all moved into the house?" she asked him. Her phone dinged yet again, but like before, Carmen ignored it.

"More or less." It was more on the less side of things, but he didn't want her offering to help him unpack. That was because he wasn't sure he'd do that just yet. He was renting the guesthouse on Matt's ranch, and Gabriel didn't know how long he'd be there.

"And the job?" Carmen went on. "Is that more or less, too, as far as you being settled into it?"

"More," he admitted. He was still a cop, which meant he was doing the only job he'd ever wanted to do. After he'd gotten injured, he'd thought that carrying another badge would never be an option. But Matt had given him that option, and Gabriel had snapped it up.

"Well, that's good," Carmen concluded, and when she shifted to Rosalie, Gabriel thought Carmen might be ready to launch into some chitchat. He was going to have to nip that in the bud.

He took out his phone to show Carmen the photo he'd transferred from Derwin's phone to his. "This was in Hamish's grave," he explained in case Derwin or one of her callers hadn't spelled it out. "No coffin, just this."

Carmen plucked her reading glasses from their perch on her head, and she read the inscription aloud. "'Ha Ha, Carmen. I got the last laugh.'"

Gabriel figured that would cause her to sigh, maybe even get mad. Or hurt. But her reaction surprised him. She smiled. "So, that's where this ended up. I always wondered."

Rosalie exchanged a puzzled glance with Gabriel, but he sure as heck couldn't provide her with any answers.

"You knew about the silver box?" Gabriel pressed.

His great-aunt didn't hesitate with her confirming nod. "It was a gift from my cousin, one of the few members of my family who didn't boycott the wedding. It's an antique, meant to hold trinkets."

"How'd it end up in the grave?" he asked when Carmen fell silent.

She shrugged and handed Gabriel back his phone. "I'm guessing Hamish put it there when he faked his death and burial. I noticed it was missing shortly after the funeral."

Rosalie made a soft sound, no doubt one of surprise. Gabriel was right there on the same page with her. "Hamish isn't dead?" he managed to say.

Another shrug from Carmen. "Maybe. I don't know for sure one way or the other. But he wasn't dead when this box went in his grave."

Gabriel didn't come out and insist that his great-aunt add a thorough explanation to that statement. He just waited until she'd had a long sip of her beer. Then she motioned for them to move to the small, shaded seating area at the end of the porch. Since it was hot and this conversation might take a while, Gabriel didn't object. However, he did object—silently, anyway—to how the seating arrangements had worked out.

Carmen took the only chair, leaving the swing seat for Rosalie and him. The very small swing seat that put them shoulder to shoulder and hip to hip. That position seemed to please Carmen because she smiled and then appeared to rethink her expression when Gabriel scowled.

"About a year after Hamish *died*," Carmen said, putting the last word in air quotes, "I found a receipt from a jewelry store in San Antonio. I was confused because as you well know Hamish wasn't the jewelry-buying type. So, I called the store and told the clerk who answered that I was Hamish's widow and asked about the purchase. Well, it turned out not to be an actual purchase but the receipt for engraving services. The store still had the records, so the clerk read off the inscription."

"You must have been shocked," Rosalie said when Carmen fell silent.

"Oh, I was. But then I got to thinking as to what could have happened, and I recalled Hamish's old drinking buddy, Elroy Merkins. He's a mortician in San Antonio," Carmen added, giving him a flat, knowing look.

Gabriel immediately connected the dots. Hamish had died of a heart attack in San Antonio while visiting Elroy. Or rather, he'd seemingly died of a heart attack. Elroy had been the one to call Carmen and deliver the news. Elroy had also been the one to handle all the funeral and burial arrangements.

Well, hell.

Gabriel could see how all of this had played out. Two drinking buddies, one of them a miserable codger who had apparently wanted to get the last ha-ha laugh on his wife by faking his death, and then…what?

Going on to lead another life?

If so, Gabriel wished he could throttle the jerk for making everyone, especially his wife, believe he was dead. It didn't matter that Carmen was seemingly better off without him. Nope. Didn't matter. If Hamish had wanted to end his marriage and leave, then he should have done it the old-fashioned way, by telling her the truth and asking for a divorce.

"Did Elroy falsify the death certificate?" Gabriel snapped, ready to go arrest the fellow jerk. Then he remembered the guy would be in his late eighties or maybe not even alive.

Carmen shook her head. "There wasn't a death certificate. Elroy told me he'd take care of it, and since there wasn't any life insurance and the Silver Springs Ranch was all in my name, I forgot about it. By then, Hamish and I had been living very separate lives. He had his bank account, and I had mine."

"Did you ever contact Elroy and ask him what'd happened?" Gabriel pressed. He leaned forward. Not the best idea he'd ever had because his arm brushed across Rosalie's left breast. He pretended not to notice.

"No," Carmen said in the same tone she might use if

she'd decided not to purchase a particular brand of beer. "I mean, what would be the point? Hamish clearly didn't want to be here. Didn't want to be with me," she added, and he heard the change in her tone. The slight hitch in her breath.

"I'm sorry," Rosalie and he said at the same time. Also at the same time, they reached to pat Carmen's hand and did a whole lot more inadvertent touching. Rosalie's thigh rubbed against his. Her elbow caught his chest. Their legs touched.

Carmen waved that off. "Old water, old bridge."

Maybe, and while no one ever thought Carmen and Hamish had been madly in love and happy, this had to sting at least a little. But Gabriel immediately rethought that. Once upon a time, they must have been in love. Must have been happy. If not, they wouldn't have married. So, the stinging had to be more than a little and had likely gone on for years.

"Resentment and bitterness can fester," Carmen continued as if reading Gabriel's thoughts. "Hamish couldn't make the ranch work. I couldn't have kids. And he didn't get the respect that I hadn't known he wanted from marrying a Parkman."

"I'm sorry," Rosalie repeated, probably because she didn't know what else to say.

Carmen stayed quiet a moment and then seemed to pull herself back to her usual cheery self. "I suppose you'll look for Hamish?" she asked.

Gabriel nodded. He'd also check to see if any laws had been broken. Of course, since it'd been nearly fifteen years, the statute of limitations would apply and likely no charges would stick. Still, he thought Hamish should have to face up to what he'd done.

"Oh, well," Carmen said on a sigh. "Hamish won't thank

you for that. Resentment and bitterness," she repeated. Then she looked at them. "You know, Hamish thought you two were repeating our history. He went on and on about how the Parkmans were never going to accept anyone with Mc-Cloud blood into their family."

Rosalie looked at him, the questions and surprise in her eyes, but Gabriel knew he wasn't having that same reaction. That was because he'd been on the receiving end of Hamish's rant about Carmen and Rosalie's gene pool.

And Gabriel suspected Hamish had taken the rants and warnings a step further.

One *huge* step further.

If his suspicions were right, it was even more reason for Gabriel to track down the man and demand the truth. Because he had another suspicion that Rosalie's caution toward him wasn't something he wanted to undo. Especially now. He had barely qualified as good enough for her when he'd been a football star and a semi-golden boy. There was nothing golden about him now, and he sure as hell wasn't a star.

"Hamish was wrong," Carmen said, yanking Gabriel's attention back to her. "He should have never tried to come between you two. It's obvious you're a match made in…" She stopped, chuckled. "Well, maybe not in heaven but a match made in Last Ride, anyway. That's sort of like heaven."

Gabriel would have disagreed with that if he could have figured out a way to do it without insulting Rosalie. While he sat there, more than a little dumbfounded, his great-aunt continued.

Carmen smiled again as her gaze skirted around her property. "You should take over the Silver Springs Ranch."

She'd tacked on that last part so fast that it took a while

for it to sink in. To sink in and mentally slug him in the face. "Are you all right? Is this ranch too much for you——"

Carmen gave him a reassuring smile. "I'm fine. Just old, that's all. I've been thinking about moving into one of those little cottages in town that my cousin Evangeline has set up."

Gabriel remembered Evangeline. A hippie-type do-gooder who'd given away most of her share of the Parkman fortune. "What cottages?" he asked.

"It's a retirement-type area on Webster Street," Rosalie provided, setting her beer bottle on the tray. She'd only had a few sips, he noted. "Evangeline bought some empty lots and did fundraisers to build cottages."

"Sort of like a transition between being at home and assisted living," Carmen provided just as her phone dinged with yet another text. She smiled when she looked at the screen. "I should go inside and make some calls to let everyone know that I'm not dissolving into a puddle of grief."

Carmen stood, signaling an end to the meeting, and she kissed Gabriel's and Rosalie's cheeks. "Don't let Hamish get the last laugh when it comes to the two of you," she murmured, gathering up the tray. "Don't throw away a second chance because of the likes of him," she said before heading inside.

Rosalie and he got up as well. "What did she mean by that?" she asked. "How did Hamish try to come between us? And why would Carmen think he'd gotten the last laugh on us?"

Gabriel considered how to respond to that and went with the truth. Well, the partial truth, anyway. "Despite Hamish's sour nature, he was close to my dad and thought Last Ride wasn't a good enough place for him, that he'd have more opportunities in a bigger city." Since his dad had been an electrician, that was possibly true.

"What did that have to do with us?" she pressed as they got into the truck. He turned on the engine and cranked up the AC. It seemed as if Rosalie had been about to tack on another question to that, but she stopped. "Hamish thought if you left Last Ride, then your folks would, too. I mean, since all your siblings had already moved away."

"Bingo," Gabriel confirmed. "Needless to say, Hamish didn't see the town as any sort of heaven."

"No," she softly agreed, but there seemed to be a question at the end of her single-word response. A question Gabriel didn't especially want her to ask. He didn't want to get into the part he was pretty sure Hamish had played in their past.

"Old water, old bridge," he grumbled under his breath. It'd been meant as a reminder for him to shut up and move on.

He did the first. Had trouble with the second.

He shut up all right, but Gabriel looked at her and saw she was already looking at him. Studying him. Maybe getting ready to ask that question. Maybe sorting through memories of them.

Gabriel was doing some memory sorting, too, which meant he was doing the exact opposite of "moving on."

Nope.

He was more in sitting still and idling mode because he certainly wasn't driving back to town. Instead, he was remembering the first time he'd kissed Rosalie. Recalling in nth details all the fooling around they'd done. It'd been a damn hard challenge not to take her virginity when she'd offered it up to him. But even then, he hadn't been an idiot and had known something like that would come with big-assed strings attached. Besides, he wasn't the love-'em-and-leave-'em type.

He shook his head to clear it and reached to put the truck into gear. Just as Rosalie reached for him. Without taking her eyes off him, she slid her hand around the back of his neck. She didn't move in, didn't make it a kiss.

But Gabriel did.

He blew every vow he'd just made about keeping his hands and mouth off Rosalie, and he kissed her.

CHAPTER THREE

WHILE ROSALIE STOOD at her kitchen window and drank her iced tea, she considered glancing down at her feet to make sure they were on the floor. She was certain they were, but she'd had this amazing floating feeling since Gabriel had kissed her in his truck the day before.

Of course, she would have experienced much more than just the giddy floating if he'd pressed things and invited her back to his place, but he hadn't. He'd kissed her, stopped and cursed—in that order. Then he'd continued to mutter more profanity, all aimed at himself, as he'd driven back not to his place but into town. He hadn't mentioned the kiss, or anything else, for that matter. He'd just driven as if his only mission was to get back to work.

And away from her.

Once they'd reached the police station, where she had left her car in the parking lot, Gabriel had done more muttering, this time to tell her he'd keep her updated about Hamish, and then he'd disappeared inside the building.

Rosalie very much wanted that update on his great-uncle. Wanted another kiss or two as well, but now that she'd had some time and distance from Gabriel, she knew he'd made the right decision to stop the mistake-kiss before it could turn into something bigger. Neither one of them was willing to trust their hearts to each other again.

She frowned.

And realized that was a pile of malarkey.

Her body was seriously on board with the whole heart-risk thing, and her mind was quickly starting to agree. Old water, old bridge. Old heat, new heat. The scalding attraction she'd felt for Gabriel was definitely still there. It was nudging and pushing her in his direction, but she forced herself to play out this particular scenario.

If Gabriel and she picked up where they'd left off fifteen years ago, it would lead to sex. No doubts about that. Then more sex. Again, she had no doubts as to that outcome. She was equally certain that the sex would be amazing and leave her with the best feet-off-the-ground feeling ever.

But then what?

She kept rolling that question around in her head and considered the possibility that things would fizzle out between them. After all, they couldn't just have sex 24/7. Eventually, they'd have to deal with the same obstacles they'd dealt with when they'd been eighteen.

Except those obstacles had changed.

She'd already failed to live up to her parents' expectations and was perfectly okay with that, whether or not they ever would be. Gabriel might be okay with their proverbial stink eye, too, since he was thirty-three and was probably no longer as concerned about such things.

One obstacle, though, might be that he was possibly involved with someone else, but after some thought, Rosalie was able to dismiss that, too. If he had been in a relationship, word of it would have already gotten out, and his great-aunt wouldn't have given them that look. A look that was a seal of approval, a green light to leave and go fool around.

So, no real obstacles.

Well, other than Gabriel still seemed unhappy with her over their breakup. He hadn't been so unhappy, though, that it'd stopped him from kissing her, and that was something she wouldn't forget.

But maybe Gabriel could.

After all, he'd been the one who'd walked away and left Last Ride. He might not be able to do that now with his job, but there was more than one way to put an end to things.

She heard the vehicle pull into her driveway, and Rosalie automatically scowled. It was probably someone stopping by to ask her what was going on with the search for Hamish or another flower bouquet delivery from Reggie.

Neither of which she wanted.

The visitors and calls about Hamish had scaled back considerably since the news had broken the day before. So had Reggie's flowers. He was only sending one bouquet every other day now. Deliveries that she refused each time, but that hadn't stopped him from continuing to send them.

Rosalie set her glass of iced tea on the counter and headed to the front of the house. Not that she had far to go since her place wasn't that big. It took her only eleven steps to get from the kitchen to the door.

She was prepared to tell the delivery driver to return the flowers to Reggie or explain to whichever nosy neighbor that she had no news to share. But when she threw open the door, it wasn't someone from Petal Pushers, the local florist, or someone on the hunt for fresh gossip. It was the feet-floating creator himself.

Gabriel.

He was wearing another of those great-fitting shirts, a blue one this time, and he had on his cop's face. It was just as attention-getting as his regular expression. Then again, everything about Gabriel got her attention.

Rosalie automatically dropped back a step to let him in. Automatically stopped breathing for a second or two as well. Gabriel had that effect on her. It was as if her body had become so preoccupied with him that it forgot how to make sure she drew air into her lungs.

"I'm not here to kiss you again," Gabriel said straightaway as he came inside, moving in such a way so that they didn't accidentally touch each other. "But I owe you an apology—"

Rosalie closed the door, and in the same motion, she came up on her tiptoes and kissed him so he didn't have a chance to finish that. She wasn't sure who was more surprised about that, Gabriel or her, but she thought she might have won that particular prize.

She kept the mouth-to-mouth contact short and sweet. Well, as sweet as it could be, considering her mouth was on Gabriel's.

"There," she said as if proving a point. Exactly what point, she didn't have a clue, though. "Now I owe you an apology, too, so that makes us even."

His eyes were hot, like the rest of him, and he aimed all that hotness at her. She expected him to start counting out all the reasons why a kiss like that shouldn't happen again. And maybe that was what he had planned. But the argument seemed to vanish before he even got out a word of it.

"Two things," he said, using his cop's voice to go along with his cop's expression. "Reggie Dalton paid me a visit this morning to tell me that you two would be getting back together soon."

Crap on a cracker.

Once Rosalie had gathered enough breath to voice a response, she made a low snarling sound that she knew was very much like a growl. "No, we're not getting back together. He cheated on me. Not that I'm telling you anything I'm positive you haven't already heard, but I walked in on him when he had his hand up his dental assistant's skirt. I don't think he was trying to help her fix the elastic in her panties, either."

Gabriel's quick nod let her know that, yes, he had indeed already heard that. "Reggie seems to believe you'll forgive him for that."

"I won't," she assured him without a drop of hesitation and with a whole lot of conviction.

He stared at her, as if trying to decide if that was true. It was, but Gabriel might be doing this assessment so he could be sure he wasn't horning in on someone else's relationship. Obviously, that wasn't something Reggie's dental assistant had ever considered, but in hindsight, Rosalie believed the woman had done her a favor. Best for her to have seen Reggie's true colors before they set a date and went through with the *I do*s. If that'd happened, Rosalie was certain she would have soon been needing the services of a divorce lawyer.

"So, it's really over between the dentist and you," Gabriel finally said. But he didn't move in to kiss her or anything.

Instead, he took out his phone and lifted the screen to show her a photo. Not the one he'd taken of the silver box at the cemetery but of an elderly man with a mop of frizzy gray hair. Even though she'd never seen Hamish wear his hair that way, she instantly recognized his face.

"You found him." She hadn't expected that—not this soon, anyway. "You found your great-uncle." Rosalie took the phone and had a closer look. It appeared to be a DMV photo.

"That was taken nine years ago in Dallas," Gabriel explained. "The license has expired, and Hamish didn't renew it."

That sent her gaze locking on to his to see if he was

about to tell her that Hamish was dead, this time for real, but Gabriel shook his head. "He's alive, still in Dallas, where he collects his monthly Social Security payment and apparently lives quite comfortably after winning the lottery shortly after he left Last Ride. He goes by his middle name, Clyde, these days."

"Alive," Rosalie repeated, and apparently better off financially than he had been when he'd lived here. "Carmen knows?" she asked.

"Yeah. I stopped by and told her before coming over here. She handled the news—" he paused "—okay."

Okay didn't sound okay enough to Rosalie, and she made a mental note to call the woman and arrange a visit so she could check on her. After all, none of this would have happened had she not gone out to the cemetery to get a photo of the tombstone. Or at least it probably wouldn't have happened so soon, anyway. Hamish's tombstone was at the far back of the cemetery, and it might have been weeks or even months before someone noticed it.

"There's no record of Hamish having a phone, but he could be using prepaid ones," Gabriel went on. "With no way to call him, I contacted an old friend of mine in Dallas PD, Lieutenant Miguel Rodriguez, and he sent one of his uniforms out this morning to do a face-to-face check on Hamish. When Hamish didn't respond to the knock on his door, the officer left a message with his neighbor."

So, Hamish likely knew by now that his secret was out, and Rosalie wondered how he would react to that. And how Carmen would handle it if Hamish decided to contact her. She doubted the woman would just be *okay* with it.

Rosalie felt the surge of emotion. Not the heated attraction for Gabriel this time, but anger, and she heard herself make that snarling sound. Hamish had done a low-down dirty thing by abandoning his wife, faking his death and leaving her that ha-ha inscription in his fake grave. If he'd wanted to end his marriage, he shouldn't have done it the cowardly way and made a joke out of it.

"The SOB needs to pay for what he's done," she grumbled. "Can you arrest him for something, for anything?"

Gabriel shook his head again, but she saw the emotion flare in his eyes, too. "As far as I can tell, he hasn't broken any laws, but trust me, I'm looking into what he's been doing for the past fifteen years. I'm looking hard."

She didn't doubt that and was about to ask him if this latest news on Hamish had gotten around town, but her phone dinged with a text from Alma Parkman, the president of the Last Ride Society.

In light of what's happened with Hamish lying through his teeth and all, please come in and draw another name to research, Alma had messaged.

Apparently, Rosalie wasn't the only one angry about what the man had done. "If he comes back to Last Ride, Hamish won't be getting a visit from the Welcome Wagon," Rosalie remarked.

When Gabriel didn't respond to that and when he just continued to stand there and look at her, Rosalie studied his face. "I'm sorry," she said. "I was thinking about how much this is probably bothering Carmen, but you're having to deal with it, too."

Gabriel seemed to dismiss that. "What made you decide to break up with me in a letter instead of telling me in person?"

Rosalie was sure she gave him a puzzled look, and it took her a moment to make the abrupt shift in the conversation. "You mean what made *you* decide to break up with *me* in a letter instead of telling *me* in person?"

And just like that, she was yanked back fifteen years ago when that had happened. The tears, the crushed heart. All of it. It was probably because of the *all of it* emotion that she didn't clue in to the way that Gabriel was staring at her. Not with an apology or a nod to confirm he'd phrased his question wrong. No, he seemed frustrated or something.

A frustration that grew by leaps and bounds when he cursed.

Groaning, he stepped away from her, cursed some more and lifted his eyes to the ceiling for a moment. "You got a letter that you believed was from me?" he finally managed to ask.

She opened her mouth to correct him and say the letter was indeed from him, but Rosalie rethought that. She nodded. "I got it the day after graduation," she verified. "And you got one that you believed was from me?"

With his nod, there was a chorus of groans and cursing from both of them, but Rosalie got specific with her profanity. She cursed Hamish because he was the obvious culprit in this. He was the bitter jerk who thought he was saving his great-nephew from the same bitterness by playing the opposite of a matchmaker.

For crap's sake.

Rosalie started pacing and kept up the cursing, trying to wrap her mind around this cut-to-the-bone deception. For the first time in fifteen years, she also wished she'd kept the heart-stomping letter so she could yank it out and try to understand why she had fallen for something like this.

"What did I supposedly write in the letter you got?" she snarled.

Muscles tightened and flexed in his jaw. "I didn't read past the first line. It said *I'm breaking up with you so you can have the life that'll make you happy.* What did yours say?"

Rosalie groaned because that was exactly how her letter had started as well. Unlike Gabriel, though, she'd read the entire thing. Many, many, many times. In fact, she'd read it so often while crying that the paper had been splotched with very sad-looking tearstains.

"You didn't notice the letter wasn't in my handwriting?" he asked.

Rosalie didn't even have to think about her answer. "No, but then, I'd never gotten a letter from you. Cards, yes, where you just signed your name. You didn't notice the letter you got wasn't in my handwriting?" she countered.

He shook his head. "But like I said, I didn't get past the first line." Gabriel paused. "Truth is, I'd been expecting the breakup. You were heading off to college. I was leaving to join the Air Force so I could be a military cop. And I didn't think you'd want to wait around for me while I got my life on track."

"I would have waited," Rosalie muttered.

She heard the words leave her mouth, and she cringed. She definitely should have kept that little confession to herself. Because it sure as heck wouldn't do any good now. It would only serve to make Gabriel feel like cow dung. Of course, she was feeling like dung as well, and she wished she could give Hamish a well-placed kick that would drop him to his knees and make him feel some of this crappiness, too.

Rosalie kept pacing and tried to make sense of this. Her entire adulthood had been shaped by that letter from a lying sack of, well, crap. Gabriel's, too.

Or rather, it'd been sort of shaped, anyway.

Even without the letter, Gabriel would have probably

left Last Ride. He hadn't kept it secret that he'd wanted to join the Air Force. No. The only thing he'd kept to himself was how, or if, she would fit into his future.

"I would have never asked you to wait," Gabriel said.

That stopped Rosalie in her tracks, and she looked at him. And there it was. The confirmation on his face that even without Hamish's lies, the breakup would have happened anyway. Of course, she could have pressed him to take her with him, but even at the oh so young age of eighteen, Gabriel had apparently been able to see the flaws in that particular plan.

He'd moved three times during that first year, twice for training and then to a base overseas where the military didn't send families. Rosalie knew that thanks to the steady stream of gossipers who'd seemingly loved filling her in on Gabriel's new life. Yes, she could have maybe participated in that life in some way, but it would have been a challenge for her to finish college. An even bigger challenge to try to find teaching jobs as she followed him from base to base overseas.

And then there would have been the biggest challenge of all.

Her, leaving the only place she'd ever wanted to call home. She hadn't wanted to merely come back to Last Ride for visits. No. She'd wanted to live here, had wanted to teach here, surrounded by family and traditions that sometimes could be overwhelming. But at other times, they had anchored her when she'd needed it.

For Gabriel, that anchor had obviously felt too heavy instead of just the right amount of steady.

That realization calmed her anger some. Some. Though she still wanted Hamish to pay for his deception. But hindsight being twenty-twenty and all, she could see that Gabriel's leaving hadn't been the man's fault.

Or hers.

His leaving had been about him taking the path that he thought would make him happy.

"Yeah," Gabriel said as if reading her thoughts. More likely, he was simply reading her body language, and he'd no doubt seen the fight and anger inside her melt away.

Rosalie could see the same in him. The *what's done is done* acceptance. But she could see something else. He was right there, standing in her living room while wearing that chest-clinging shirt. And his Last Ride deputy's badge.

A badge he'd accepted because maybe he'd decided this town wasn't a deadweight around his neck after all.

"There are no obstacles," she said, and Rosalie immediately saw that he didn't have a clue what she was talking about.

However, he did have a clue what she was about to do when she went to him. He braced, not in a defensive way, but as if he'd known all along what was about to happen. And what was about to happen was a kiss.

He reached for her. She reached for him. Gabriel was faster than she was, though, and he hooked his arm around her waist, snapping her to him. His mouth landed on hers just as her breasts landed on his chest. All in all, she couldn't have asked for more. Well, not at the moment, anyway.

The heat slid through her, from head to toe. Yes, Gabriel could make her hot everywhere, and a single kiss from him could kick things straight to foreplay. That was the good thing, and the bad, about this not being their first kissing rodeo with each other. He already knew how to play around with her mouth to make this heat skyrocket to the next level.

Unlike so many of their other make-out sessions, they

weren't in the confines of a truck. They had room to move, and Gabriel moved her all right. He turned her, pressing her back against the wall, and he managed to do that without breaking the kiss. A kiss he'd deepened in the best way possible. In fact, everything about this was the best way possible.

Except for the ringing.

At first, Rosalie thought the sound was only in her ears, but when Gabriel tore his mouth from hers and cursed, she realized it was his phone. Apparently, he didn't think he could just ignore it, what with him being a deputy on duty and all, so he yanked the cell from his pocket. No cursing, though, when he saw the name on the screen.

She saw it, too. Miguel Rodriguez. And she remembered that was his friend in Dallas PD. The one who'd sent an officer to check on Hamish.

"I, uh, need to take this," Gabriel said, hitting Answer and shifting away from her. He didn't put the call on speaker, but she had no trouble hearing the other cop when he spoke.

"I just got an interesting call from your great-uncle's neighbor," the lieutenant said. "Apparently, about five minutes ago, he saw Hamish leave his house with a suitcase. He got into a car. Not driving," he quickly added, "but as a passenger. You think Hamish might be trying to run?"

"Maybe," Gabriel answered after a long pause. "He might think he's on the verge of being arrested."

"Is he on the verge?" Lieutenant Rodriguez came out and asked. "Have you found anything we can use to charge him with something?"

"Nothing. His friend, the mortician, who no doubt helped him fake his death, passed away a couple of years ago. His son took over the business, but he said there were no records on Hamish."

So, a dead end. Literally. But even if the mortician had still been alive, he might not have been willing or able to tell Gabriel any more than he'd already learned. Nor would he have necessarily faced any criminal charges because of the statute of limitations.

"All right," the lieutenant muttered. "The neighbor said he'd call us when and if Hamish returns, but I won't be sending out any other officers unless I hear different from you. And speaking of hearing from you, have you considered my offer?"

Gabriel glanced at her and shifted his position so that he was turned slightly away from her. "Haven't had a chance to even think about it."

"Well, get on with it," Rodriguez said with a chuckle. "I'm sure if you need any waivers for passing the physical, we can work around that. Think about it. Better pay and you and me teaming up again. Just say the word, and I'll make sure the job is yours."

Everything inside Rosalie went still. All right. That was an obstacle she hadn't seen coming. She'd obviously been wrong about Gabriel not being able to work on a big-city police force.

"I'll get back to you," Gabriel replied, glancing at her again. "Keep me posted about Hamish."

He ended the call but stared at the phone for a couple of seconds before he slipped it back into his pocket.

"Are you, uh, thinking about…?" She stopped, regrouped. Then fessed up to him. "I overheard your conversation. Small house, big ears," Rosalie added, trying to lighten her tone.

"Miguel and I served together on a couple of assignments," Gabriel said after his own pause and what appeared to be his own regrouping. "He wants me to work there in Tactical Investigations, tracking down fugitives."

It took her a couple of seconds to find her voice. First, Rosalie had to tamp down the sickening dread that once again she was going to have to watch Gabriel leave Last Ride. "Uh, that sounds interesting. And important."

She doubted he'd have assignments here that met that level of importance. Well, not on a level to compete with Dallas PD, anyway. His cases would certainly be important to the citizens of Last Ride.

"Rosalie," he murmured, her name coming at the end of a heavy sigh. Maybe a sigh he intended to follow up with an apology, but if an *I'm sorry* was coming, it got cut off by the knock at her door.

Still feeling numb and frazzled at the same time, she opened the door without thinking. And she instantly regretted it. Because Reggie was on her porch. Reggie, wearing his white dentist coat and looking somewhat numb and frazzled himself.

"Oh," Reggie said, his wide-eyed gaze sliding from her to Gabriel. "Oh," he repeated, and it sounded like a *what the heck is going on here?* question.

No way did she owe this cheating scumbag an explanation as to why Gabriel was in her house and why she probably looked as if she'd just been kissing him. Which she had been.

"What do you want, Reggie?" she asked and didn't bother to take the annoyance and irritation out of her voice.

Every time she saw him, she got the same neon flash in her head—of him doing panty play with his assistant. Reggie, though, apparently got a flash of a whole different sort. He flicked an annoyed glance at Gabriel and turned back to her.

"I'm here to ask you to go to the high school reunion with me this weekend," Reggie threw out there, and he said it with a smile as if she'd never walked in on panty-gate. "And before you say no," he added, just as she was about to say no, "think of it like this. Being with me will put a stop to all those ugly rumors about Gabriel and you."

Gabriel took one very slow, very menacing step toward Reggie. "What ugly rumors?" he asked. His tone was menacing, too.

She had to hand it to Reggie—he stood his ground and looked Gabriel straight in the eye. "That Rosalie is on the rebound and nursing a broken heart, and that you're taking advantage of that to try to get in her pants."

Rosalie groaned. "And was it you who started that rumor?" she demanded.

"No." Reggie pulled back his shoulders and looked genuinely offended. "Of course not. I defended you. I said there was no way you'd fall for something like that, not after Gabriel dumped you and broke your heart."

"Gabriel didn't dump me," she snarled, realizing it was true. Well, true-ish, anyway. In large part he'd left because of Hamish's letter.

Reggie looked at her with overly sympathetic eyes that conveyed he knew the way things had gone down and that he was there for her. "The fastest way to quell the rumor is to be seen at the reunion with me. And, of course, for you not to fall for the fast one Gabriel's trying to pull."

Oh, the anger came. It came in one fast, rolling wave that collided into her and had her seeing red. Apparently, it washed away any hesitation in her blurting what leaped from her mouth.

"FYI, what you did was a hell of a lot worse than Gabriel leaving. You. Cheated. On. Me," she spelled out. Rosalie jabbed her index finger at Reggie. "And I can't go to the reunion with you because I'm going with Gabriel."

CHAPTER FOUR

YOU DON'T HAVE to do this, Gabriel read from the text Rosalie had just sent him

It wasn't the first time she'd given him that particular option, either. For the last two days, she'd been repeating variations of it through other texts and calls. She'd also added so many apologies that Gabriel had lost count.

However, he hadn't lost count of just how many times he'd gotten pissed off when Reggie had tried to pressure Rosalie into going to the reunion dance with him by insisting he could stop "ugly rumors."

Gabriel hadn't actually heard such rumors with his own ears, but he didn't doubt they were floating around out there. Also didn't doubt that Reggie had been fueling them as a way to get Rosalie to come back to him. That had only pissed Gabriel off even more, and if Rosalie hadn't lied and said she was going with him, he would have asked her on the spot.

Of course, now he had doubts about doing this.

Not doubts about coming to Rosalie's rescue. She almost certainly could have handled her own rescue, but he'd been glad to help. No, his doubts centered around the fact that this wasn't a good idea since it could crank up the gossip mill about them. Which would almost certainly happen once they stepped inside the high school gym where the reunion was being held. Still, it was too late to back out now, and that was the reminder running through his head when he knocked on Rosalie's door to pick her up for their date.

She answered the moment he knocked, an indication she'd been right there, waiting for him. One look at her, and Gabriel's tongue landed in the vicinity of the porch floor. Oh, man. He was toast.

Rosalie was wearing a red dress that hugged every one of her curves, and she'd ditched her ponytail tonight. Her blond hair tumbled over her shoulders in loose curls that made him want to reach out and touch them. Then again, there really wasn't any part of her that he didn't want to touch right now.

"You look…" they said at the same moment. Then stopped. Waited a heartbeat. "Amazing," they finished, again at the same moment.

So, she obviously approved of his "dressy casual" choice of black jeans and white button-down shirt. Probably approved of him, too, judging by the way her gaze skimmed over his body. That wasn't a good thing. Because this mutual admiration could turn to something scalding hot if they weren't careful.

Gabriel felt a little foolish when he offered her a wrist corsage, one he'd picked up from Petal Pushers just minutes earlier. He'd originally ordered one with pink roses, but the florist had informed him that he should choose something that would better coordinate with Rosalie's red dress. Something that was apparently all over town because folks had seen her pick up said dress from the dry cleaner's. Folks had described it as the color of the apple Eve had sampled in the Garden of Eden and that it fit her like second skin.

They hadn't been wrong.

She smiled when he slipped the corsage onto her wrist, and maybe she was remembering they'd done something very much like this for their senior prom and then the graduation dance. Memories. No way to rid yourself of them, but they were playing into this because so many of those memories were good. In fact, they had been right up to the very end.

Since he'd figured out that Hamish had written breakup letters to them, Gabriel had been playing the what-if game. Involuntarily playing it, that was, and he had wondered just where Rosalie and he would be now if Hamish hadn't butted in. It was sort of a small-town Texas version of *It's a Wonderful Life*, but instead of wondering what it would have been like for them to have never met, he was wondering about the opposite.

Where would they be now if he'd stayed?

What kind of people would they have been had he never put on a military uniform and she'd had to endure daily criticism from her parents about her choice to be with him?

It was a question all right, and he had to admit it was possible Rosalie and he would have stayed together. Just as possible, though, that they'd have split up, but Gabriel knew without a doubt Hamish had been wrong about the inevitable bitterness. It just wasn't there.

Heck, if Gabriel didn't feel bitterness over the way his military career had turned out, and he didn't, then he wouldn't have those feelings toward this woman who'd been his first love.

And his only.

That thought didn't settle well in his gut, and he pushed it aside, focusing on something that settled very well indeed. He kissed her. Not a long, deep one that his body wanted, but just a little taste. It was enough to make her smile and caused her already sparkling eyes to sparkle even more.

But some of the sparkle faded when she opened her mouth to say what he figured she was about to say.

"Yes, I'm sure I want to go to the reunion with you," he said, cutting her off at the pass.

"Even though it'll give folks something to talk about?" she countered.

"Even though," he assured her. "This is Last Ride. Talk is inevitable." And, yes, Rosalie and he were getting more than the lion's share of it.

"FYI, I've heard the rebound talk that Reggie mentioned," she said.

So had he. "Are you on the rebound?" he came out and asked.

She sighed, took her purse from the foyer table and followed him out onto the porch so she could lock up. "No, and that's the sad part."

Gabriel hadn't expected that answer. "Sadder than you walking in on your fiancé with his hand in another woman's panties?"

"In a way. I just wasn't that torn up after the breakup," she said, and he led her to his truck. "I should have been because, hey, engaged to him and all that." She paused. "But after I got past the initial shock of seeing him with another woman, I felt relief. And vindication."

He was sure he gave her a blank look. "You're going to have to explain that."

"Well, my parents thought Reggie was the one, and while I knew he wasn't perfect, I kept thinking that I was in my thirties and that maybe it was time to settle down. But what I was doing was settling, not settling down. Big difference."

Yeah, it was, and that difference explained why Gabriel had never married. He'd liked a couple of women, could have probably pushed it to being in love with one of them, but he always figured falling in love shouldn't require pushes like that.

"I had convinced myself that I loved Reggie and could have the perfect life with him," she went on. "But when the bubble burst, it was liberating. I could do a proverbial nanny nanny boo boo at my parents for pushing me to marry a cheater, and I could see that my life was already perfect."

For some reason, that tightened his chest. Did that mean Rosalie had ditched all plans for another serious relationship, for a chance to find that no-push required to fall in love?

"Perfect," he repeated, mulling that over.

"Sure. I have my own house, a job I love, and I live in a town I love. Not many people get that."

No, they didn't, and when it all came together, then *perfect* did indeed apply.

"I still have to put up with texts from my mom," she went on, "telling me not to get involved with you again. But I'd get those no matter where I lived or what job I had."

Gabriel had figured her mother wouldn't keep her disapproval about him to herself. "How many texts are you talking about?" he asked.

"Two or three every day. Apparently, my mom is worried I might sow some wild oats with you or use you to get back at Reggie. I would never do that." Rosalie stopped, shrugged. "Well, I wouldn't use you or anyone else to get back at Reggie, anyway."

She sighed, looked at him, and he heard the unspoken signal that she was done revealing her heart to him. But Gabriel wouldn't forget a word of what she'd said. He couldn't add to her nearly perfect life. In fact, if he pushed—there was that word again—he could cause her a boatload of unhappiness. That should stop him from wanting her so much.

It didn't.

"So, what's going on at the police station?" she asked.

He doubted this was just small talk. After all, they had competition for the most gossiped about topic right now. "We're getting several calls an hour for Hamish sightings," he told her.

Rosalie's eyebrow lifted. "People have actually seen him?"

"No," he couldn't say fast enough. "People *think* they've seen him. So far, the sightings have turned out to be any man in town over the age of eighty, an odd-shaped haystack, a pitchfork in the haystack and Elmer Gentry's bull calf that had gotten a shirt from the clothesline stuck on his head."

She frowned. Made a face. Then smiled. "This must be trivial compared to your previous duties."

Gabriel shrugged. "All in all, my first week on the job has been, well, varied and interesting."

Now she just looked confused, as if he might be lying. He wasn't.

"Everybody thinks being a military cop is about dodging bullets and going into combat," he explained as he drove toward the school. "Most of the time, it's not. I started out just like many rookie cops by responding to domestic calls, making DUI arrests, going on patrol and doing lots of paperwork. Later on, after I made rank, I went on some deployments, but when I was stateside, I supervised the younger cops and coordinated the more serious criminal investigations with the local civilian authorities."

He glanced at her as she processed that. "But you were shot," she murmured, as if the mere subject was taboo.

"I was but not in combat. It was a domestic dispute. I was shot by a young airman who'd been aiming a gun at his equally young, terrified wife." He could say the words now and not have them feel as if someone had punched him. Or shot him again. "You don't want to hear this, not with us about to go into a party."

"I want to hear it if you want to tell me," she insisted.

"But I don't want to bring back bad memories for you."

Gabriel nodded but didn't say anything until they reached the school. He parked far away from the building where he could see people milling around, and he got out of his seat belt so he could unzip his jeans.

Even though the only illumination was coming from a lamppost, he saw the surprise in her eyes. Surprise mixed with heat. Which pleased him. Even now, she responded to him, and he would try to add to that heat later, but for now, there was something he wanted to show her.

Even though he immediately realized that yanking down his pants probably wasn't his brightest idea.

Still, Gabriel maneuvered and shifted his position on the seat until he could get his jeans down past his boxers and to his thigh. She couldn't miss the scar because it hadn't faded to the healed stage yet. Might never. He'd accepted that. But he still watched Rosalie's reaction to it.

She didn't gasp, say she was sorry or some of the other things people said when they found out he'd been injured in the line of duty. She simply touched her fingers ever so gently to it.

"It still hurts?" she asked.

"Sometimes. Not now, though."

Especially not now. Then again, pain wasn't his go-to response when Rosalie's hand was mere inches from his boxers. Which meant she was mere inches from the place where she used to touch him.

Reggie wasn't the only one who'd done the hands-in-the-pants stuff. Nope. They'd gotten damn good at pleasuring each other.

"You didn't take my virginity," she said out of the blue. Her eyes met his, but she kept her hand on his thigh. "You wanted me. I was sure of that."

"You were sure because it was true," he verified.

And while this was probably the worst time to dole out his logic, because of the location of her hand and because he had his jeans hiked down, he did owe her an explanation.

"I was still trying to work out how I could leave Last Ride and not hurt you," he said. "I just didn't feel it was right to have sex with you, then walk away." He stopped, groaned and pulled up his jeans. "That makes me sound more honorable than I was. Trust me, there were plenty of times I wanted to pretend you wouldn't get hurt and go ahead and finish what we'd started."

She stayed quiet a moment. "We did do a lot of *starting*, didn't we?" Rosalie asked, not in a sad-trip-down-memory-lane kind of way. "And some finishing in our own way." She was smiling a little now.

"Yeah, we did." He felt himself smiling, too. Felt the urgent need to lean in and kiss her.

So that was what Gabriel did.

He touched his mouth to hers and lingered there just to savor the moment. There was plenty to savor. Plenty to taste. So that was what he did, too. He kissed her, letting the heat catch fire and go into a long, slow simmer where time just seemed to stop. His heart sure didn't stop, though. It began to rev. So did other parts of him, but Gabriel just kept on kissing her.

A sudden blast of laughter had them pulling apart, and for a moment Gabriel thought someone had caught them. It wouldn't have been the first time. But in this case, the laughter hadn't been aimed at them. It'd come from a group of their former classmates who were making their way into the gym. Judging from the blare of the music when they opened the door, the reunion party was already in full swing.

There was absolutely nothing in that building that he wanted more than being with the woman sitting beside him.

"I don't want to be here," Rosalie said, looking up at him. "Do you?"

"No, I don't," Gabriel assured her, and he was already calculating just how fast he could get her back to her house.

And into her bed.

CHAPTER FIVE

Rosalie had no doubts that Gabriel and she would soon be the talk of Last Ride, since there was a good chance that someone had seen them arrive at the reunion and then quickly leave.

All that kissing they'd done in his truck likely would have been noticed, too. But she didn't care. Didn't mind having to deal with morning-after gossip. She just wasn't going to let that interfere with her night with him. For fifteen years, she'd lamented that she'd never done the deed with Gabriel, and now she was.

Heck, maybe two deeds or even more.

It wasn't easy, but they managed to keep their hands off each other during the short drive from the high school back to her house. They even waited until they'd gotten inside, which prevented her neighbors from getting a peep show. But once they were in her foyer, the restraints snapped, and they went after each other.

She'd missed this kind of clawing hunger. The urgency. The need. A need that had never been this strong with anyone but Gabriel. Part of her wanted to blame what she was feeling on the searing, pent-up heat, on the fact that she'd never had all of him, but it felt like more.

So much more.

And speaking of more, Gabriel gave her plenty of that, starting with that first hot kiss. It wasn't the gentle touching of mouths as he'd initiated earlier in the truck. Nope. This was a different kind of foreplay. One with the desperate edge to get past the start and onto the finish, and that edge was contagious.

She didn't mind the desperation one bit because she was right there with him. Later, once they'd burned off some of this heat, they could slow down for round two, but this first time had to happen now.

The touching started, but they didn't break the kiss to get on with that. Rosalie slid her hands down his chest, silently cursing the shirt that was in between them. She fixed that by going after his buttons until she had the skin-to-skin contact she desperately needed.

Gabriel clearly had some needs, too, because he zoomed in on her zipper, and even though it ran from nape to butt, he got it down in one fluid move. More moving, also fluid, and he slid the dress off her. Rosalie had just a moment to feel the silk slink down her body and pool at her feet. A moment because Gabriel frazzled her brain by shoving down the cups of her bra and kissing her breasts.

She moaned in pleasure.

This was familiar territory for him, and he obviously hadn't lost his touch with his mouth and tongue. He gave her a really enjoyable reminder of how they'd passed the time during some of their high school make-out sessions.

Breathless now and with her body revving, Rosalie gave him a couple of reminders. She went after his zipper, lowered it and slid her hand inside his boxers. He was huge, hard and ready.

Now it was Gabriel who grunted with pleasure. And he cursed her, too, but it made her laugh because she knew what kind of sweet torture this was.

Mindful of his injury, Rosalie kept up the touching while

she began backing him toward her bedroom, very thankful for her small house because it didn't take them long to get there. She pushed him back on her bed, following on top of him, and kissed him with all the heat she'd stored up for the last fifteen years.

Gabriel must have had some pent-up heat of his own, because he flipped her onto her back, and he tackled her underwear. Except he put his own spin on getting her naked. He kissed and used his tongue on every inch of her that he uncovered when he shimmied off her bra and panties. Each touch of his mouth skyrocketed the heat until Rosalie was worried she would climax before they got around to the actual deed.

She did something about that.

After another flip, Gabriel was beneath her again, and she got busy getting him naked. Oh, what an adventure. All those toned and tight muscles were hers to play with, and she had to admit that time was on her side for this. Gabriel had filled out in all the right places, and she had a lot more of him to explore than she had when they'd been teenagers.

Getting on with that exploring, Rosalie took a page from Gabriel's foreplay book and kissed the parts of him that she stripped. His chest. Stomach. And, yes, then the prize.

He cursed her again, grimaced with that sweet pleasure that she was feeling just by tasting him. But apparently, Gabriel thought this particular pleasure was too sweet, because he turned, and she found herself beneath him again. She didn't mind.

Because now they were naked body to naked body.

She did curse, though, when he leaned over and started fumbling with his jeans that she'd just taken off him. It took her a couple of seconds to realize he was getting a condom from his wallet. Good grief. She'd forgotten all about safe sex. Thankfully, though, Gabriel hadn't.

He got on the condom, which involved touching her with the back of his hand. She doubted it was intentional, but he had her seeing stars and some constellations. He had her very close to that climax that she was trying to stave off. She had the romantic notion of them doing this together, an explosive, perfectly timed release that might cause some earthquakes.

And the romantic notion was a drop in the bucket compared to the real deal.

Gabriel pushed inside her, and then he went still for a couple of seconds. Maybe to give her time to adjust, maybe to give himself that time. Maybe just to savor. One look at him, and she decided it was the latter, because he was staring down at her as if she were the sun, the moon. The big, shiny prize that he'd finally gotten.

She got a big, shiny prize, too, and it got even shinier when he started to move inside her. Those delicious thrusts that kept pushing her toward the brink. Since the brink was exactly where she wanted to go, she didn't even try to hold on.

Not that she could have.

Gabriel could have easily finished her off then and there, but he added a flourish. He kissed her, long and deep, before he gave her that final push. And, yes, the brink happened, and she got to experience what she'd fantasized about for fifteen years. Gabriel shot her straight to the moon.

And then he went with her.

With her breath still uneven, Rosalie lay beneath Gabriel and felt the slack floating of her body. Oh, yes. Gabriel and she had indeed managed that whole romantic-notion deal.

She figured it was rare for sex to live up to such notions and fantasies, but Gabriel had defied the odds.

In the back of her mind, a little kernel of sadness formed, because it didn't seem possible that they could re-create what'd just happened. Then he kissed her, and the kernel of doubt vanished. They could definitely re-create this, maybe very soon if he had any more condoms.

"I'll be right back," he whispered to her, kissing her again before he headed off to the bathroom.

Rosalie just lay there, grinning like an idiot when she caught sight of his bare butt. Yes, she was up for another round of that. However, her smiling ground to a halt when she heard her phone ding with a text. Her phone that was obviously still in her purse that was now somewhere on the living room floor. She tried to ignore it, but since Gabriel was still in the bathroom, she hurried to get it.

Then she cursed when she saw the text was from Reggie.

Just wondering when you'll be here at the reunion, the message said, and he'd added some party emojis, probably to make it appear like a lighthearted, jovial comment.

It wasn't. He was likely there and had heard she'd driven off with Gabriel. In fact, Reggie probably knew she'd taken Gabriel home and that they had picked up where they'd left off. And that meant it was time to spell out something. Or rather, repeat something.

Quit texting me, she replied with no emojis whatsoever. Get a life. I have. It's over, and I'm blocking you.

Something she should have done months ago. Tomorrow, she'd go to Petal Pushers and demand they not deliver any more flowers. That should finally make things sink in that she wasn't going back to him. Ever. Even if things didn't work out between Gabriel and her, and the odds were high they wouldn't, then she wasn't going to settle for Reggie. Or any other man, for that matter.

She went back into her room to find a naked Gabriel in her bed. That brought back her smile.

"Everything okay?" he asked, tipping his head to her phone that she was still holding.

Rosalie nodded. "Just tying up some loose ends. It won't take me long," she assured him.

Now he grinned and tucked his hands behind his head. "Then I'll just sit here and admire the view."

She had a moment of panic since—hey, body flaws galore, including the extra pounds on her thighs. But since Gabriel seemed to be smiling at those flaws, she didn't rush to cover up. Instead, Rosalie fired off a text to her mother.

I'm sowing wild oats with Gabriel. Don't judge or I'll give you details you don't want to hear.

She didn't have to wait long for a response, but it did take her a couple of seconds to interpret her mother's reply. Her mom had a habit of relying on autocorrect and then not checking the response before hitting Send.

Sewing goats? her mom had texted. I'm signing here. Shirley, you've thought this threw.

Translation: *Sowing oats? I'm sighing here. Surely, you've thought this through.*

Yep, I thought it through, Rosalie replied. It's what I want.

Again, her mother's reply was fast. Evan if gay be rail is going to deli?

Translation: *Even if Gabriel is going to Dallas?*

Now Rosalie did her own sighing. Yes, even if, she simply replied and muted her phone.

Of course, she'd need to give her mother more of an explanation, and she would. When she had an explanation, that was. For now, though, she didn't want to think about Dallas, and the only sigh she intended to have was when she got that second climax from Gabriel.

She tossed her phone onto the nightstand and slid back into bed with him, intending to see just how long it would take to fire him back up again. Not long, she decided, when he moved right into the kiss. Rosalie would have heated up that kiss even more.

If his phone hadn't rung.

Muttering some profanity, he pulled away from her mouth and began to riffle through his jeans that were at the foot of the bed. "It's Carmen," he relayed when he saw the screen.

He hit Answer, but unlike his earlier call with his cop pal in Dallas, she couldn't hear Carmen's end of the conversation. However, one look at Gabriel's face when he ended the call, and she knew something was wrong.

"It's Hamish?" she immediately guessed.

Gabriel nodded and pulled on his boxers. "He just showed up at the ranch, and Carmen wants us to go over there."

CHAPTER SIX

THIS WAS NOT the ending he'd had planned for his evening with Rosalie. Not when he had a second condom still in his wallet. Gabriel had figured once they'd gone through that, then they could continue to fool around the way they had back in high school.

But there was no way he could leave Carmen to deal with Hamish alone.

Gabriel had put back on his badge before Rosalie and he had hurried out of her house and started the drive to the Silver Springs Ranch. He wanted Hamish to see the badge and understand that he was looking for a reason to arrest him. Especially if Hamish was giving Carmen any hassles. When it came to his great-uncle, Gabriel's tolerance meter was at zero.

"I should have known Hamish would do something like this," Gabriel grumbled as he drove. "I should have gone ahead and moved to the ranch and put out the word I was there. That might have given Hamish some second thoughts about just showing up."

Rosalie pulled back her shoulders. *"Gone ahead and moved to the ranch?"* she questioned.

"Yeah. Carmen's moving to the cottage in town, remember? I could have gone ahead and moved in out here. And FYI, I'm not allowing her to give me Silver Springs like she wants. I'm buying it from her."

Since he was driving, he didn't stare at her when she made a weird sound, but he did give her a glance. "You're not taking the job in Dallas?" she asked.

Oh, so that was what the sound was about, and he frowned. "No. I was never going to take that job."

She looked at him as if he'd just dropped the biggest bombshell in the history of bombshells. Hell. He obviously owed her an explanation. One that would have to wait, he decided, when he pulled into the driveway of the ranch and spotted the car and driver at the side of the house. So, apparently Hamish hadn't driven himself. If he had, that would have given Gabriel the excuse to arrest him, since the man didn't have a valid license.

Hamish was sitting on the porch steps, in the very spot where Carmen had been during Rosalie's and his last visit. But his great-aunt wasn't serving beer or lemonade tonight.

Nope.

She was standing in the doorway of the house, and while she didn't look upset, or furious, she clearly hadn't welcomed Hamish inside.

Sporting the same curly helmet of gray hair that he had in his old DMV photo, Hamish got to his feet when Gabriel and Rosalie got out of the truck. Hamish didn't look upset, or furious, either. He seemed ready to do some groveling, but there wasn't enough groveling in the universe to make up for what he'd done.

Hamish held up his hands as Gabriel and Rosalie approached. "If you're going to punch me," the man said, "wait until I confess that I'm the one who sent you each breakup letters fifteen years ago."

"We know," Gabriel and she said in unison, both of their tones as flat as the look Gabriel was giving his great-uncle.

Hamish flinched, frowned and then slid his gaze from

Rosalie to him. "Not excusing what I did," Hamish said, "but I figured you were looking for a way out of Last Ride, and I gave you one with that letter."

Gabriel couldn't deny that first part. He had been trying to find a way to leave town and not hurt Rosalie in the process, but he hadn't come up with a solution. Neither had Hamish with those heart-crushing letters.

"I would have preferred Gabriel's goodbye to come from Gabriel," Rosalie snarled. "And you misspelled two words in the one you sent me. That might seem nitpicky in the grand scheme of things, but I went through the next fifteen years wondering how Gabriel had managed to get straight As in English when he'd flubbed words like *farewell* and *forget*."

"And I spent fifteen years wondering why the hell Rosalie would even use a word like *farewell*," Gabriel grumbled. Of course, until recently he hadn't wondered about it enough to consider that she hadn't even written it.

"I thought I was doing the right thing," Hamish said. "I believed you were repeating the mistakes I'd made."

That caused Carmen to make a disapproving *hmmp* sound. Rosalie huffed and rolled her eyes.

The sound and the glare Rosalie gave him didn't stop Hamish, though. "I always believed Parkman blue blood doesn't mix with McCloud," he went on, earning him a growl from Carmen this time. "Or so I thought," he quickly added. "But I was wrong."

"You think?" Carmen snapped, and she made her way onto the porch. "You thought DNA determines happiness? It doesn't."

"I know," Hamish softly agreed, and he repeated it in a whisper while shaking his head. He groaned and sank back down on the step. "I came back to see you," he continued, aiming that at Carmen. "About a year after I left, I came back and spotted you in the barn. You were smiling, obviously very happy. So, I guess that *Ha Ha, Carmen. I got the last laugh* was really a laugh on me."

"Yes, it was," Carmen agreed, but the fight was gone from her voice.

"I don't know why I was so bitter," Hamish continued. "And I blamed it on everything but myself. This ranch. Your silver-spoon family. The fact I was practically broke when I came to the marriage. After I won the lottery, I knew I wasn't miserable because I didn't have money. I knew it was on me and me alone."

"He gave me a check for a million dollars," Carmen said, showing it to them.

"Her half of the lottery I won," Hamish supplied. "It seemed only fair because I chose the numbers of her birthday." He stayed quiet for a moment and got to his feet. "Let me be a cautionary tale, Gabriel. Don't screw things up like I did."

Gabriel nearly snapped that he'd never do that, but that would have been the anger talking. Truth was, he had screwed up with Rosalie, and now he was hoping he'd get the chance to fix that.

The words seemed to have an effect on Carmen, too. She wasn't exactly misty-eyed, but she no longer looked ready to shove that check into some orifice of Hamish's body.

Hamish turned to Rosalie. "I heard you drew my name for the Last Ride Society. Mind telling me what you were going to put in your report on my life?"

Rosalie opened her mouth, probably to snarl out a laundry list of his wrongdoings, but she stopped and seemingly rethought that. "Maybe I would have said that I hoped you wouldn't blow any second chance you got. A second chance you wouldn't deserve, by the way, but hey, sometimes people get lucky."

Hamish smiled. Then he laughed. He gave Gabriel a playful jab on the arm. "You've got a good one there, Gabriel. I can see why you love her. Can see why she loves you, too."

The silence rolled in. An awkward kind of silence, because neither Rosalie nor he addressed the love thing. Gabriel held his breath, waiting to see if Rosalie would laugh and deny it. Not because that was what she would want or how she felt but because she might think it was what he wanted to hear.

It wasn't.

And Gabriel had no intentions of laughing it off, either. Because Hamish had just spoken the truth.

"Do the smart thing and don't let her get away this time," Hamish added. "If you need any help writing a makeup letter, just let me know."

Gabriel glared at him. Well, a short glare, anyway. That was still too sensitive a subject to make jokes about, but he thought it was one of those stories that could be entertaining down the road.

"I've decided I want to live out what's left of my life right here in Last Ride. I'm going to ask a Realtor to find me a house in town," Hamish announced. "Maybe someplace close to Webster Street," he added in a mumble.

Since that was where Carmen was planning on living, Gabriel looked up at his great-aunt to see how she felt about that. She shrugged. For such a simple gesture, it conveyed a lot. Carmen wasn't going to stand in the way of Hamish's return. She wasn't exactly going to welcome him back with open arms, either. Maybe never would. But Gabriel knew that wouldn't stomp on Carmen's happiness. It might not stomp on the newly found happiness Hamish had found, either.

"Good evening," Hamish said, heading to his car. "I'll be seeing y'all around. Oh, and you're welcome for my return taking some of the gossip heat off the two of you," he added.

It would indeed do that, but Gabriel figured enduring some gossip was a small price to pay for being with Rosalie.

"Are you okay?" he asked Carmen when Hamish's driver pulled away from the house.

"I'm fine," she assured him, and she managed a smile. "I'm guessing you two can say the same."

Rosalie and he weren't exactly wearing a we-just-had-sex sign, but it was possible they were putting off some kind of vibe. He kissed Carmen good-night, waited for her to go back inside, and then Gabriel slipped his arm around Rosalie to lead her back to his truck.

"What was that you said to Hamish? *Sometimes people get lucky*?" Gabriel asked.

She lifted her shoulder. "Sometimes. I'm not sure he will when it comes to reconciling with Carmen."

Yeah, that was a long shot, but life was short and sometimes filled with the best of surprises. Like now, when he stopped at the truck door and brushed a kiss on Rosalie's mouth, he got not only a shot of the heat she was capable of giving. He also felt the love.

Lucky, indeed.

Because it occurred to him that every time he'd kissed her, the love had been there. Right from the start. And it just kept on coming.

"You don't have to stay in Last Ride for me," she muttered.

He smiled, knowing it wouldn't have taken her long to

make that suggestion. After all, she'd heard him say he'd never planned on taking that job in Dallas.

"Now, that's where you're partly wrong," he said. "I want to stay for you, Rosalie. I want to be here with you for a long, long time. It's taken me a while, fifteen years or so, to figure this out, but I'm in love with you."

Now she was the one smiling. "Good. About time you saw the light. I'm still in love with you, too."

There it was, all tied up with a pretty bow. His past, his present and sure as heck his future. When Gabriel pulled her into his arms and kissed her, he made sure Rosalie was the one feeling the love.

* * * * *

1/2 6215.65

3348.43

1134 ~Vega